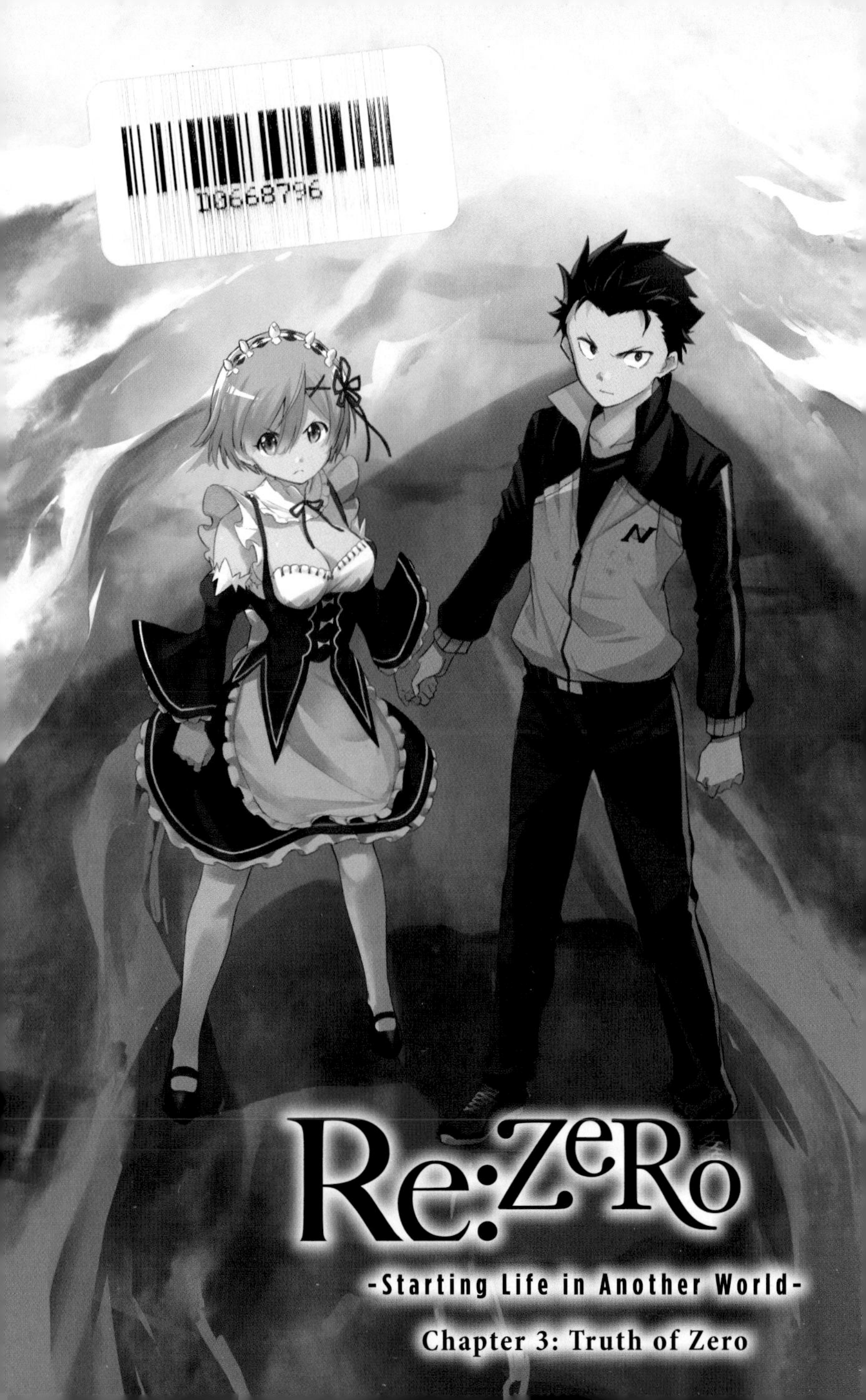

Re:ZeRo

-Starting Life in Another World-

Chapter 3: Truth of Zero

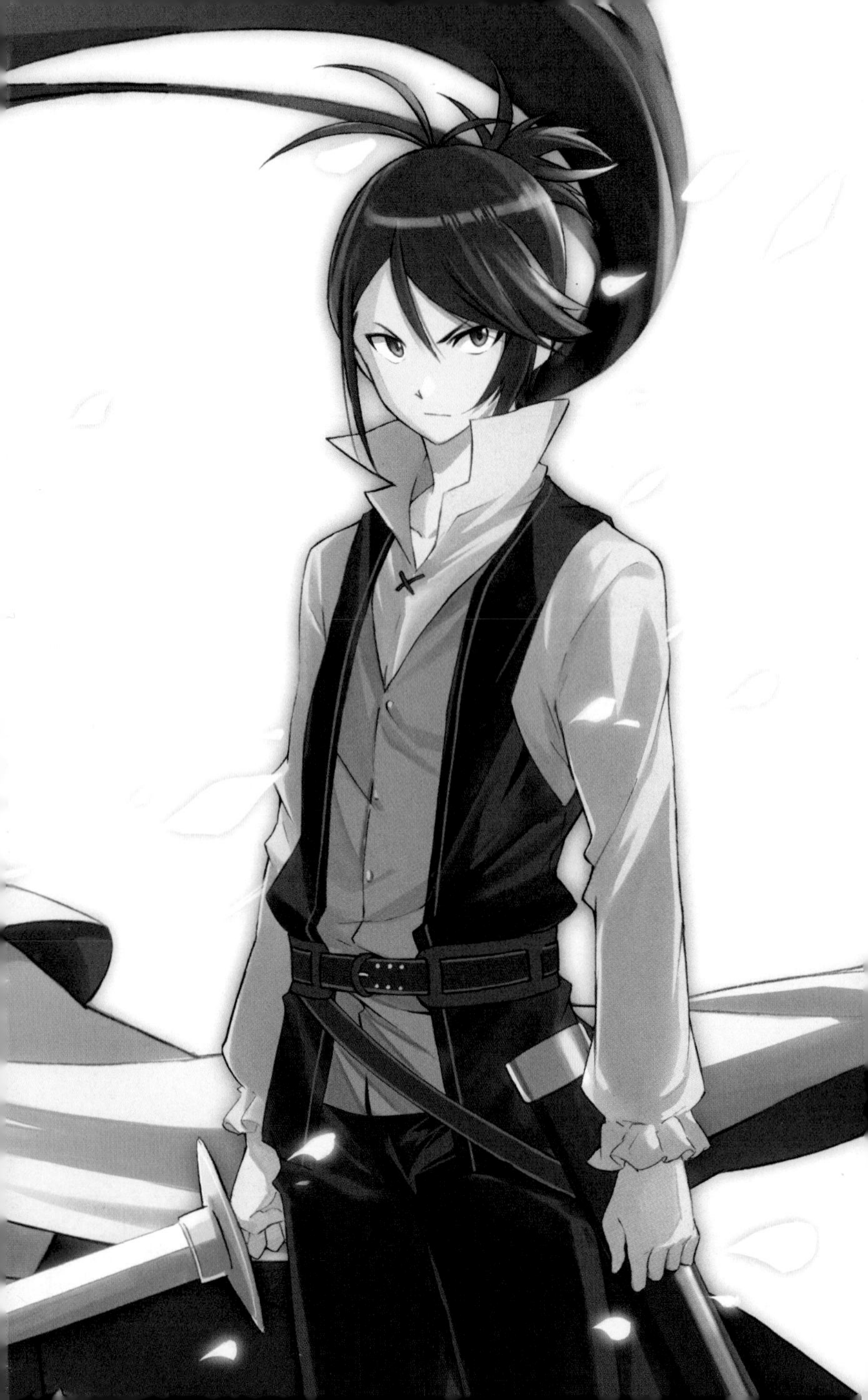

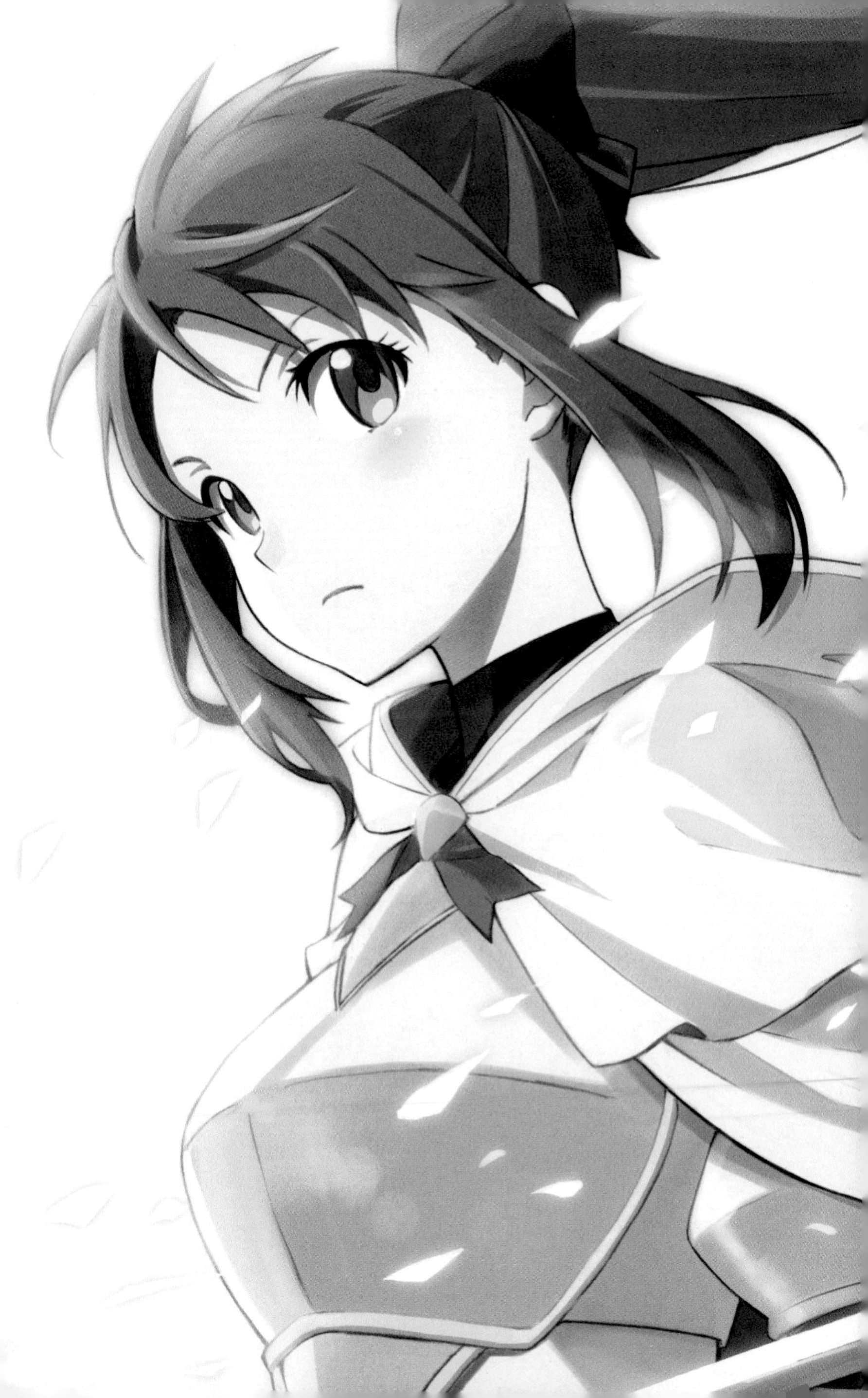

Re:ZERO -Starting Life in Another World-

Chapter 3: Truth of Zero

The only ability Subaru Natsuki gets when he's summoned to
another world is time travel via his own death. But to save her,
he'll die as many times as it takes.

Contents

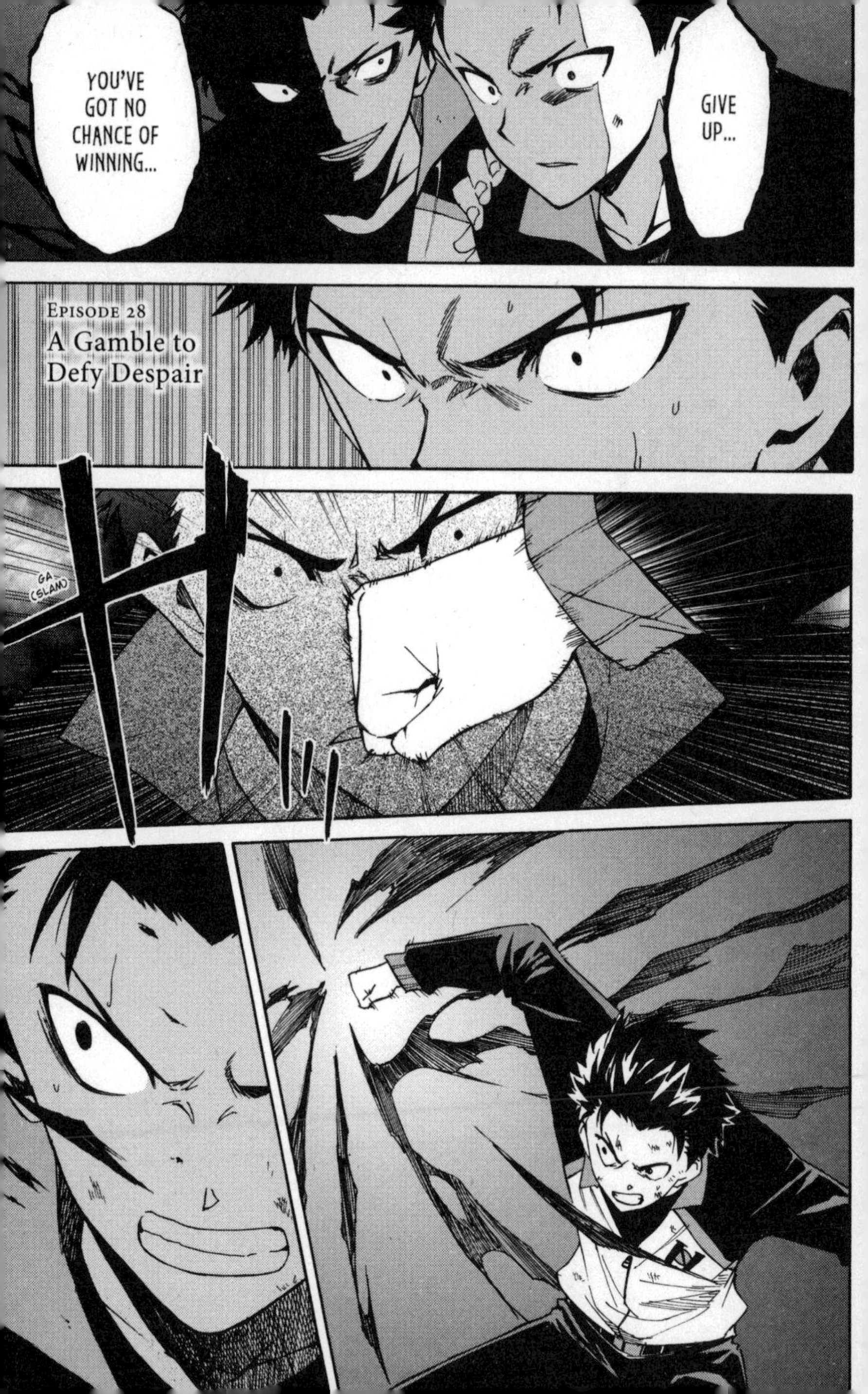
GIVE UP...
YOU'VE GOT NO CHANCE OF WINNING...
Episode 28
A Gamble to Defy Despair
GA (SLAM)

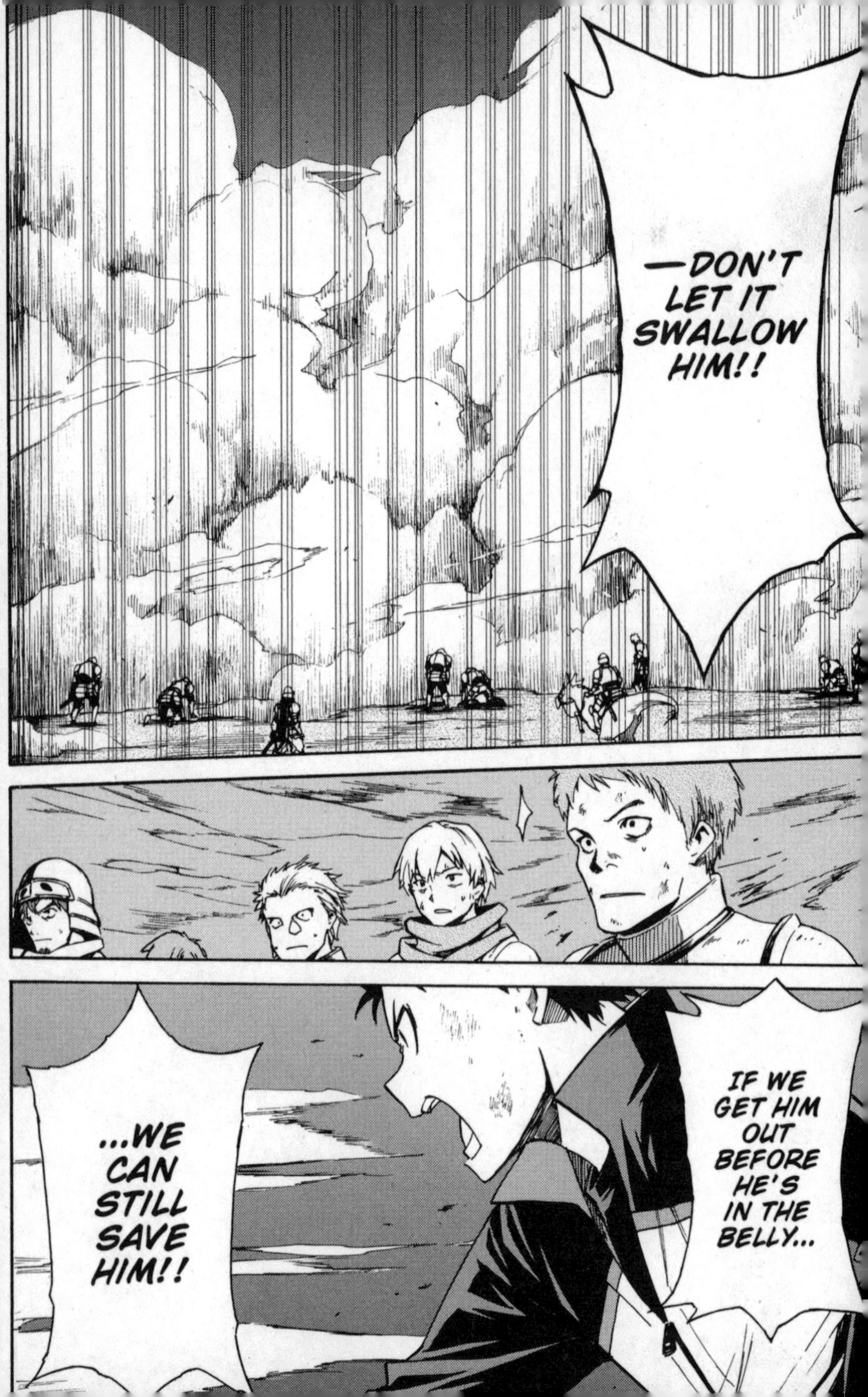
—DON'T LET IT SWALLOW HIM!!
IF WE GET HIM OUT BEFORE HE'S IN THE BELLY...
...WE CAN STILL SAVE HIM!!

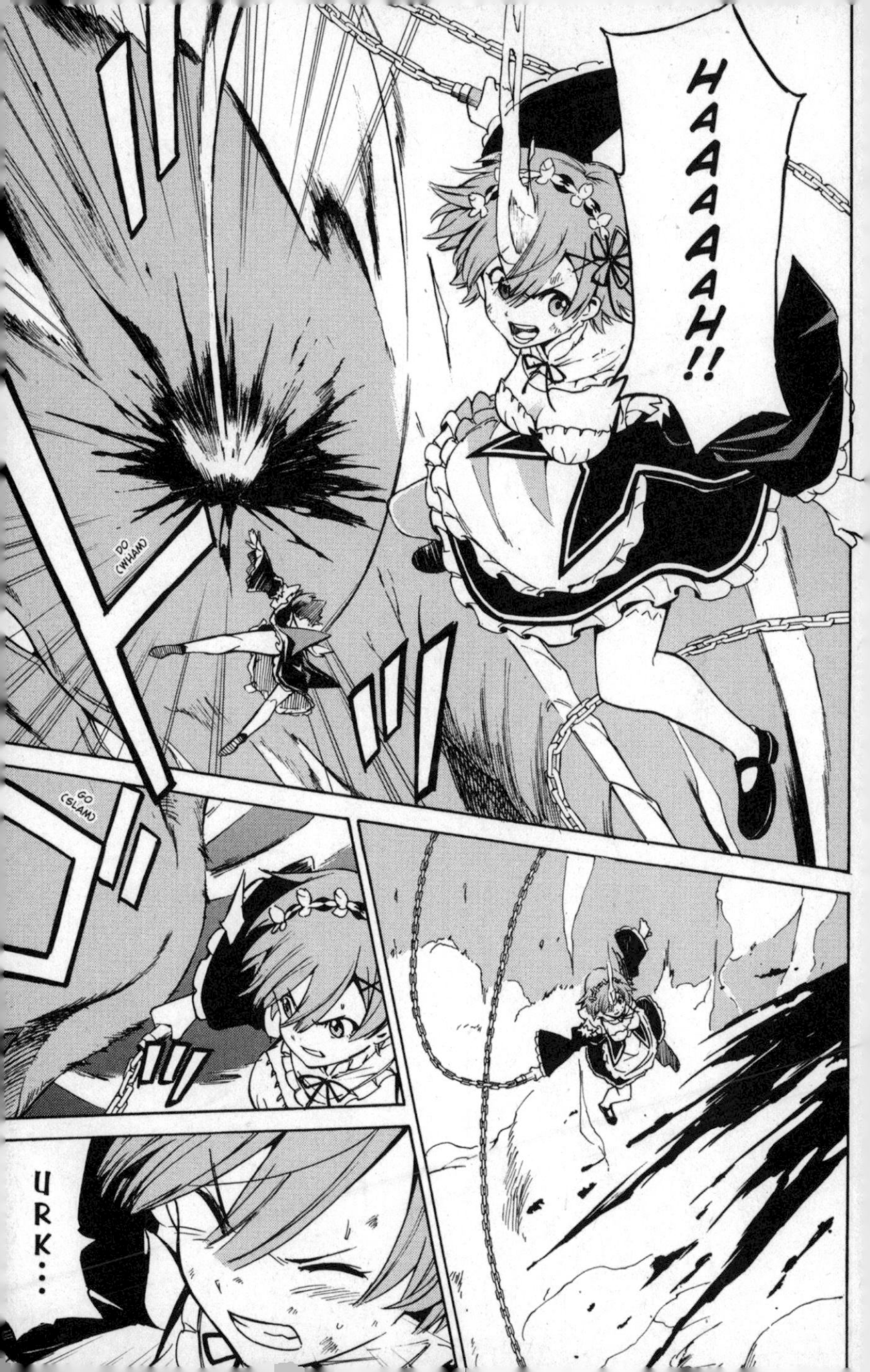
HAAAAAAH!!
DO (WHAM)
GO (SLAM)
URK...

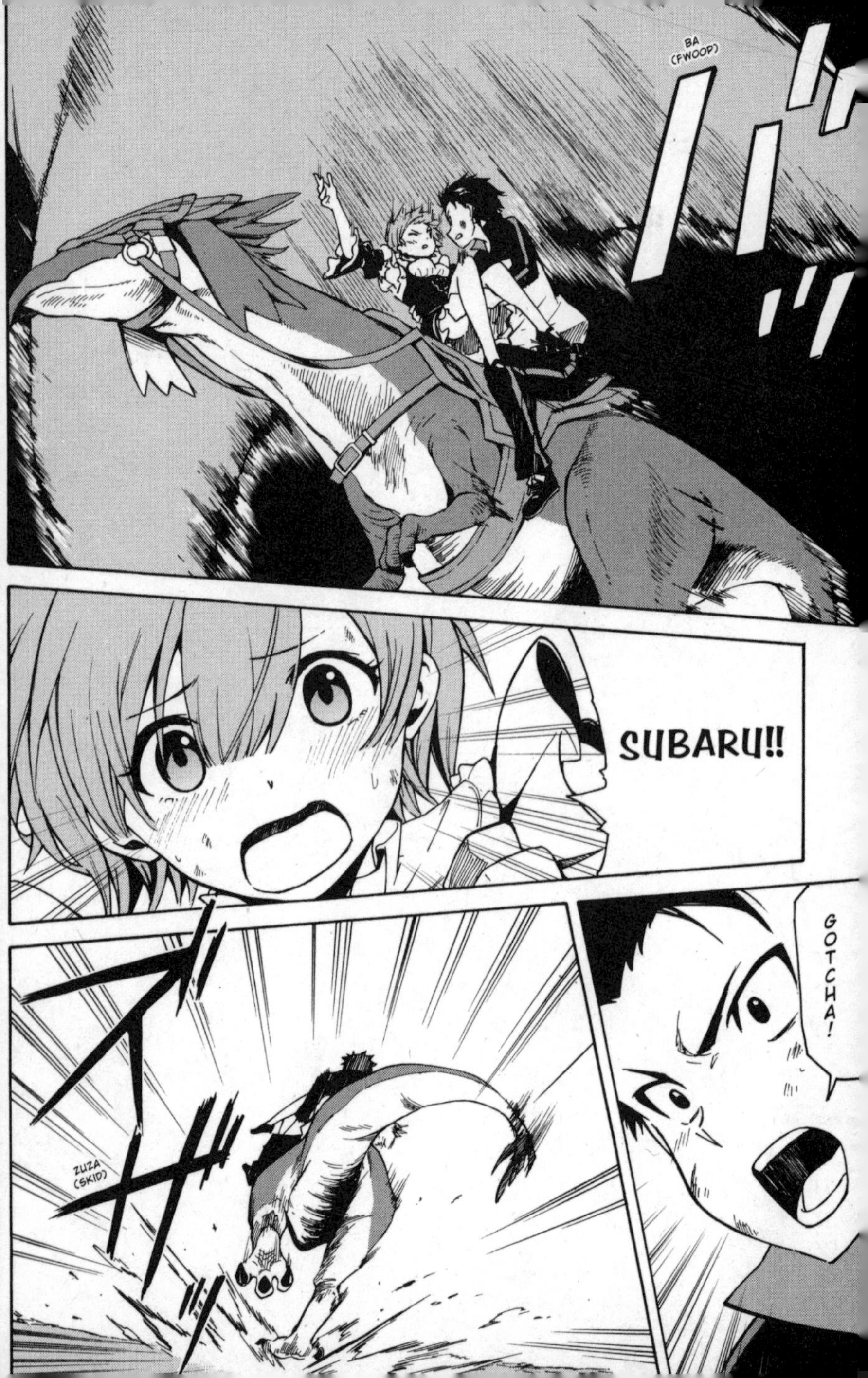
BA
(FWOOP)
SUBARU!!
GOTCHA!
ZUZA
(SKID)

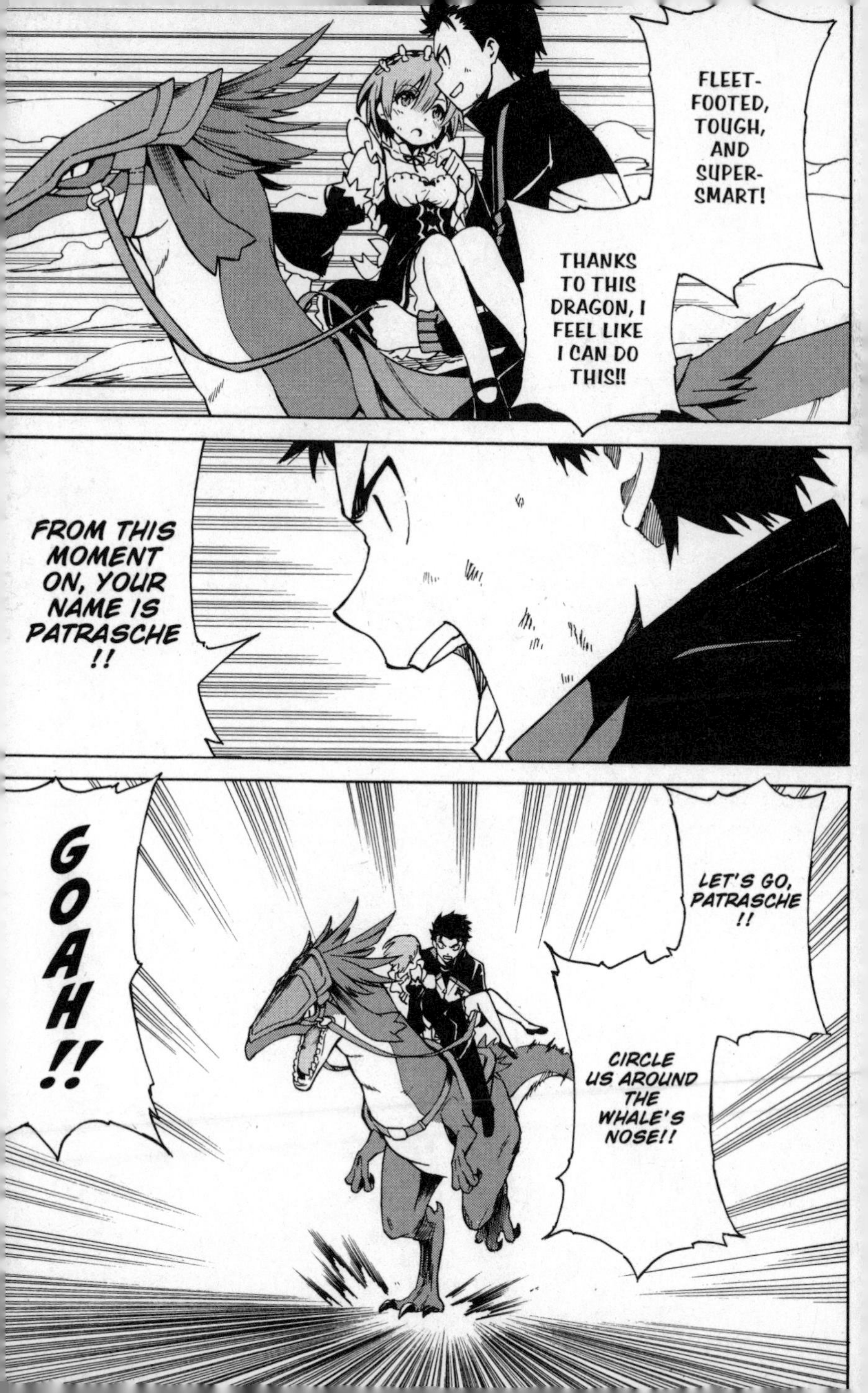
FLEET-FOOTED, TOUGH, AND SUPER-SMART!
THANKS TO THIS DRAGON, I FEEL LIKE I CAN DO THIS!!
FROM THIS MOMENT ON, YOUR NAME IS PATRASCHE!!
LET'S GO, PATRASCHE!!
CIRCLE US AROUND THE WHALE'S NOSE!!
GOAH!!

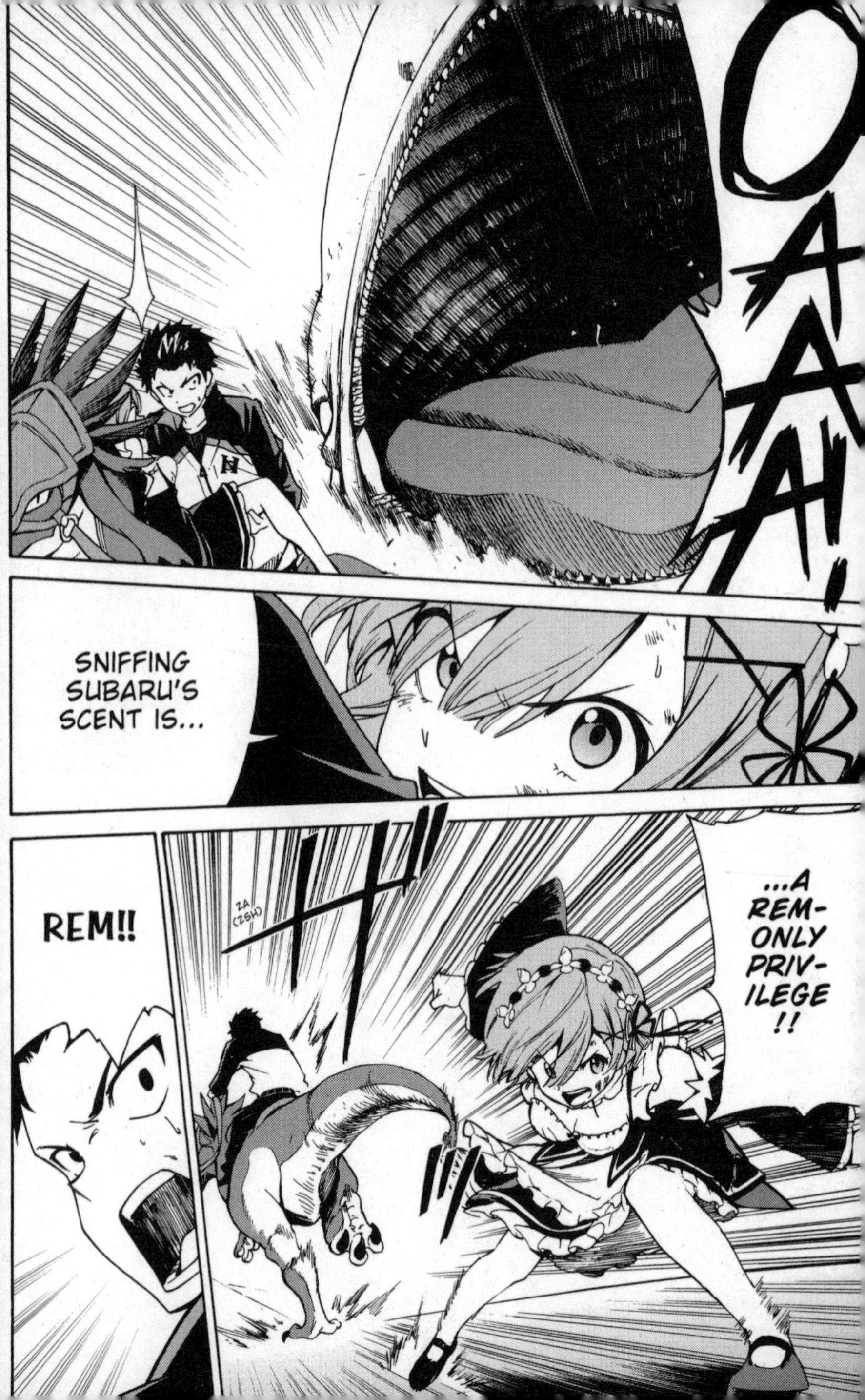

OAAA!!
SNIFFING SUBARU'S SCENT IS...
...A REM-ONLY PRIVILEGE!!
ZA (ZSH)
REM!!

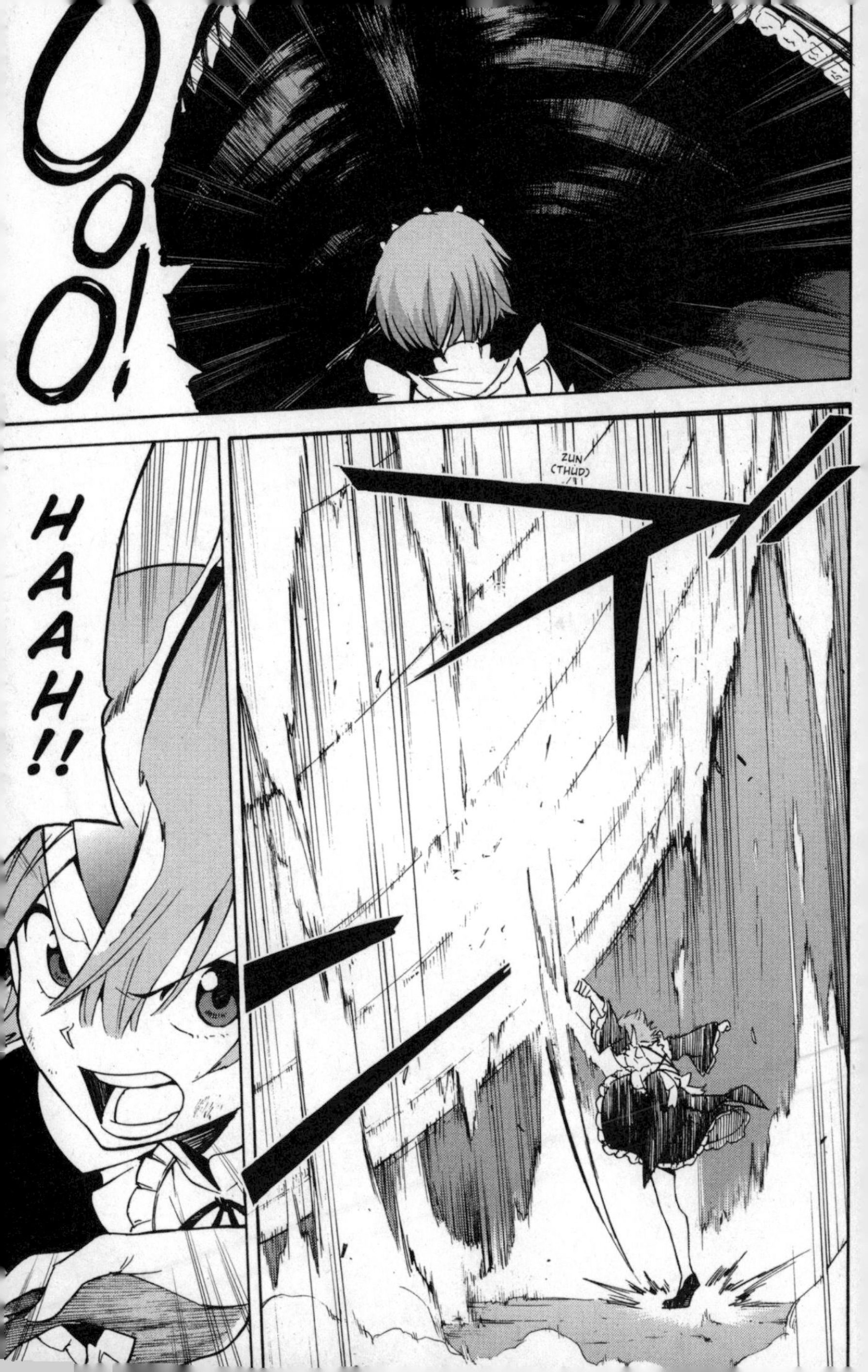
OOO!
ZUN (THUD)
HAAAH!!

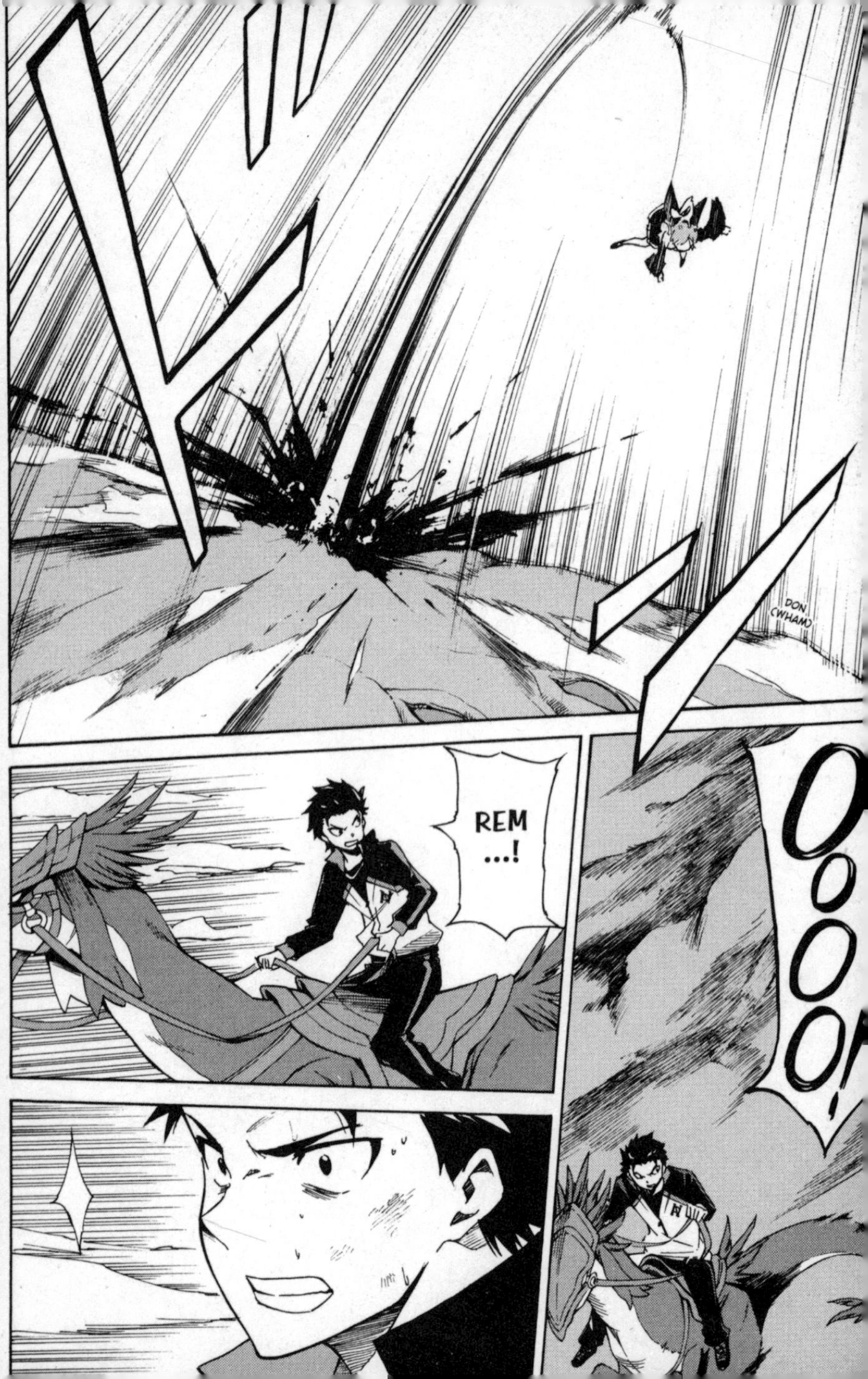
DON (WHAM)
REM ...!
OOOO!

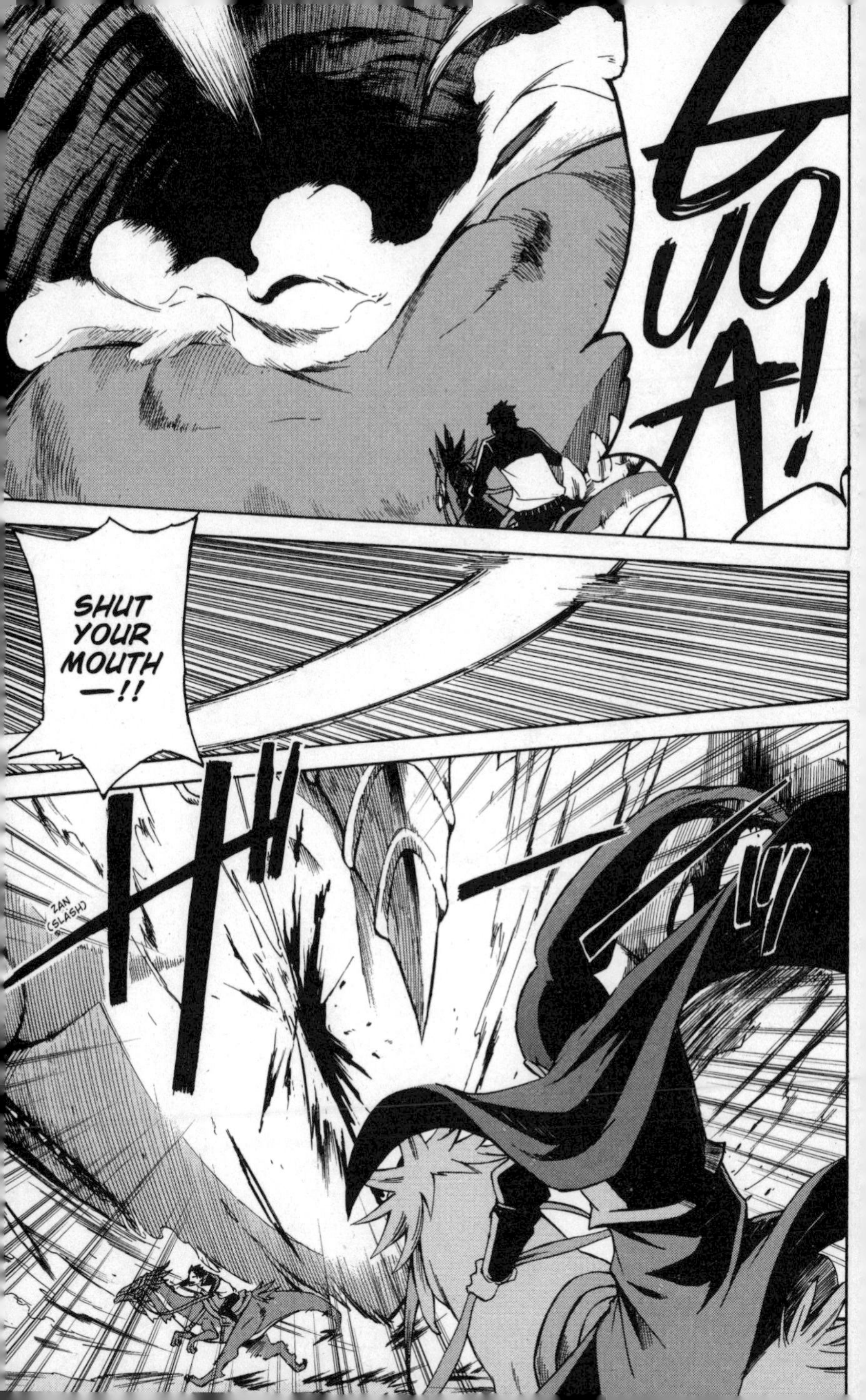
GUOA!
SHUT YOUR MOUTH—!!
ZAN (SLASH)

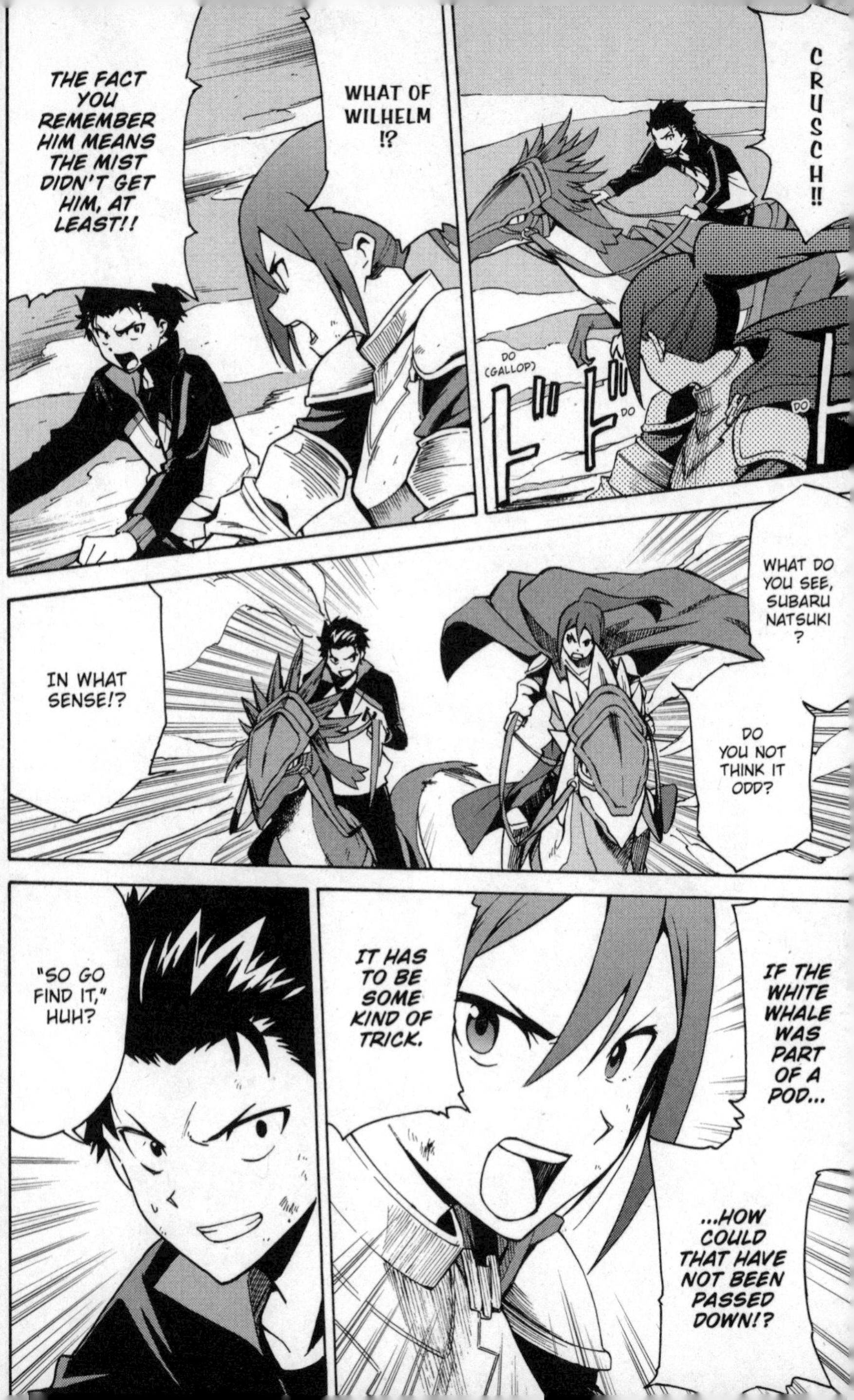
CRUSCH!!
DO (GALLOP)
DO
DO
WHAT OF WILHELM !?
THE FACT YOU REMEMBER HIM MEANS THE MIST DIDN'T GET HIM, AT LEAST!!
WHAT DO YOU SEE, SUBARU NATSUKI?
DO YOU NOT THINK IT ODD?
IN WHAT SENSE!?
IF THE WHITE WHALE WAS PART OF A POD...
...HOW COULD THAT HAVE NOT BEEN PASSED DOWN!?
IT HAS TO BE SOME KIND OF TRICK.
"SO GO FIND IT," HUH?

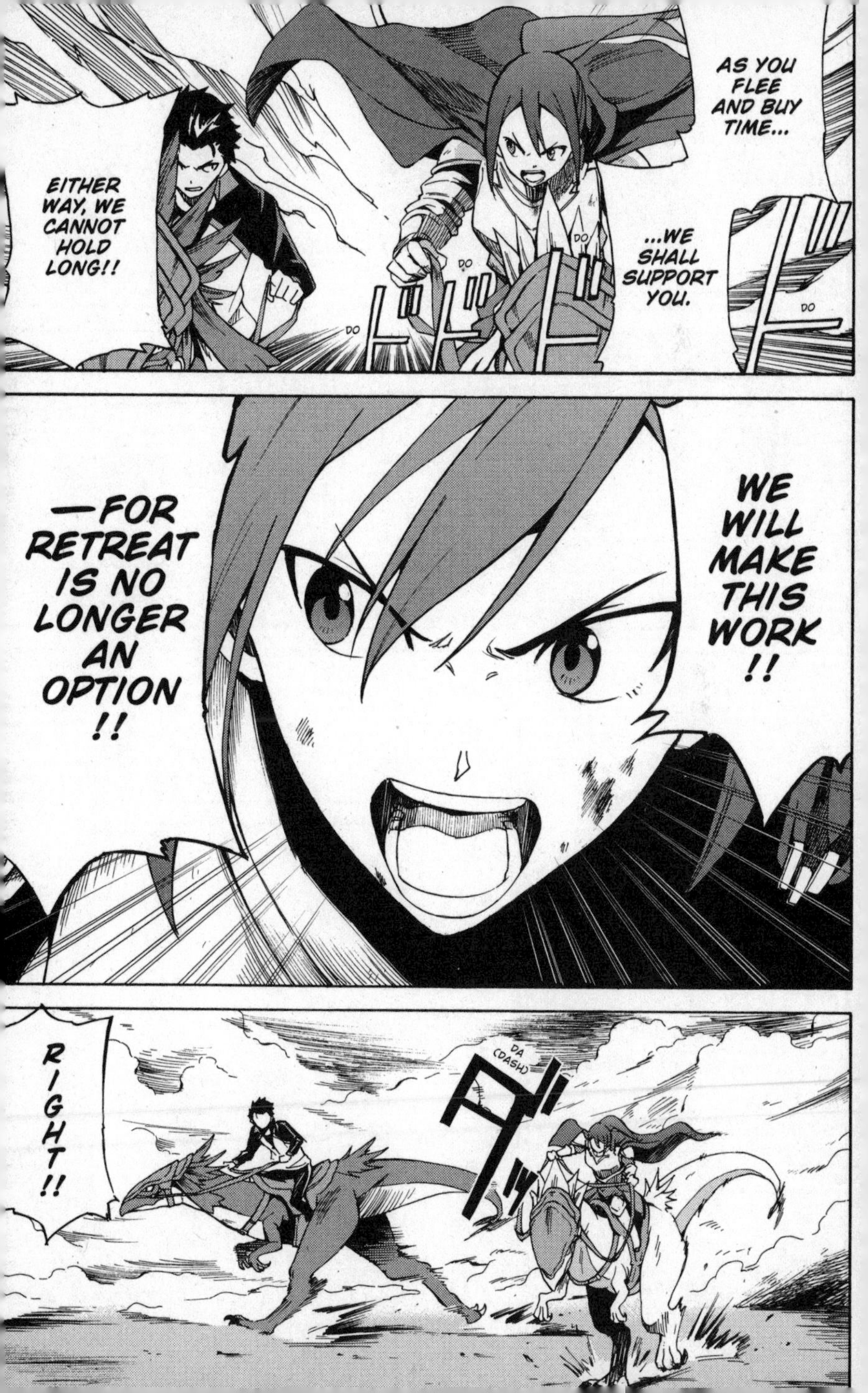
AS YOU FLEE AND BUY TIME...
...WE SHALL SUPPORT YOU.
DO
DO
DO
DO
EITHER WAY, WE CANNOT HOLD LONG!!
WE WILL MAKE THIS WORK!!
—FOR RETREAT IS NO LONGER AN OPTION!!
DA (DASH)
RIGHT!!

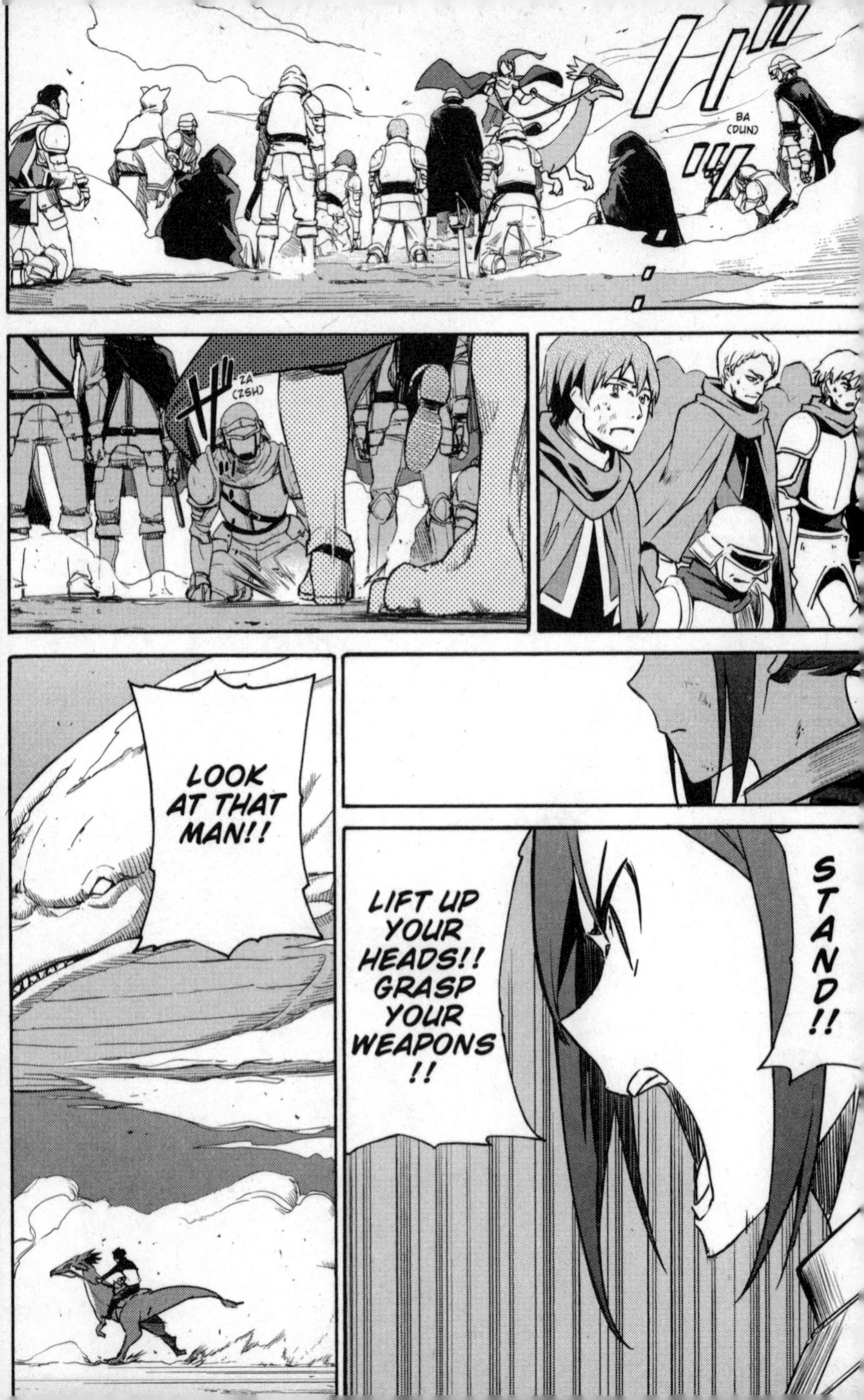
BA (DUN)
ZA (ZSH)
STAND!!
LIFT UP YOUR HEADS!! GRASP YOUR WEAPONS!!
LOOK AT THAT MAN!!

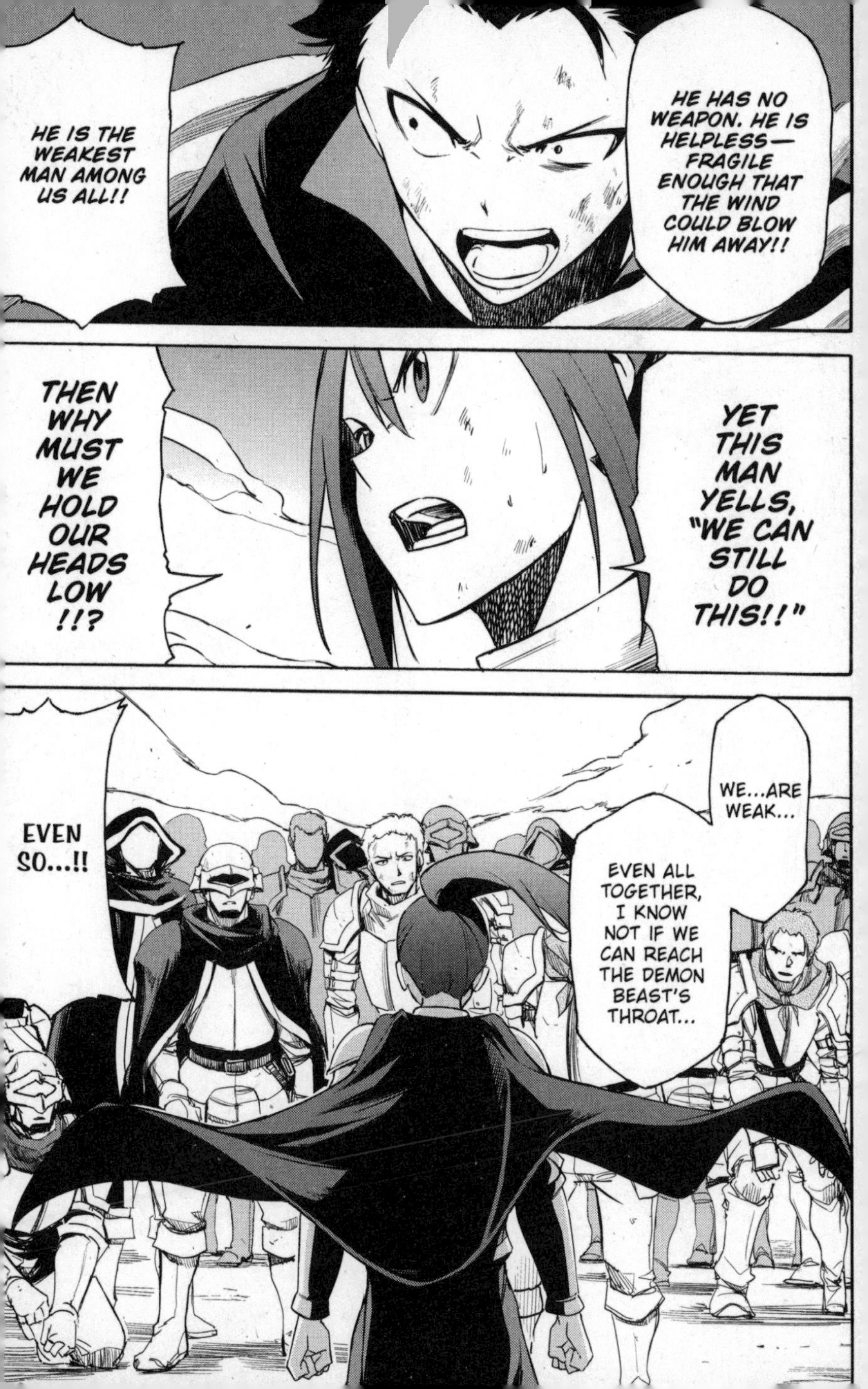
HE HAS NO WEAPON. HE IS HELPLESS—FRAGILE ENOUGH THAT THE WIND COULD BLOW HIM AWAY!!
HE IS THE WEAKEST MAN AMONG US ALL!!
YET THIS MAN YELLS, "WE CAN STILL DO THIS!!"
THEN WHY MUST WE HOLD OUR HEADS LOW!!?
WE...ARE WEAK...
EVEN ALL TOGETHER, I KNOW NOT IF WE CAN REACH THE DEMON BEAST'S THROAT...
EVEN SO...!!

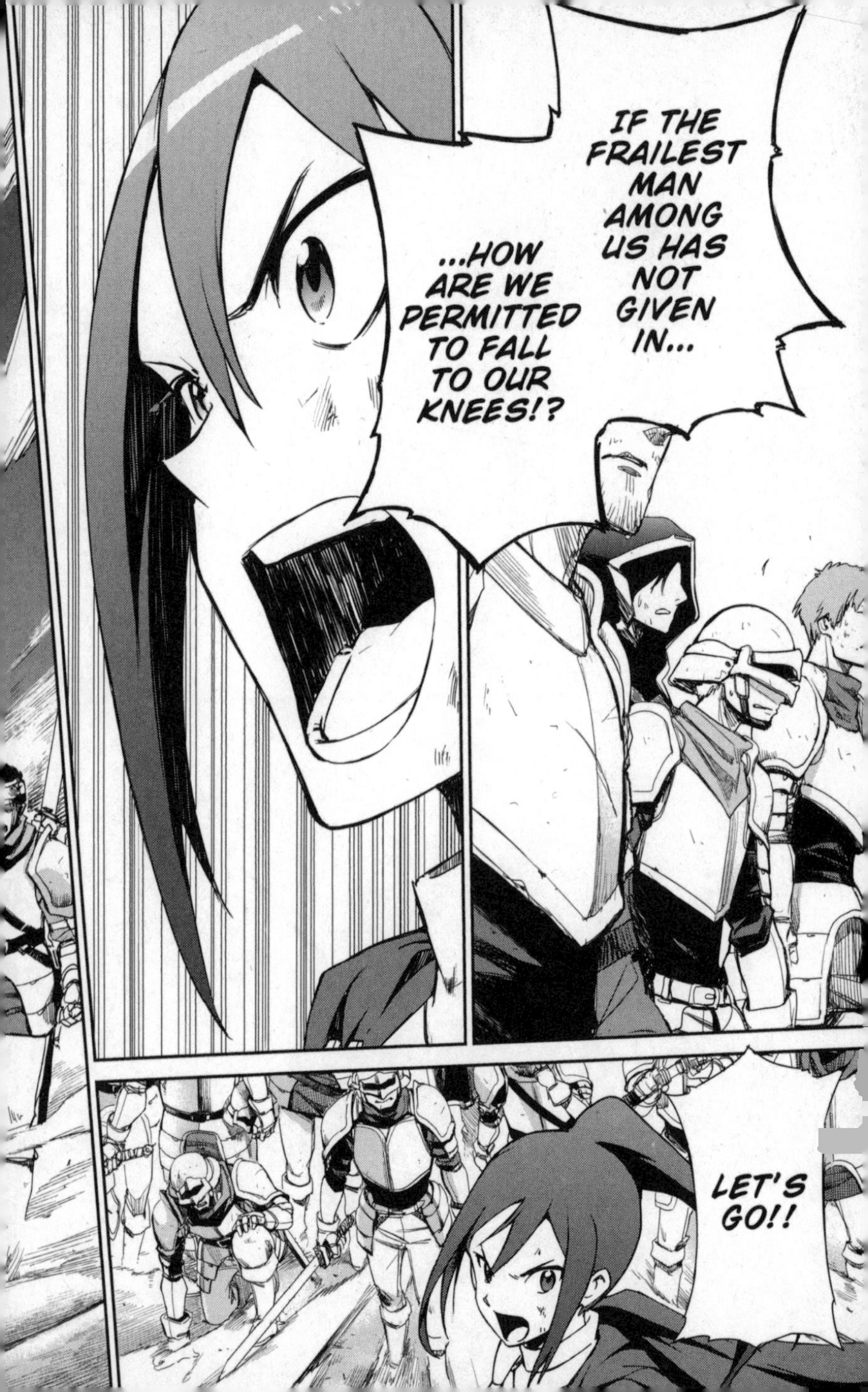
IF THE FRAILEST MAN AMONG US HAS NOT GIVEN IN...
...HOW ARE WE PERMITTED TO FALL TO OUR KNEES!?
LET'S GO!!

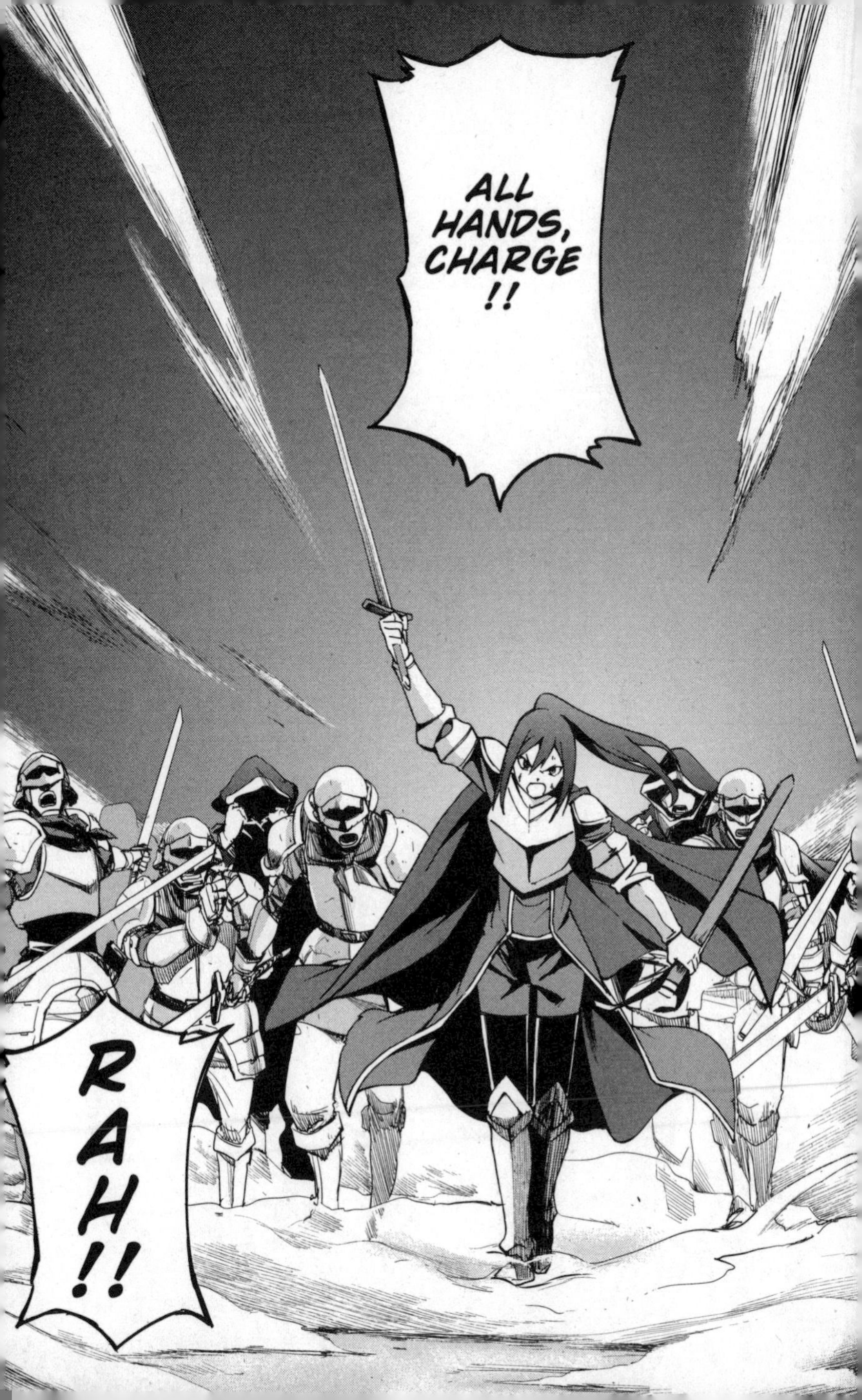
ALL HANDS, CHARGE!!
RAH!!

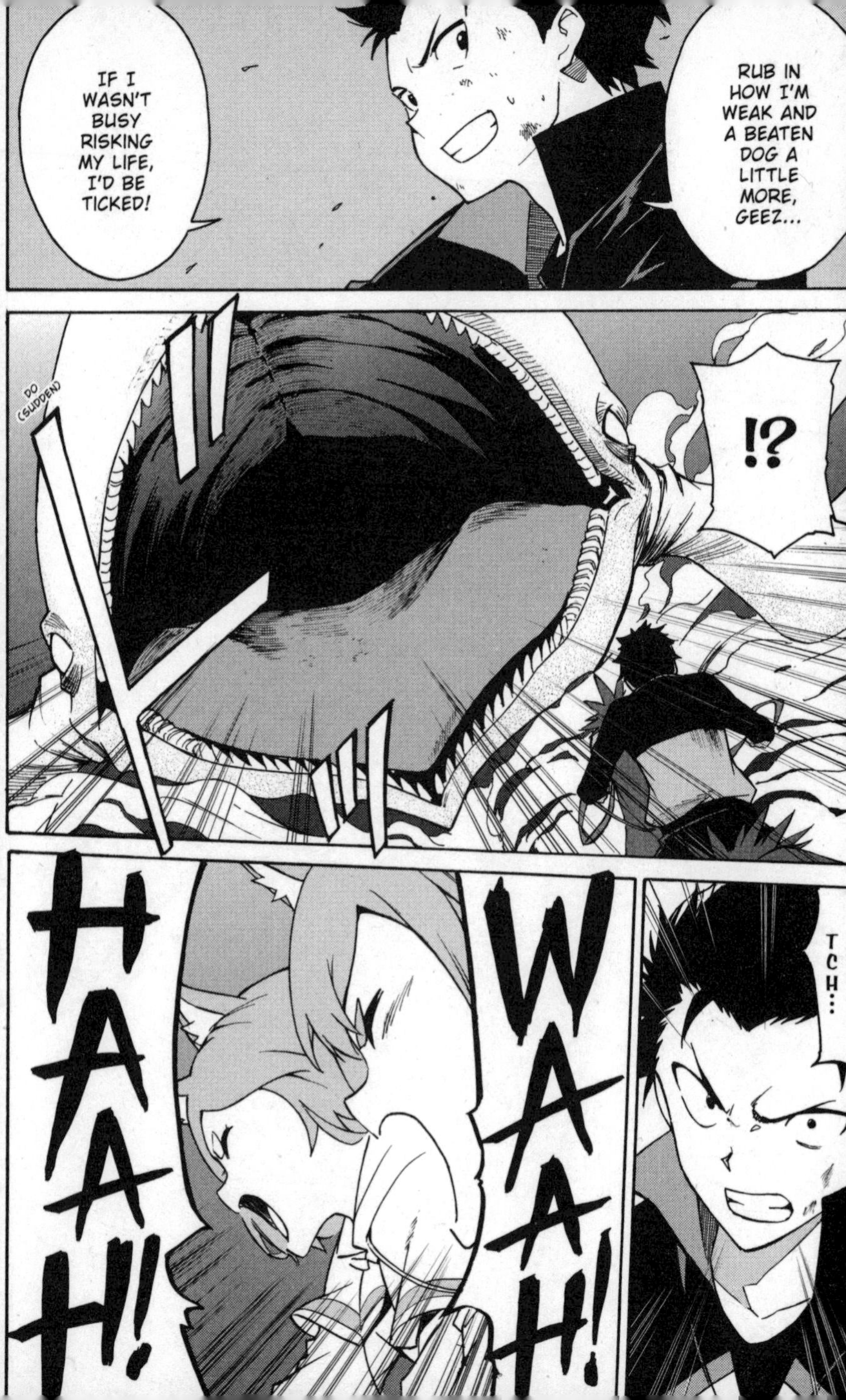
RUB IN HOW I'M WEAK AND A BEATEN DOG A LITTLE MORE, GEEZ...
IF I WASN'T BUSY RISKING MY LIFE, I'D BE TICKED!
!?
DO (SUDDEN)
TCH...
WAAAH!
HAAAH!

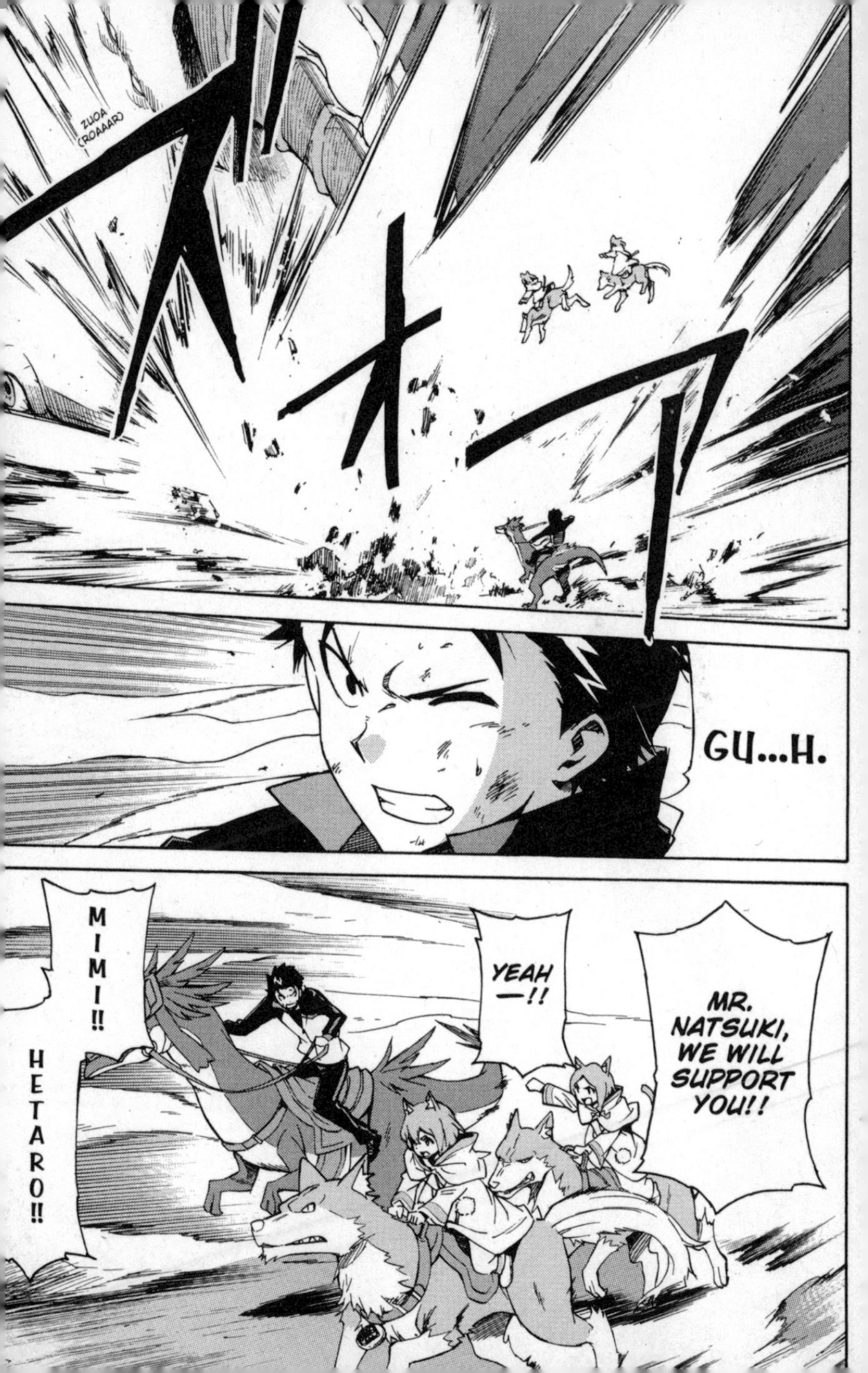
ZUOA (ROAAAR)
GU...H.
MR. NATSUKI, WE WILL SUPPORT YOU!!
YEAH—!!
MIMI!!
HETARO!!

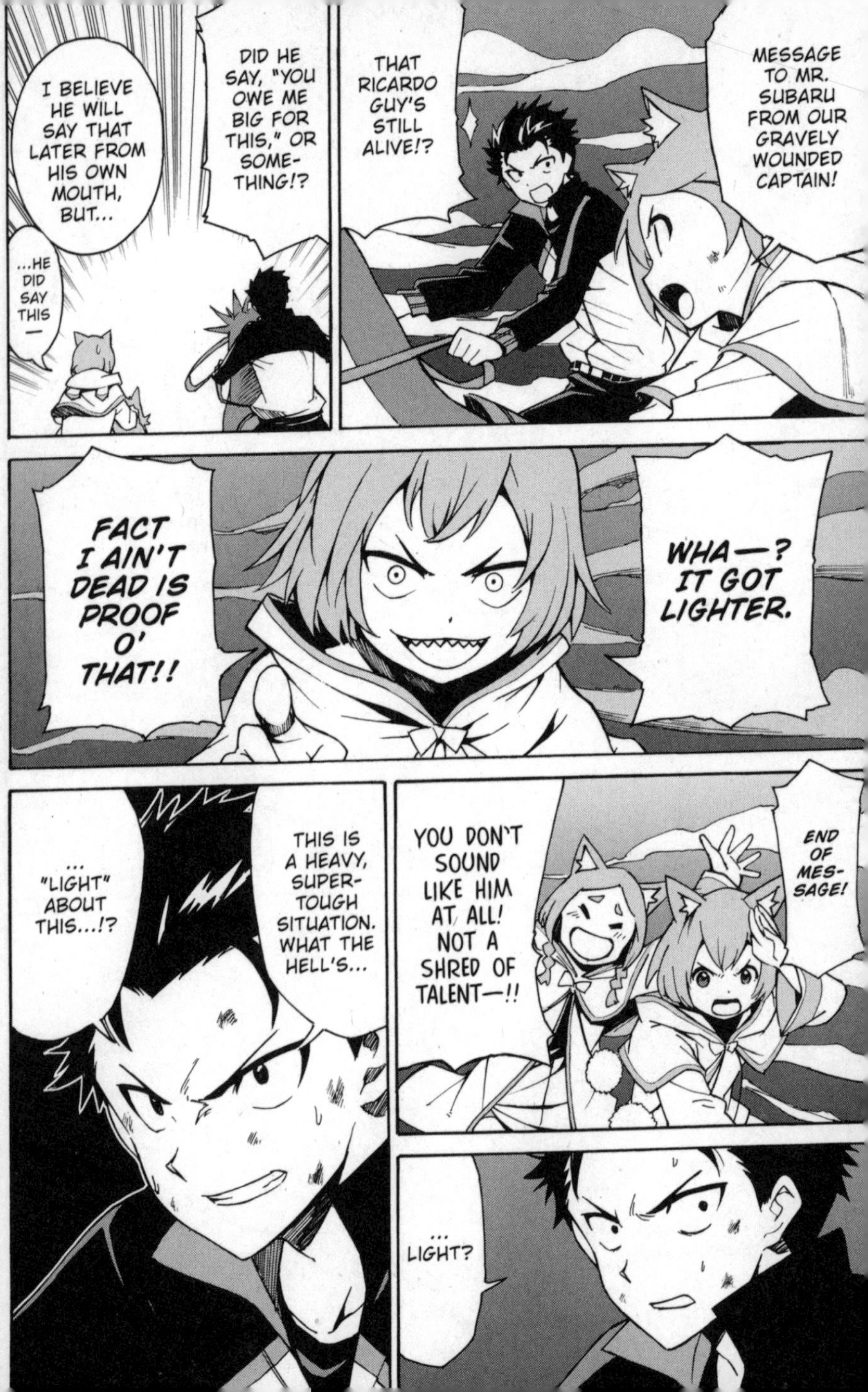

MESSAGE TO MR. SUBARU FROM OUR GRAVELY WOUNDED CAPTAIN!
THAT RICARDO GUY'S STILL ALIVE!?
DID HE SAY, "YOU OWE ME BIG FOR THIS," OR SOME-THING!?
I BELIEVE HE WILL SAY THAT LATER FROM HIS OWN MOUTH, BUT...
...HE DID SAY THIS—
WHA—? IT GOT LIGHTER.
FACT I AIN'T DEAD IS PROOF O' THAT!!
END OF MES-SAGE!
YOU DON'T SOUND LIKE HIM AT ALL! NOT A SHRED OF TALENT—!!
... LIGHT?
THIS IS A HEAVY, SUPER-TOUGH SITUATION. WHAT THE HELL'S...
... "LIGHT" ABOUT THIS...!?

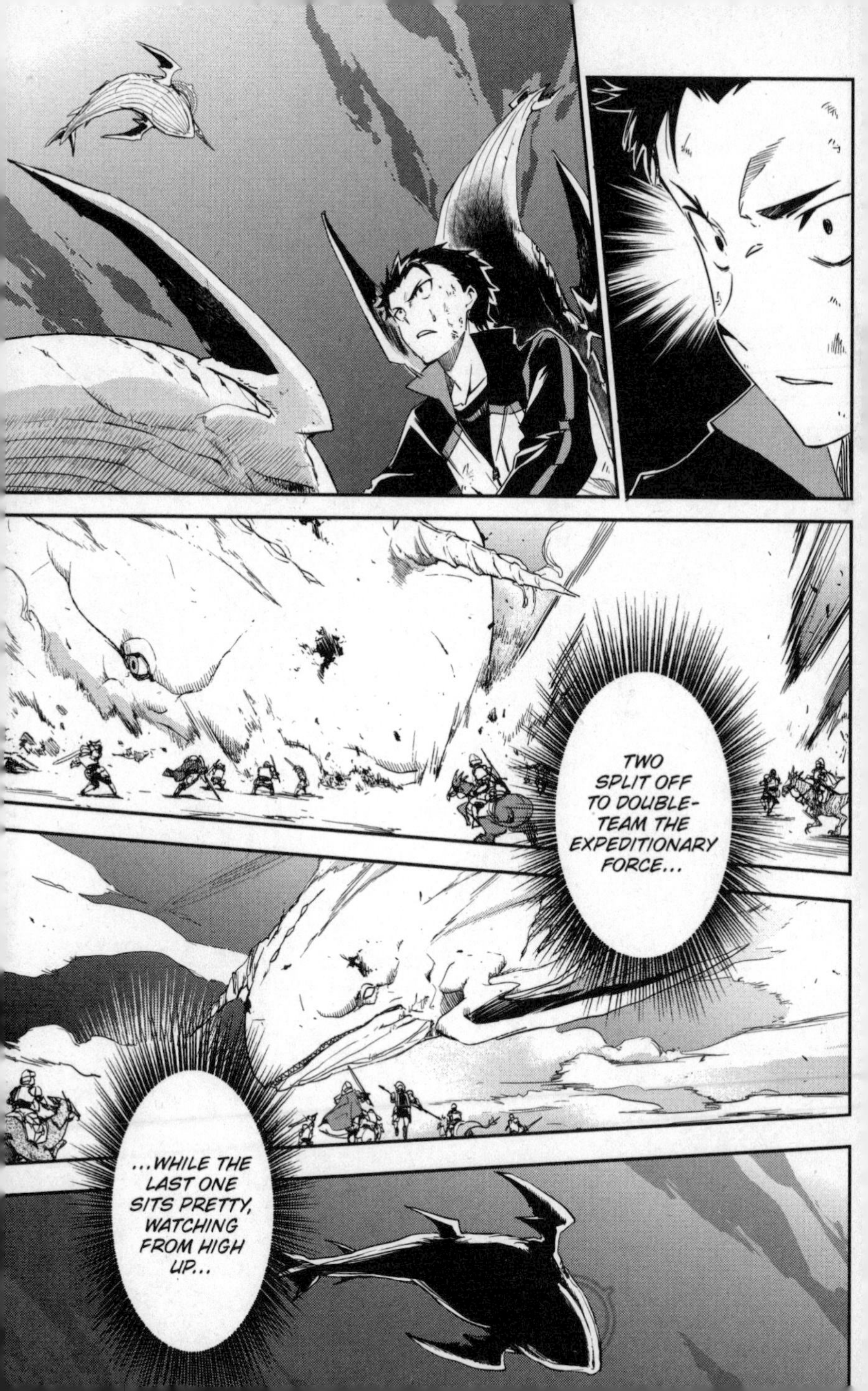
TWO SPLIT OFF TO DOUBLE-TEAM THE EXPEDITIONARY FORCE...
...WHILE THE LAST ONE SITS PRETTY, WATCHING FROM HIGH UP...

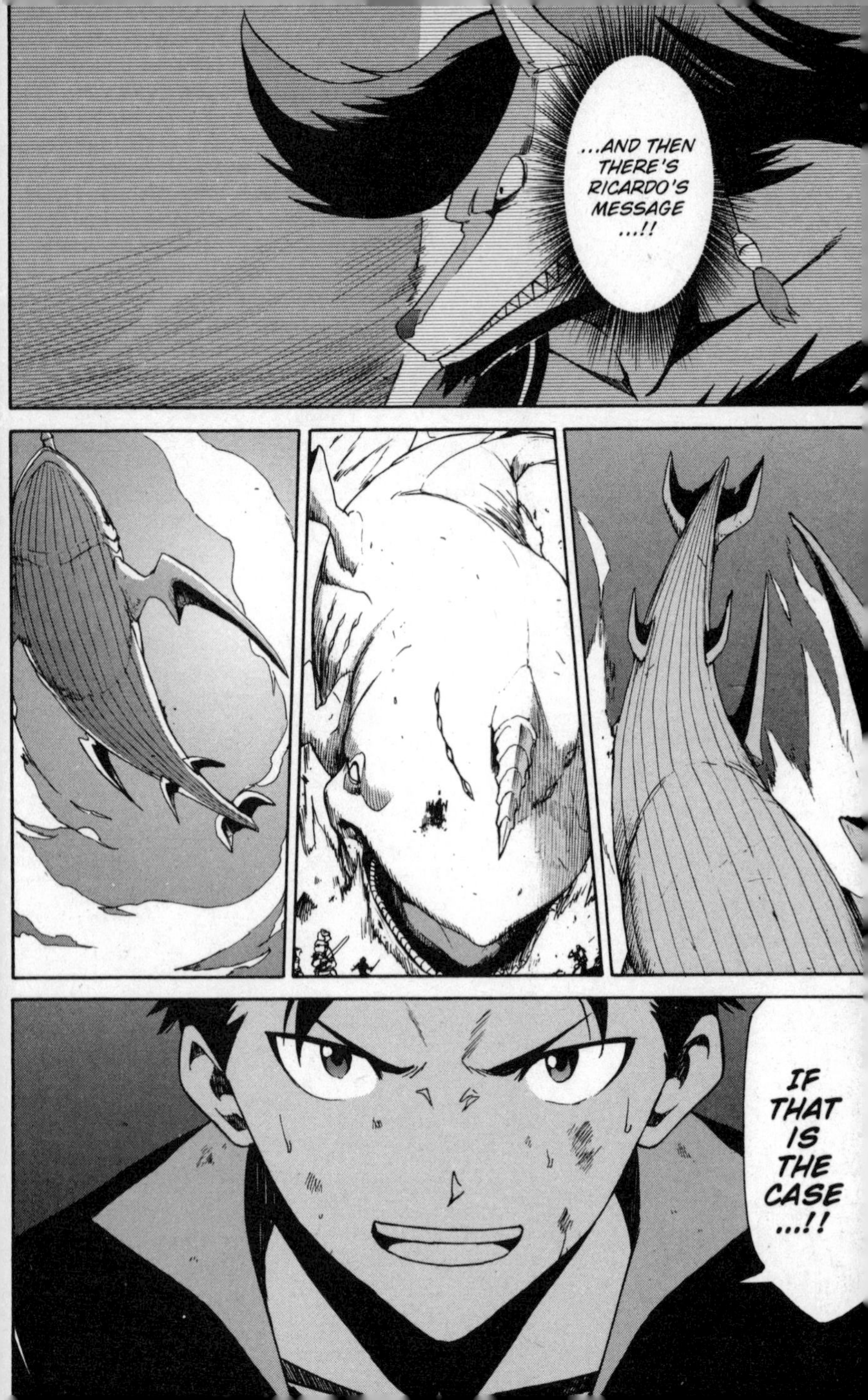
...AND THEN THERE'S RICARDO'S MESSAGE ...!!
IF THAT IS THE CASE ...!!

The only ability
Subaru Natsuki gets whe[n]
he's summoned to anothe[r]
world is time travel via h[is]
own death. But to save h[er,]
he'll die as many times
as it takes.

Re:ZERO -Starting Life in Another World-
Truth of Zero

The only ability Subaru Natsuki gets when he's
summoned to another world is time travel via his own
death. But to save her, he'll die as many times as it takes.

Truth of Zero

Re:ZERO -Starting
Life in Another World-

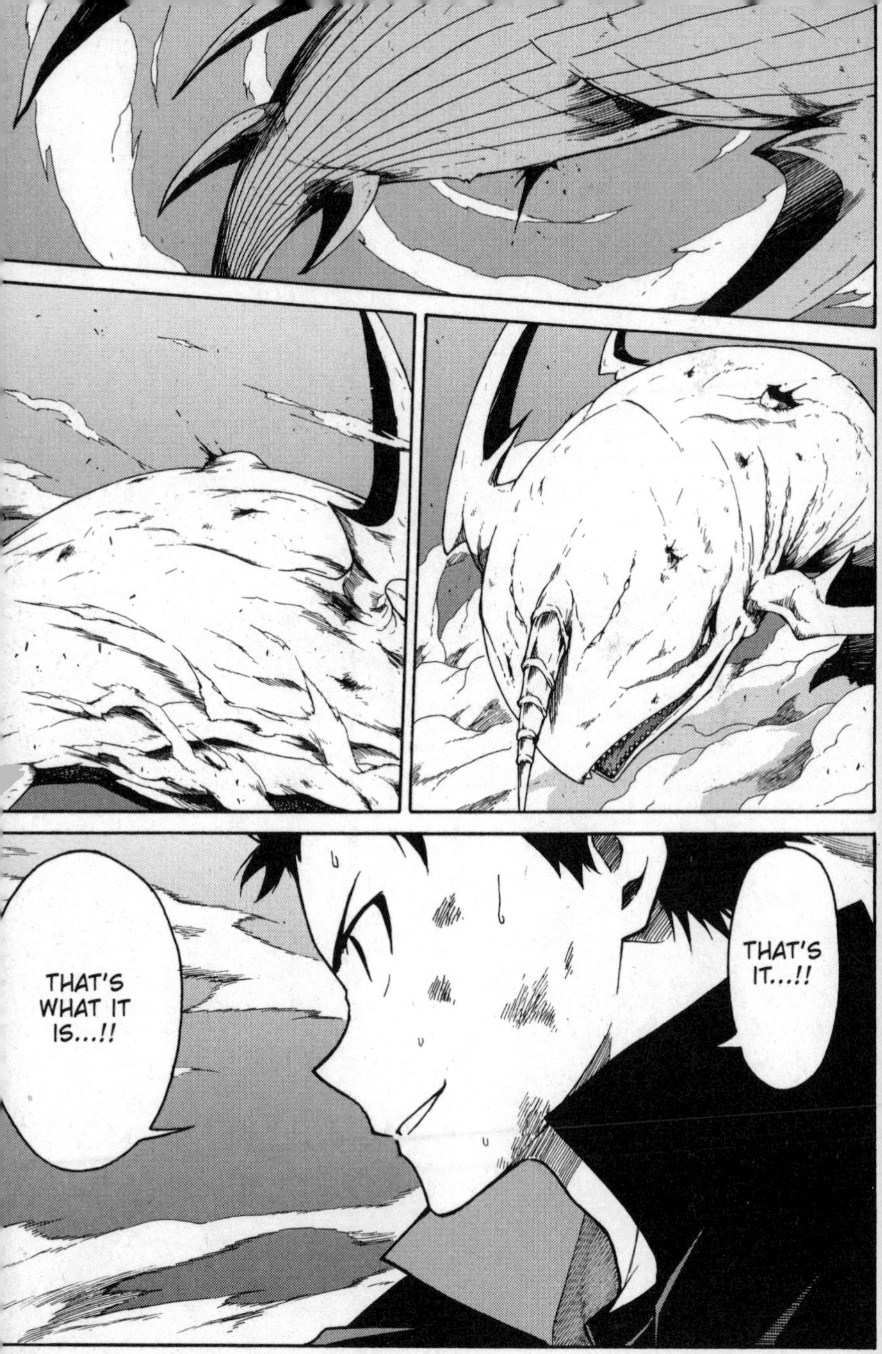
THAT'S IT...!!
THAT'S WHAT IT IS...!!

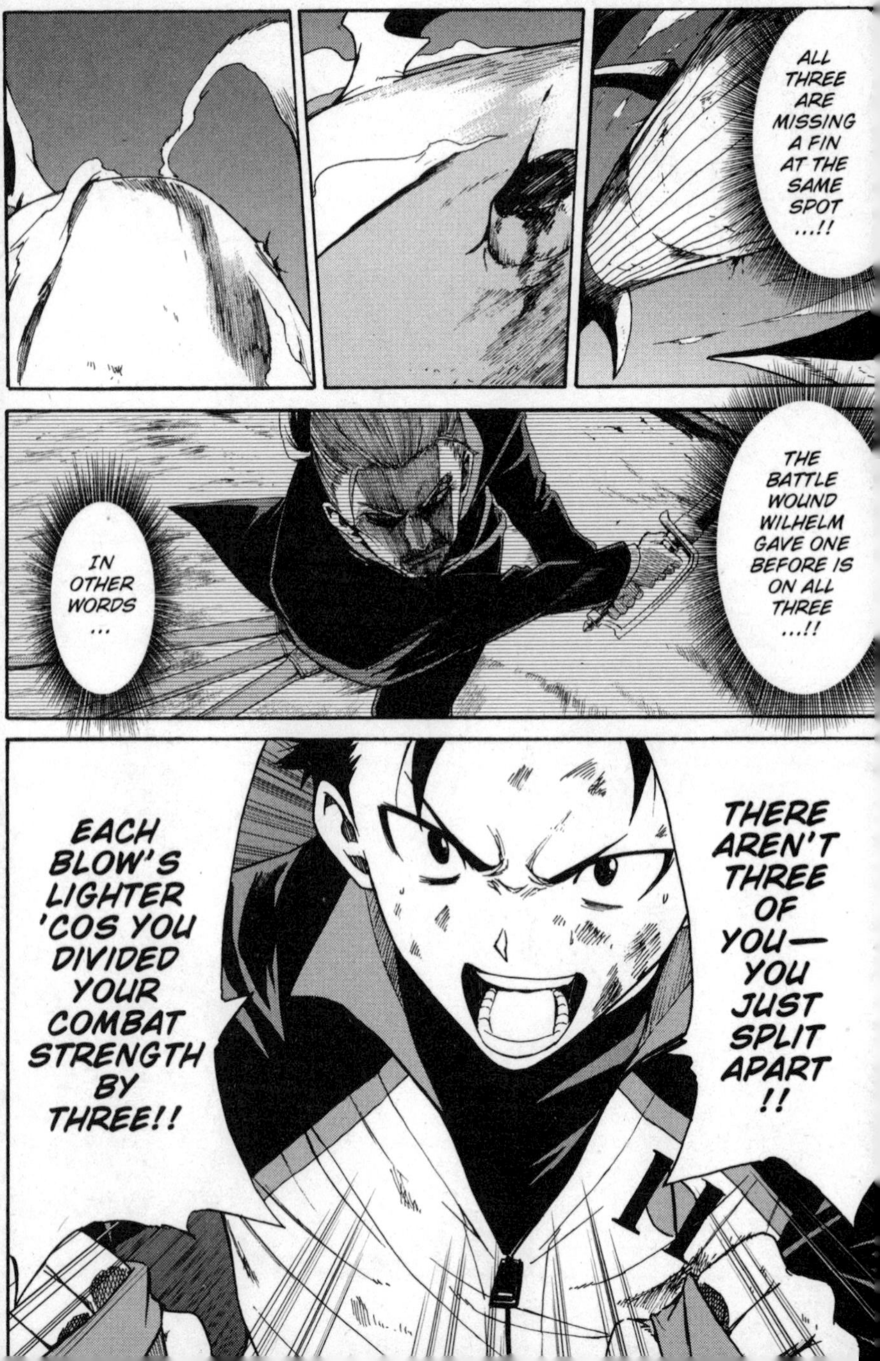
ALL THREE ARE MISSING A FIN AT THE SAME SPOT ...!!
THE BATTLE WOUND WILHELM GAVE ONE BEFORE IS ON ALL THREE ...!!
IN OTHER WORDS ...
THERE AREN'T THREE OF YOU— YOU JUST SPLIT APART !!
EACH BLOW'S LIGHTER 'COS YOU DIVIDED YOUR COMBAT STRENGTH BY THREE!!

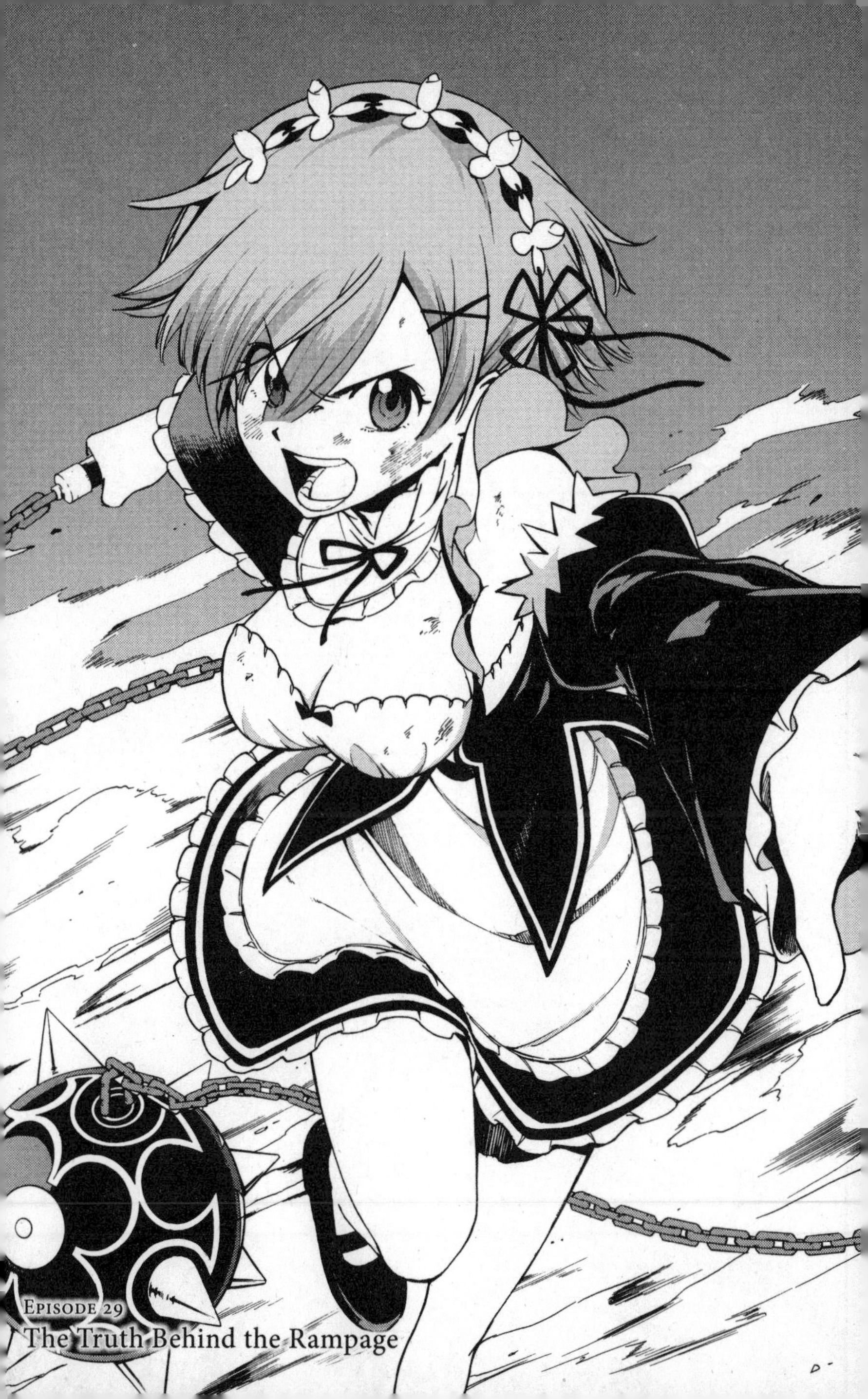
Episode 29
The Truth Behind the Rampage

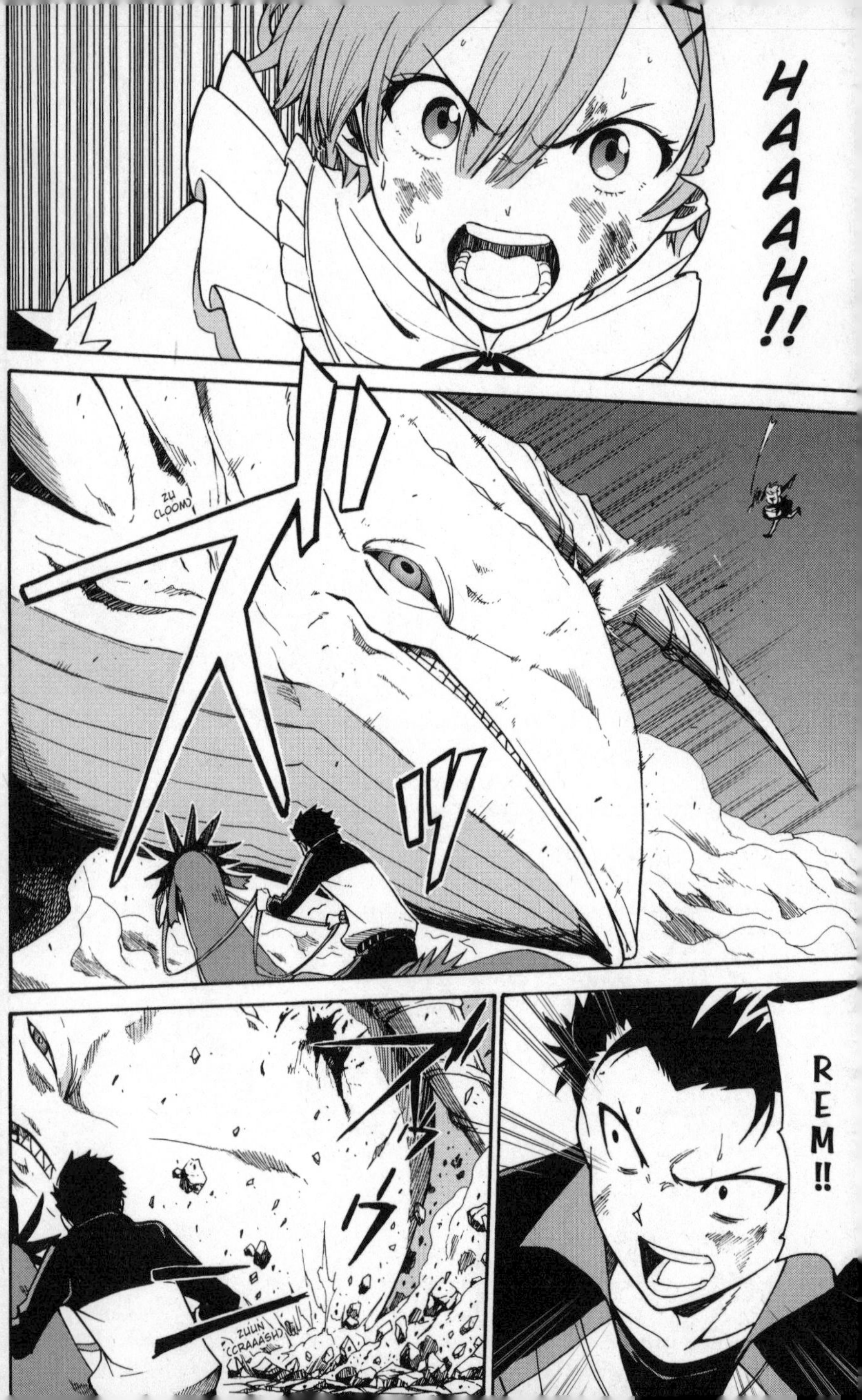
HAAAAH!!
ZU (LOOM)
ZUUN (CRAAASH)
REM!!

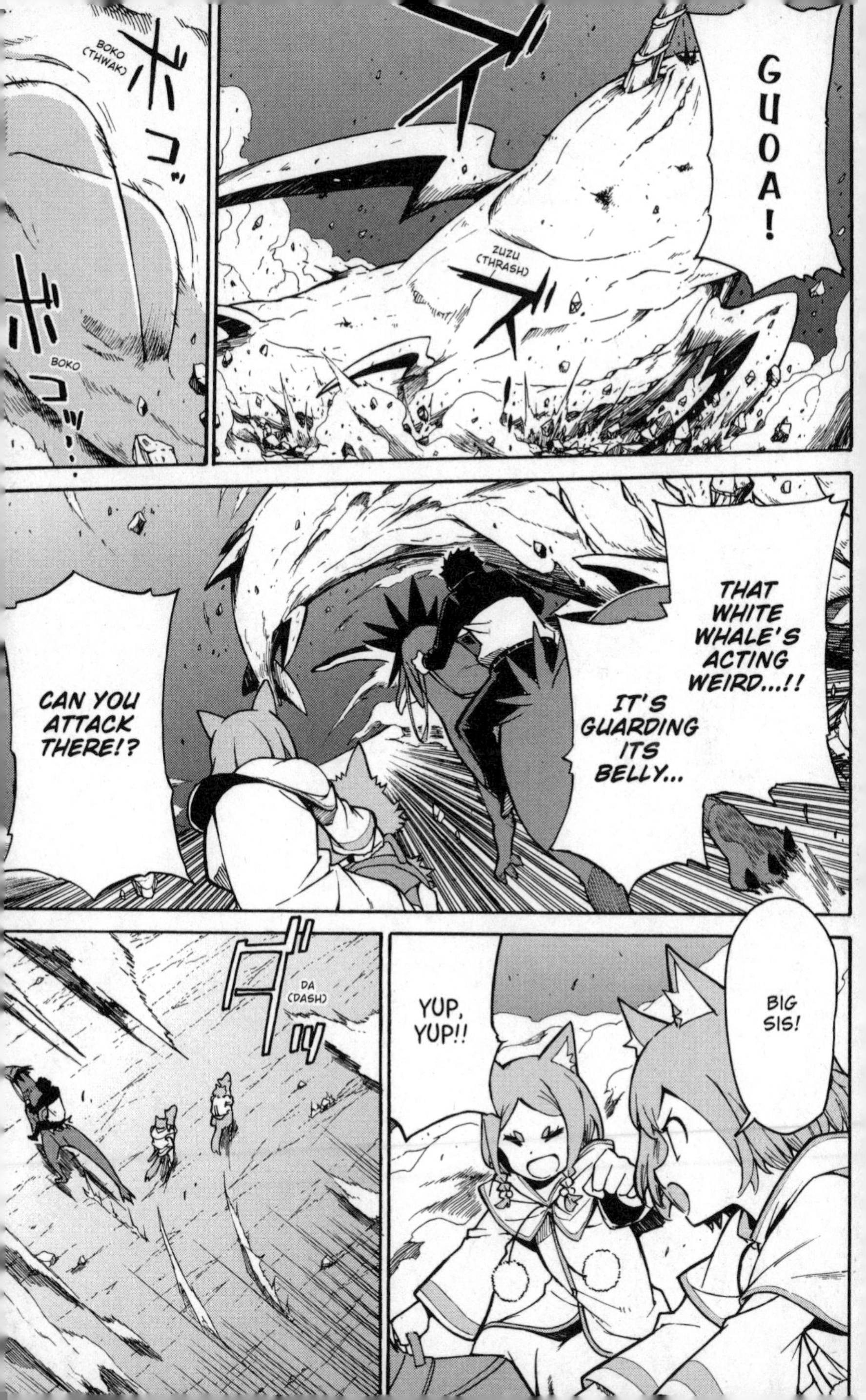
GUOA!
ZUZU (THRASH)
BOKO (THWAK)
BOKO
THAT WHITE WHALE'S ACTING WEIRD...!!
IT'S GUARDING ITS BELLY...
CAN YOU ATTACK THERE!?
BIG SIS!
YUP, YUP!!
DA (DASH)

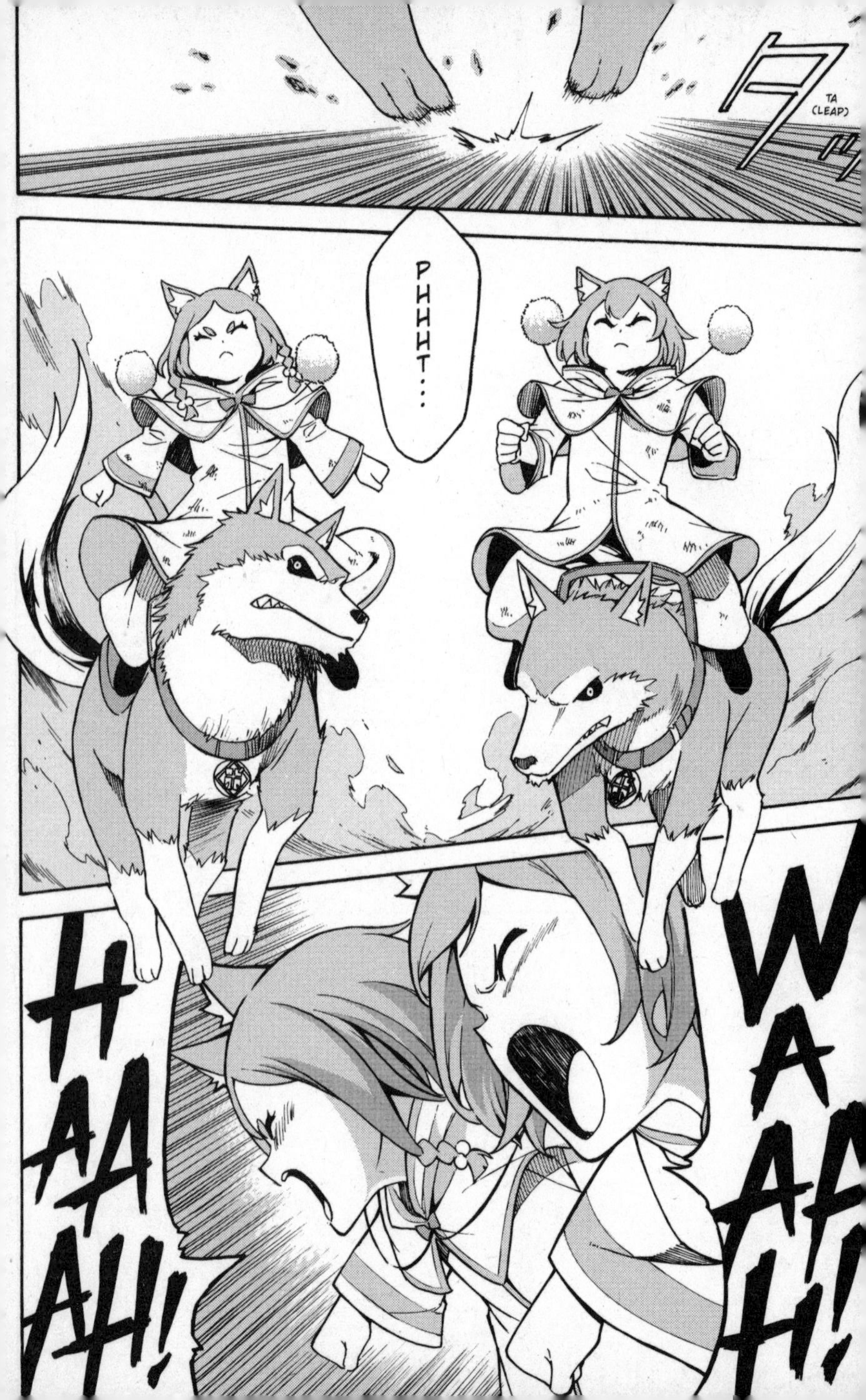

TA (LEAP)
PHHHT...
WAAAH!
HAAAAH!

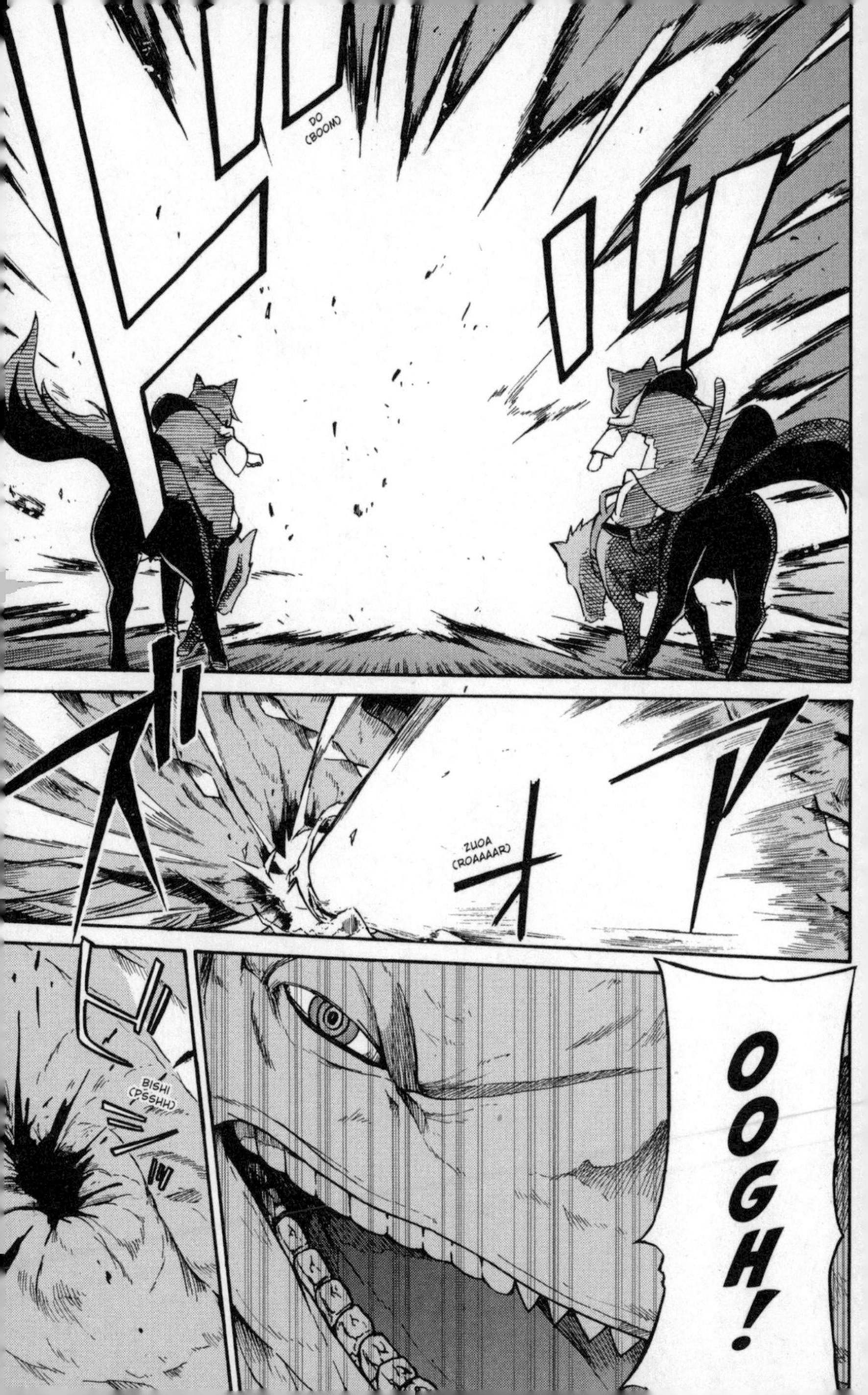
DO
(BOOM)
ZUOA
(ROAAAAR)
OOGH!
BISHI
(PSSHH)

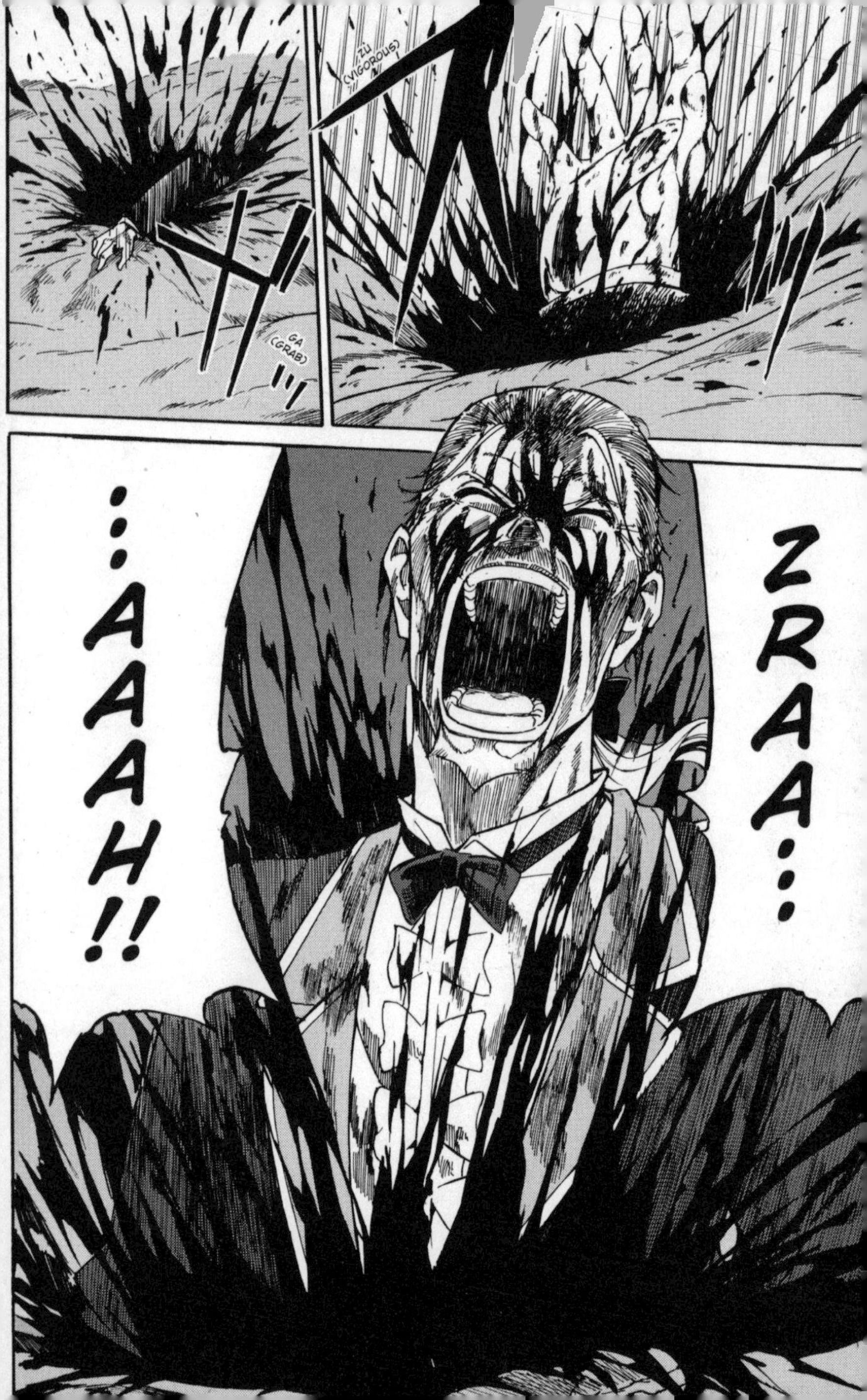
ZU (VIGOROUS)
GA (GRAB)
ZRAA...
...AAAH!!

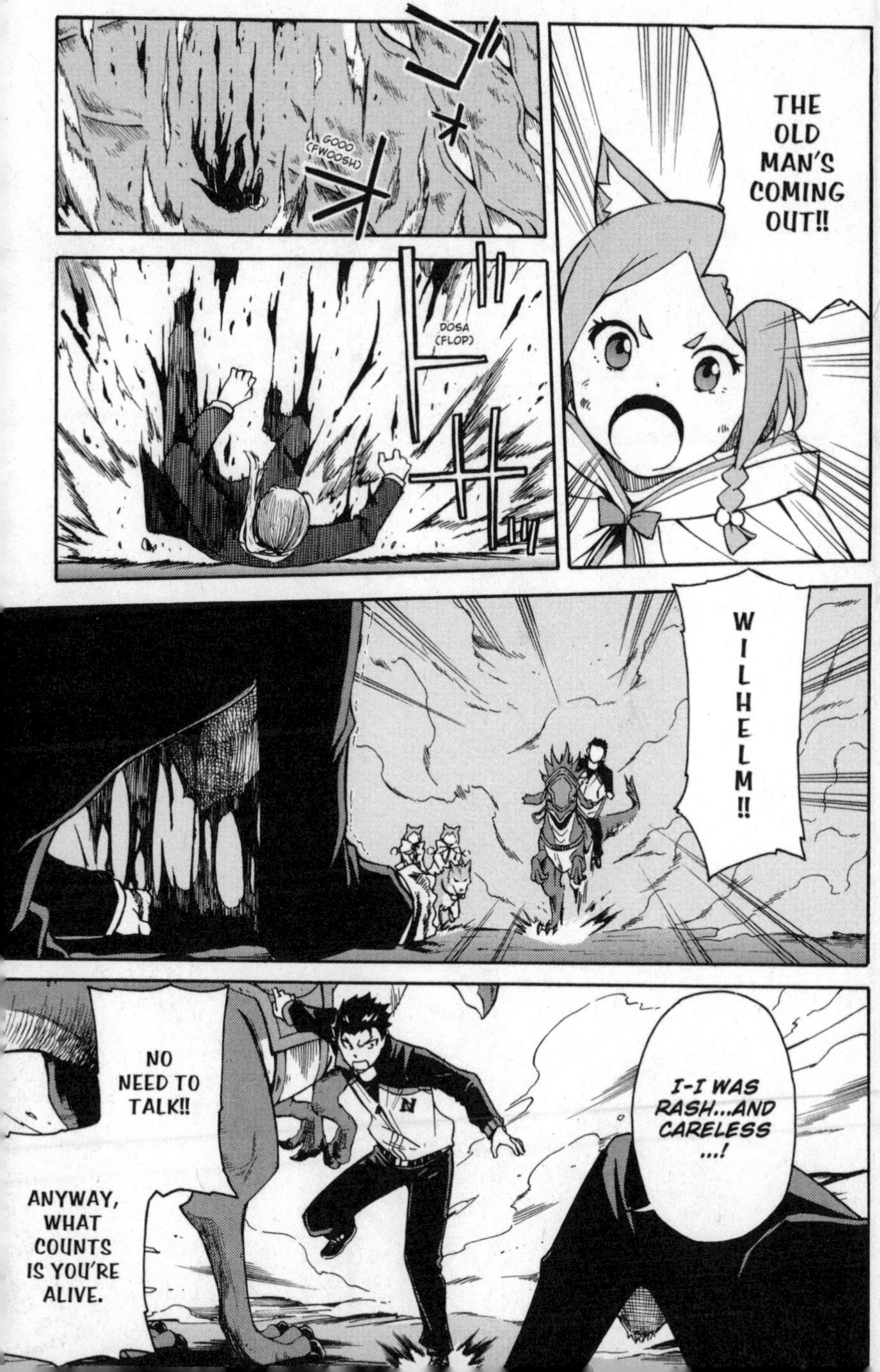
THE OLD MAN'S COMING OUT!!
GOOO (FWOOSH)
DOSA (FLOP)
WILHELM!!
I-I WAS RASH...AND CARELESS ...!
NO NEED TO TALK!!
ANYWAY, WHAT COUNTS IS YOU'RE ALIVE.

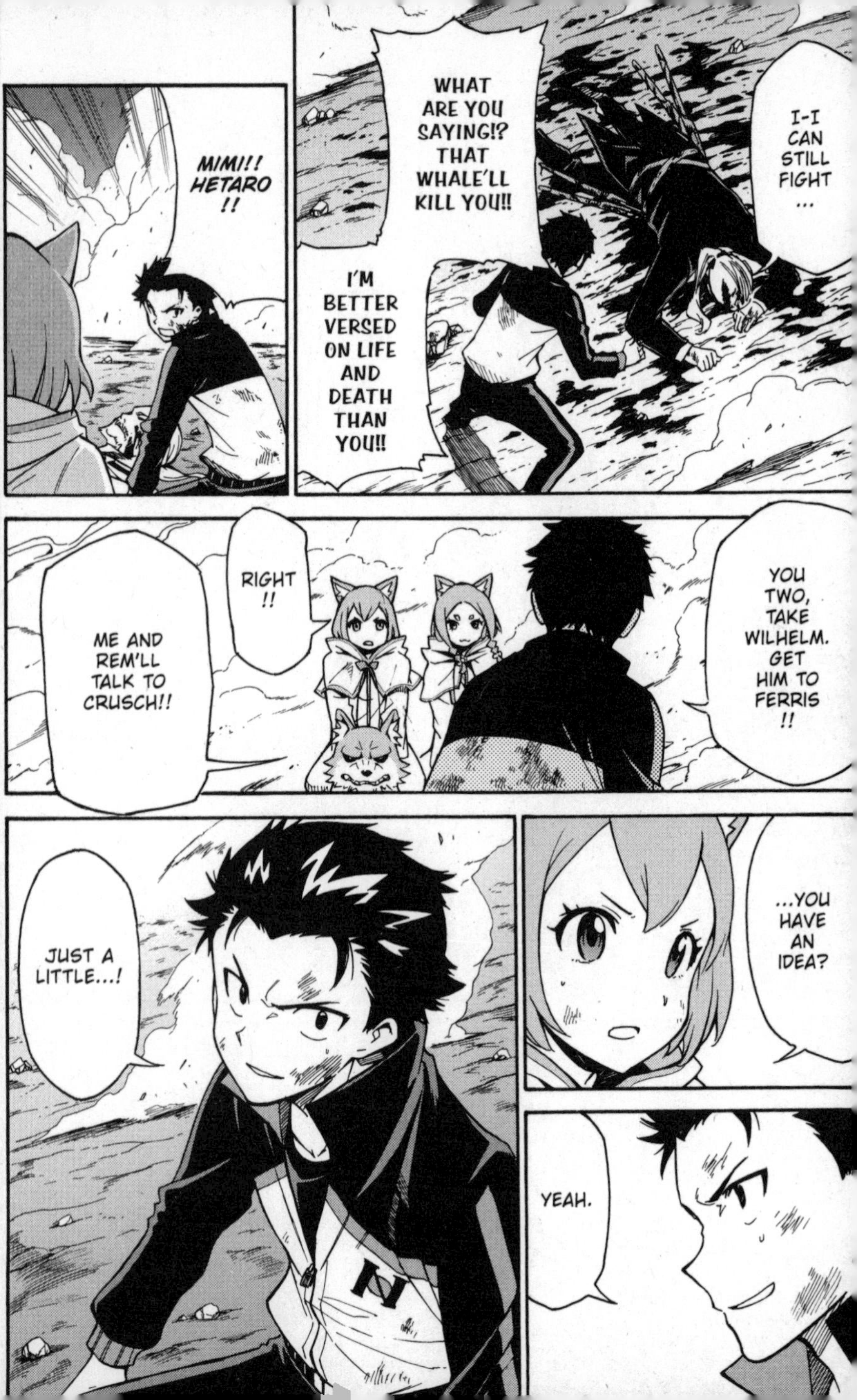
I-I CAN STILL FIGHT ...
WHAT ARE YOU SAYING!? THAT WHALE'LL KILL YOU!!
I'M BETTER VERSED ON LIFE AND DEATH THAN YOU!!
MIMI!! HETARO !!
YOU TWO, TAKE WILHELM. GET HIM TO FERRIS !!
RIGHT !!
ME AND REM'LL TALK TO CRUSCH!!
...YOU HAVE AN IDEA?
YEAH.
JUST A LITTLE...!

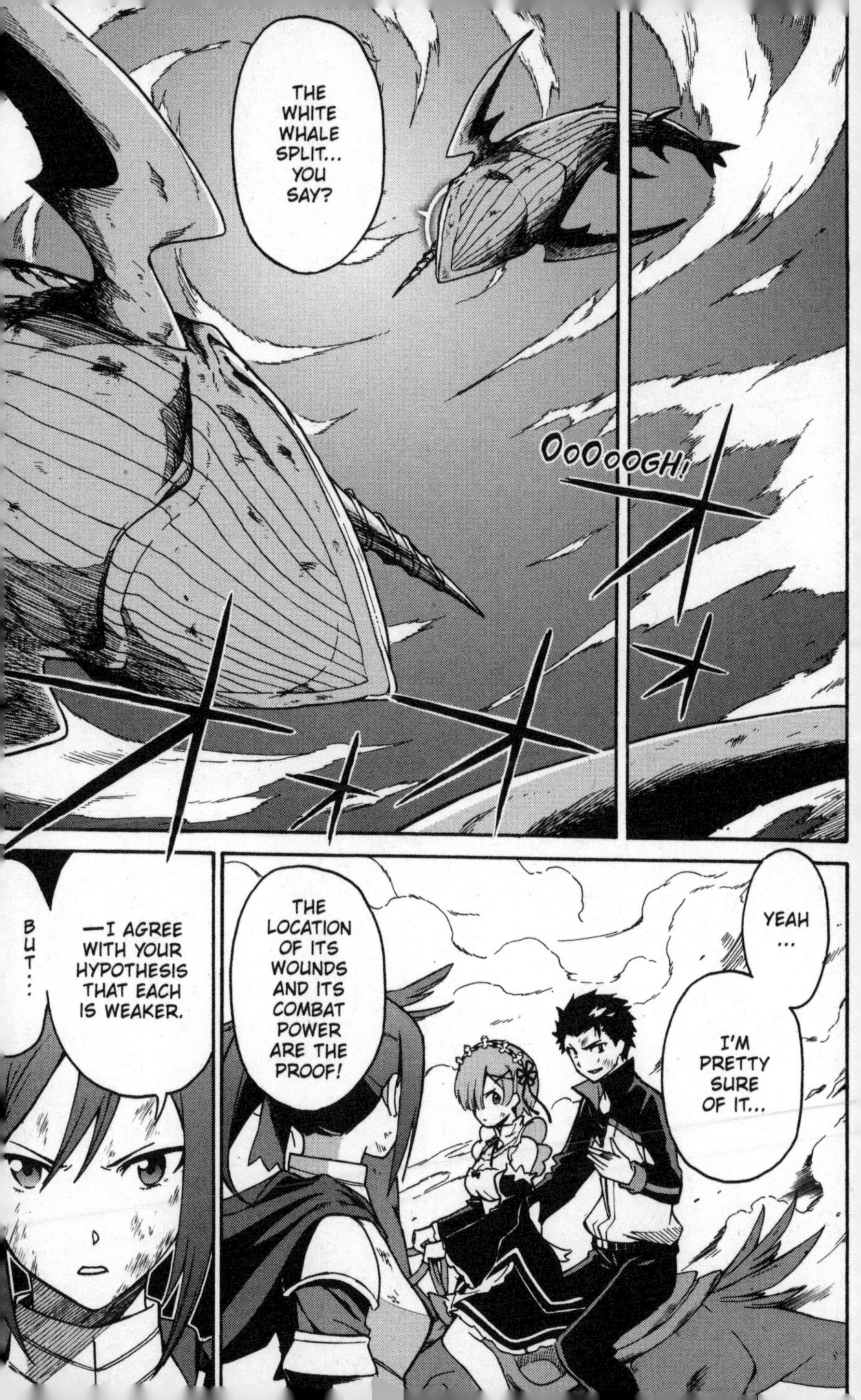
THE WHITE WHALE SPLIT... YOU SAY?
OoOooGH!
YEAH...
I'M PRETTY SURE OF IT...
THE LOCATION OF ITS WOUNDS AND ITS COMBAT POWER ARE THE PROOF!
—I AGREE WITH YOUR HYPOTHESIS THAT EACH IS WEAKER.
BUT...

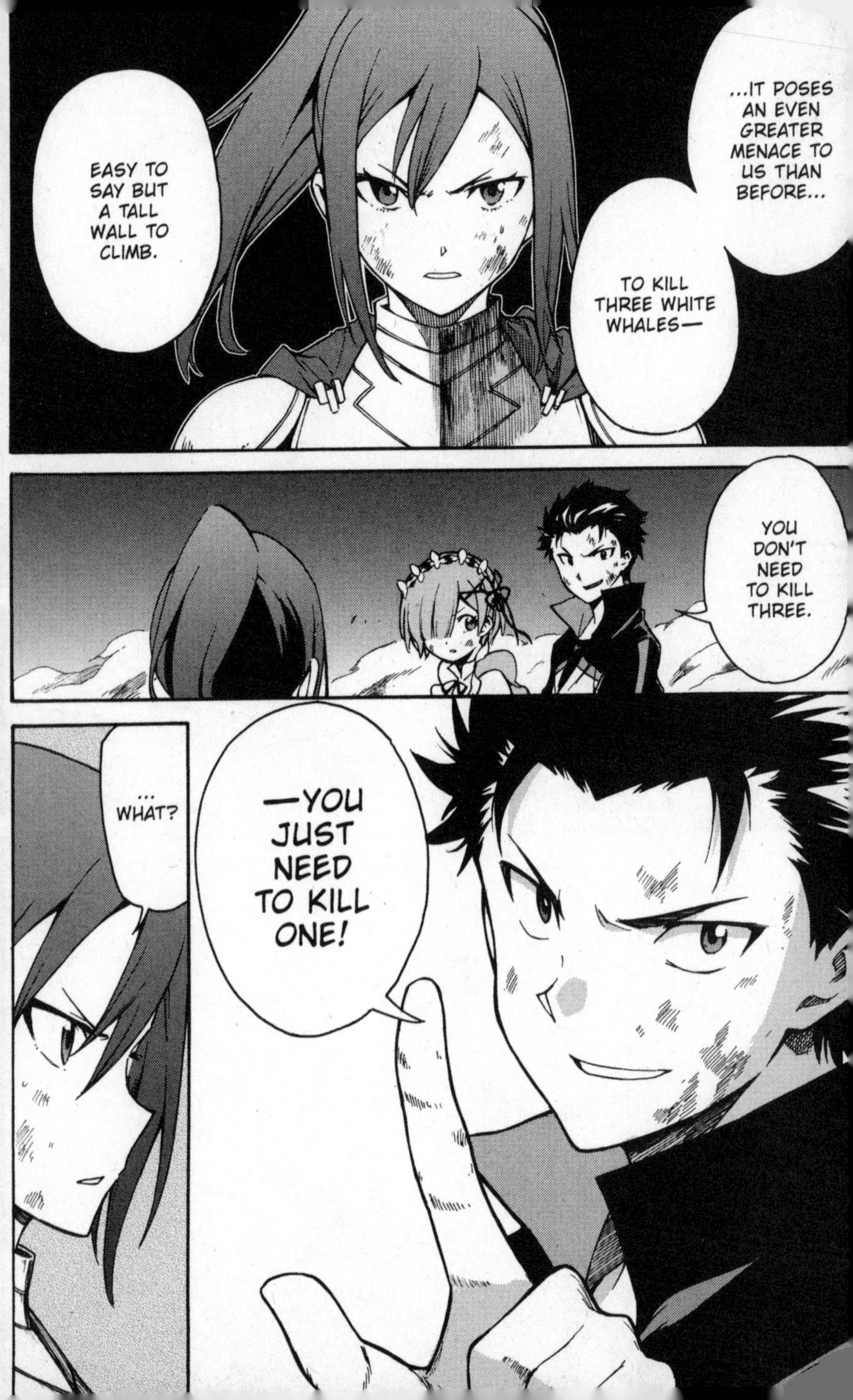
...IT POSES AN EVEN GREATER MENACE TO US THAN BEFORE...
TO KILL THREE WHITE WHALES—
EASY TO SAY BUT A TALL WALL TO CLIMB.
YOU DON'T NEED TO KILL THREE.
—YOU JUST NEED TO KILL ONE!
... WHAT?

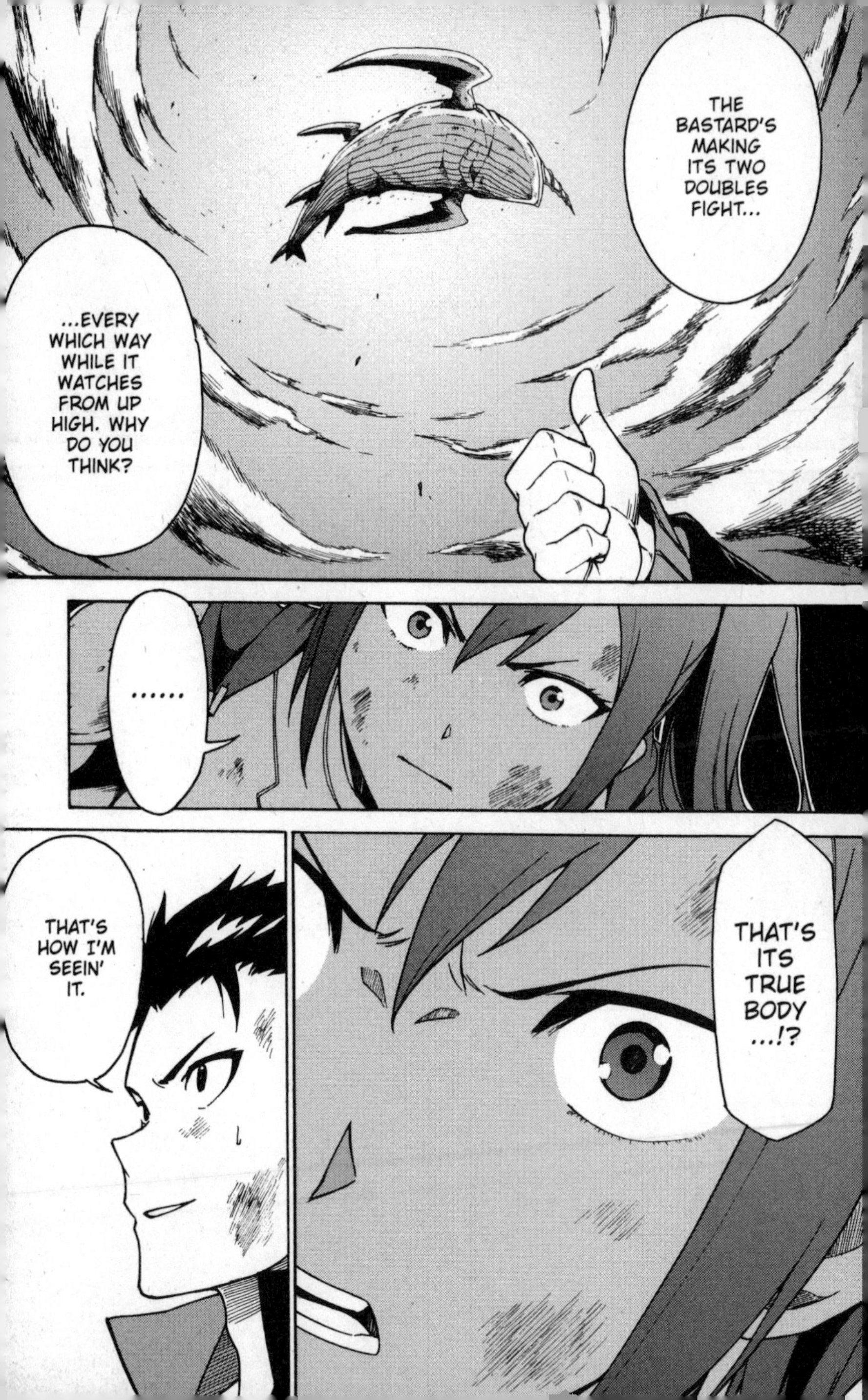
THE BASTARD'S MAKING ITS TWO DOUBLES FIGHT...
...EVERY WHICH WAY WHILE IT WATCHES FROM UP HIGH. WHY DO YOU THINK?
......
THAT'S ITS TRUE BODY ...!?
THAT'S HOW I'M SEEIN' IT.

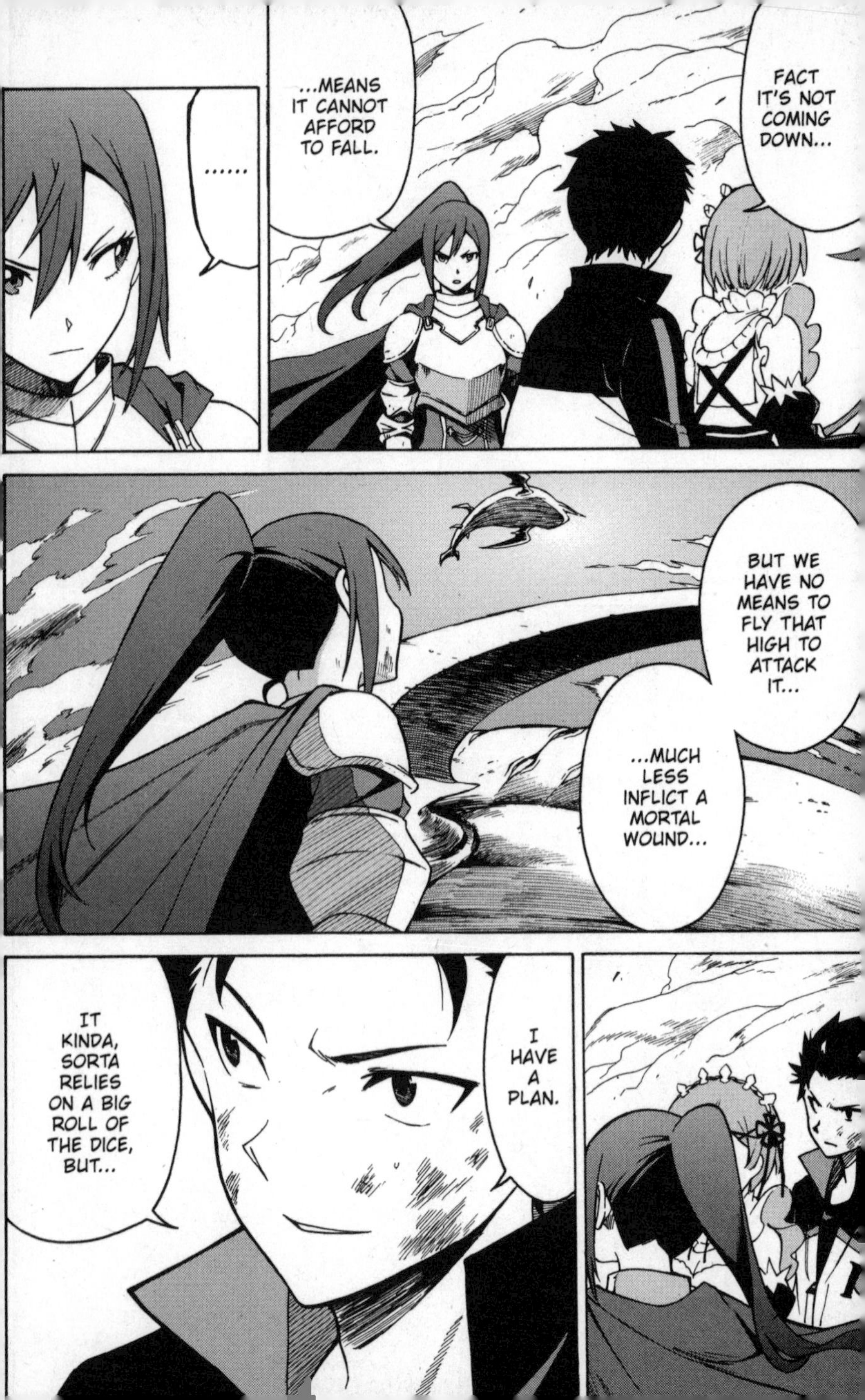
FACT IT'S NOT COMING DOWN...
...MEANS IT CANNOT AFFORD TO FALL.
......
BUT WE HAVE NO MEANS TO FLY THAT HIGH TO ATTACK IT...
...MUCH LESS INFLICT A MORTAL WOUND...
I HAVE A PLAN.
IT KINDA, SORTA RELIES ON A BIG ROLL OF THE DICE, BUT...

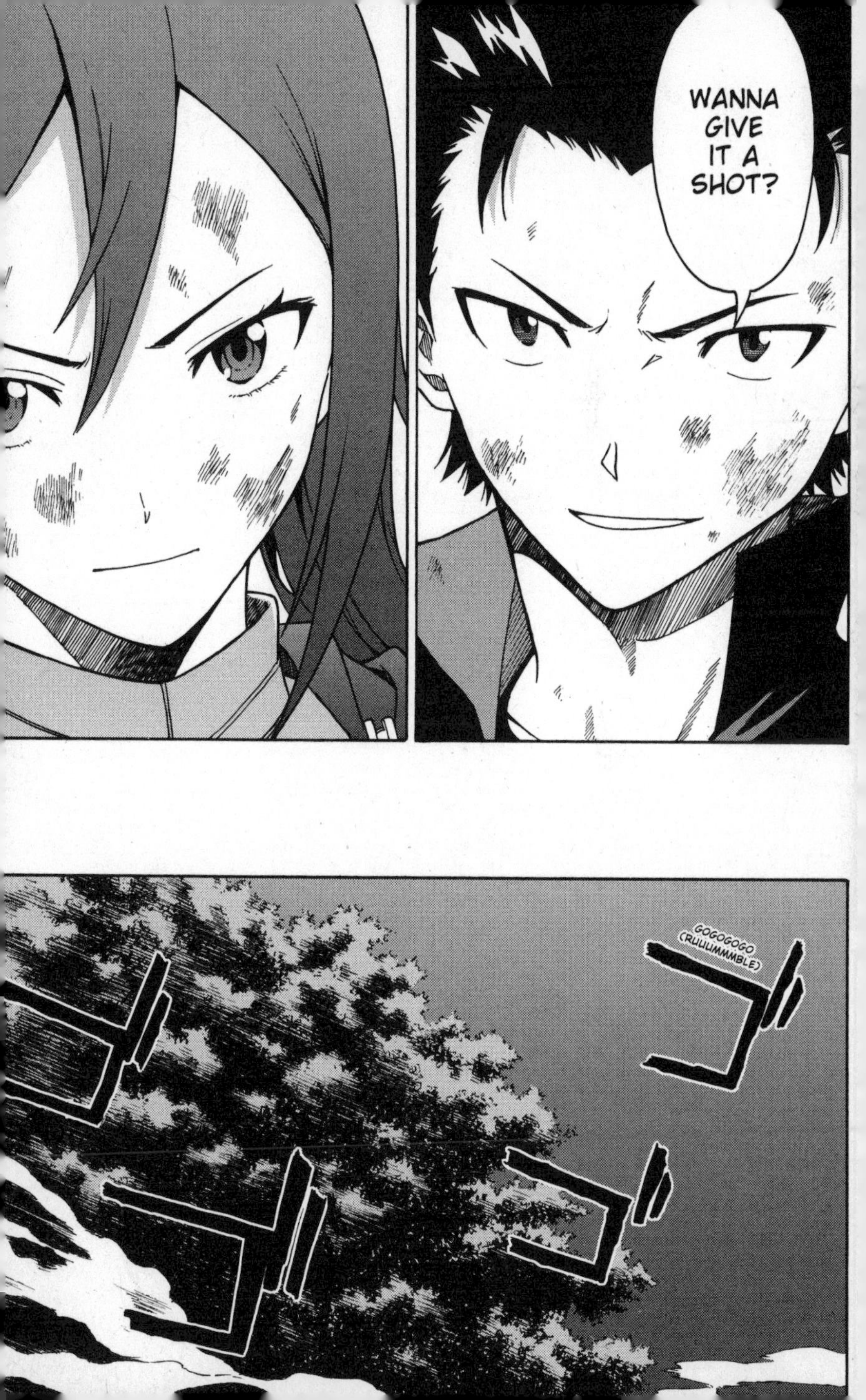
WANNA GIVE IT A SHOT?
GOGOGOGO (RUUUMMMBLE)

(OOOO)
(FWOOOO)

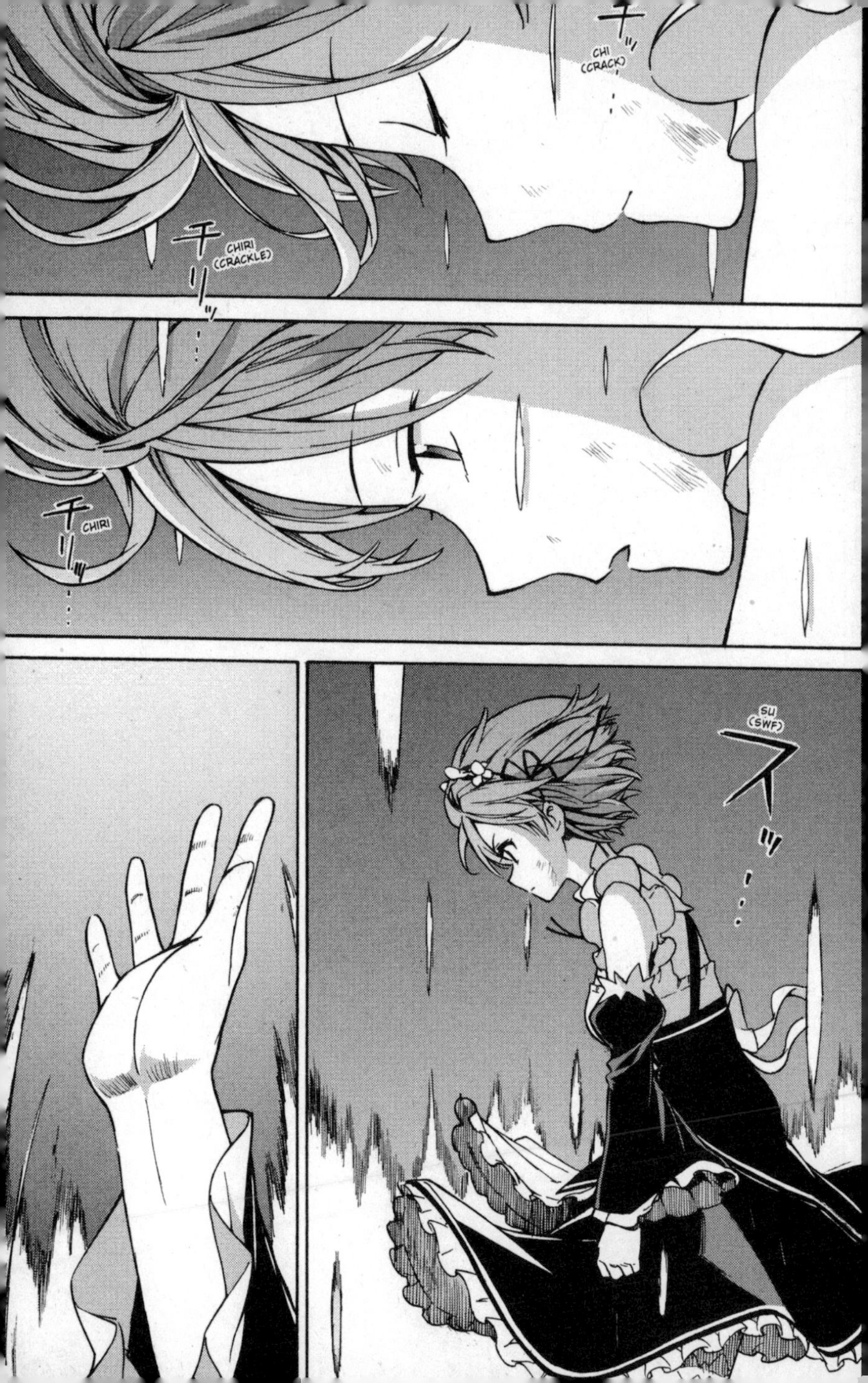
チッ
CHI (CRACK)
チリッ…
CHIRI (CRACKLE)
チリッ…
CHIRI
スッ…
SU (SWF)

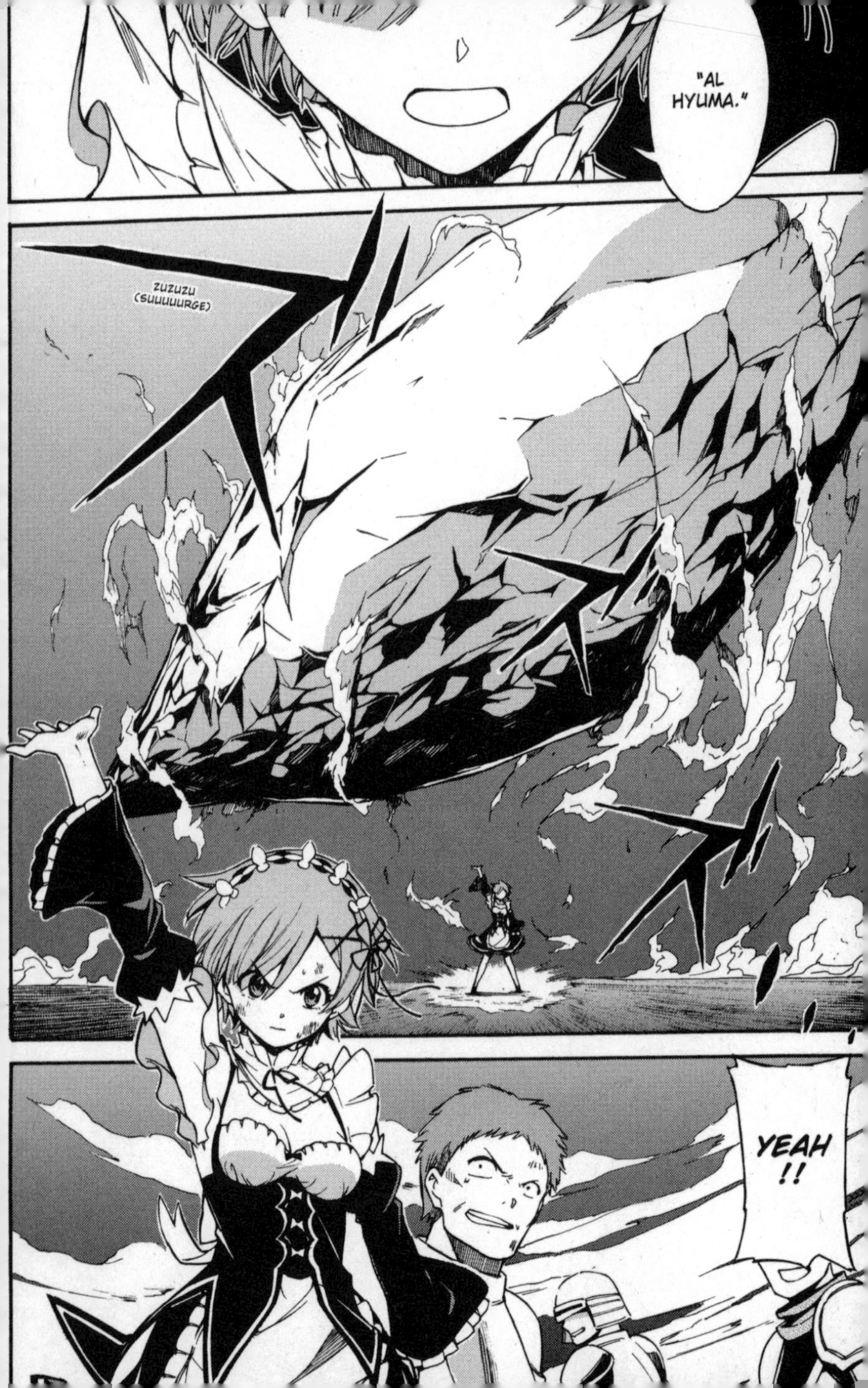
"AL HYUMA."
ZUZUZU (SUUUUURGE)
YEAH!!

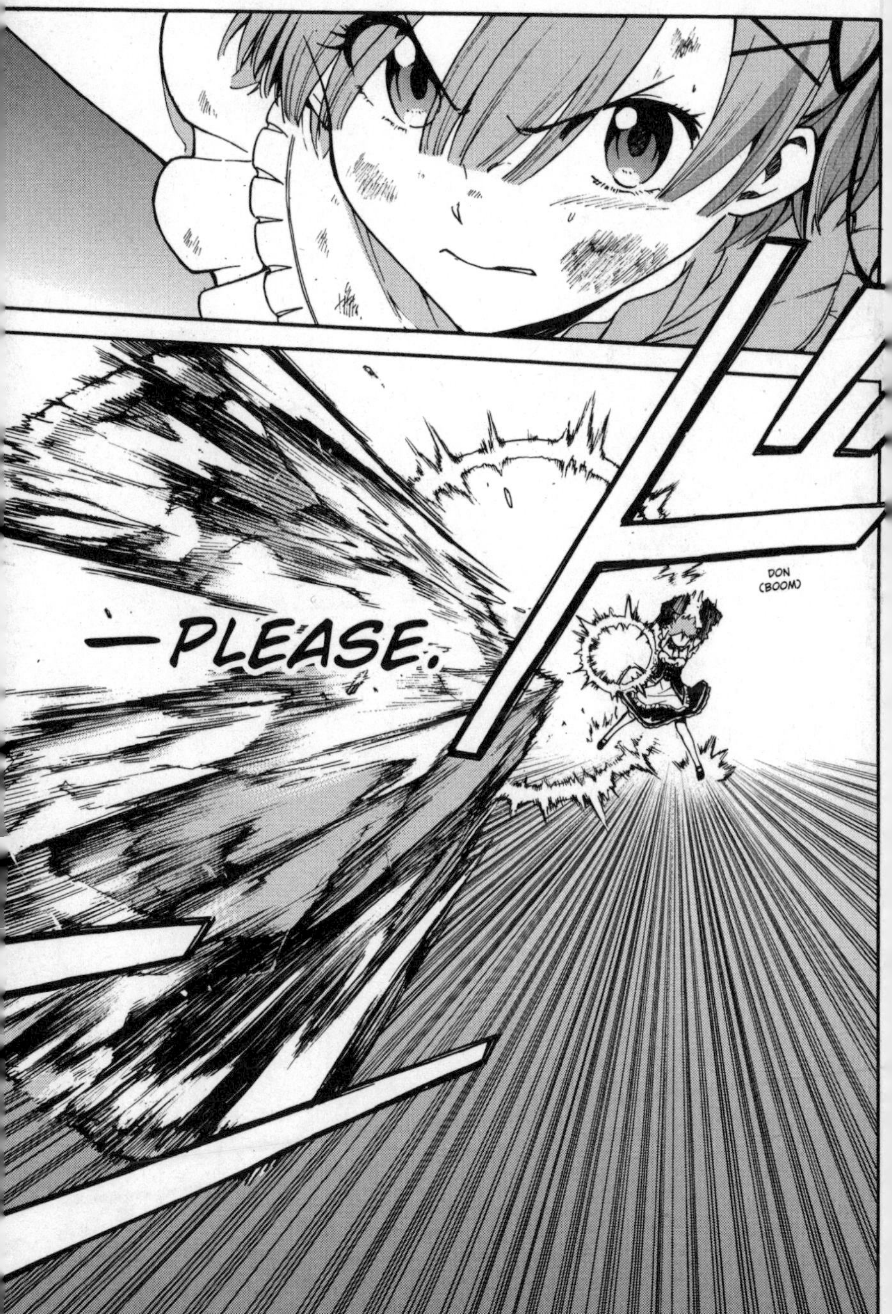
DON
(BOOM)
—PLEASE.

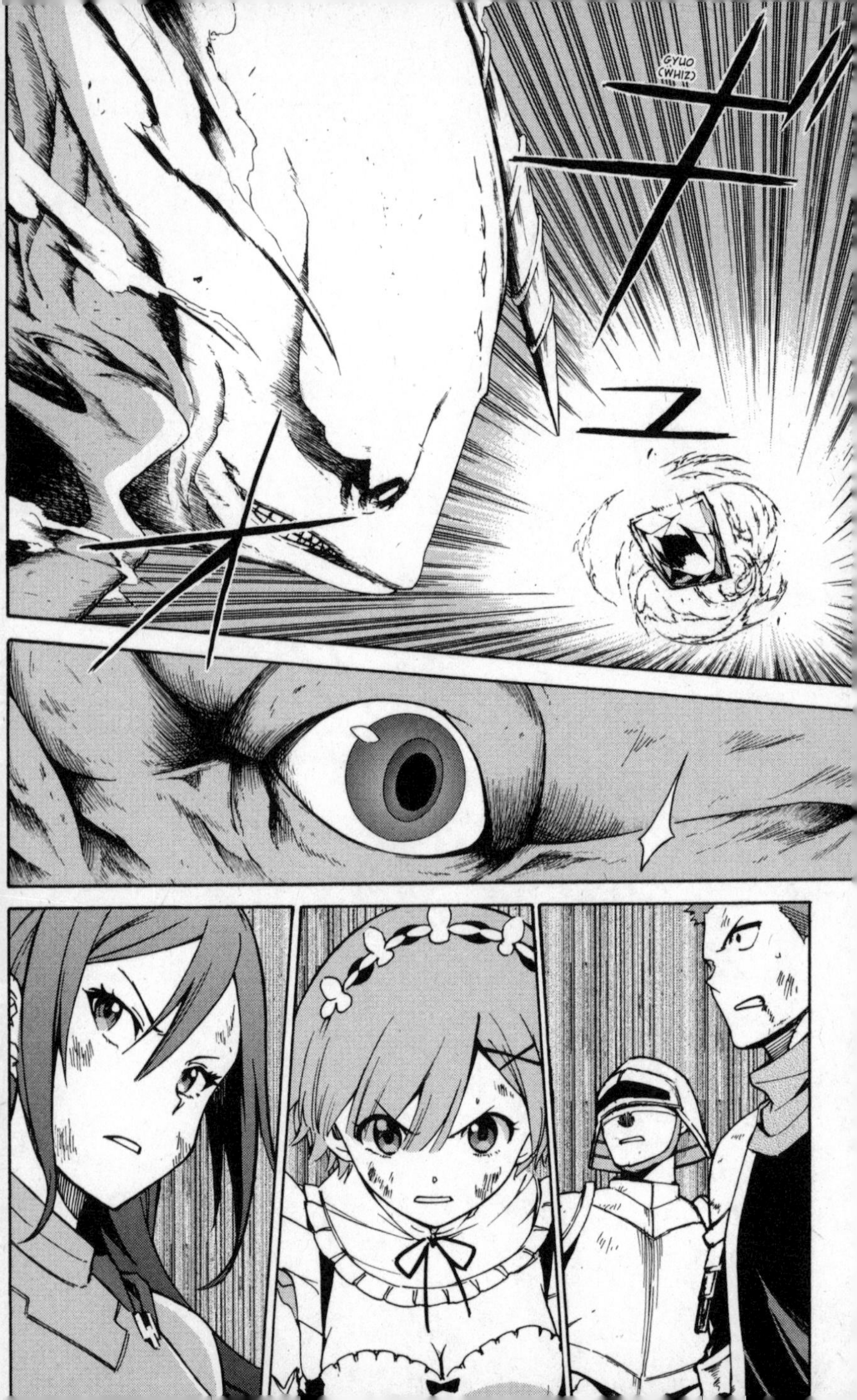
GYUO
(WHIZ)

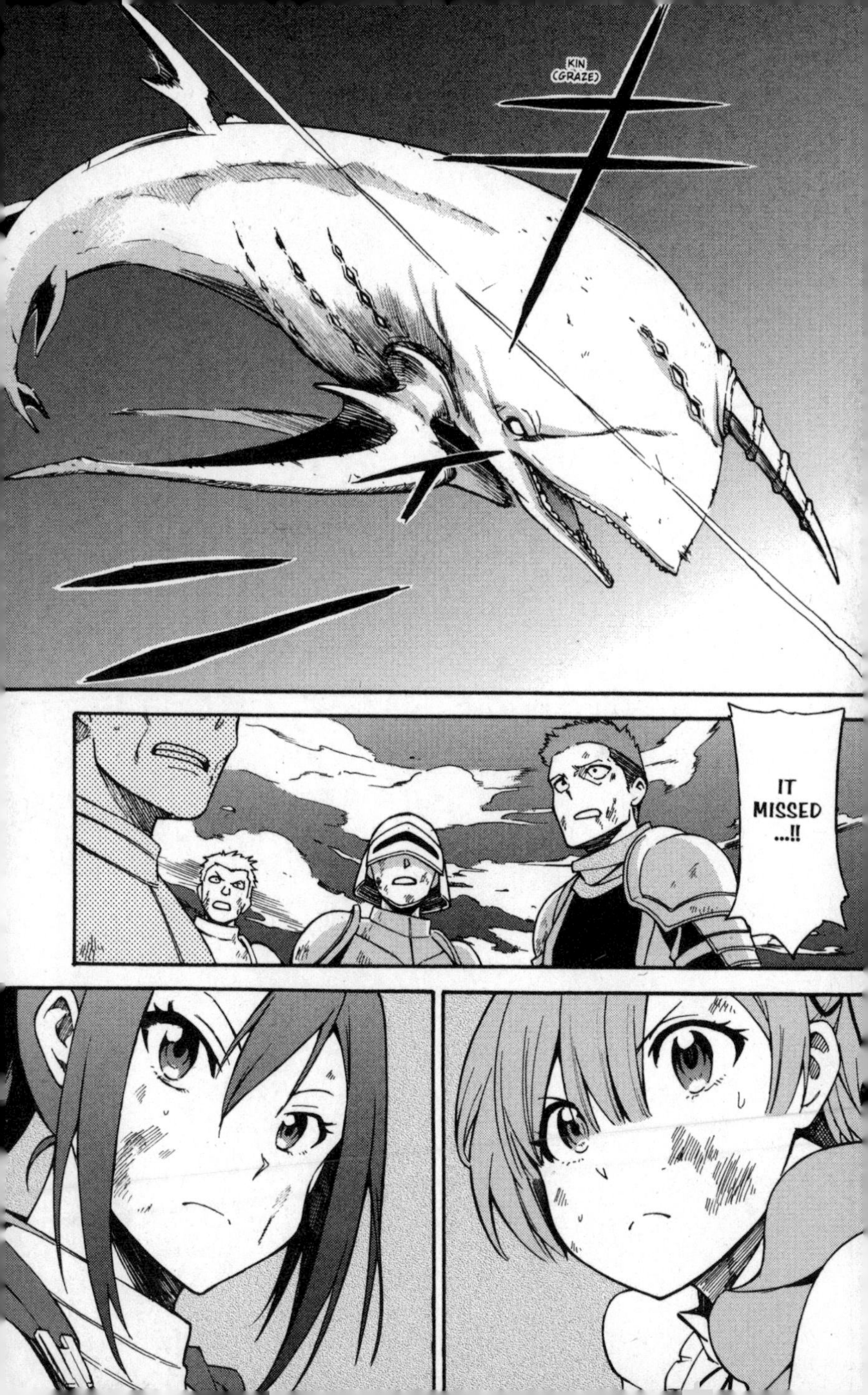
KIN
(GRAZE)
IT MISSED ...!!

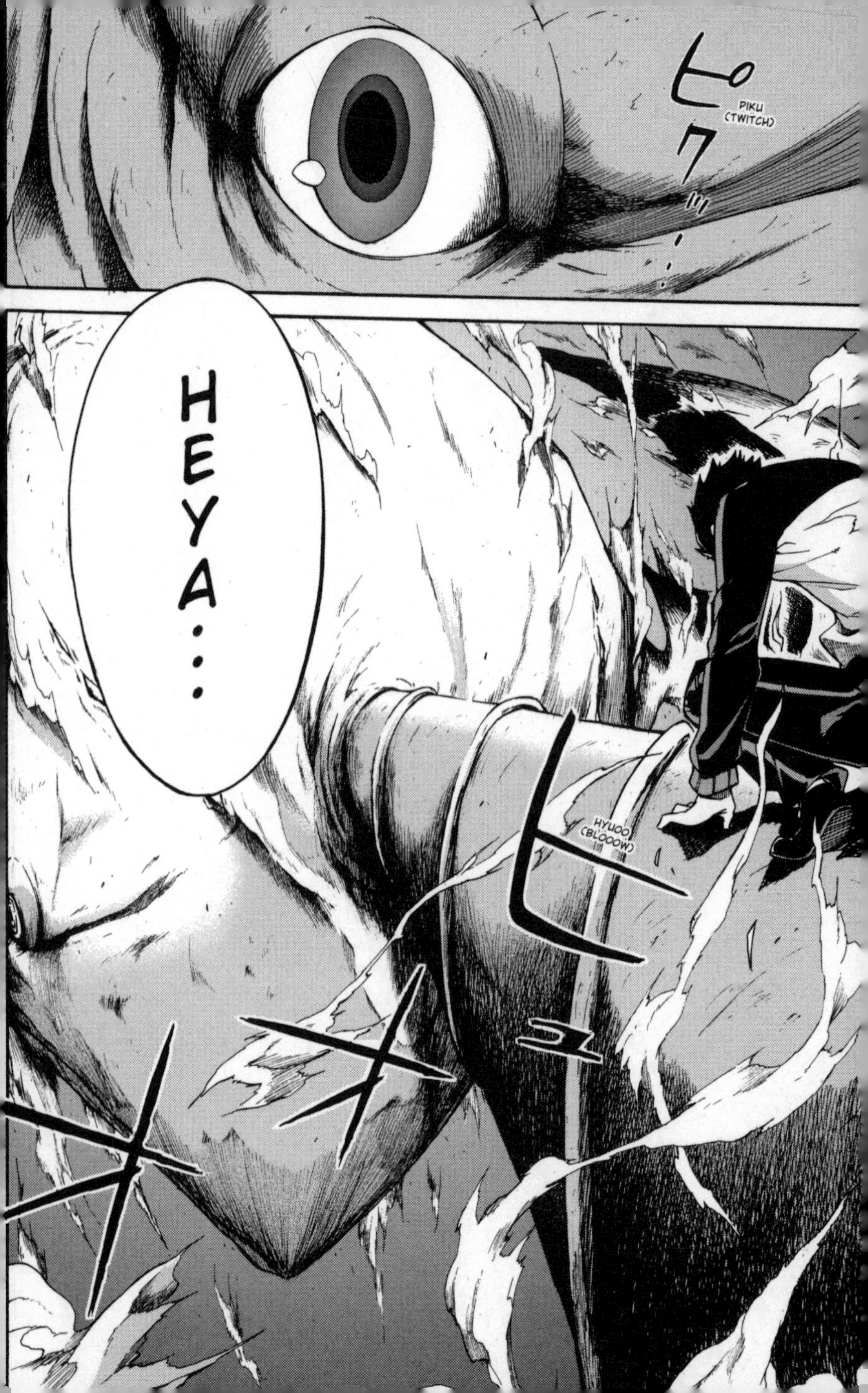
PIKU
(TWITCH)
HEYA...
HYUOO
(BLOOOW)

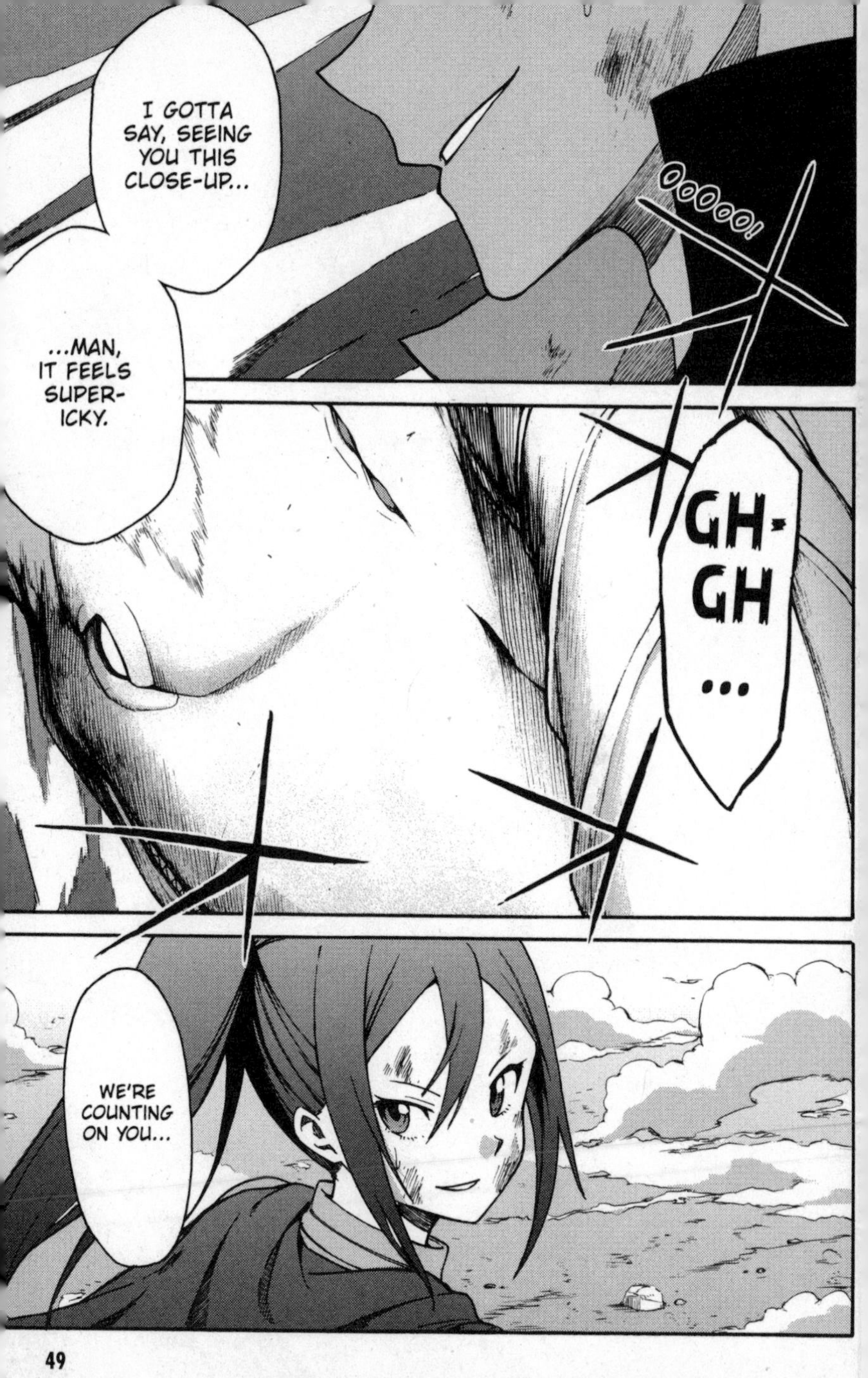
OoOoo!
I GOTTA SAY, SEEING YOU THIS CLOSE-UP...
...MAN, IT FEELS SUPER-ICKY.
GH-GH...
WE'RE COUNTING ON YOU...

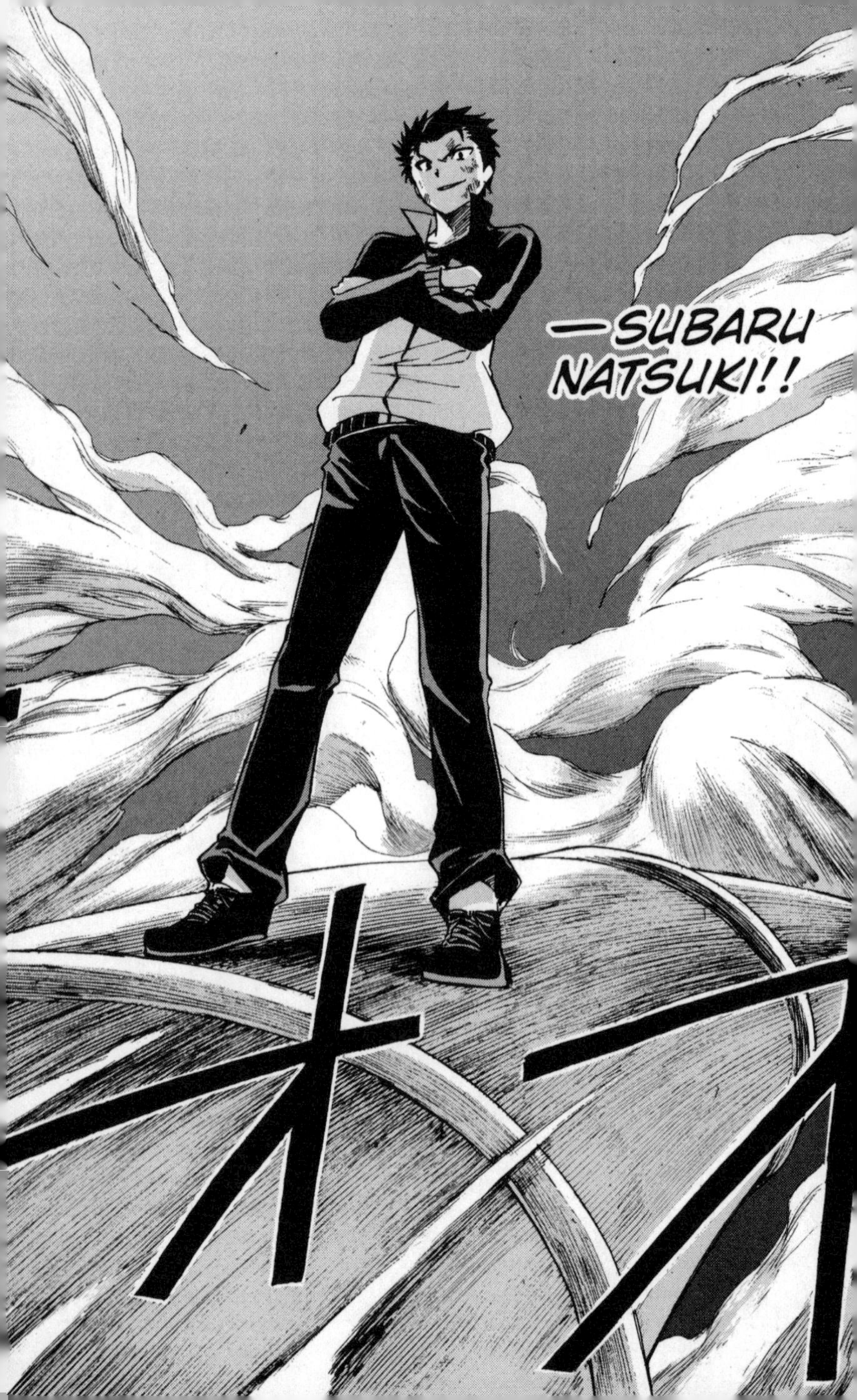
—SUBARU NATSUKI!!

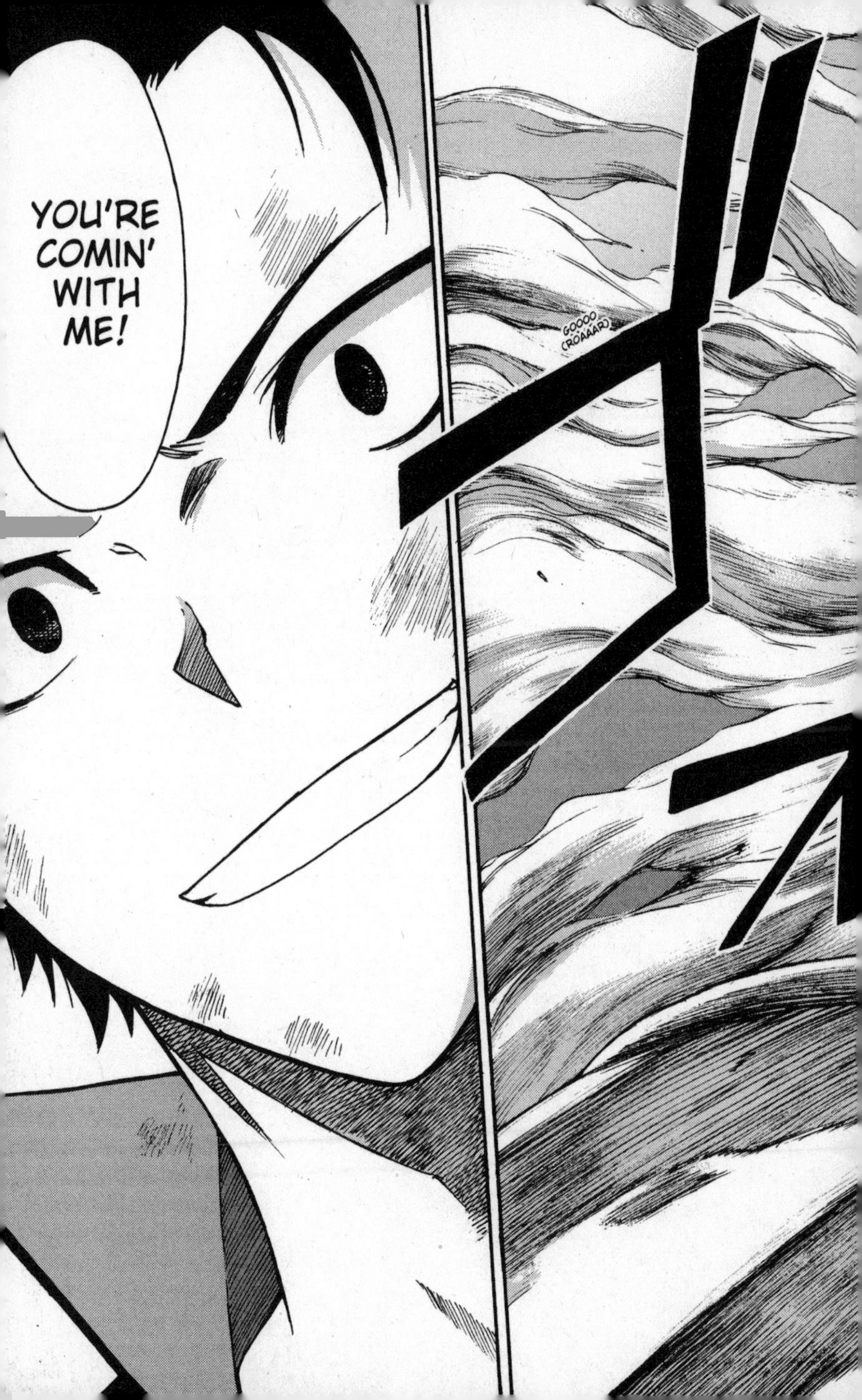
GOOOO
(ROAAAR)
YOU'RE COMIN' WITH ME!

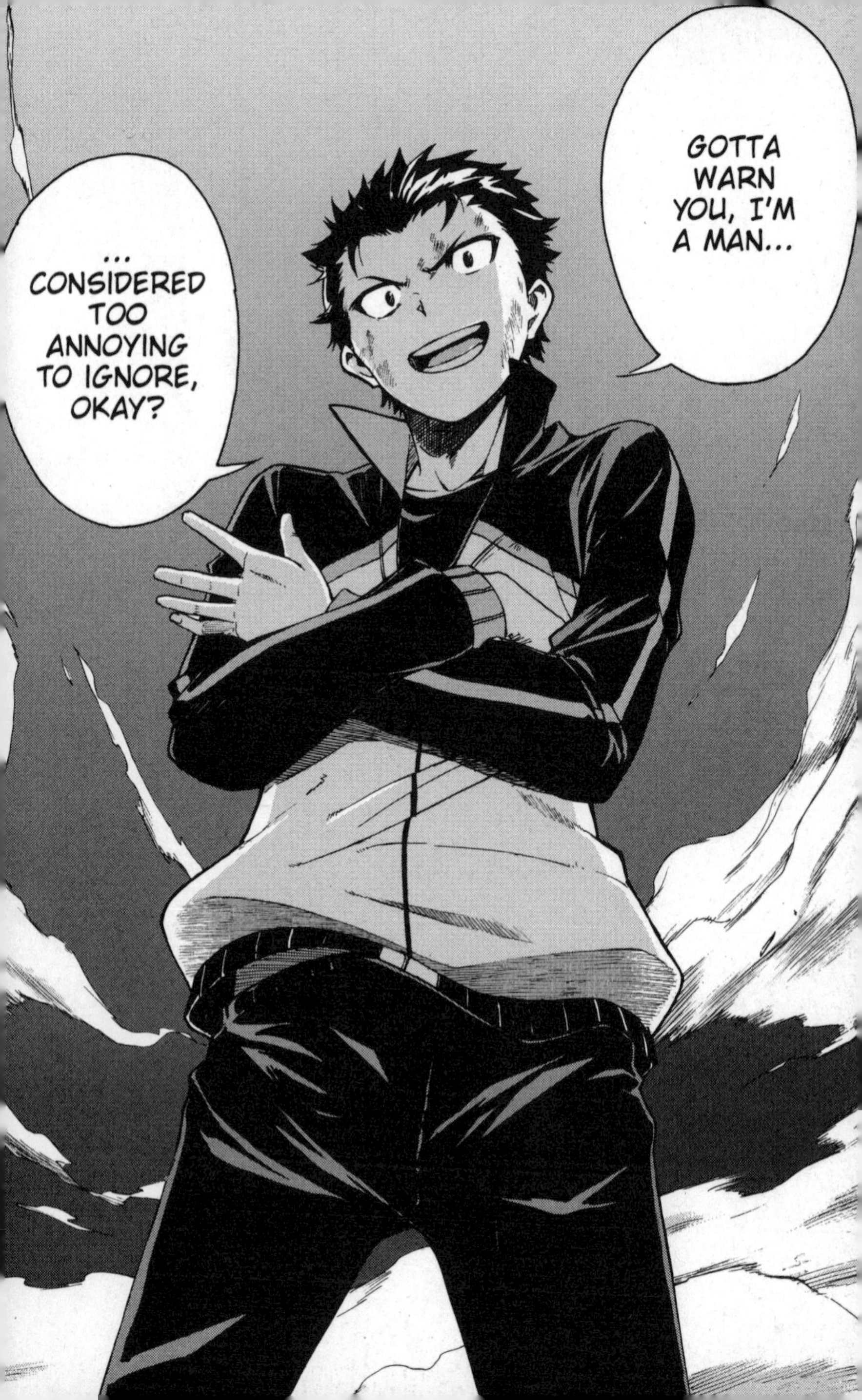
GOTTA WARN YOU, I'M A MAN...
...CONSIDERED TOO ANNOYING TO IGNORE, OKAY?

Truth of Zero
The only ability Subaru Natsuki gets when he's summoned to another world is
time travel via his own death. But to save her, he'll die as many times as it takes.

Re:ZERO
-Starting Life in
Another World-

Re:ZERO
-Starting Life in
Another World-

Truth of Zero

The only ability Subaru Natsuki gets when he's summoned to another world is
time travel via his own death. But to save her, he'll die as many times as it takes.

Episode 30
The Giant Beast Falls

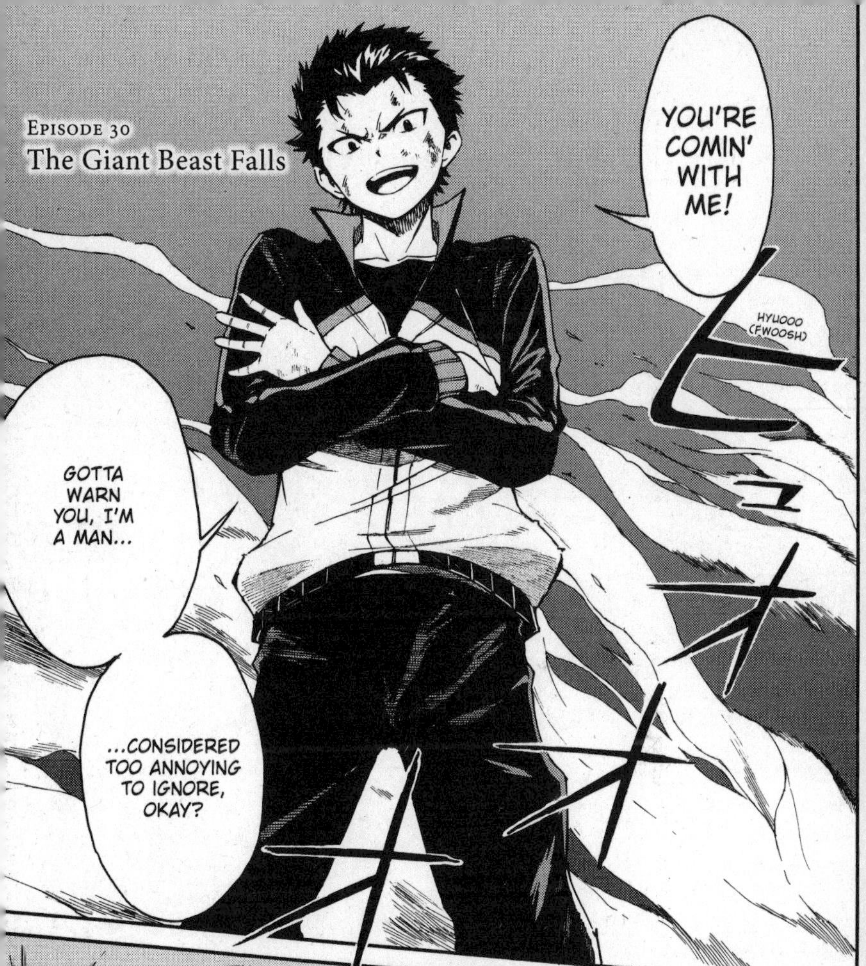
YOU'RE COMIN' WITH ME!
HYUOOO (FWOOSH)
GOTTA WARN YOU, I'M A MAN...
...CONSIDERED TOO ANNOYING TO IGNORE, OKAY?

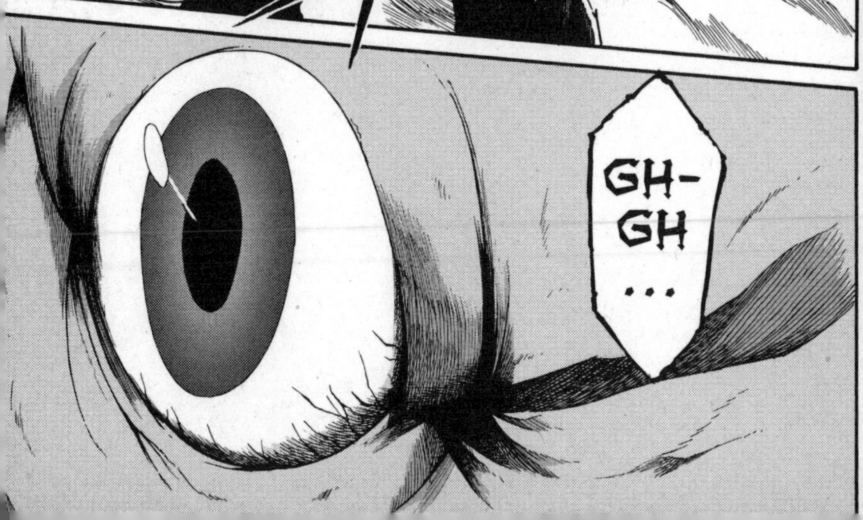
GH-GH...

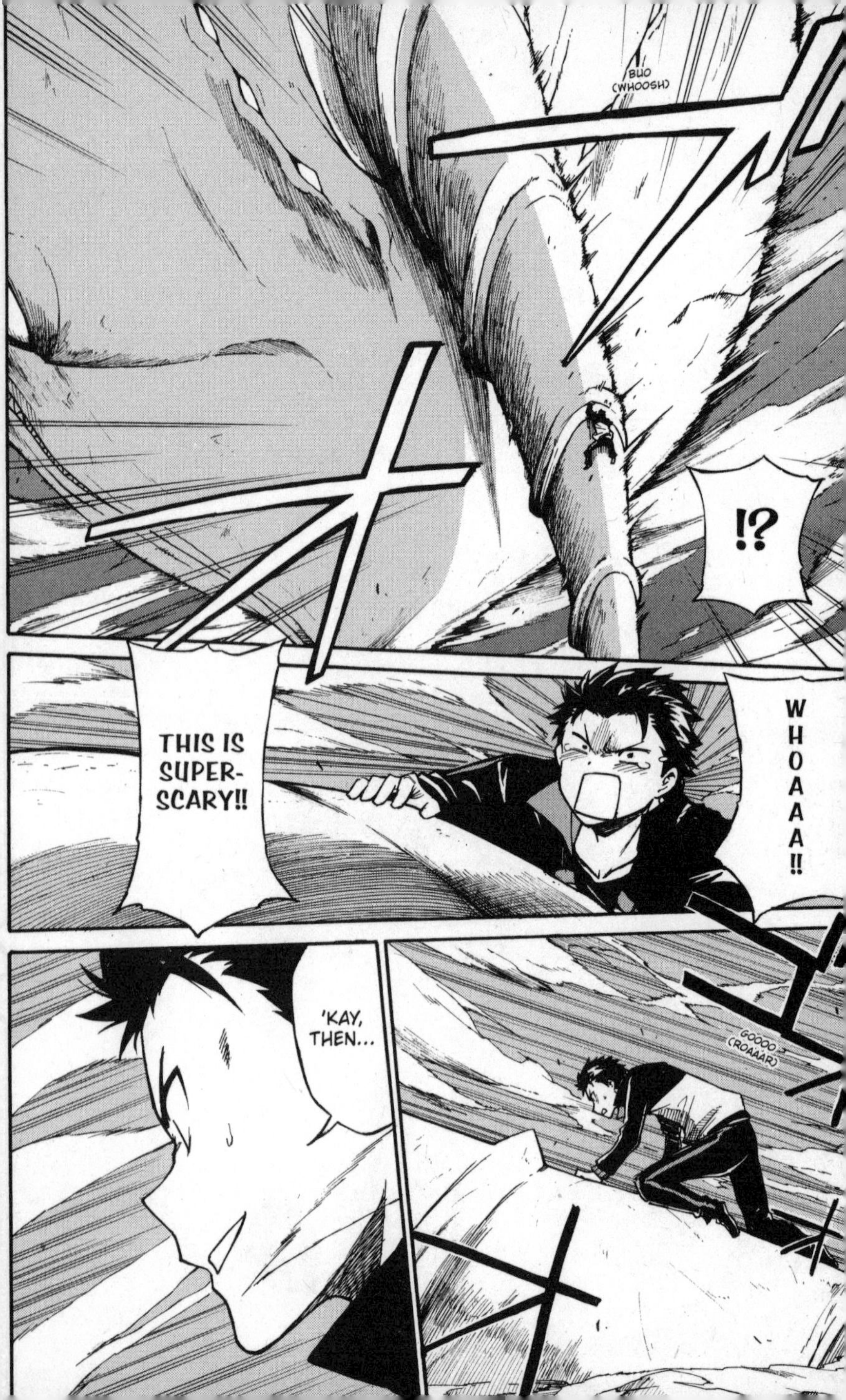
BUO
(WHOOSH)
!?
WHOAAAA!!
THIS IS SUPER-SCARY!!
GOOOO
(ROAAAR)
'KAY, THEN...

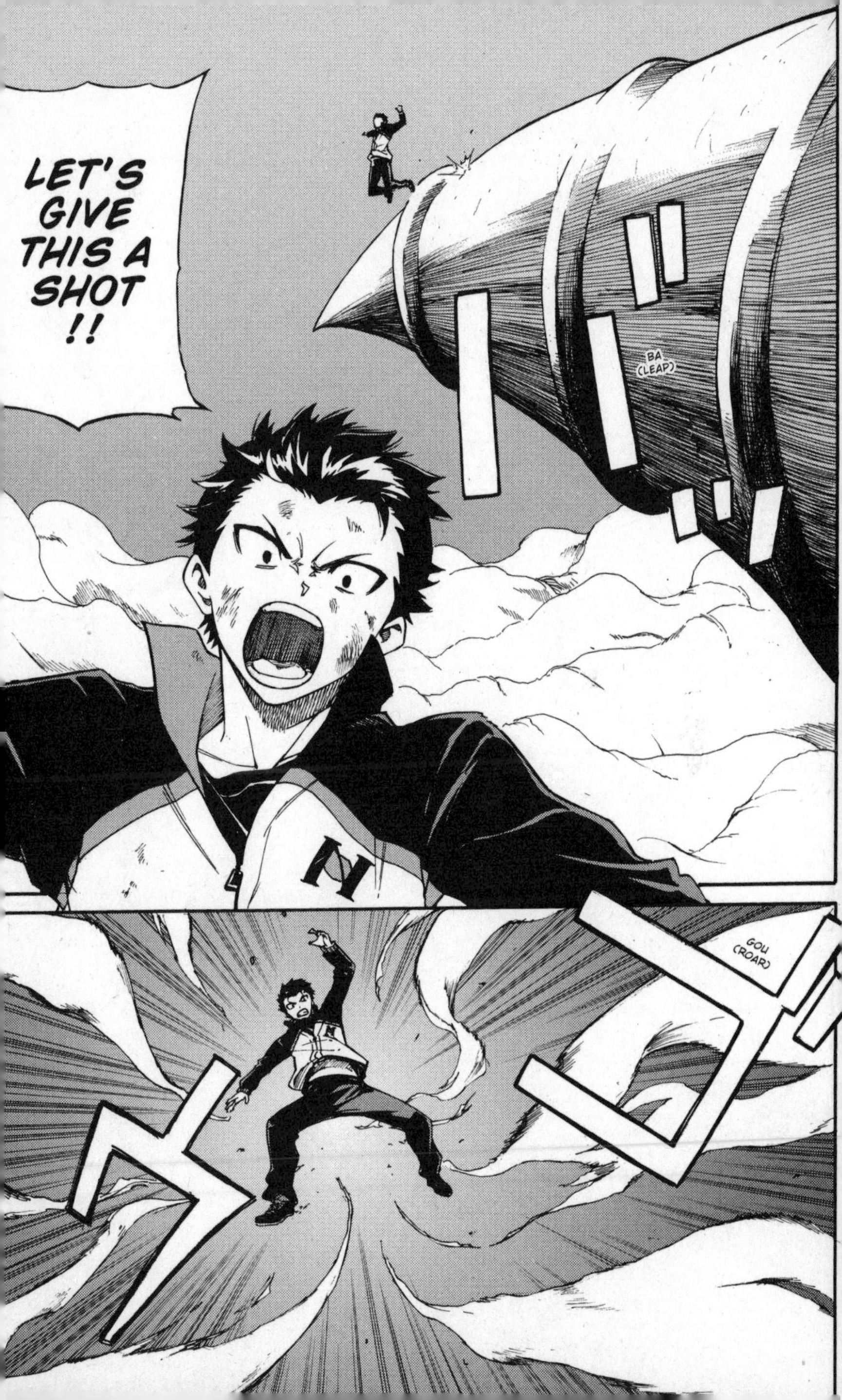
LET'S GIVE THIS A SHOT!!
BA (LEAP)
GOU (ROAR)

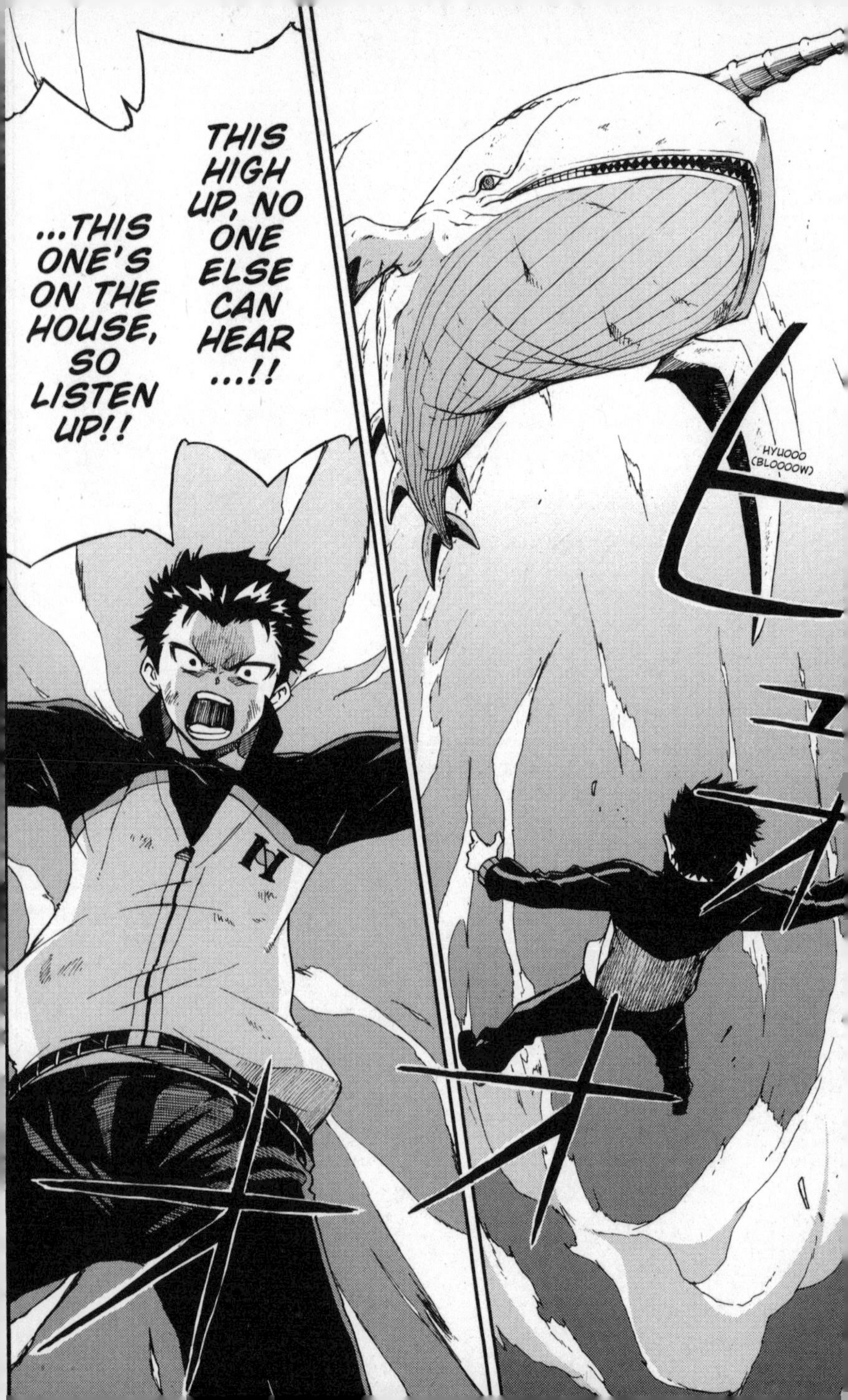
HYUOOO (BLOOOOW)
THIS HIGH UP, NO ONE ELSE CAN HEAR ...!!
...THIS ONE'S ON THE HOUSE, SO LISTEN UP!!

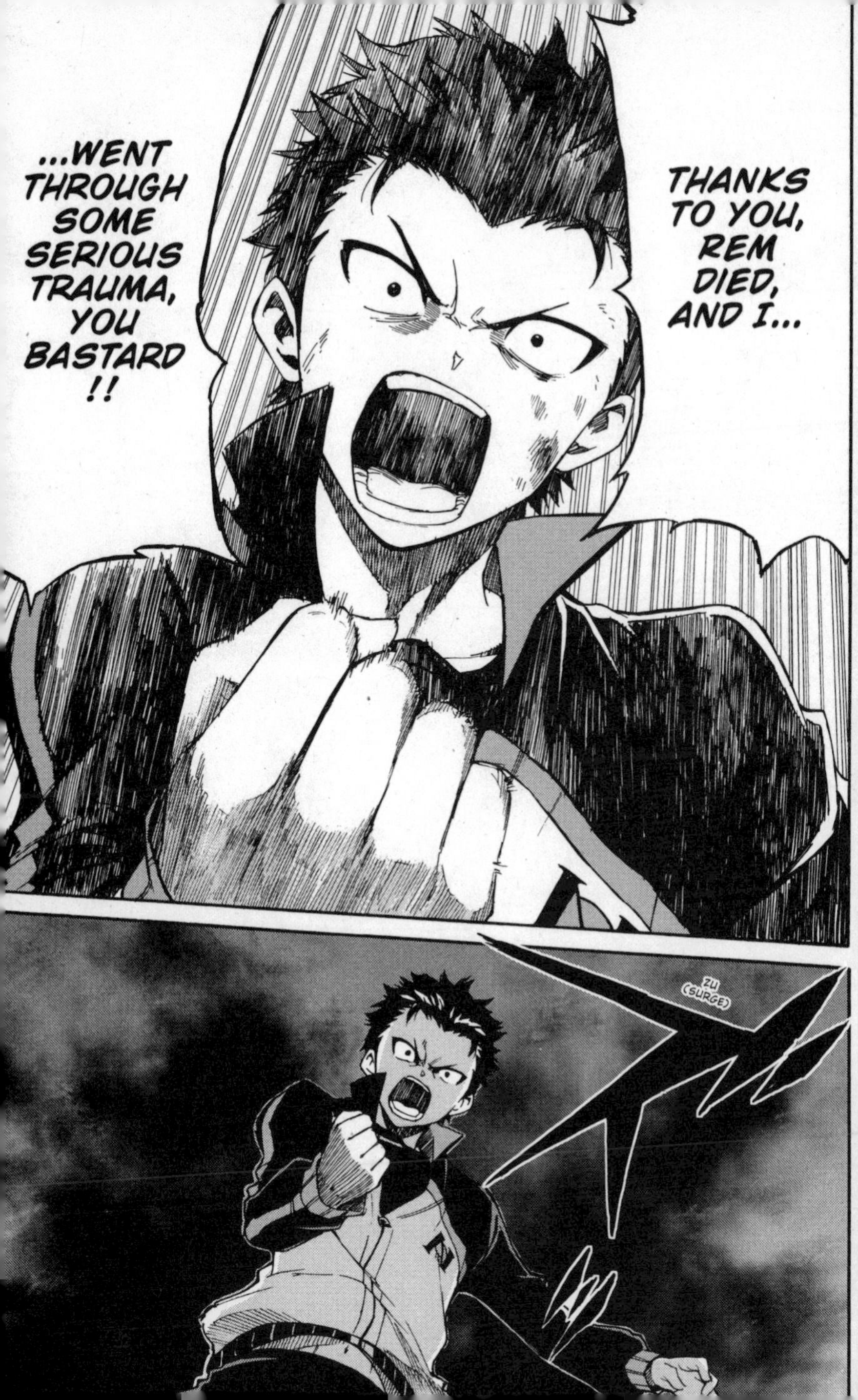
THANKS TO YOU, REM DIED, AND I...
...WENT THROUGH SOME SERIOUS TRAUMA, YOU BASTARD!!
ZU (SURGE)

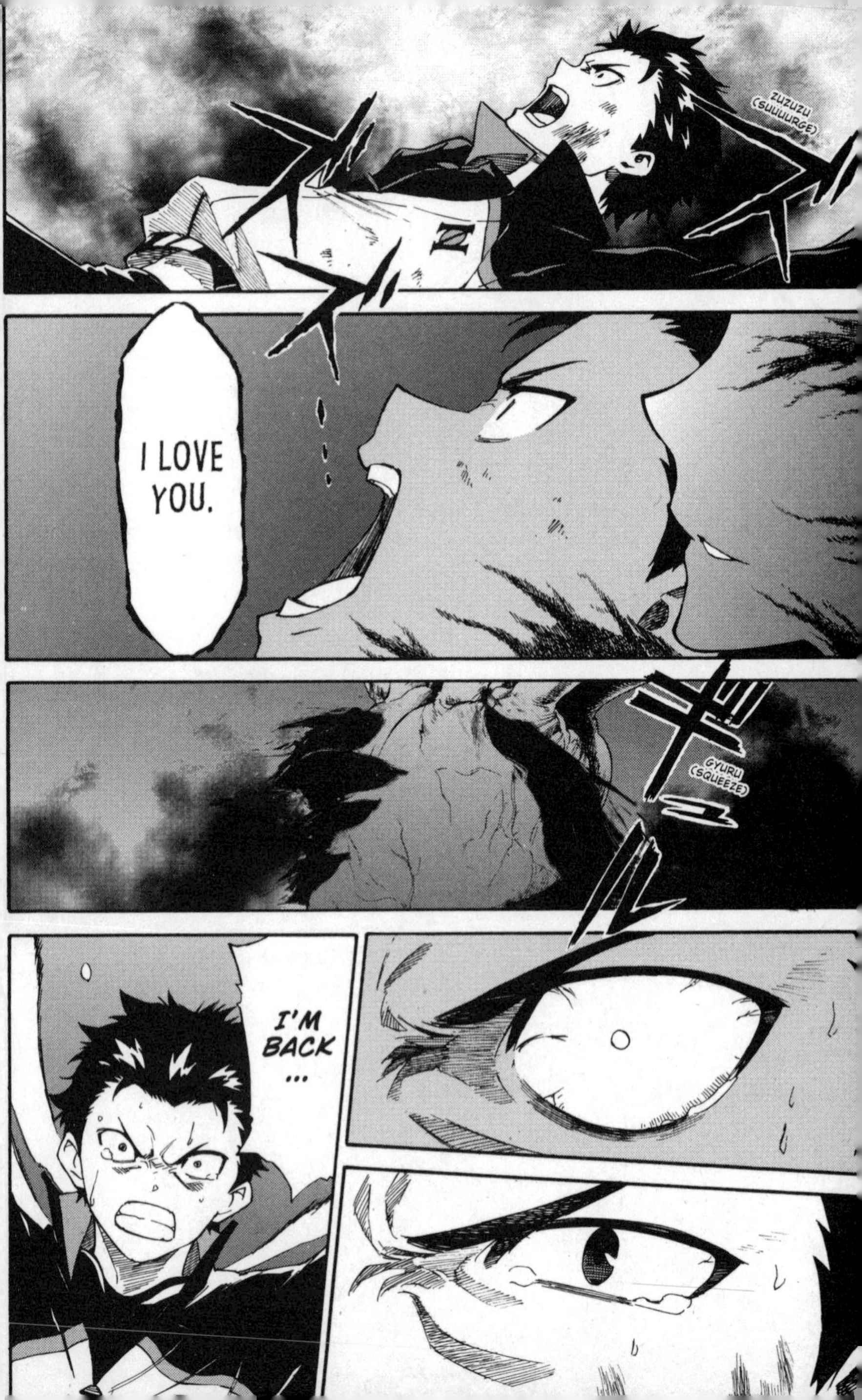
ZUZUZU (SUUUURGE)
I LOVE YOU.
GYURU (SQUEEZE)
I'M BACK ...

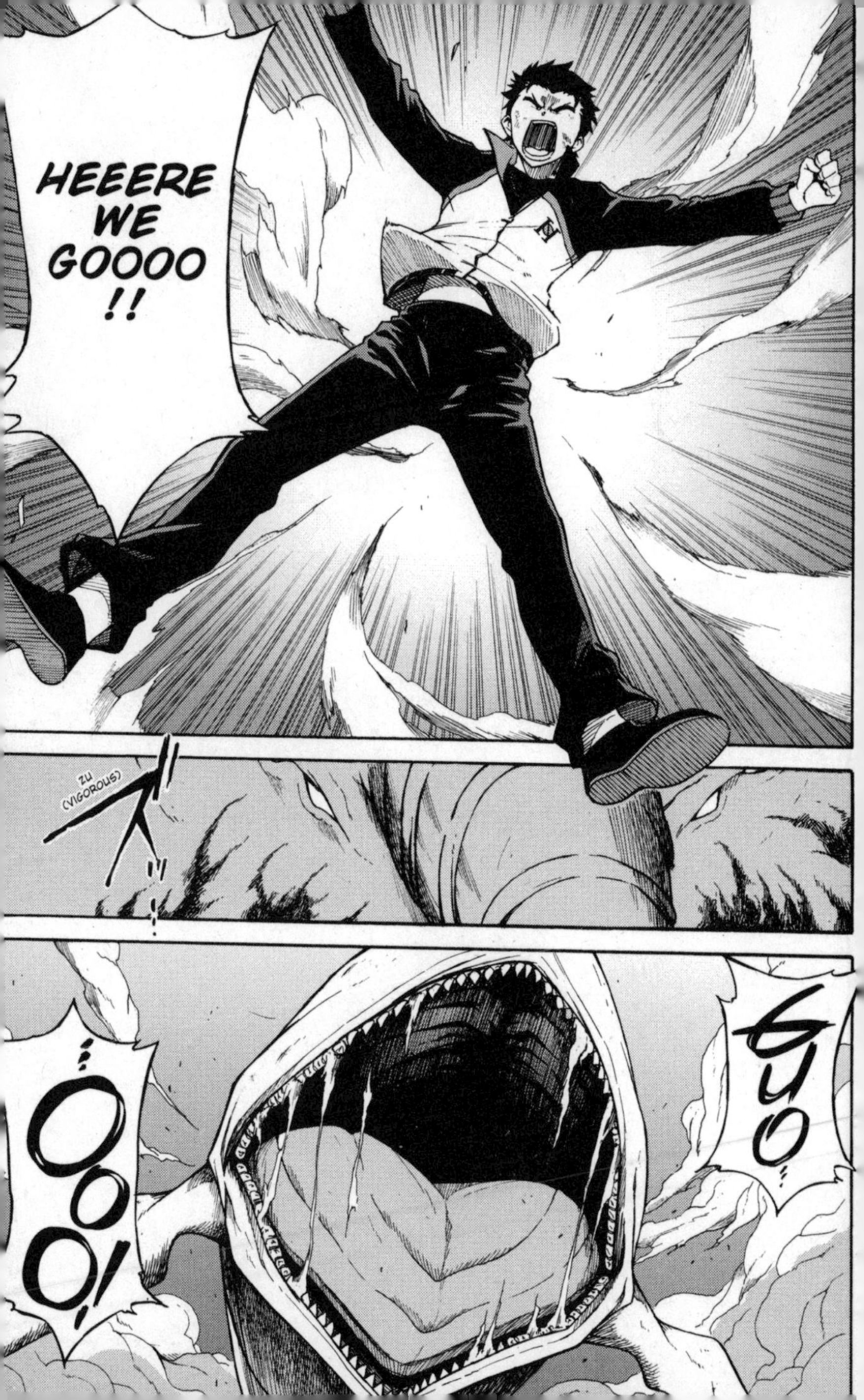
HEEERE WE GOOOO!!
ZU (VIGOROUS)
GUO...
...OOOO!

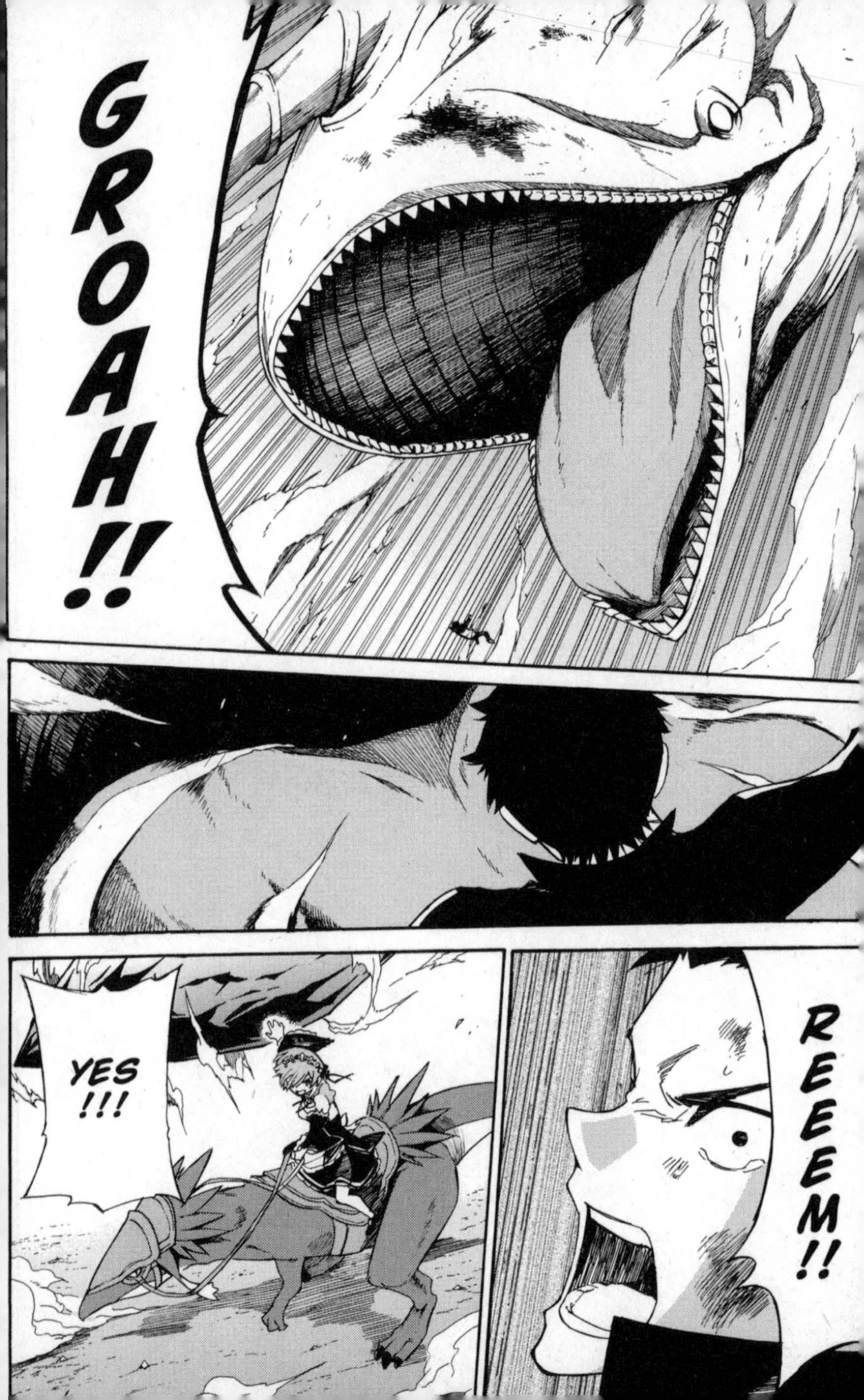
GROAH!!
REEEEM!!
YES!!!

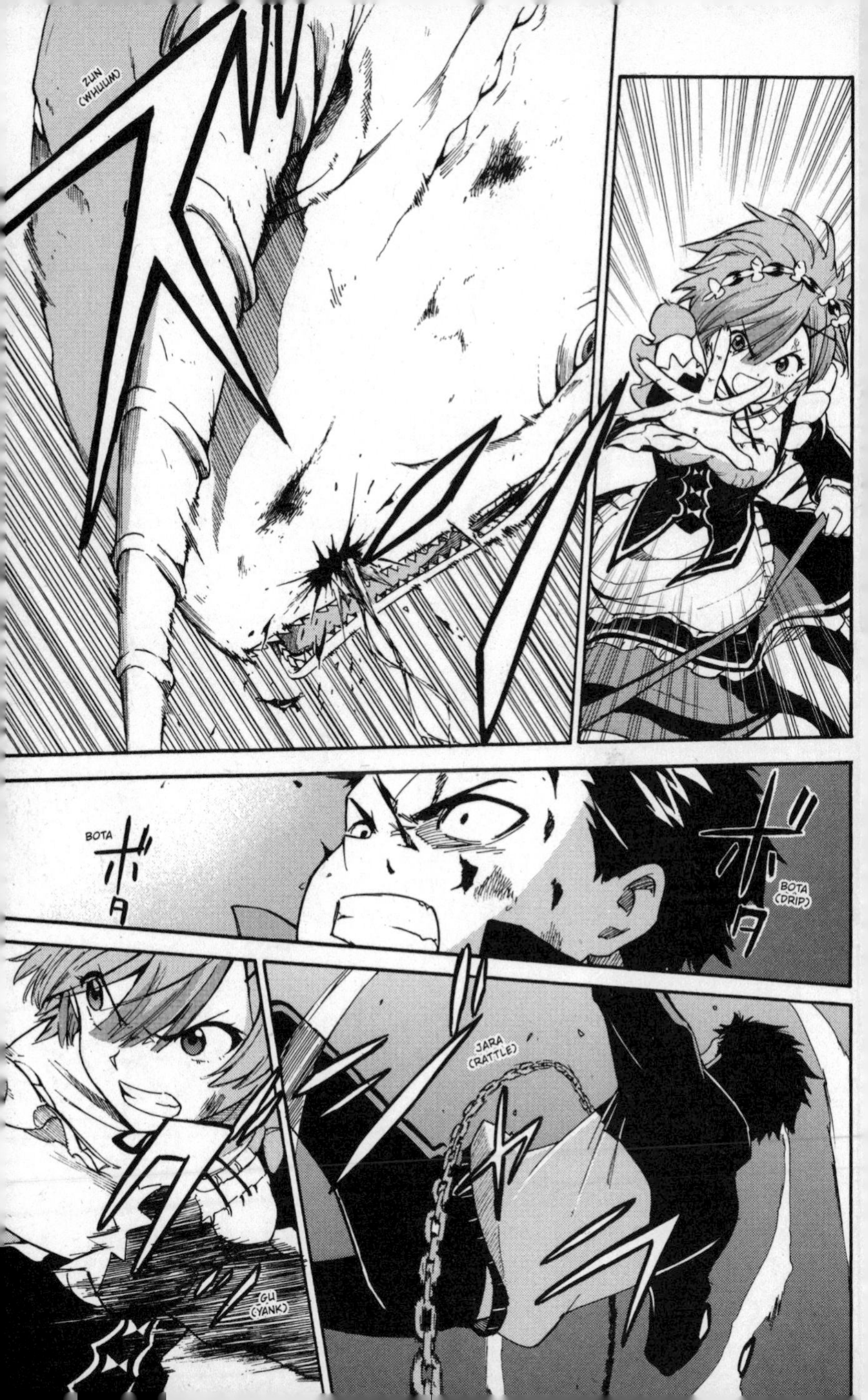
ZUN (WHUUM)
BOTA (DRIP)
BOTA
JARA (RATTLE)
GU (YANK)

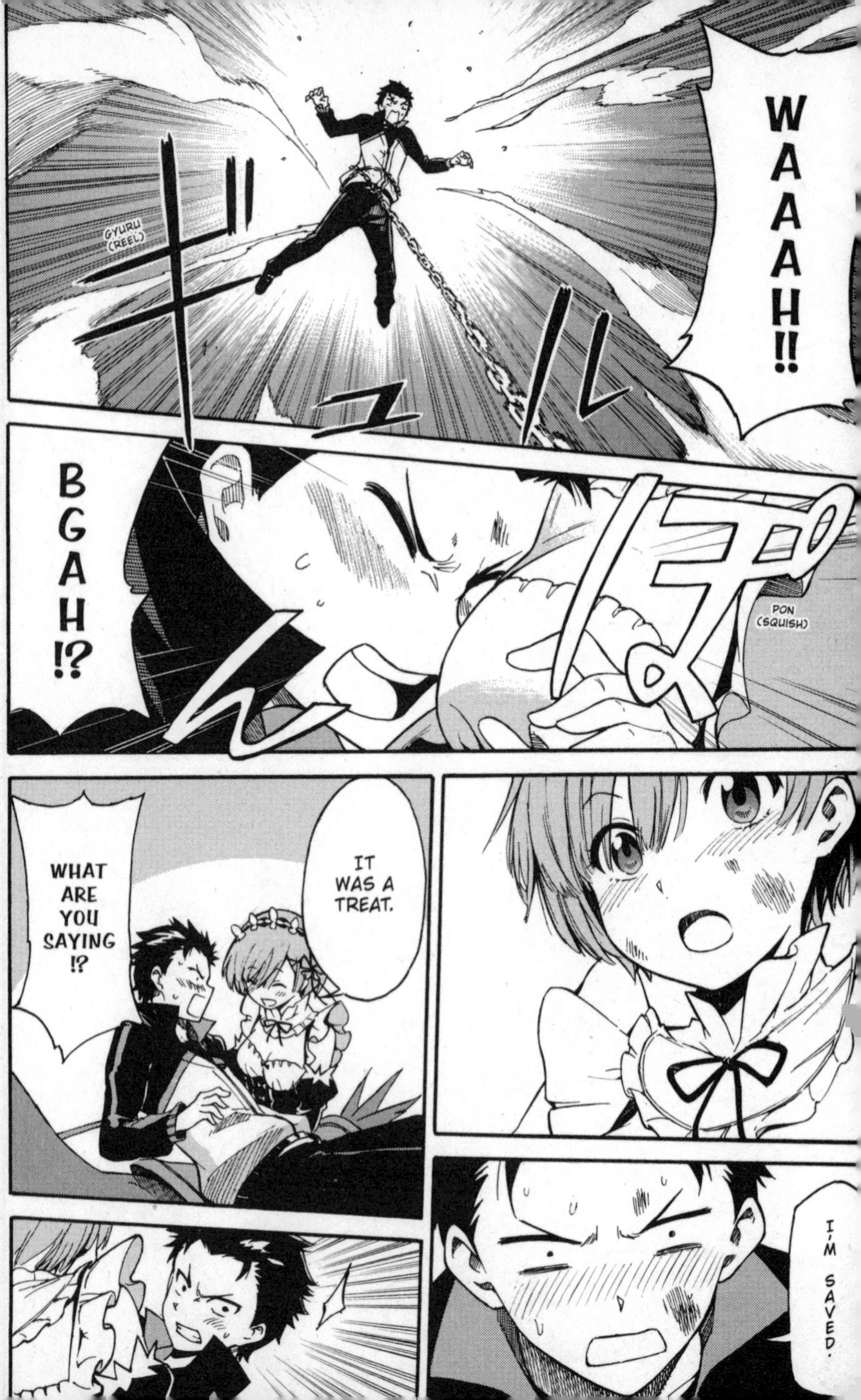
WAAAAH!!
GYURU (REEL)
PON (SQUISH)
BGAH!?
IT WAS A TREAT.
WHAT ARE YOU SAYING!?
I'M SAVED.

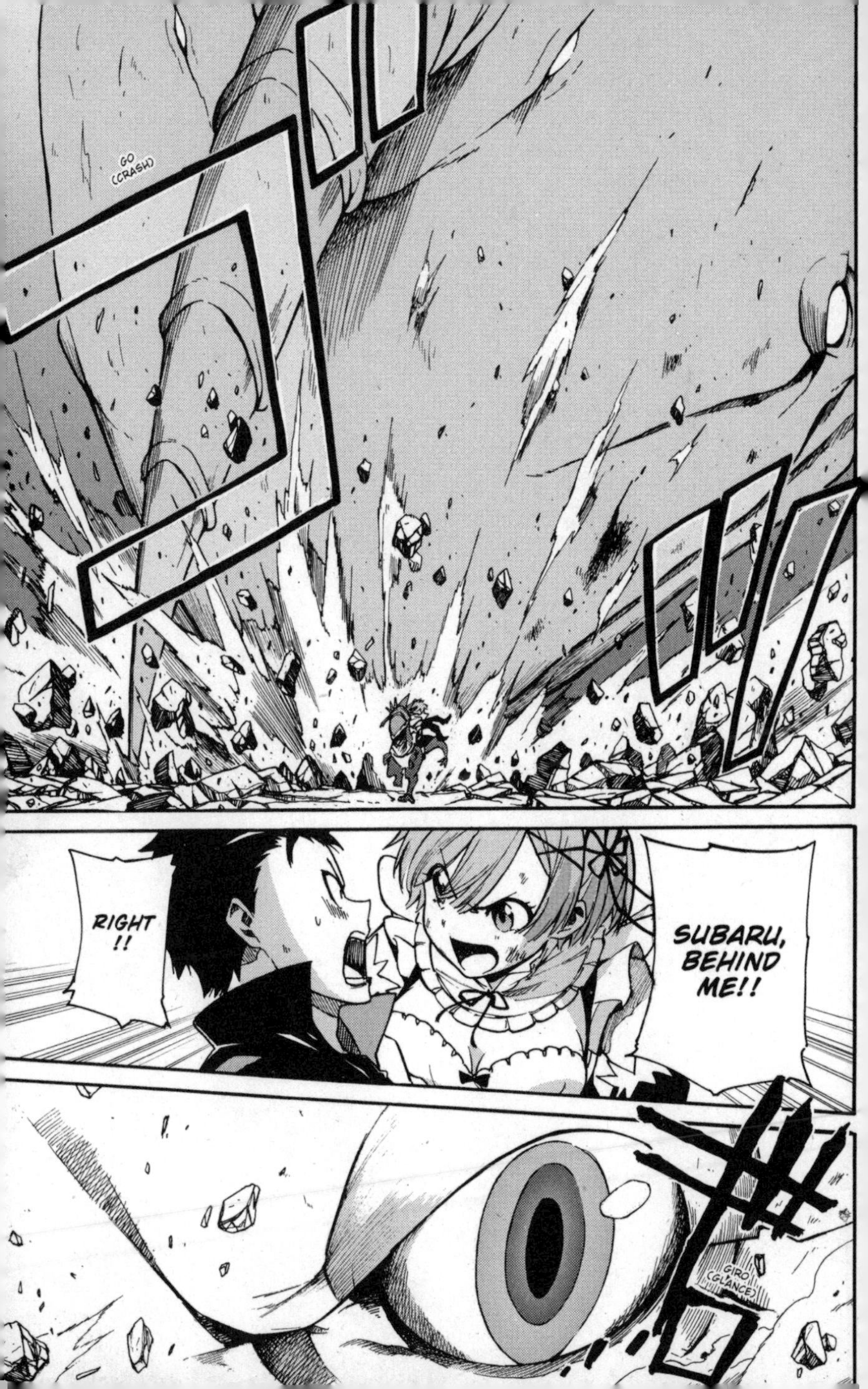
GO (CRASH)
SUBARU, BEHIND ME!!
RIGHT!!
GIRO (GLANCE)

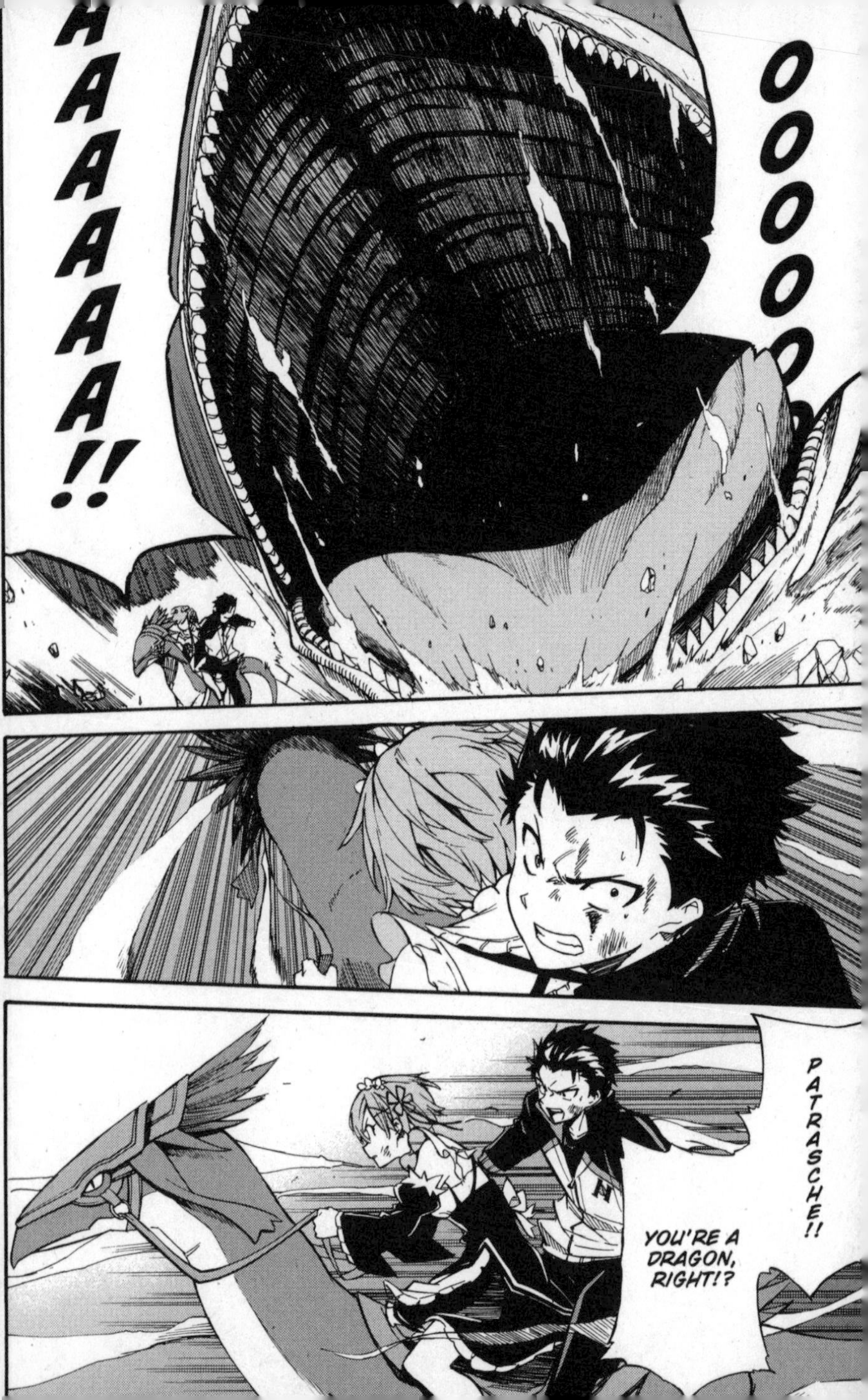
OOOOOOO
HAAAAAA!!
PATRASCHE!!
YOU'RE A DRAGON, RIGHT!?

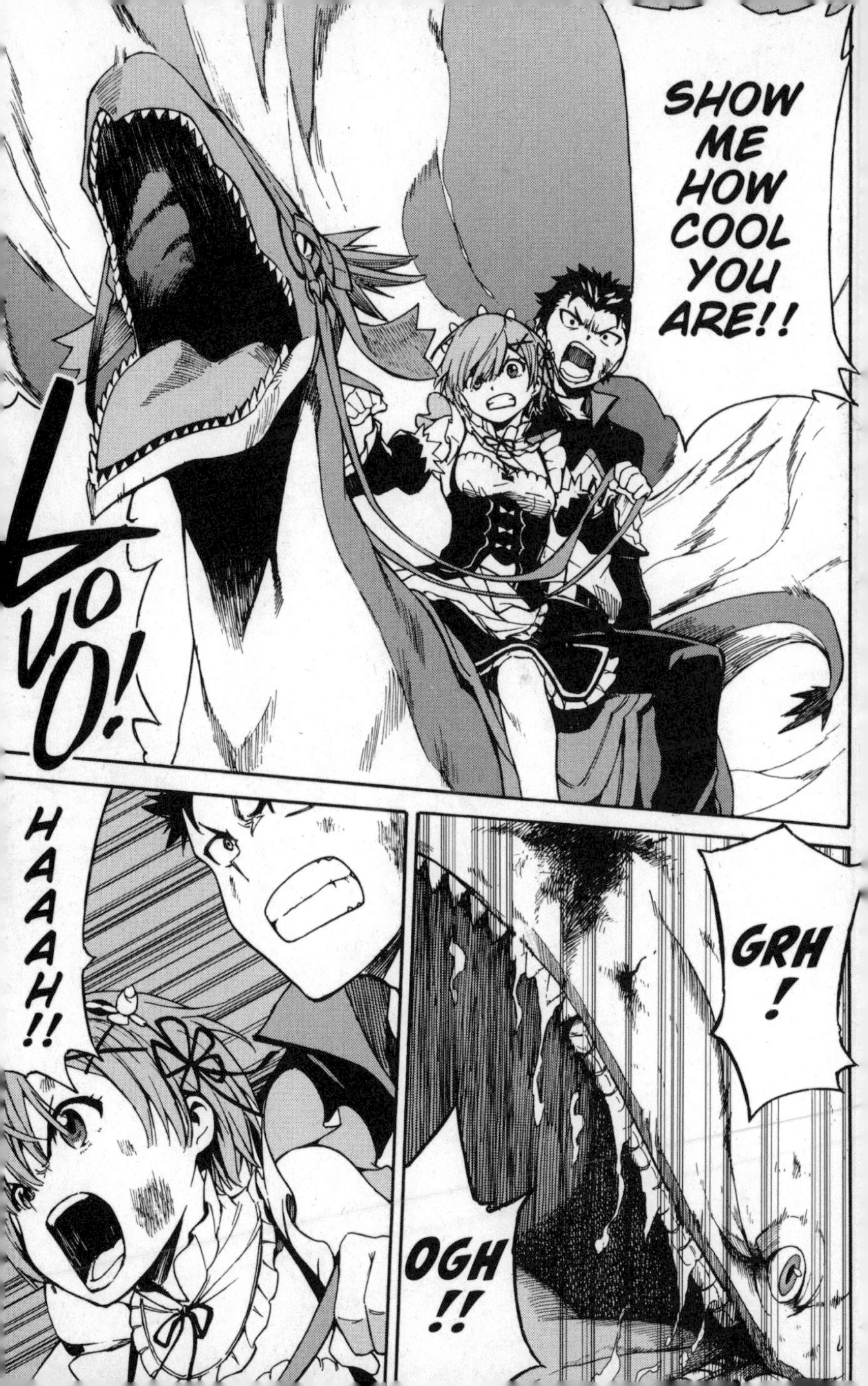
SHOW ME HOW COOL YOU ARE!!
VOO!
GRH!
OGH!!
HAAAAH!!

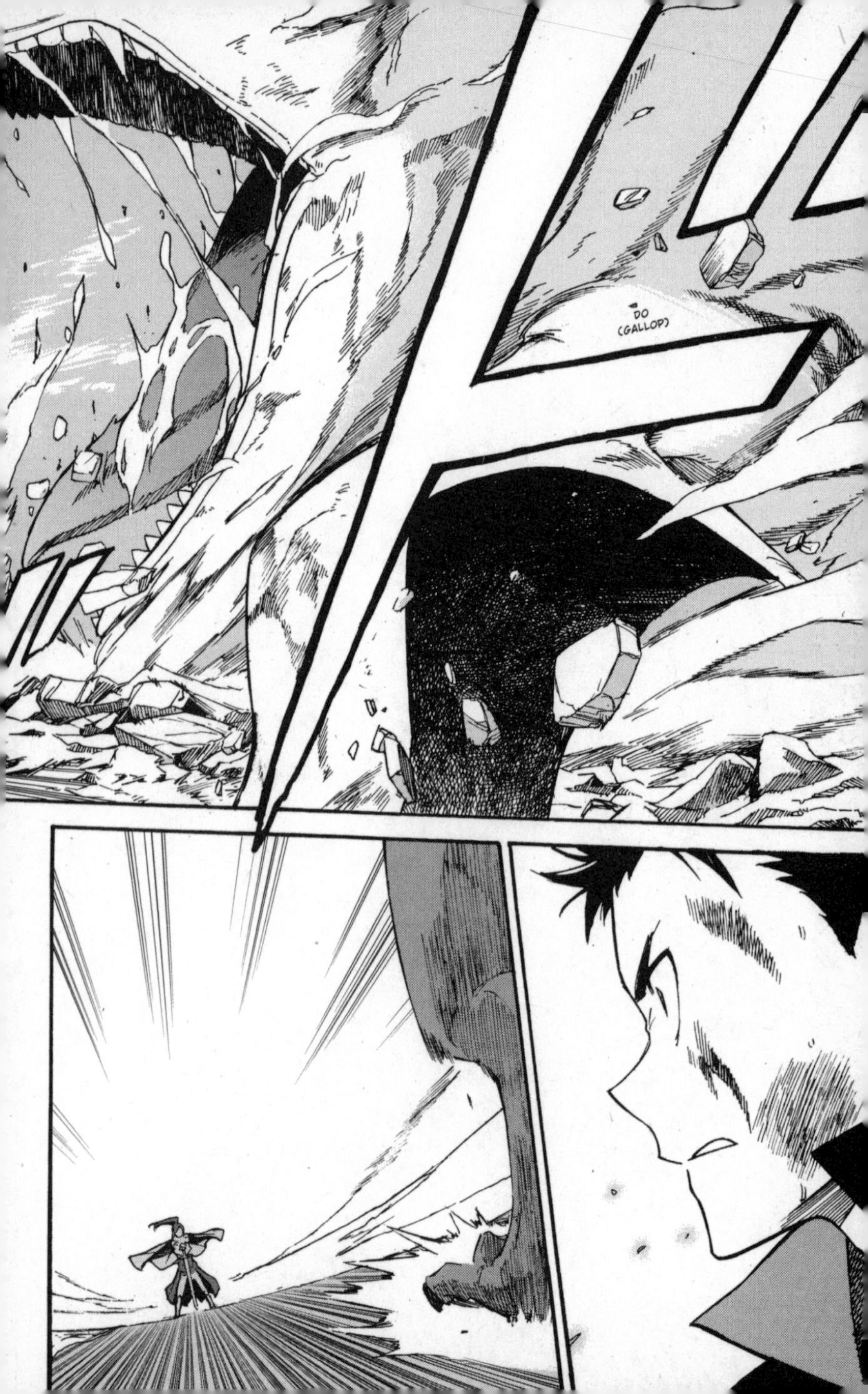
DO
(GALLOP)

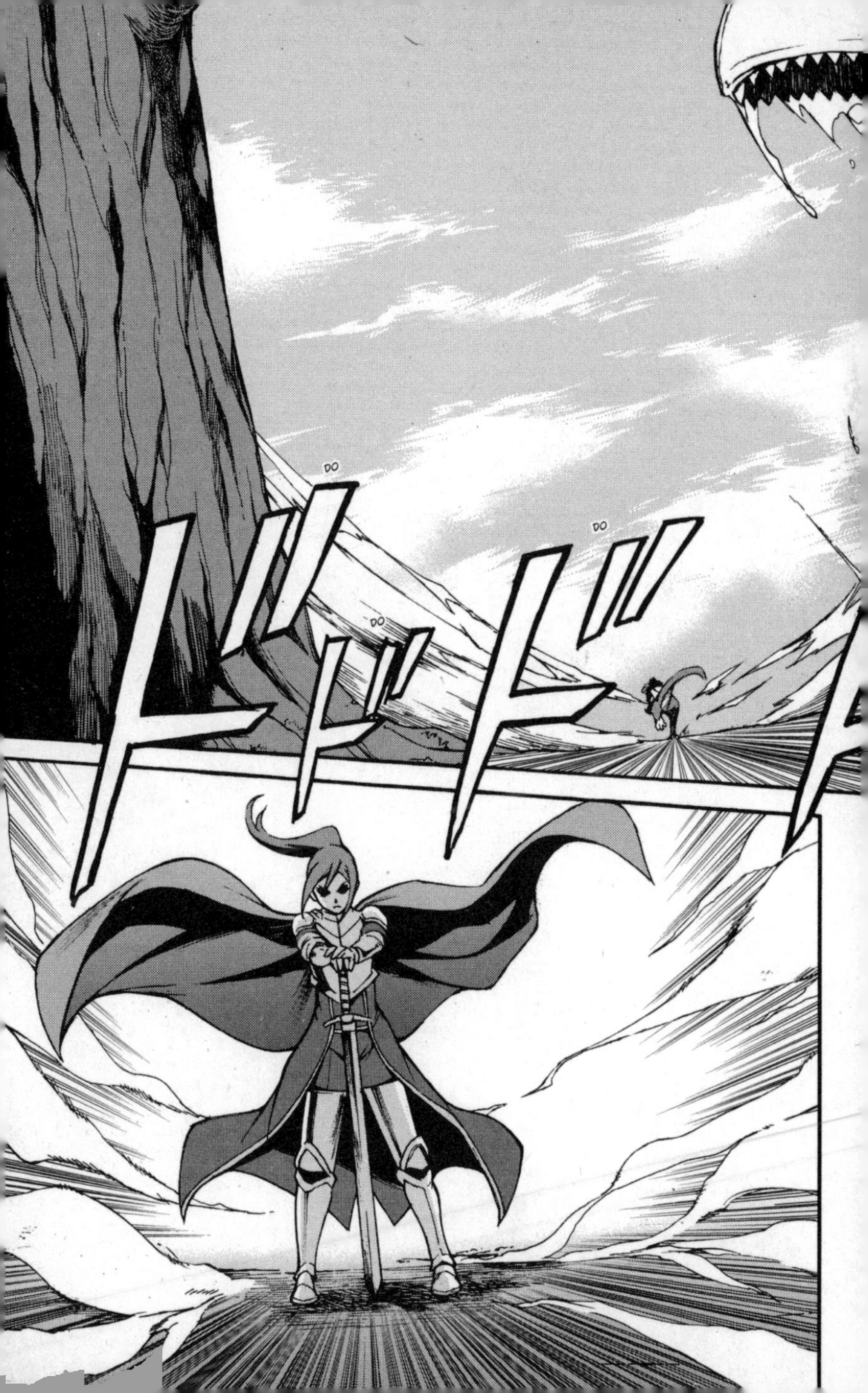
ドッドッドッ
DO
DO
DO

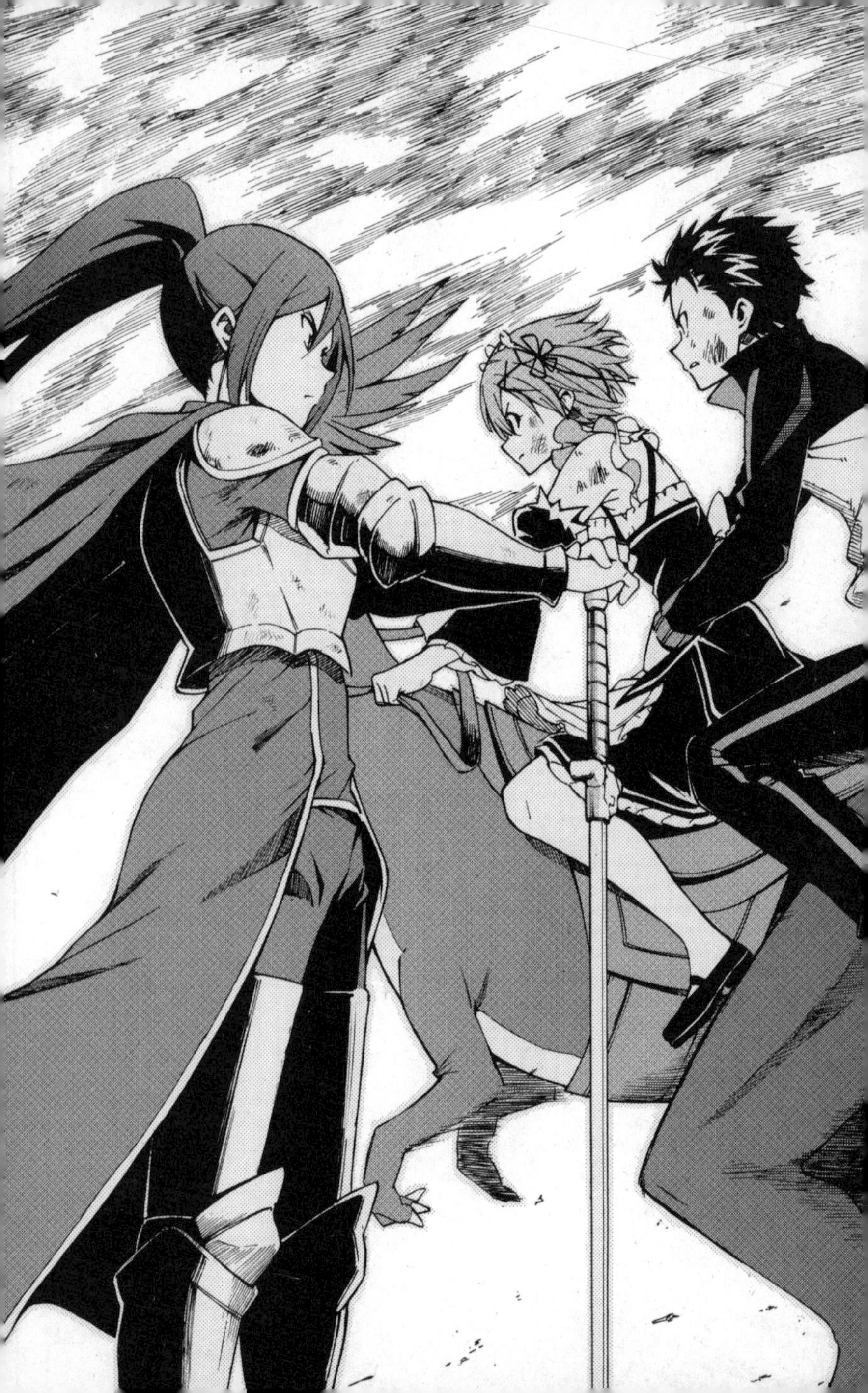

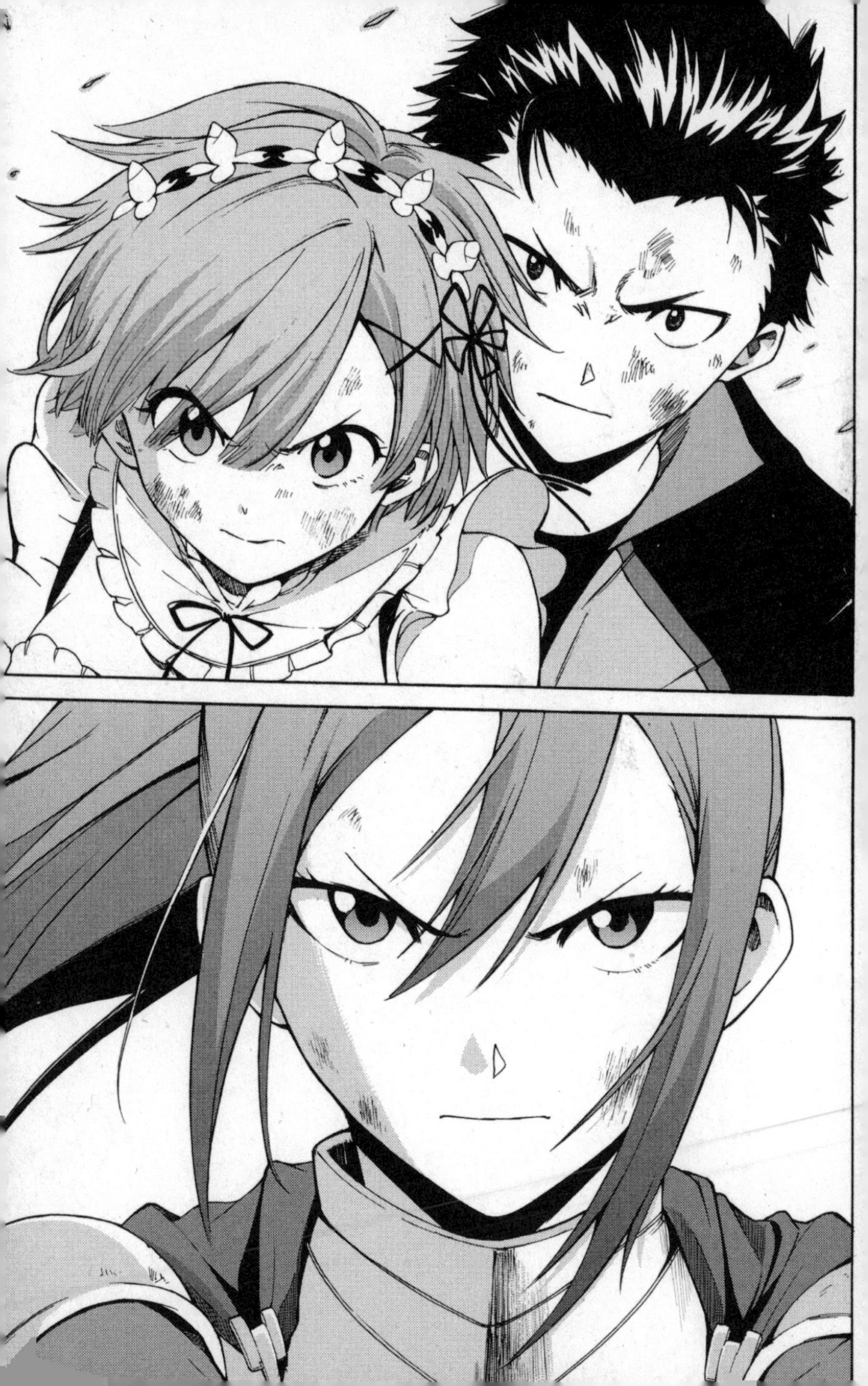

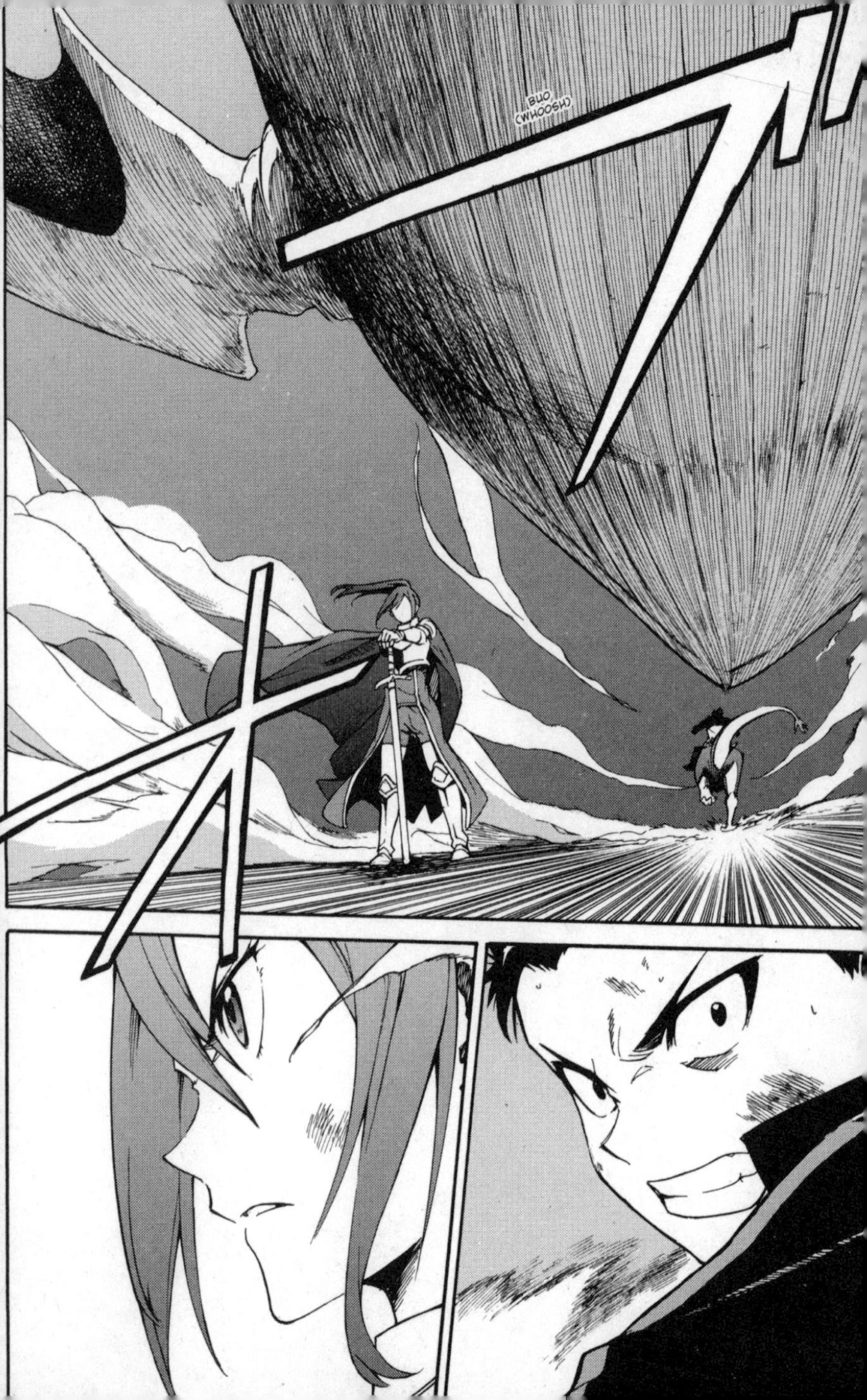
BUO (WHOOSH)

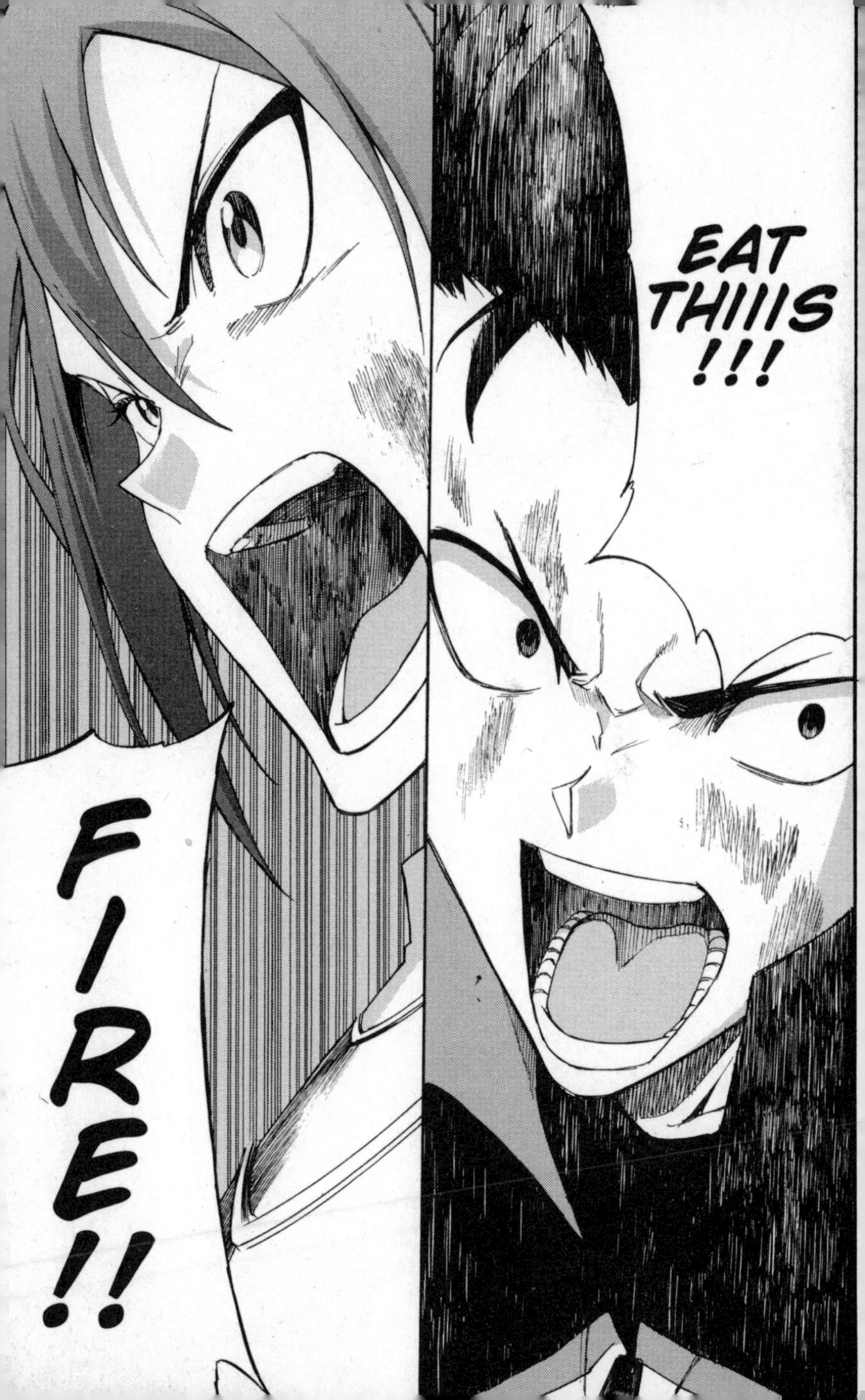
EAT THIIIS!!!
FIRE!!

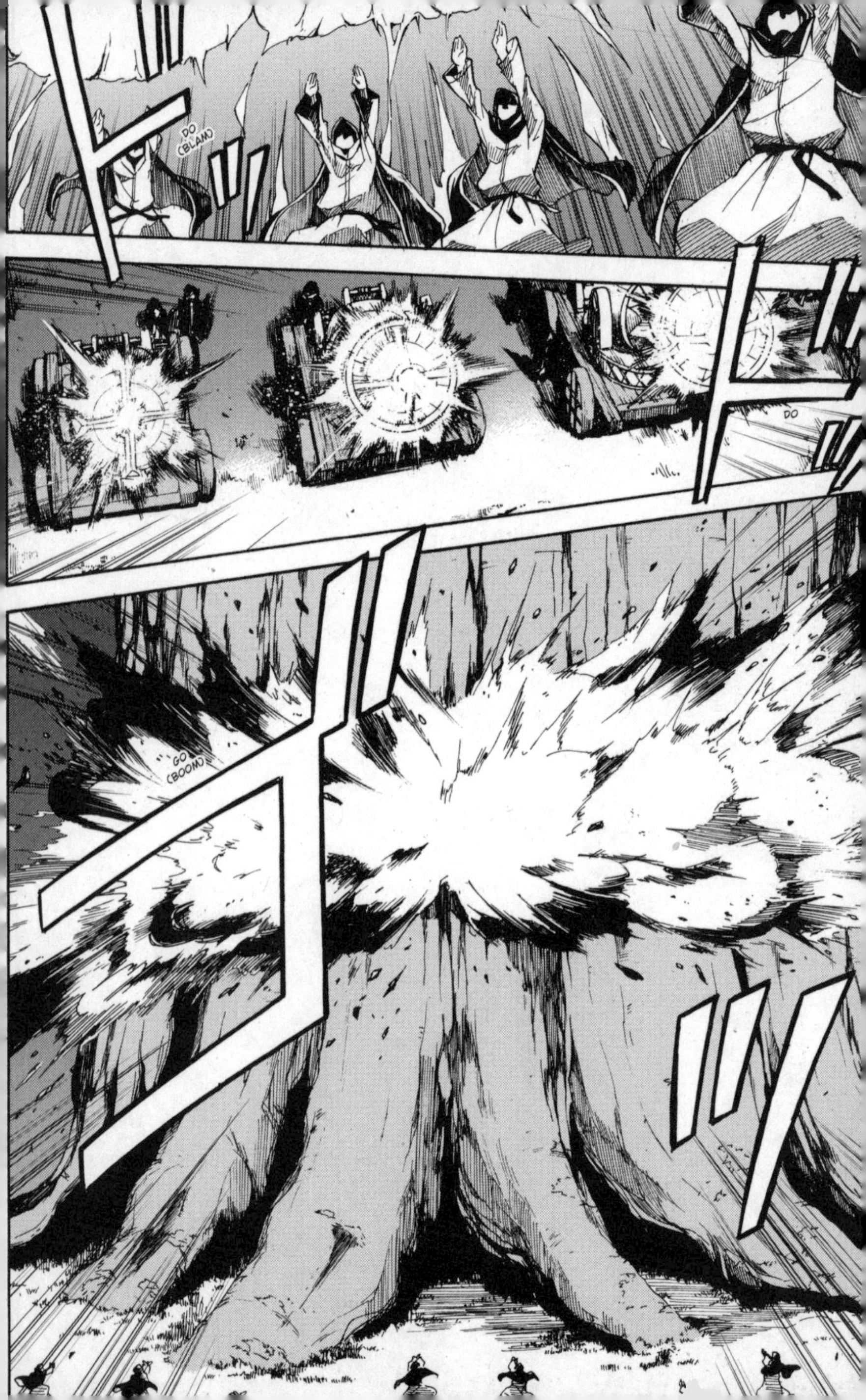
DO (BLAM)
DO
GO (BOOM)

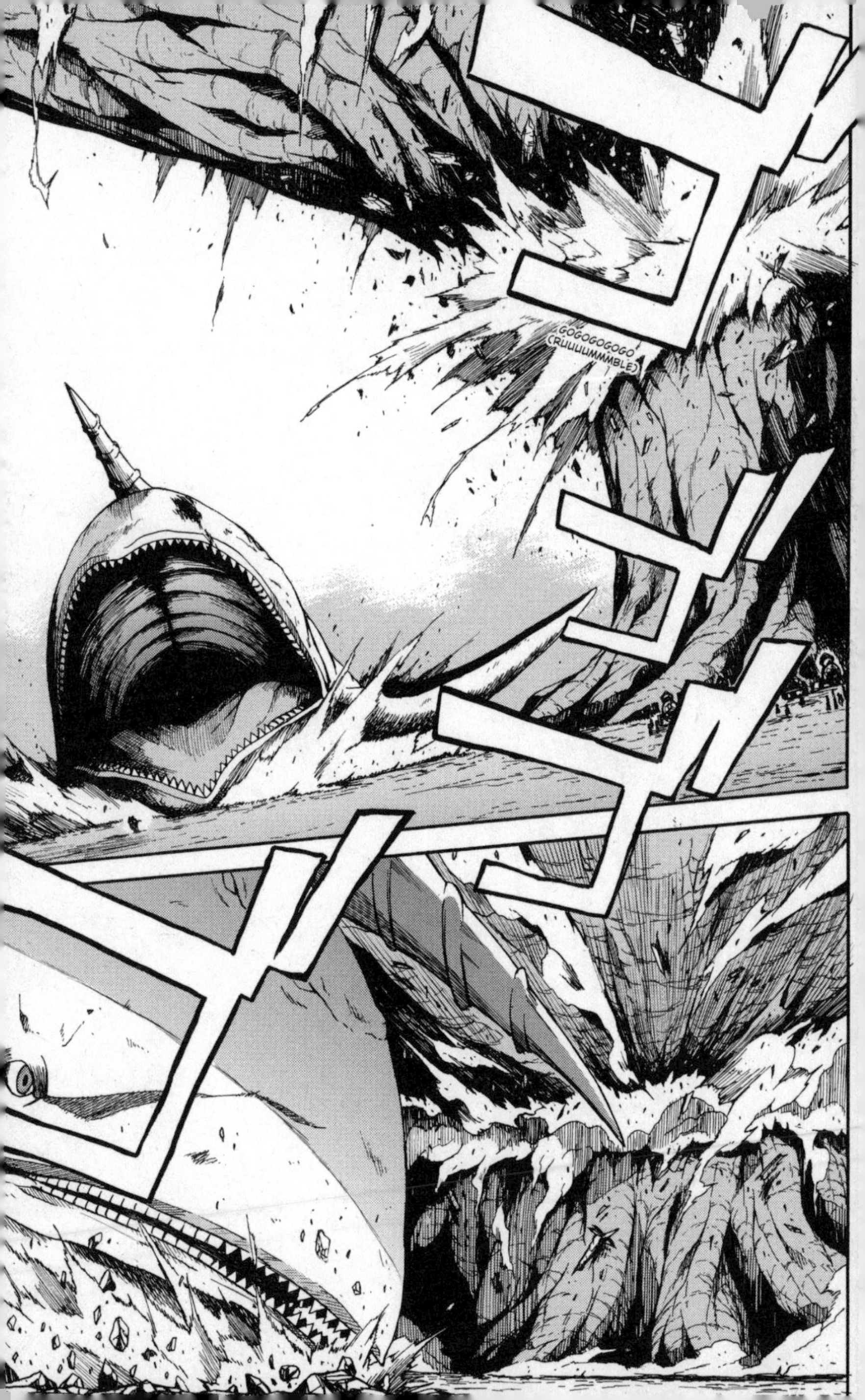
GOGOGOGOGO
(RUUUUUMMMBLE)

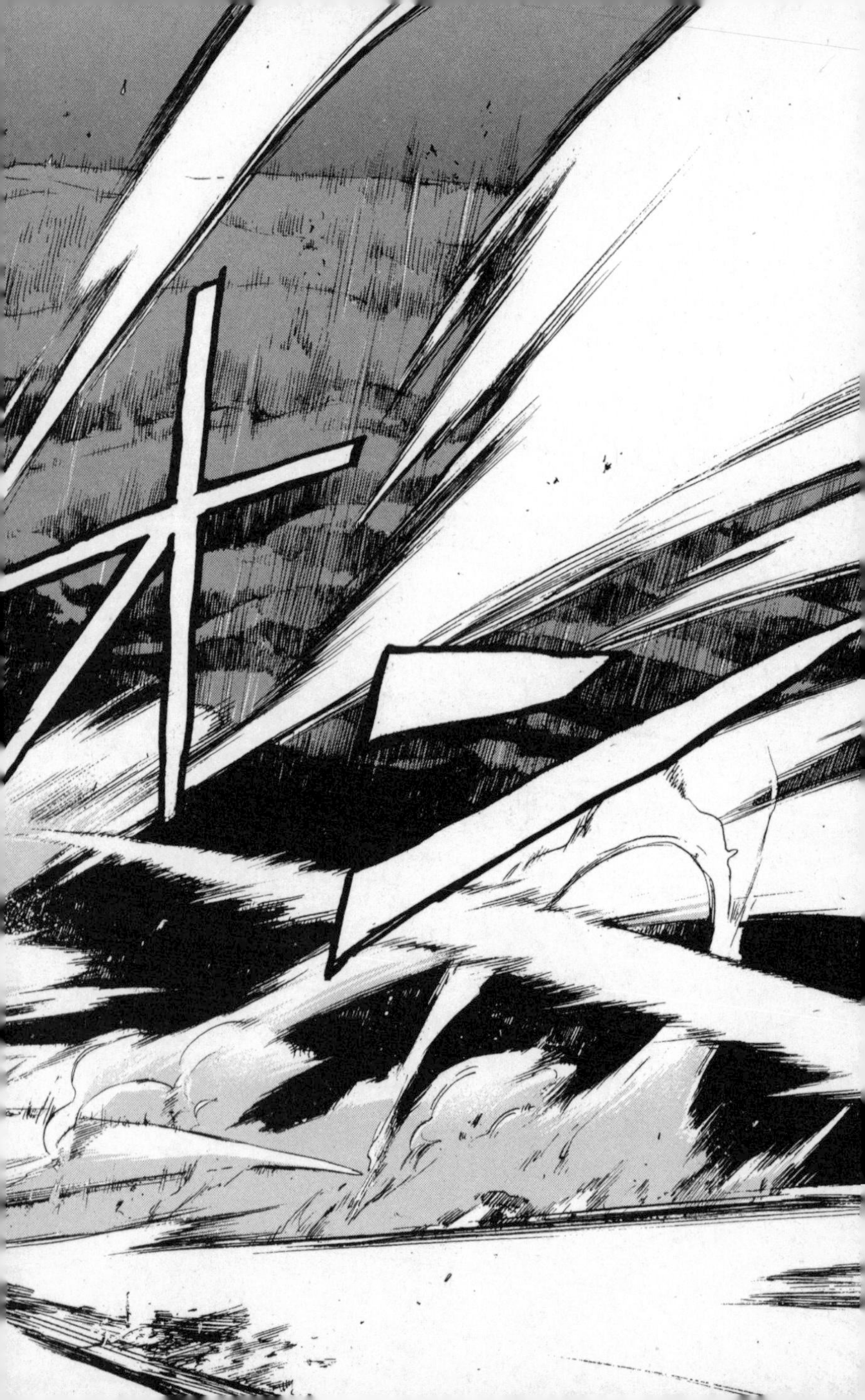

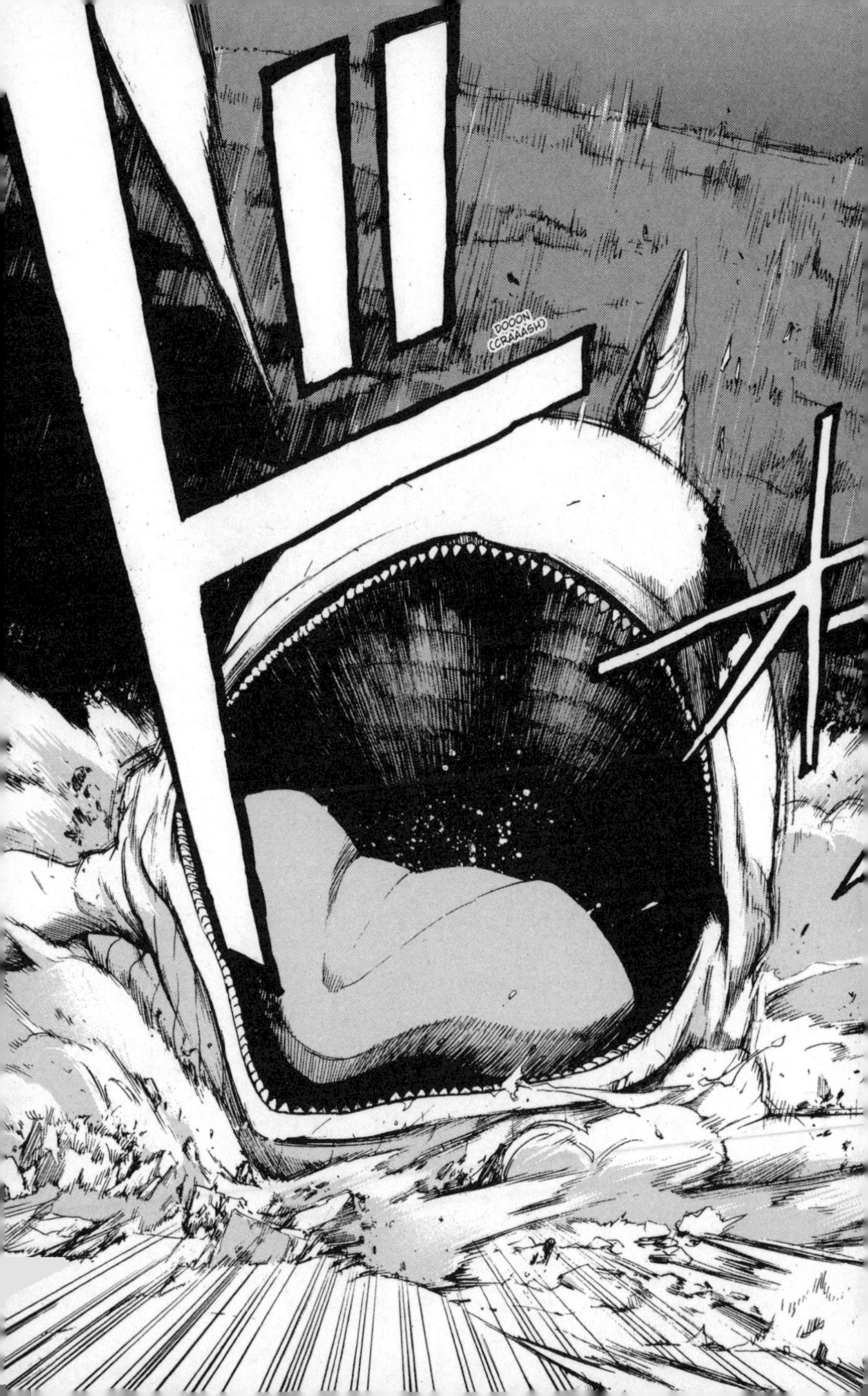
DOOON
(CRAAASH)

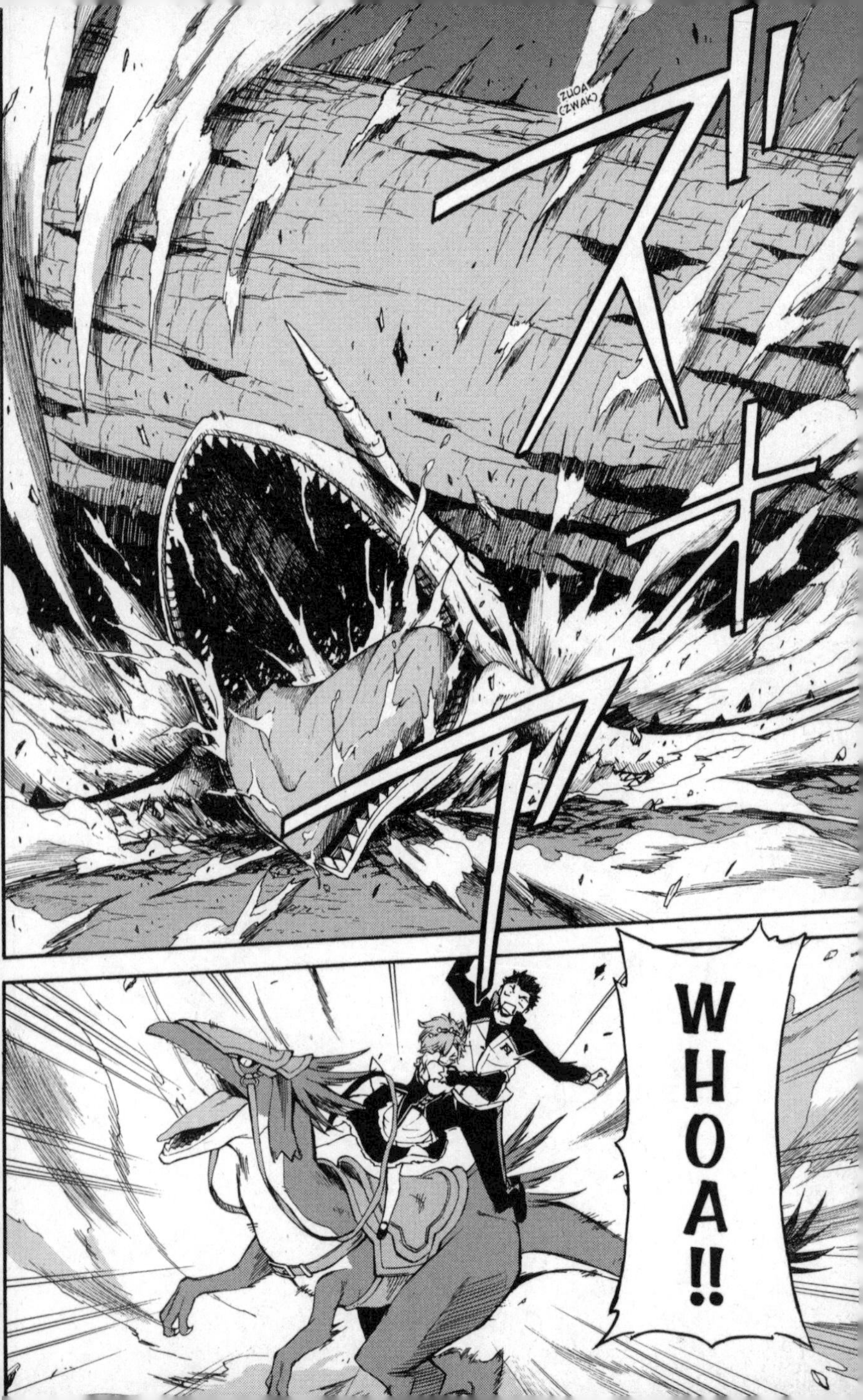
ZUOA (ZWAK)
WHOA!!

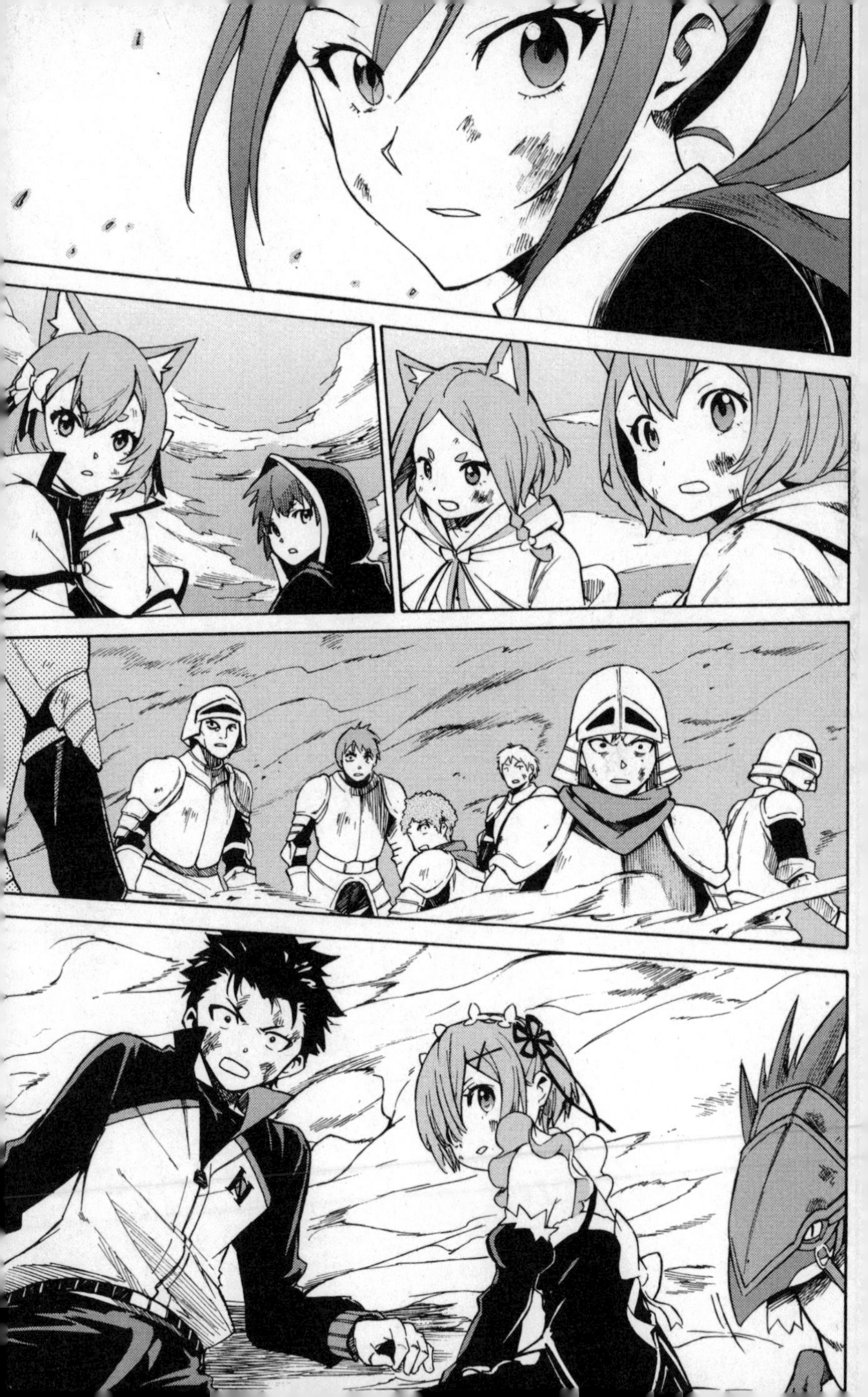

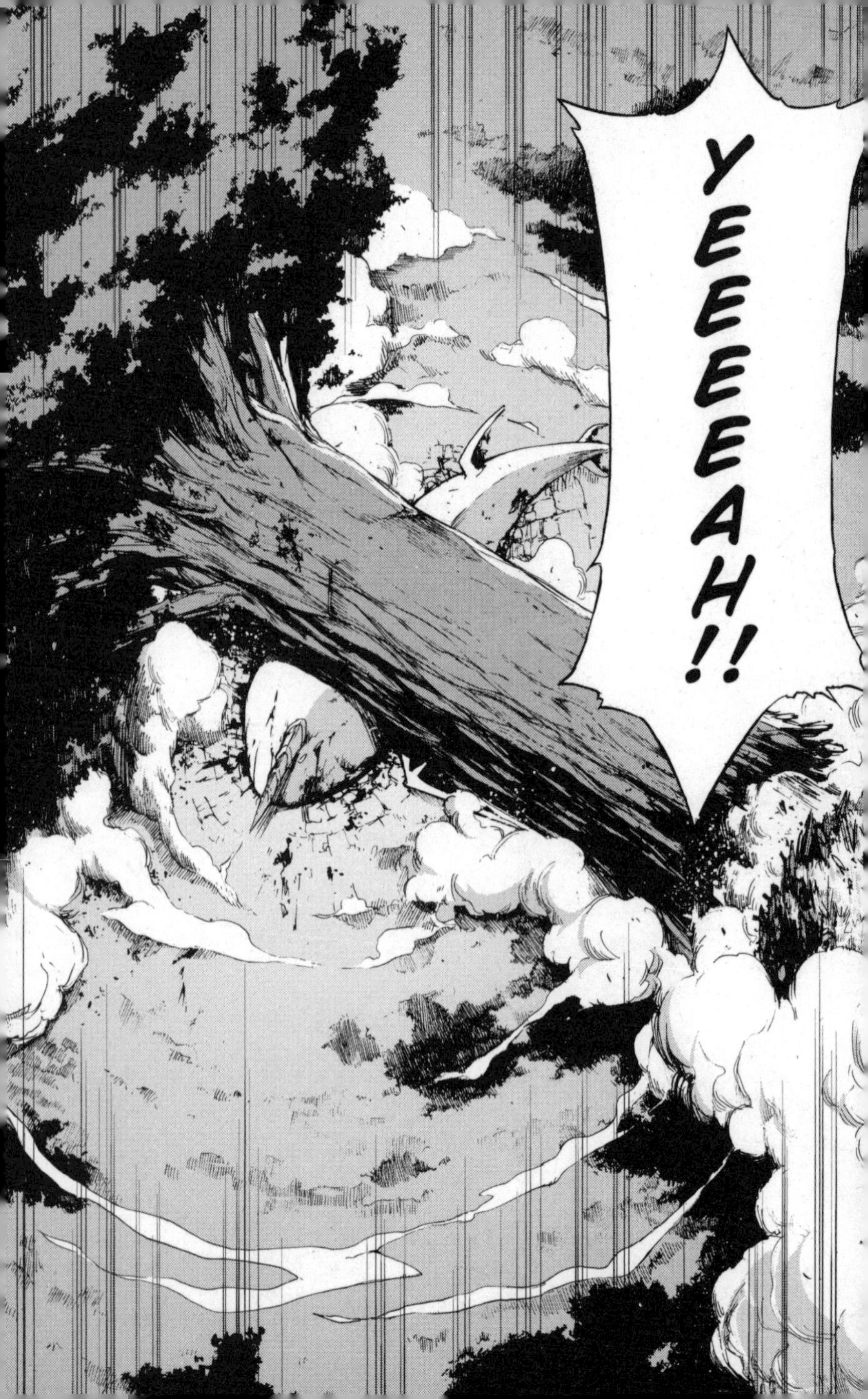
YEEEEAH!!

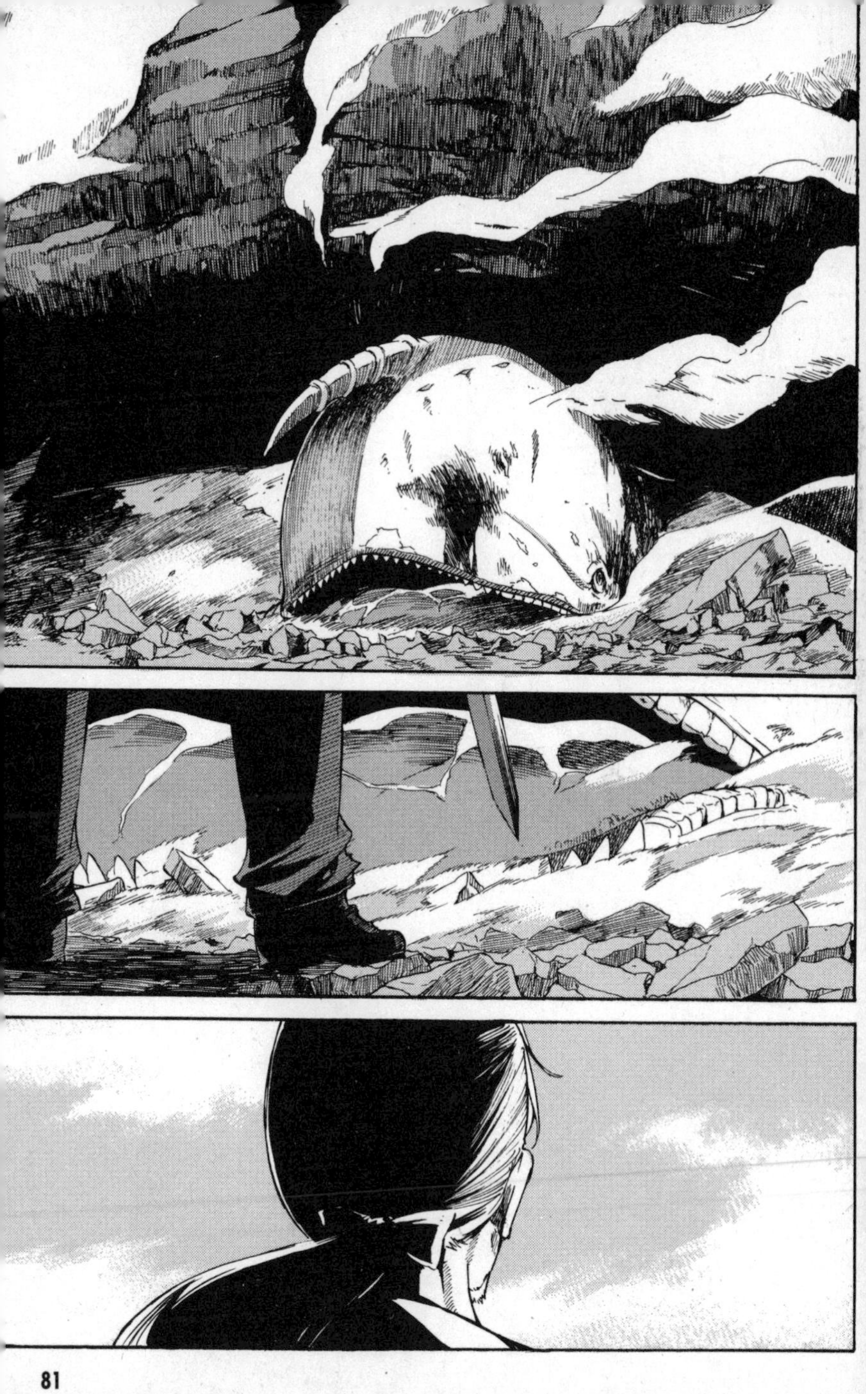

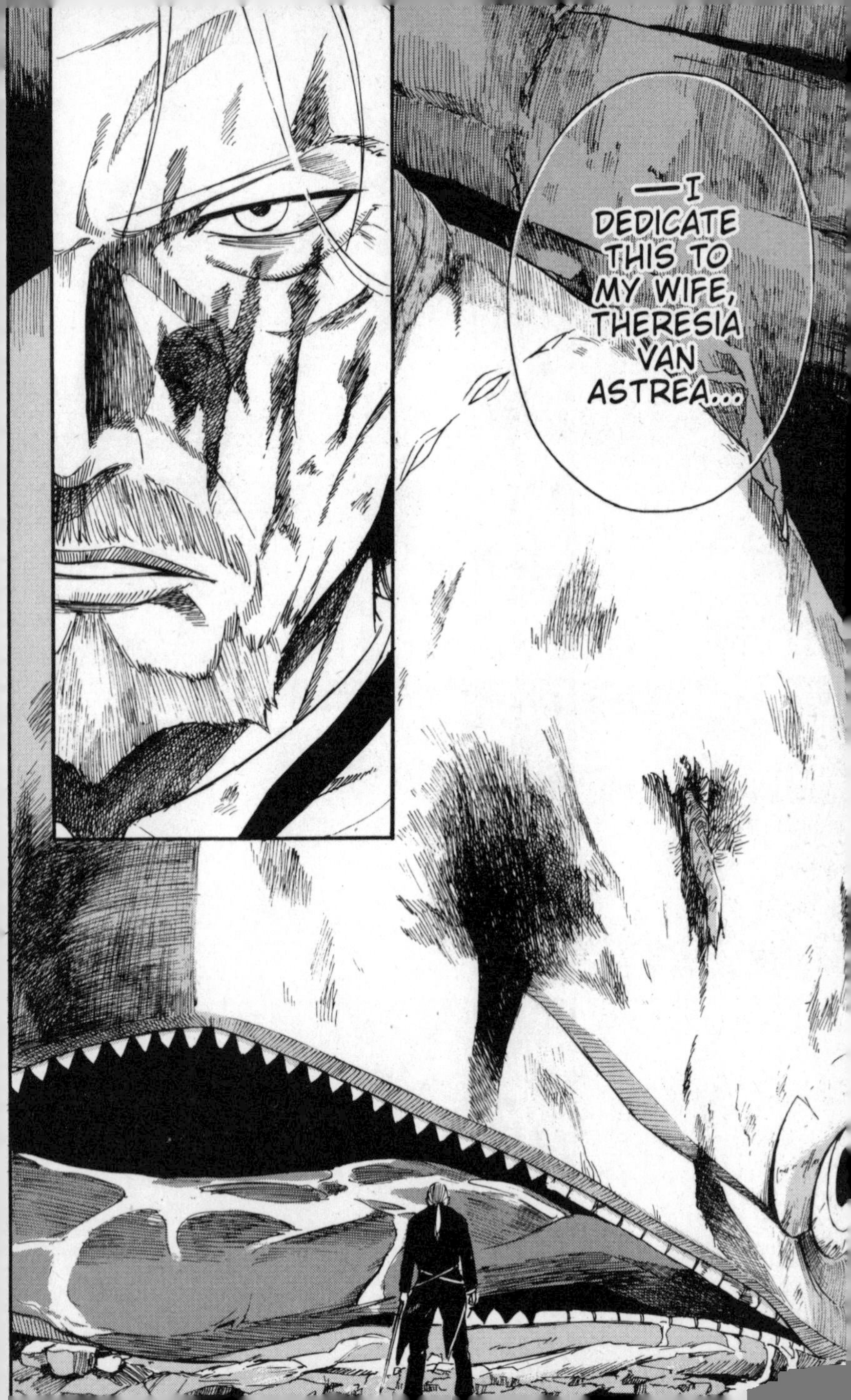
—I DEDICATE THIS TO MY WIFE, THERESIA VAN ASTREA...

Re:ZERO -Starting Life in Another World-

The only ability Subaru Natsuki gets when he's summoned to another world is time travel via his own death. But to save her, he'll die as many times as it takes.

Truth of Zero

The only ability Subaru Natsuki gets when he's
summoned to another world is time travel via his own
death. But to save her, he'll die as many times as it takes.

Re:ZERO -Starting
Life in Another World-

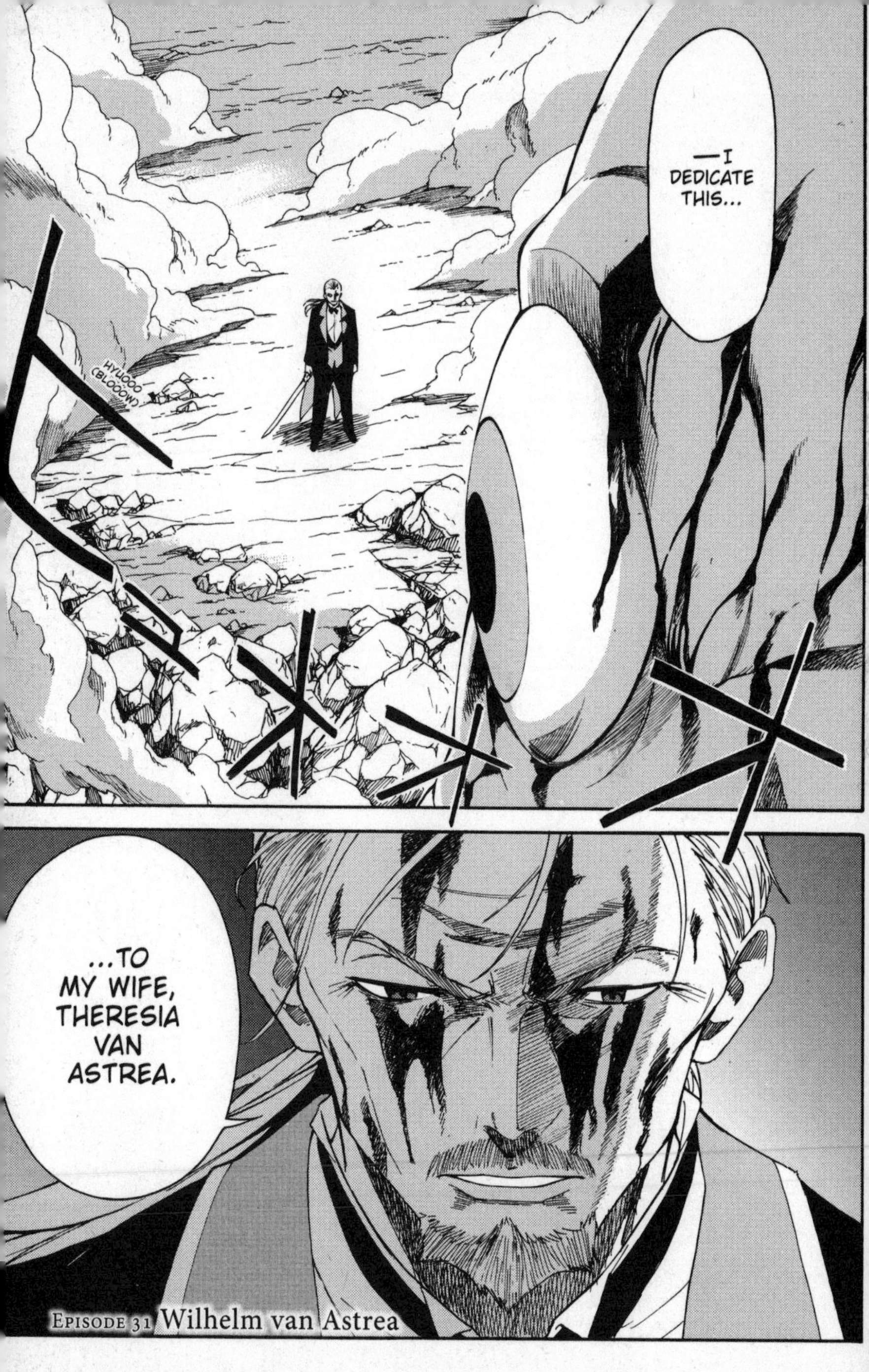
—I DEDICATE THIS...
HYUOOO (BLOOOW)
...TO MY WIFE, THERESIA VAN ASTREA.

Episode 31 Wilhelm van Astrea

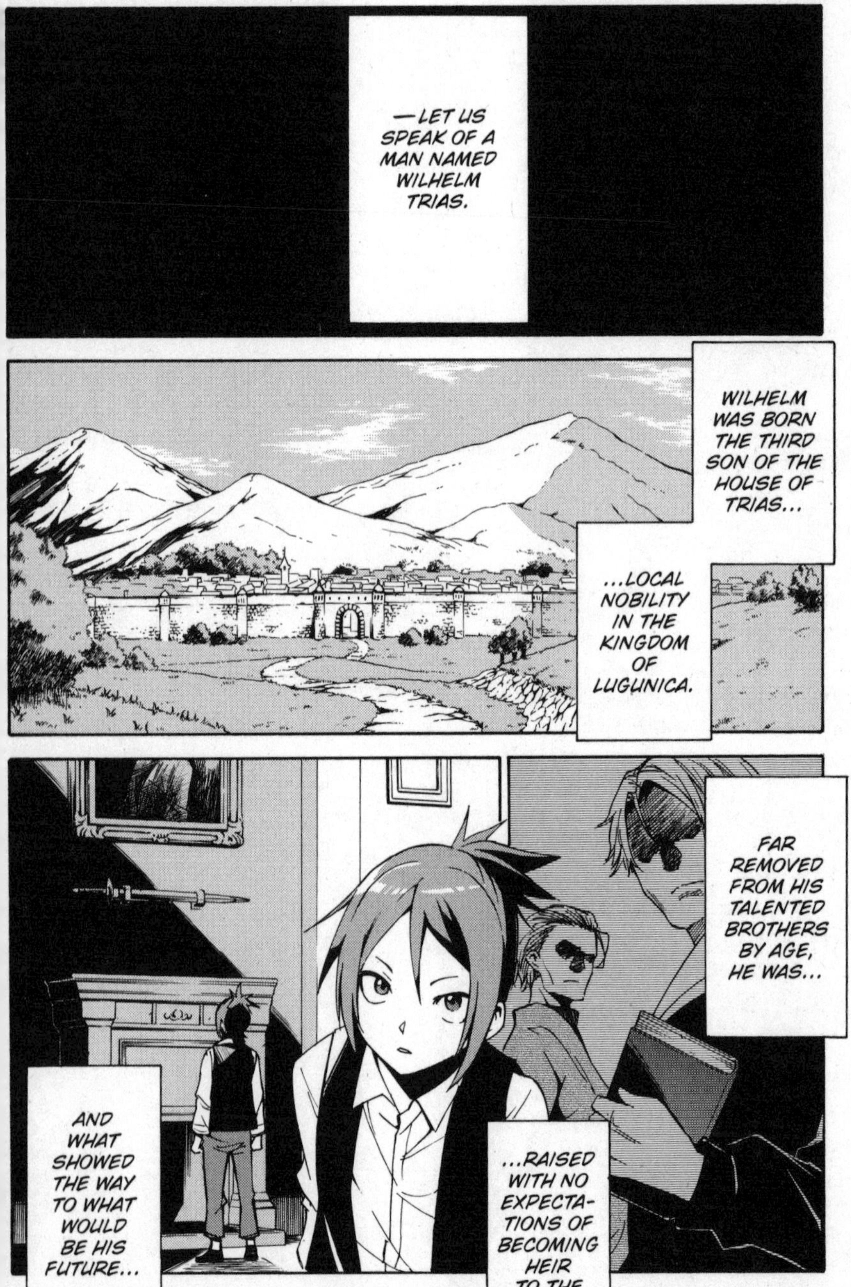
—LET US SPEAK OF A MAN NAMED WILHELM TRIAS.
WILHELM WAS BORN THE THIRD SON OF THE HOUSE OF TRIAS...
...LOCAL NOBILITY IN THE KINGDOM OF LUGUNICA.
FAR REMOVED FROM HIS TALENTED BROTHERS BY AGE, HE WAS...
...RAISED WITH NO EXPECTATIONS OF BECOMING HEIR TO THE FAMILY.
AND WHAT SHOWED THE WAY TO WHAT WOULD BE HIS FUTURE...

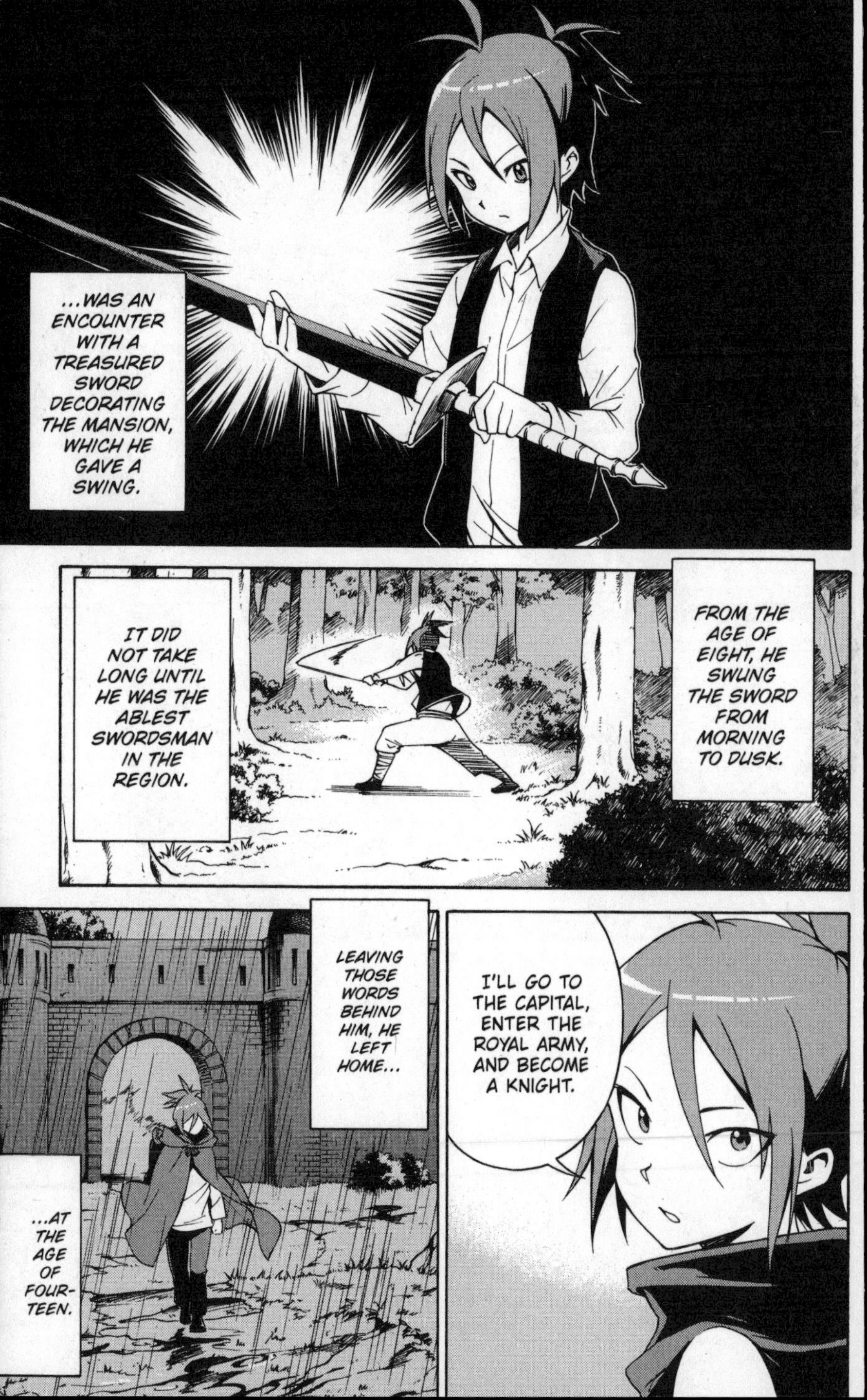
...WAS AN ENCOUNTER WITH A TREASURED SWORD DECORATING THE MANSION, WHICH HE GAVE A SWING.
FROM THE AGE OF EIGHT, HE SWUNG THE SWORD FROM MORNING TO DUSK.
IT DID NOT TAKE LONG UNTIL HE WAS THE ABLEST SWORDSMAN IN THE REGION.
I'LL GO TO THE CAPITAL, ENTER THE ROYAL ARMY, AND BECOME A KNIGHT.
LEAVING THOSE WORDS BEHIND HIM, HE LEFT HOME...
...AT THE AGE OF FOUR-TEEN.

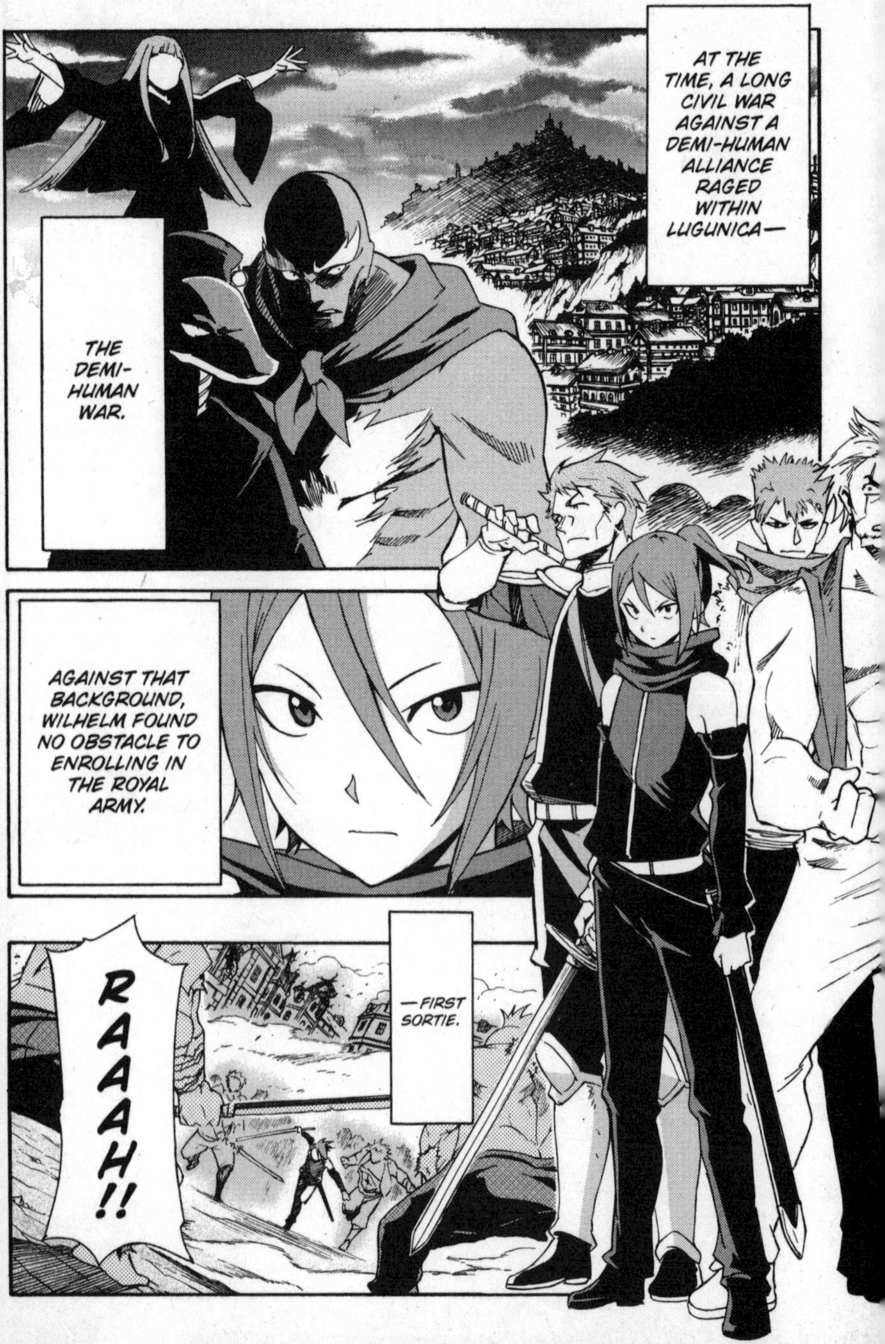
AT THE TIME, A LONG CIVIL WAR AGAINST A DEMI-HUMAN ALLIANCE RAGED WITHIN LUGUNICA—
THE DEMI-HUMAN WAR.
AGAINST THAT BACKGROUND, WILHELM FOUND NO OBSTACLE TO ENROLLING IN THE ROYAL ARMY.
—FIRST SORTIE.
RAAAAH!!

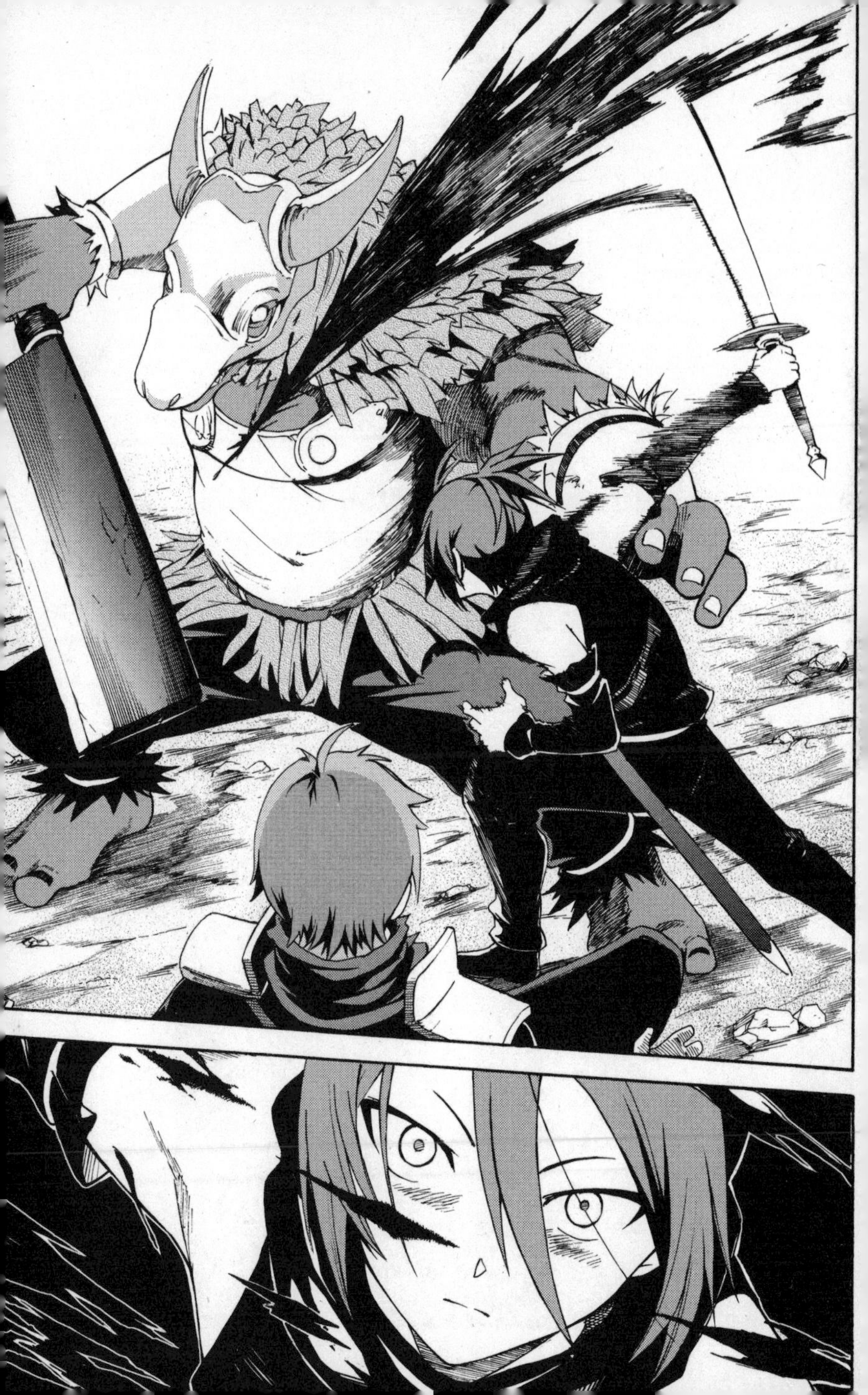

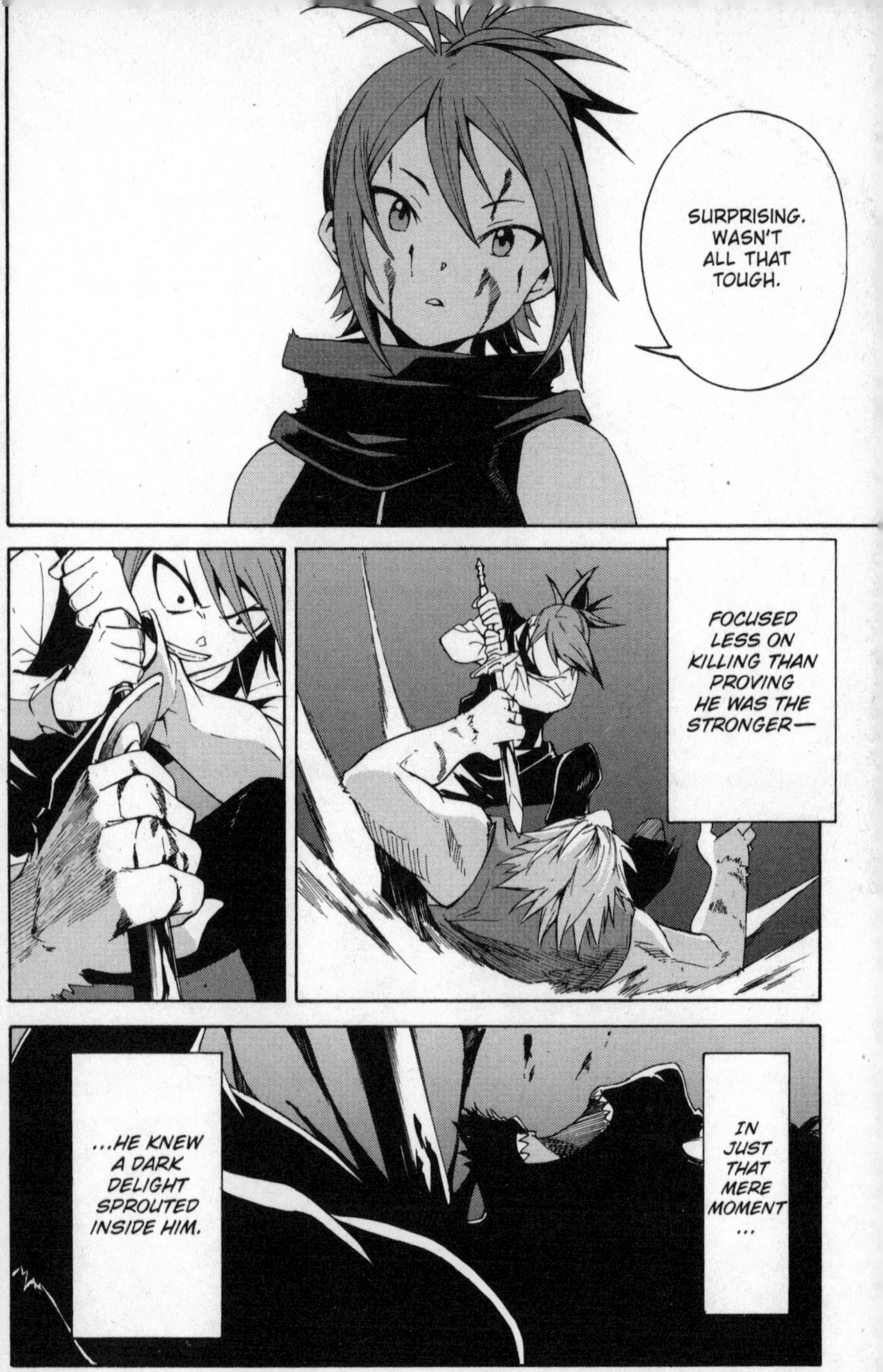
SURPRISING. WASN'T ALL THAT TOUGH.
FOCUSED LESS ON KILLING THAN PROVING HE WAS THE STRONGER—
IN JUST THAT MERE MOMENT ...
...HE KNEW A DARK DELIGHT SPROUTED INSIDE HIM.

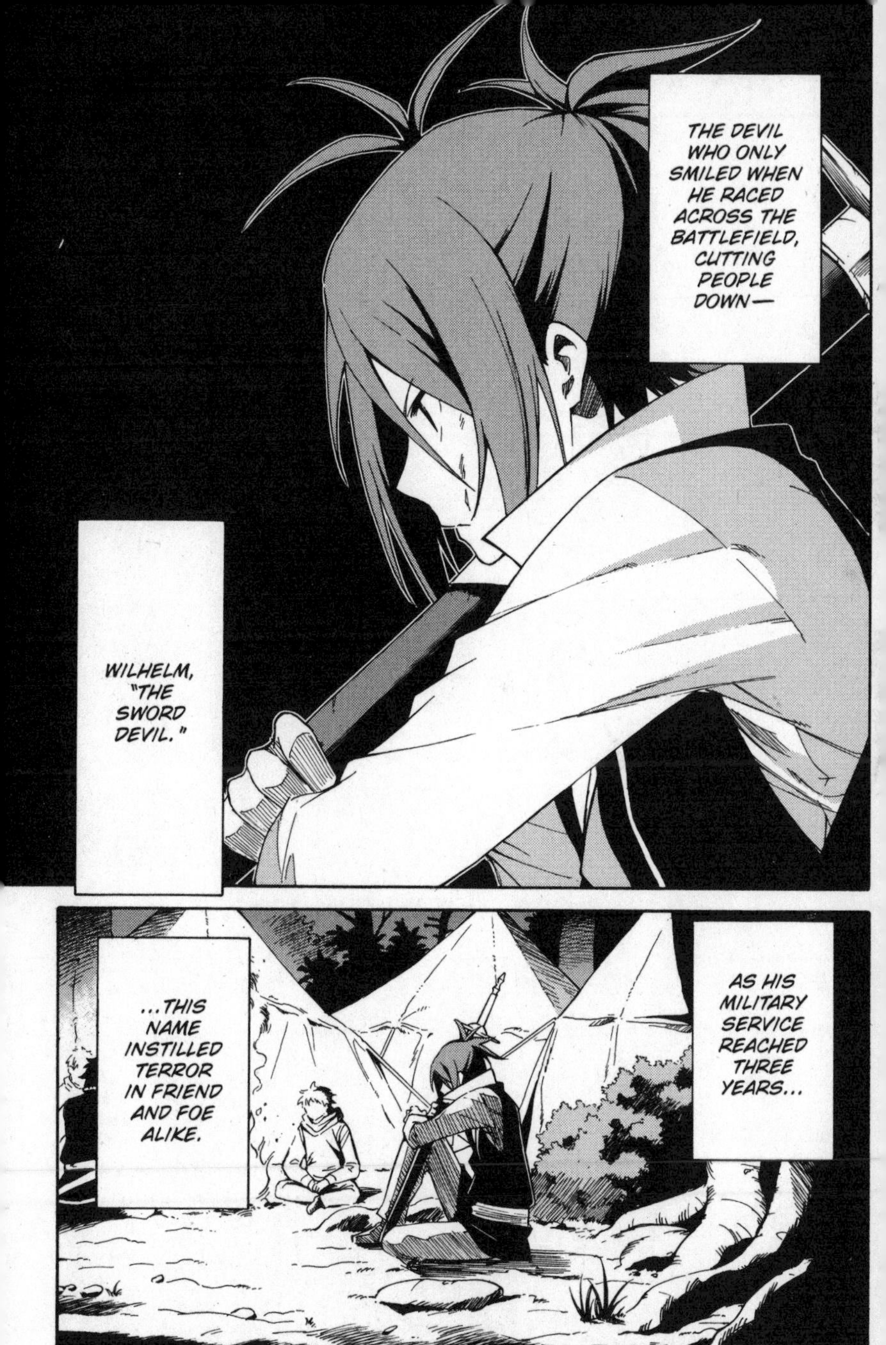
THE DEVIL WHO ONLY SMILED WHEN HE RACED ACROSS THE BATTLEFIELD, CUTTING PEOPLE DOWN—
WILHELM, "THE SWORD DEVIL."
AS HIS MILITARY SERVICE REACHED THREE YEARS...
...THIS NAME INSTILLED TERROR IN FRIEND AND FOE ALIKE.

— THERE SHE WAS, WITH LONG AND FLOWING RED HAIR...

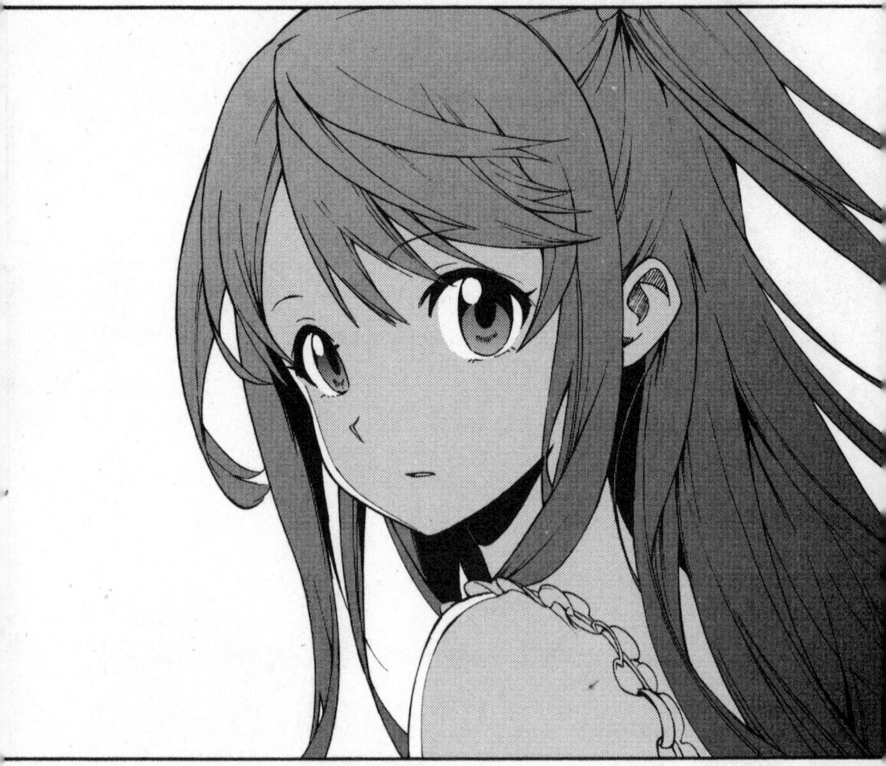

A GIRL WITH A MOST COMELY PROFILE.

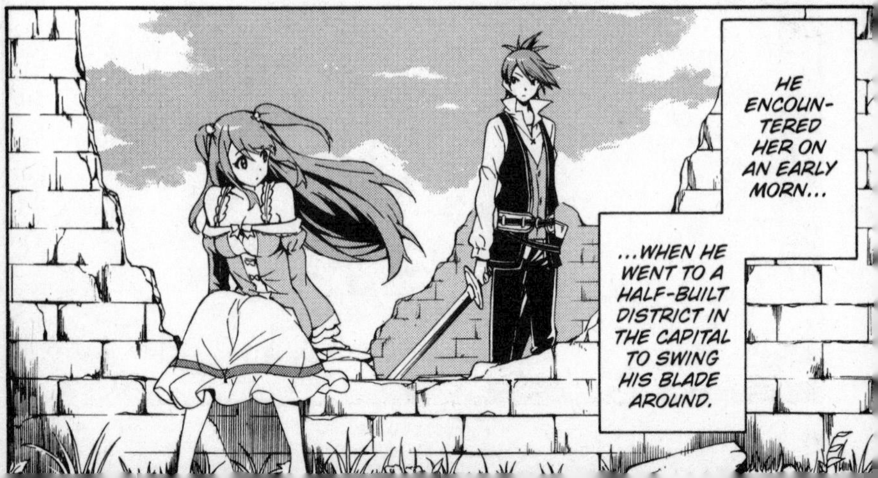
HE ENCOUN-TERED HER ON AN EARLY MORN...
...WHEN HE WENT TO A HALF-BUILT DISTRICT IN THE CAPITAL TO SWING HIS BLADE AROUND.

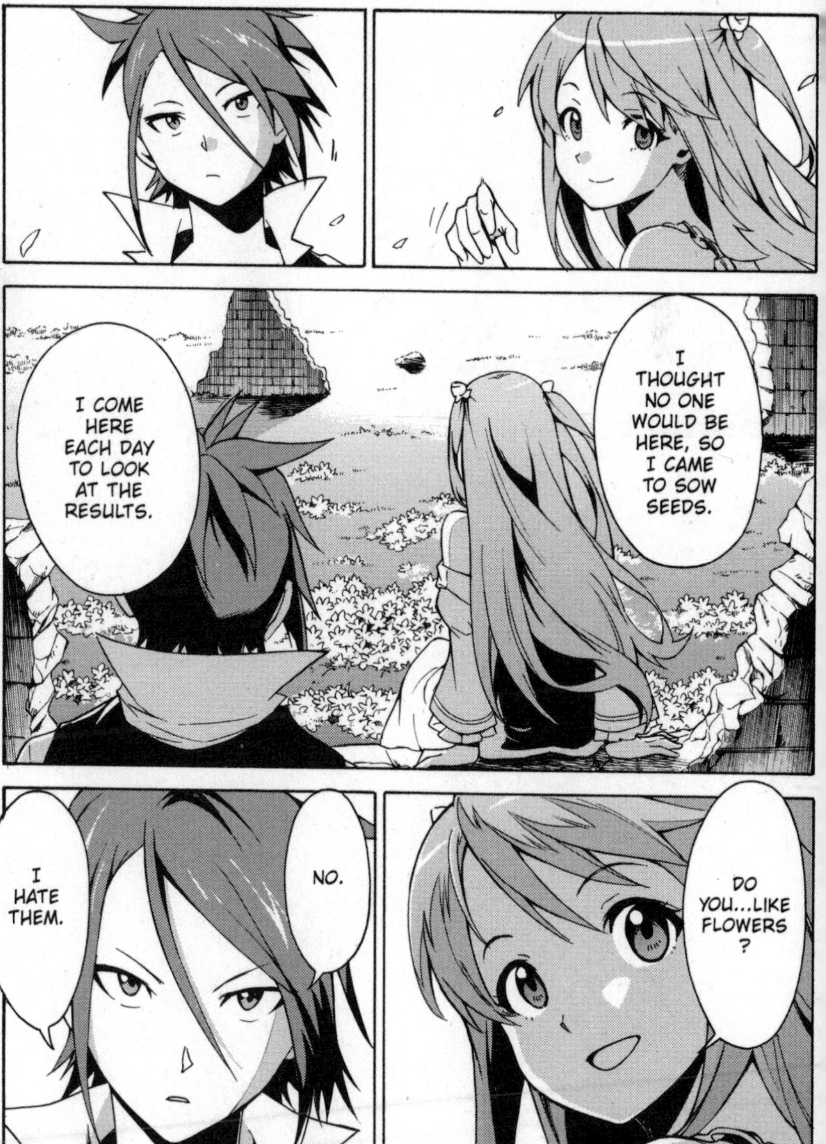
I THOUGHT NO ONE WOULD BE HERE, SO I CAME TO SOW SEEDS.
I COME HERE EACH DAY TO LOOK AT THE RESULTS.
DO YOU...LIKE FLOWERS?
NO.
I HATE THEM.

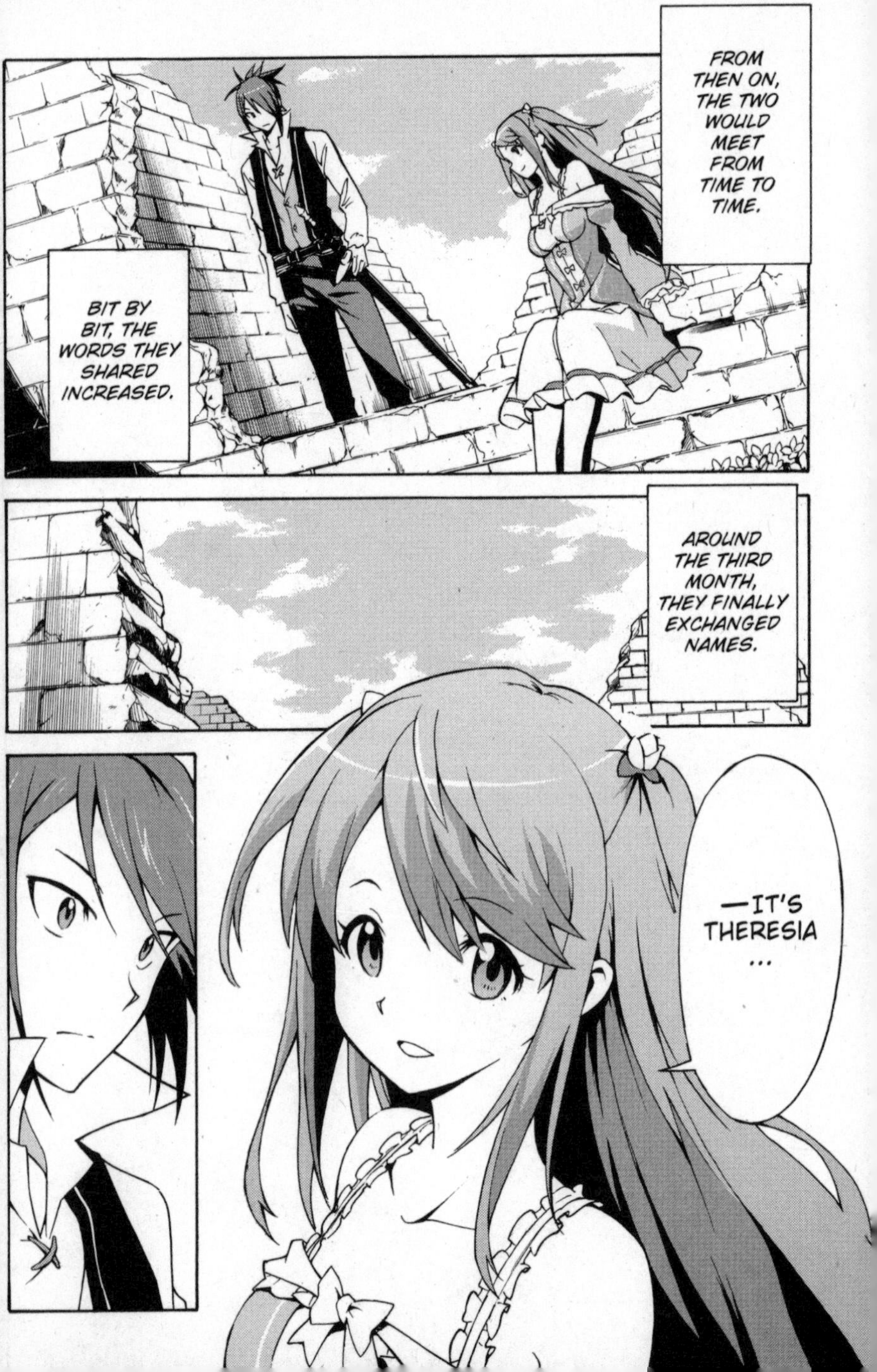
FROM THEN ON, THE TWO WOULD MEET FROM TIME TO TIME.
BIT BY BIT, THE WORDS THEY SHARED INCREASED.
AROUND THE THIRD MONTH, THEY FINALLY EXCHANGED NAMES.
—IT'S THERESIA ...

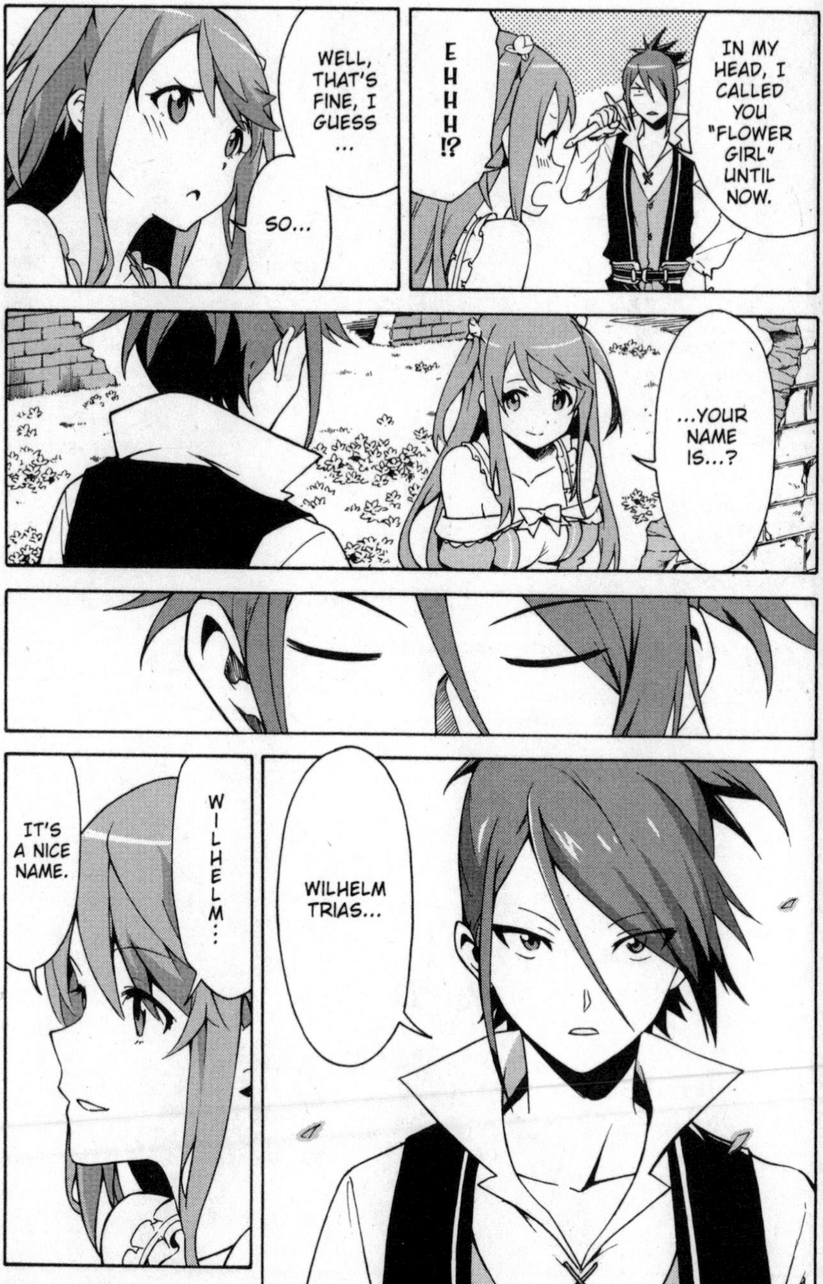
IN MY HEAD, I CALLED YOU "FLOWER GIRL" UNTIL NOW.
EHHHH!?
WELL, THAT'S FINE, I GUESS...
SO...
...YOUR NAME IS...?
WILHELM TRIAS...
WILHELM...
IT'S A NICE NAME.

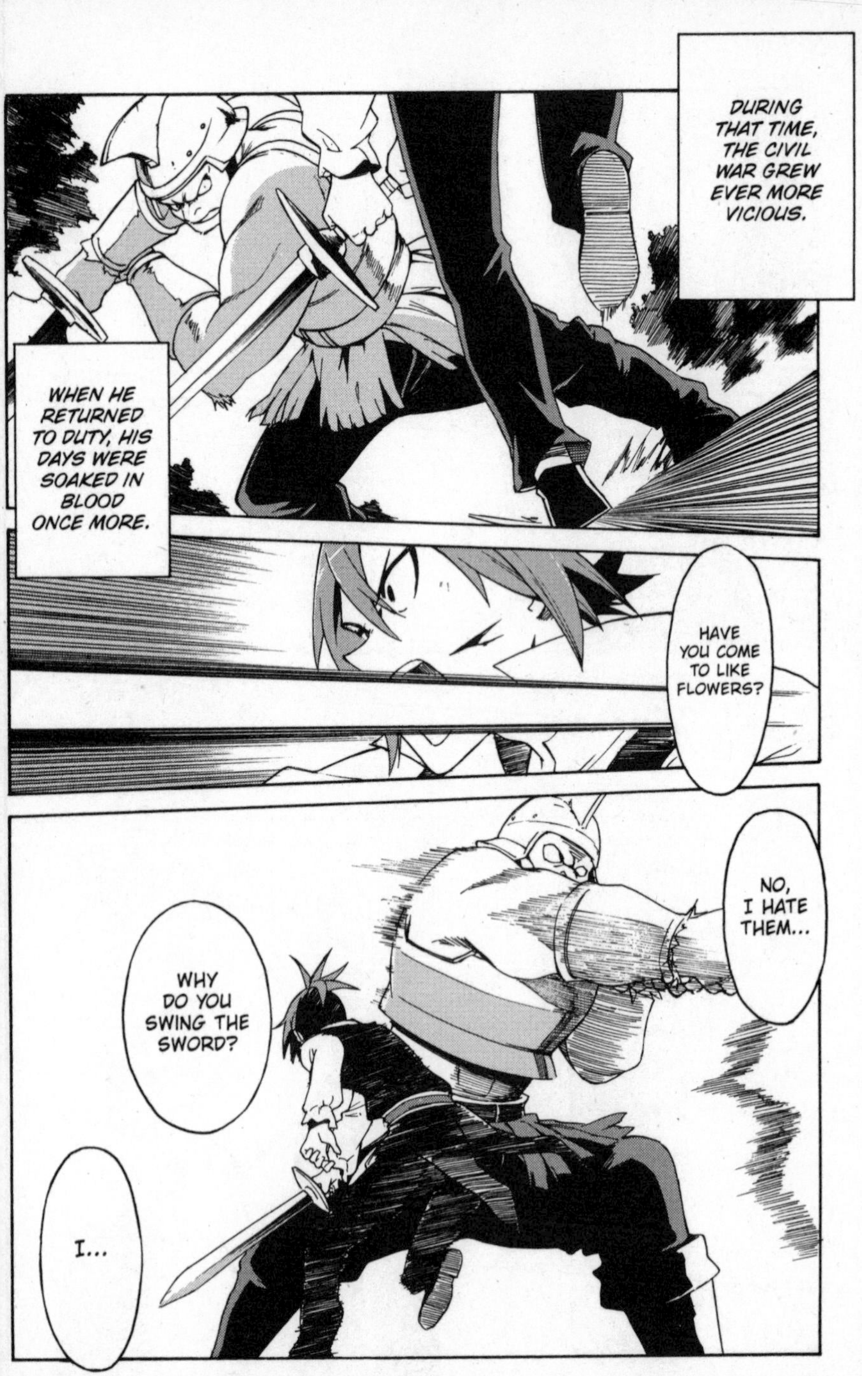
DURING THAT TIME, THE CIVIL WAR GREW EVER MORE VICIOUS.
WHEN HE RETURNED TO DUTY, HIS DAYS WERE SOAKED IN BLOOD ONCE MORE.
HAVE YOU COME TO LIKE FLOWERS?
NO, I HATE THEM...
WHY DO YOU SWING THE SWORD?
I...

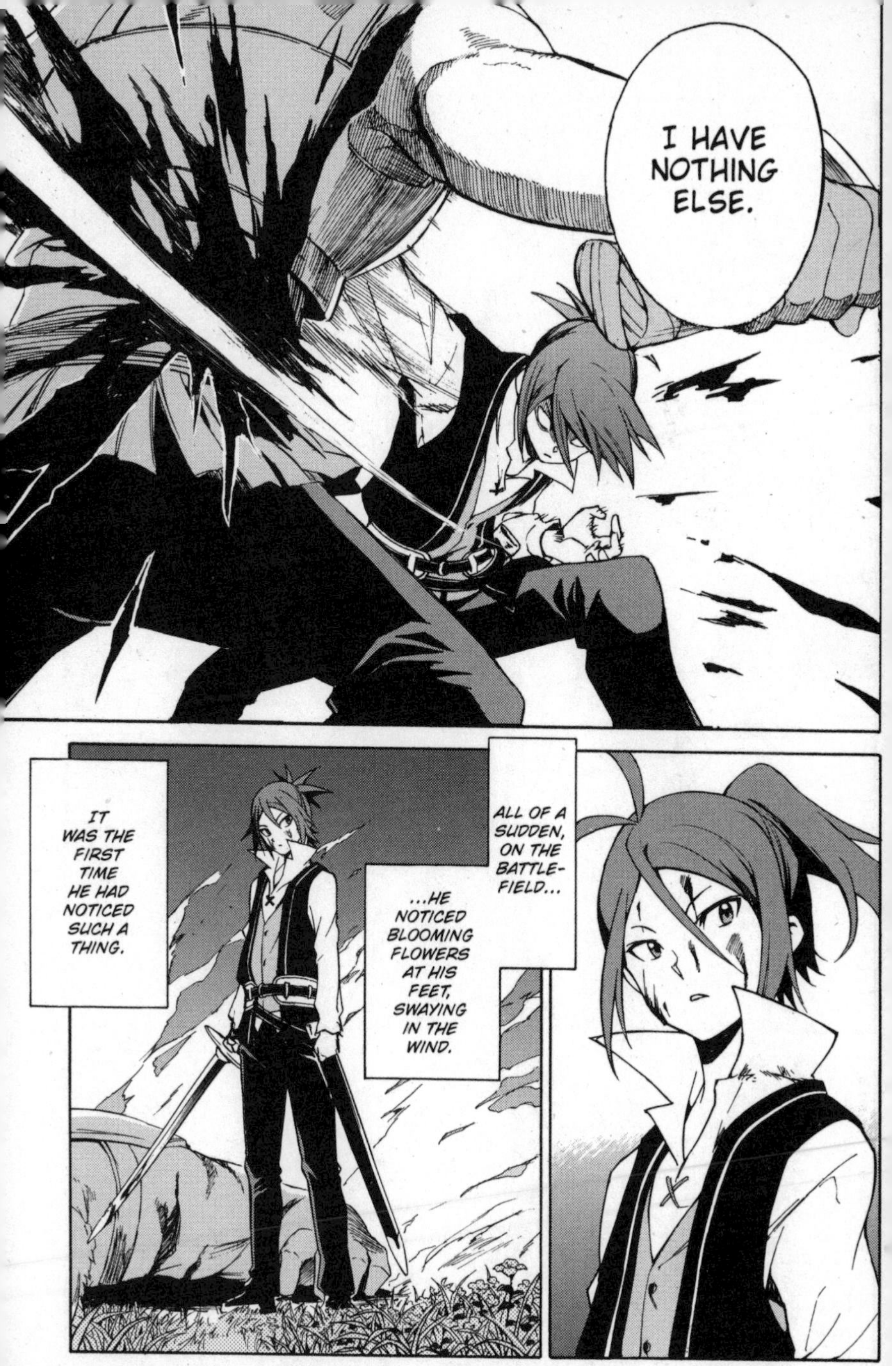
I HAVE NOTHING ELSE.
ALL OF A SUDDEN, ON THE BATTLE-FIELD...
...HE NOTICED BLOOMING FLOWERS AT HIS FEET, SWAYING IN THE WIND.
IT WAS THE FIRST TIME HE HAD NOTICED SUCH A THING.

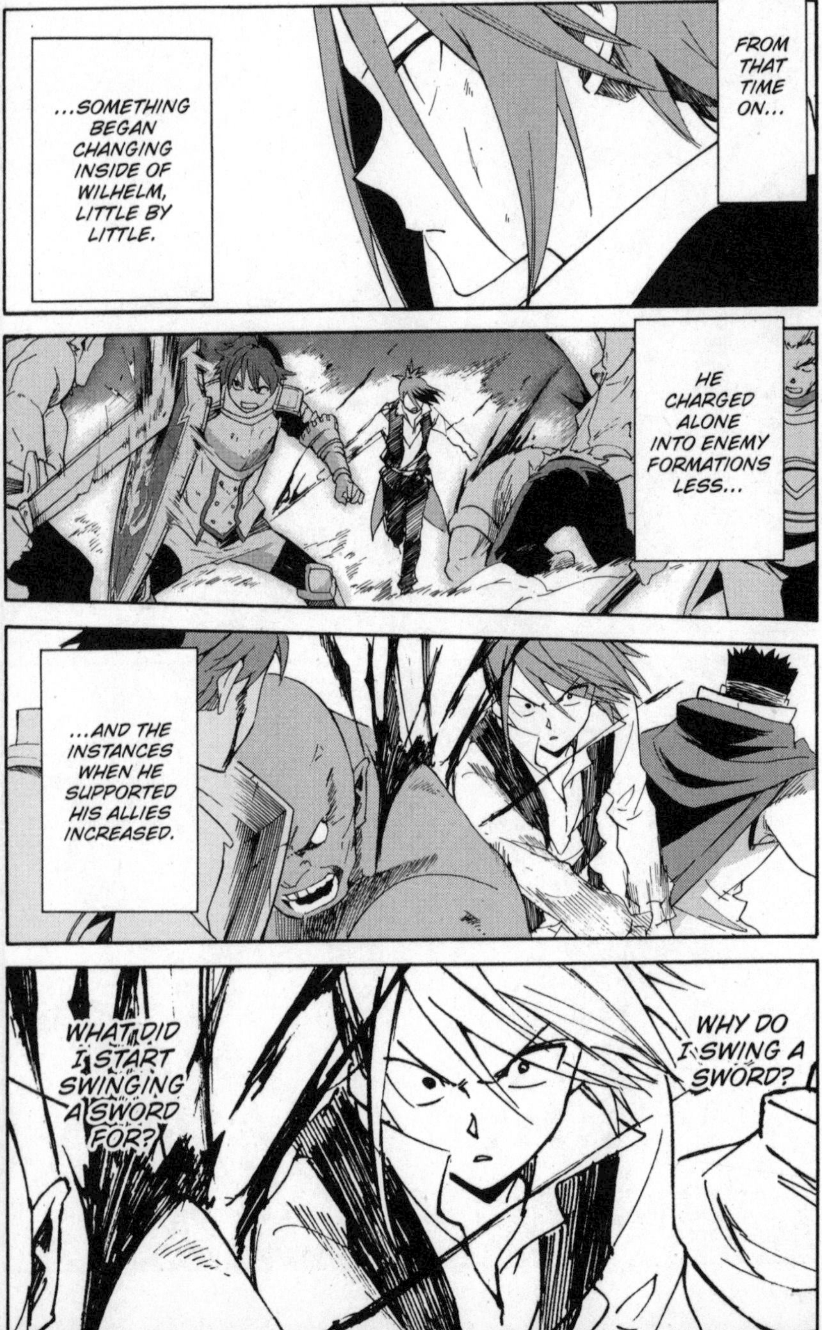
FROM THAT TIME ON...
...SOMETHING BEGAN CHANGING INSIDE OF WILHELM, LITTLE BY LITTLE.
HE CHARGED ALONE INTO ENEMY FORMATIONS LESS...
...AND THE INSTANCES WHEN HE SUPPORTED HIS ALLIES INCREASED.
WHY DO I SWING A SWORD?
WHAT DID I START SWINGING A SWORD FOR?

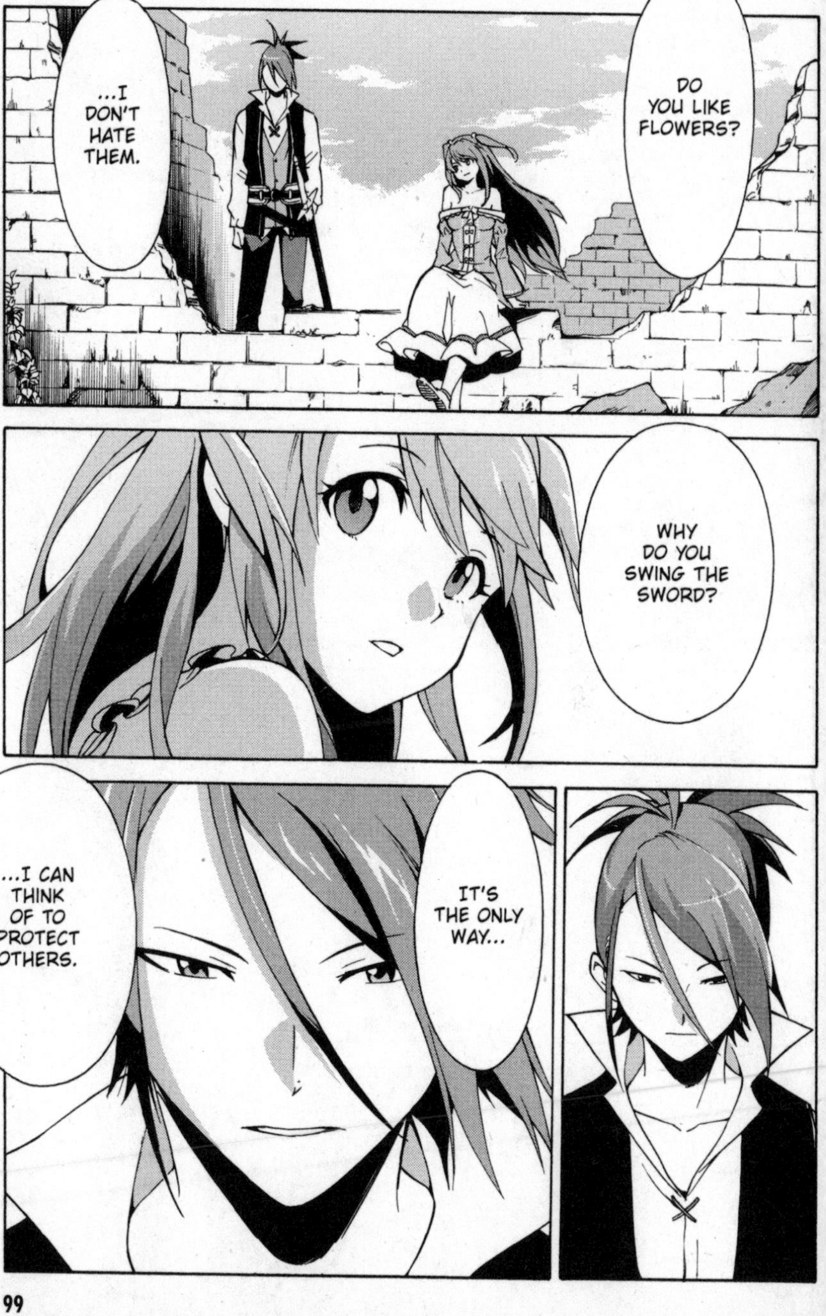
DO YOU LIKE FLOWERS?
...I DON'T HATE THEM.
WHY DO YOU SWING THE SWORD?
IT'S THE ONLY WAY...
...I CAN THINK OF TO PROTECT OTHERS.

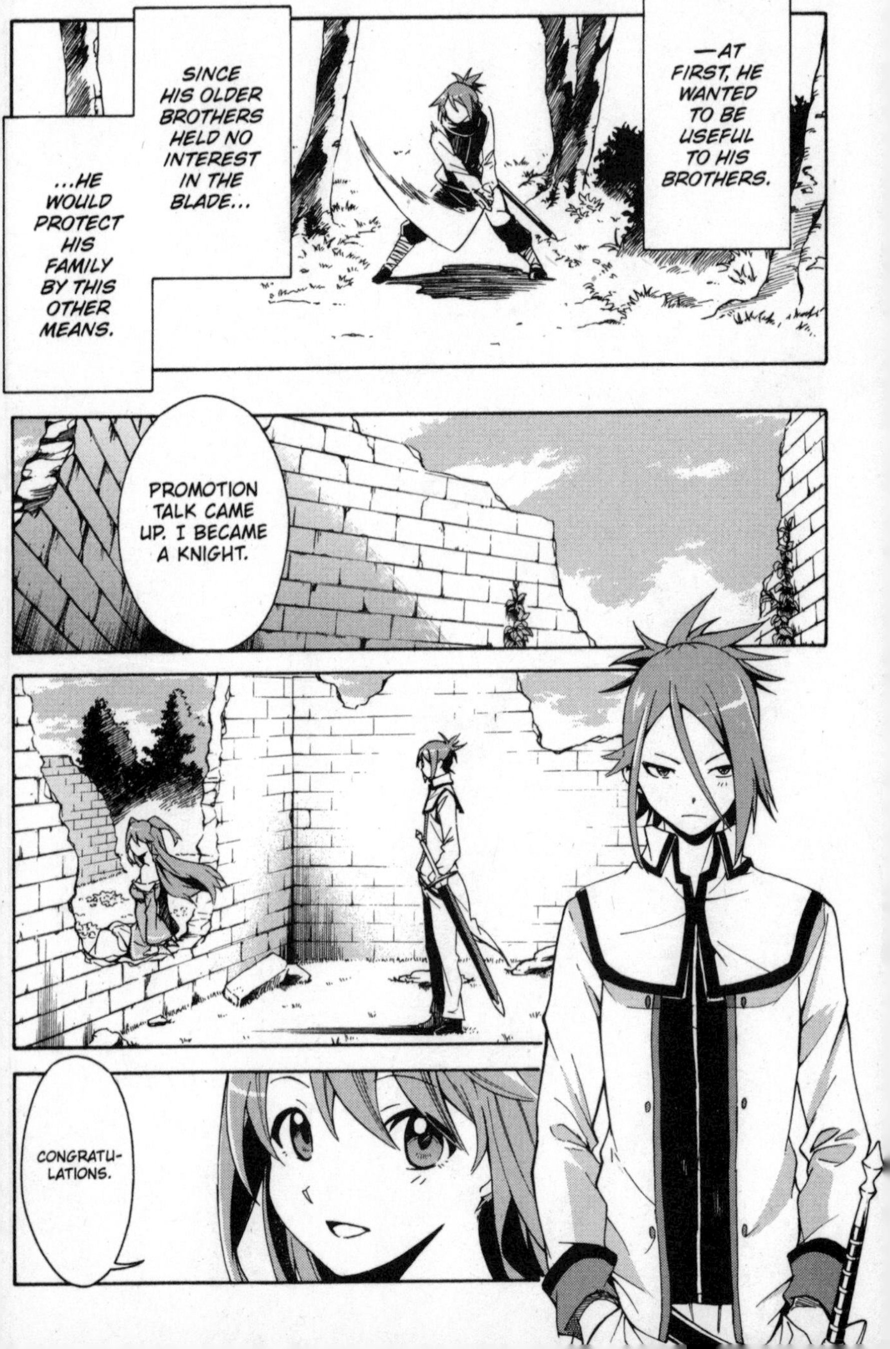
—AT FIRST, HE WANTED TO BE USEFUL TO HIS BROTHERS.
SINCE HIS OLDER BROTHERS HELD NO INTEREST IN THE BLADE...
...HE WOULD PROTECT HIS FAMILY BY THIS OTHER MEANS.
PROMOTION TALK CAME UP. I BECAME A KNIGHT.
CONGRATULATIONS.

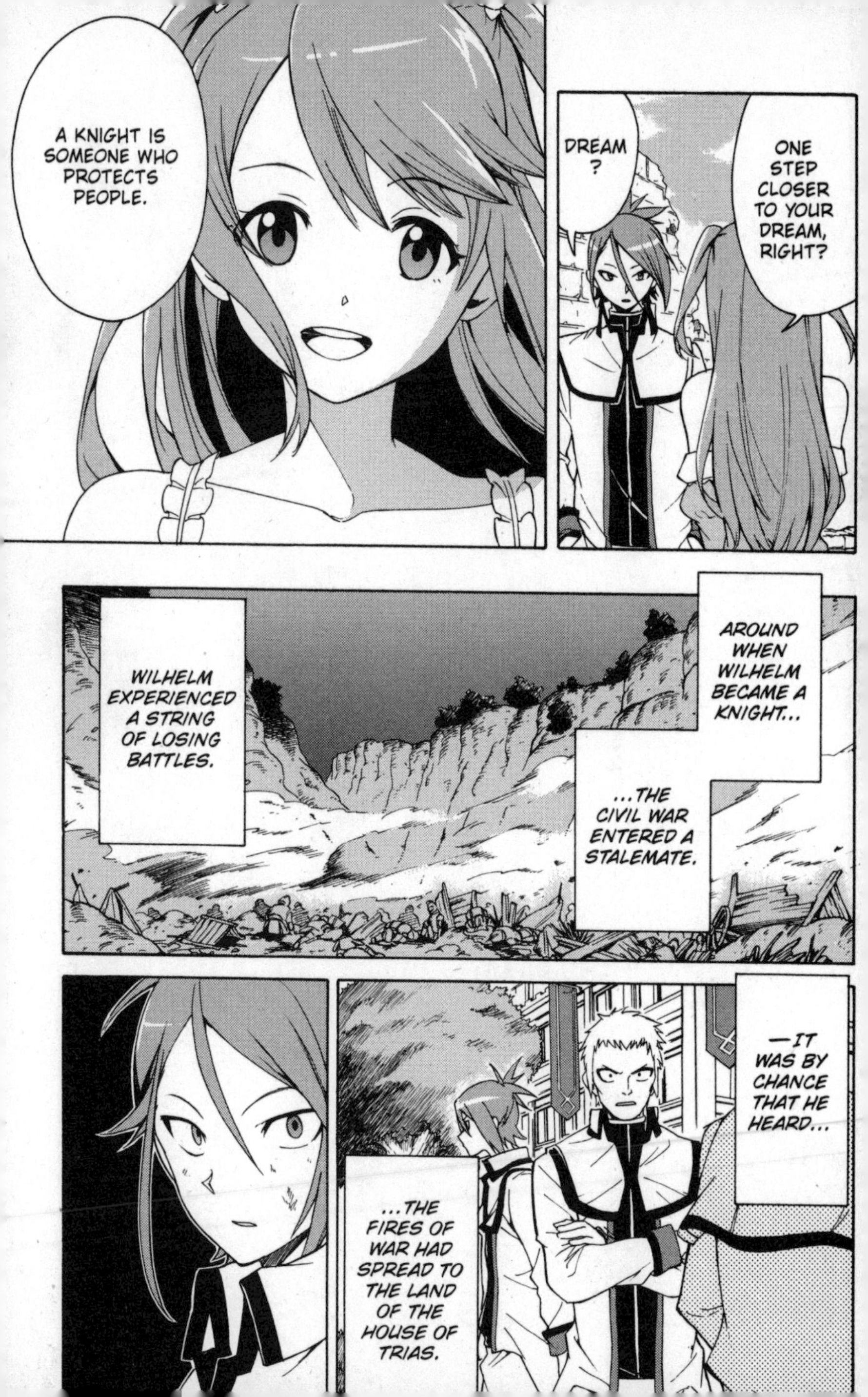
ONE STEP CLOSER TO YOUR DREAM, RIGHT?
DREAM ?
A KNIGHT IS SOMEONE WHO PROTECTS PEOPLE.
AROUND WHEN WILHELM BECAME A KNIGHT...
...THE CIVIL WAR ENTERED A STALEMATE.
WILHELM EXPERIENCED A STRING OF LOSING BATTLES.
—IT WAS BY CHANCE THAT HE HEARD...
...THE FIRES OF WAR HAD SPREAD TO THE LAND OF THE HOUSE OF TRIAS.

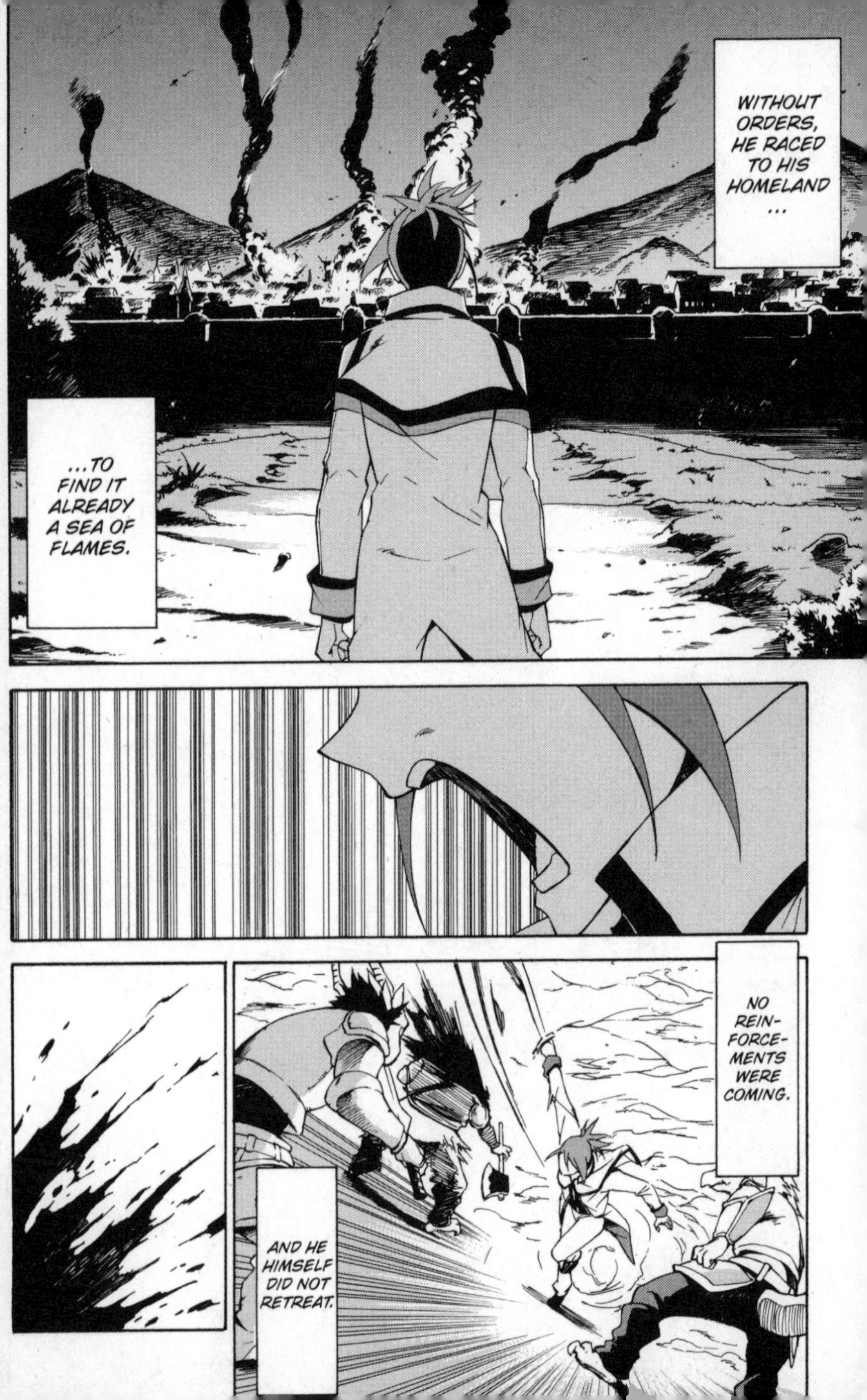
WITHOUT ORDERS, HE RACED TO HIS HOMELAND ...
...TO FIND IT ALREADY A SEA OF FLAMES.
NO REIN-FORCE-MENTS WERE COMING.
AND HE HIMSELF DID NOT RETREAT.

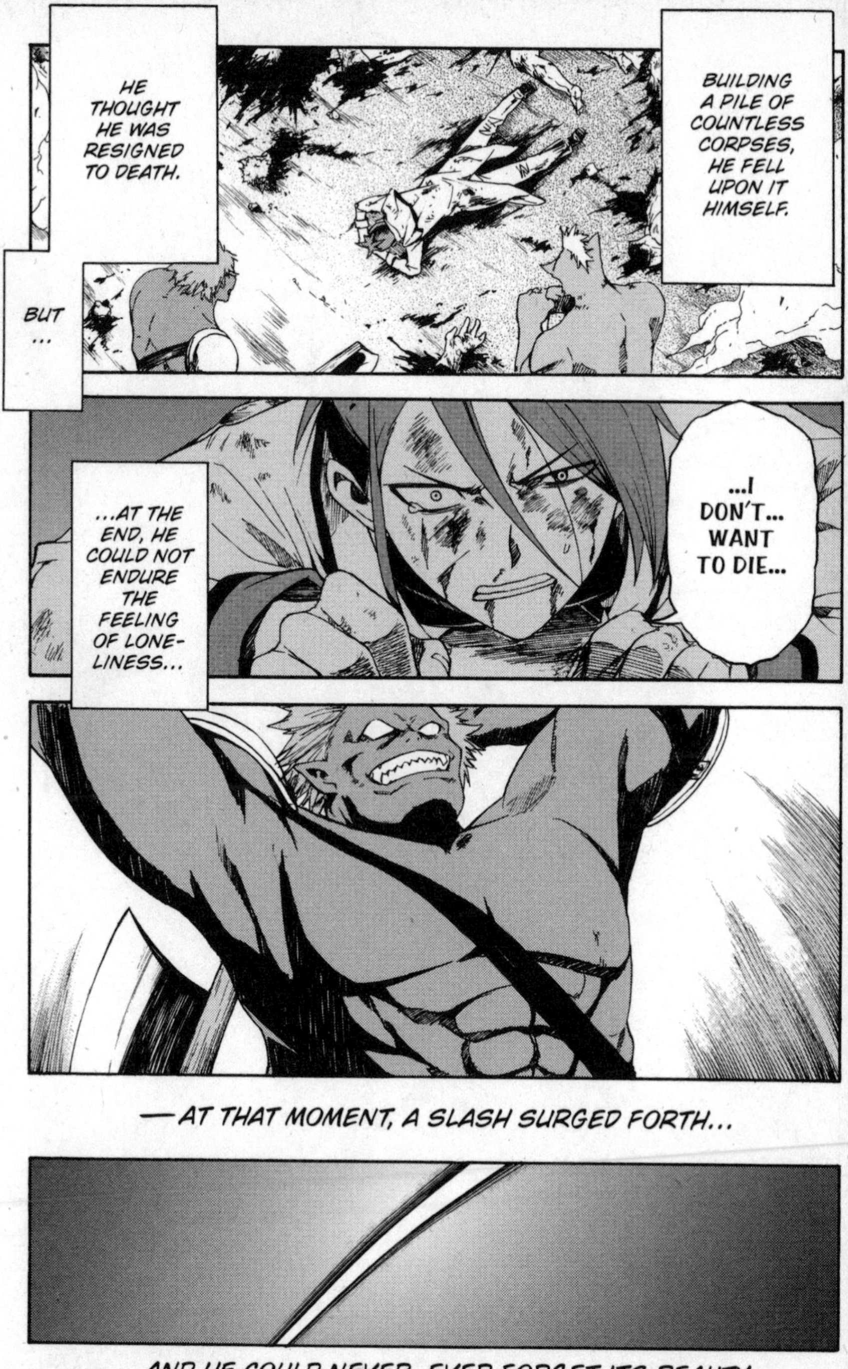
BUILDING A PILE OF COUNTLESS CORPSES, HE FELL UPON IT HIMSELF.
HE THOUGHT HE WAS RESIGNED TO DEATH.
BUT ...
...I DON'T... WANT TO DIE...
...AT THE END, HE COULD NOT ENDURE THE FEELING OF LONE-LINESS...
—AT THAT MOMENT, A SLASH SURGED FORTH...
...AND HE COULD NEVER, EVER FORGET ITS BEAUTY.

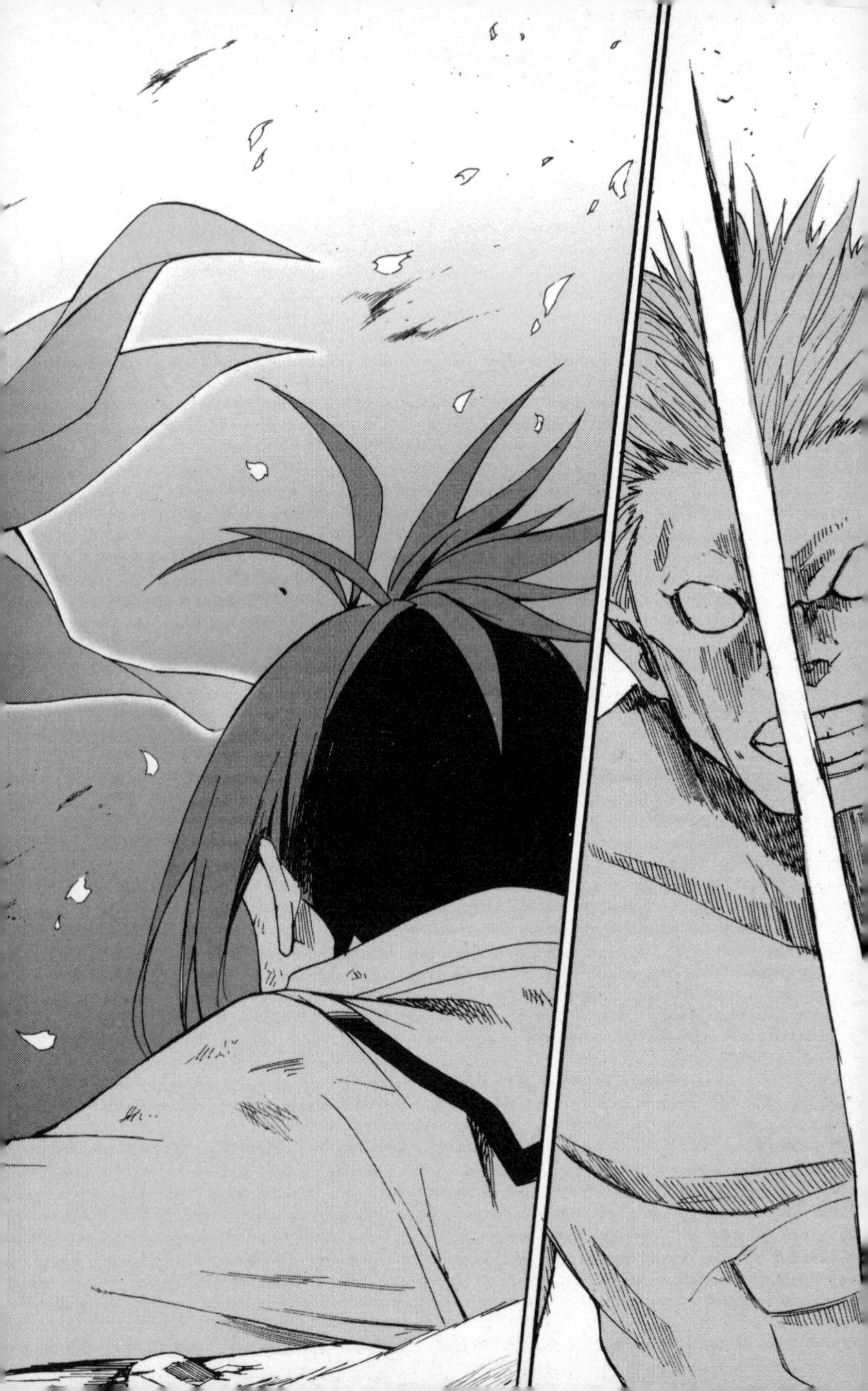

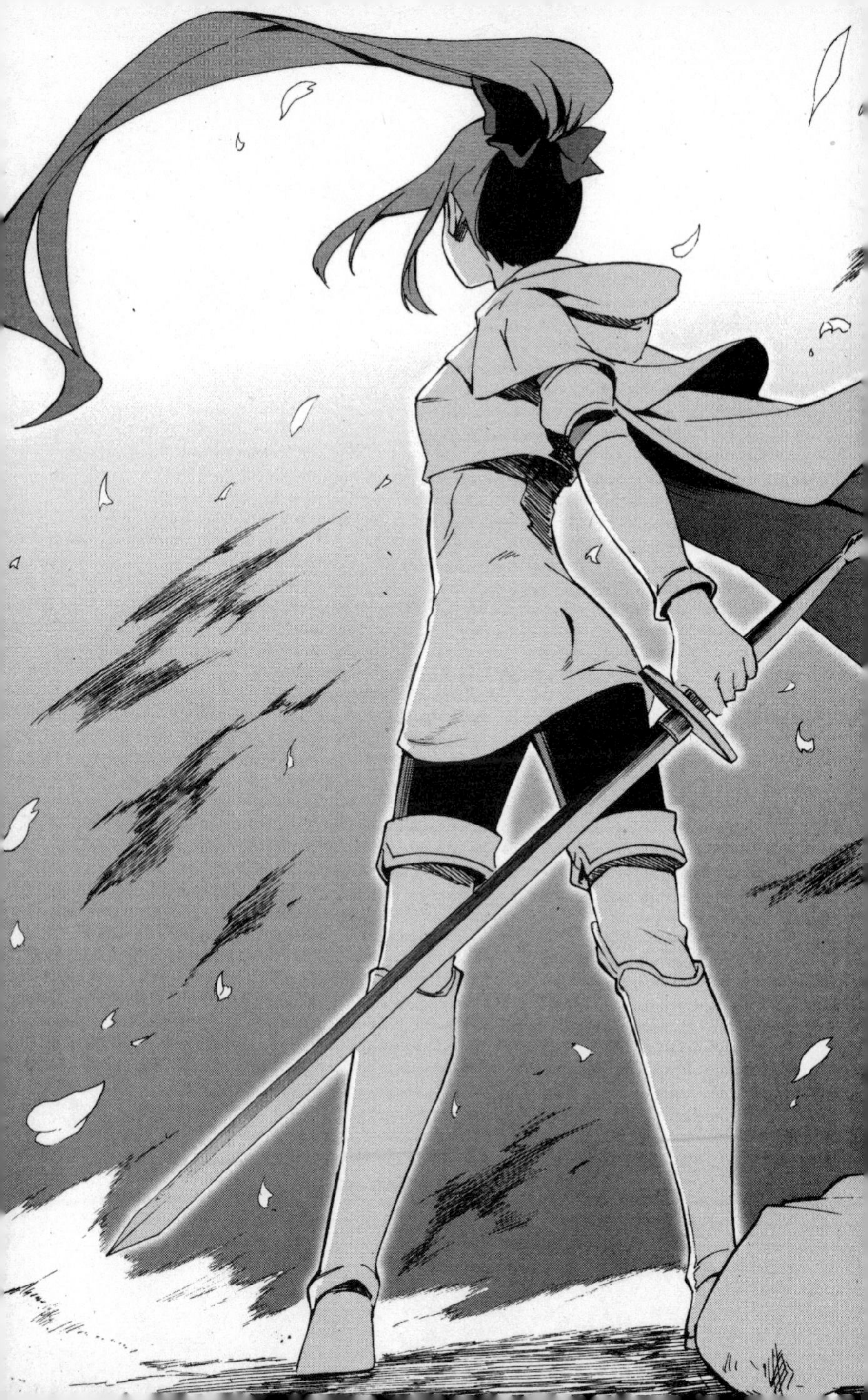

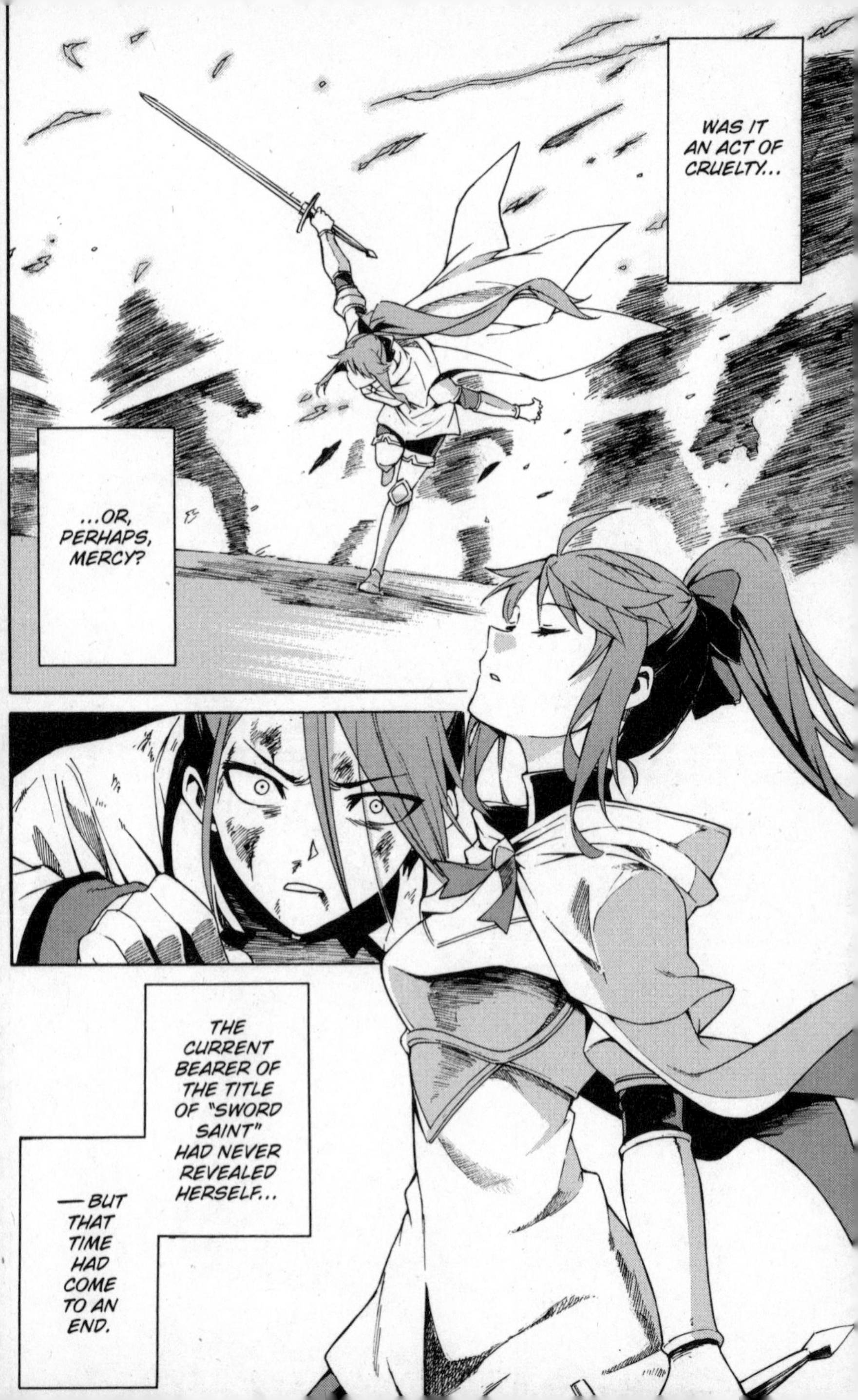
WAS IT AN ACT OF CRUELTY...
...OR, PERHAPS, MERCY?
THE CURRENT BEARER OF THE TITLE OF "SWORD SAINT" HAD NEVER REVEALED HERSELF...
—BUT THAT TIME HAD COME TO AN END.

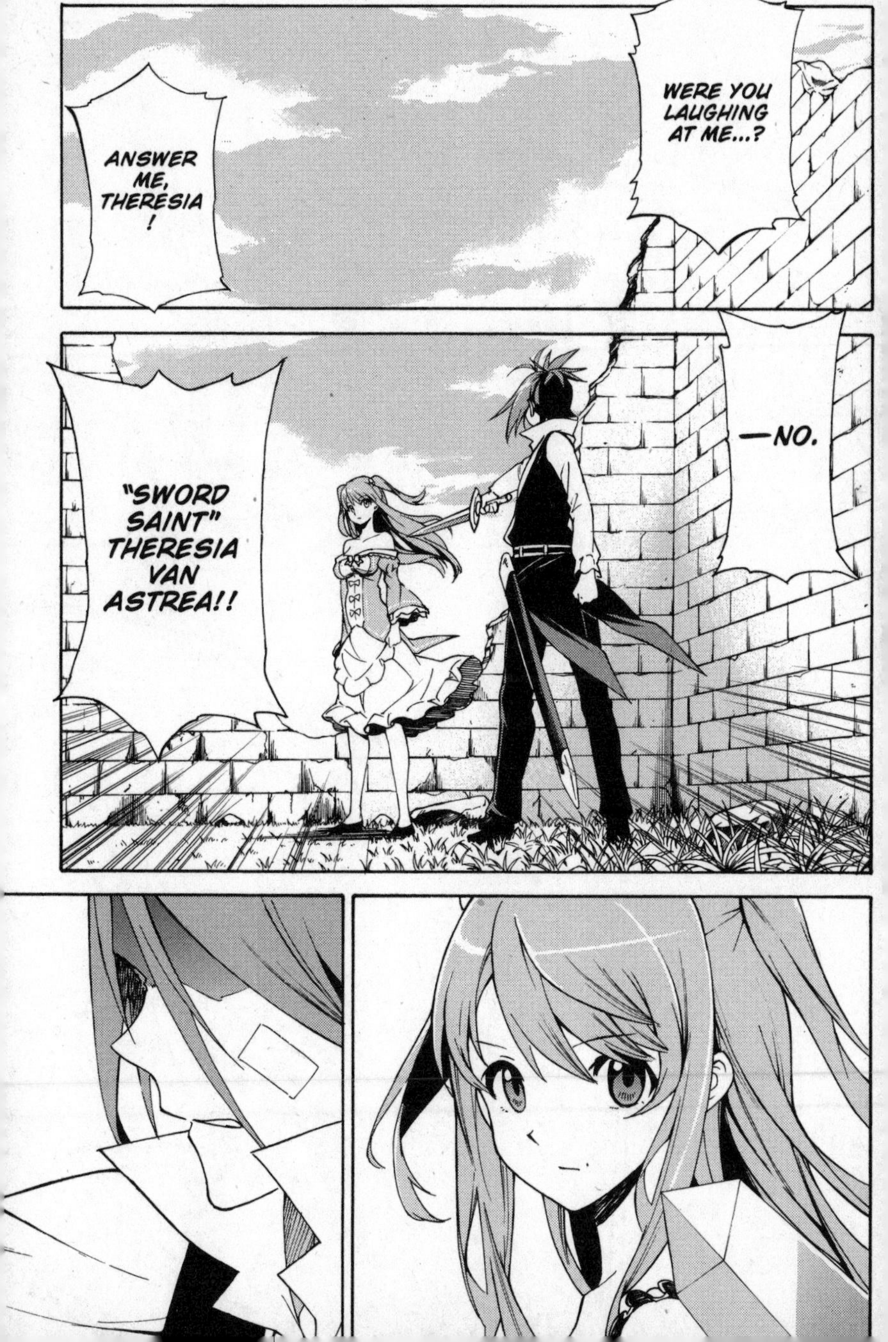
WERE YOU LAUGHING AT ME...?
ANSWER ME, THERESIA!
—NO.
"SWORD SAINT" THERESIA VAN ASTREA!!

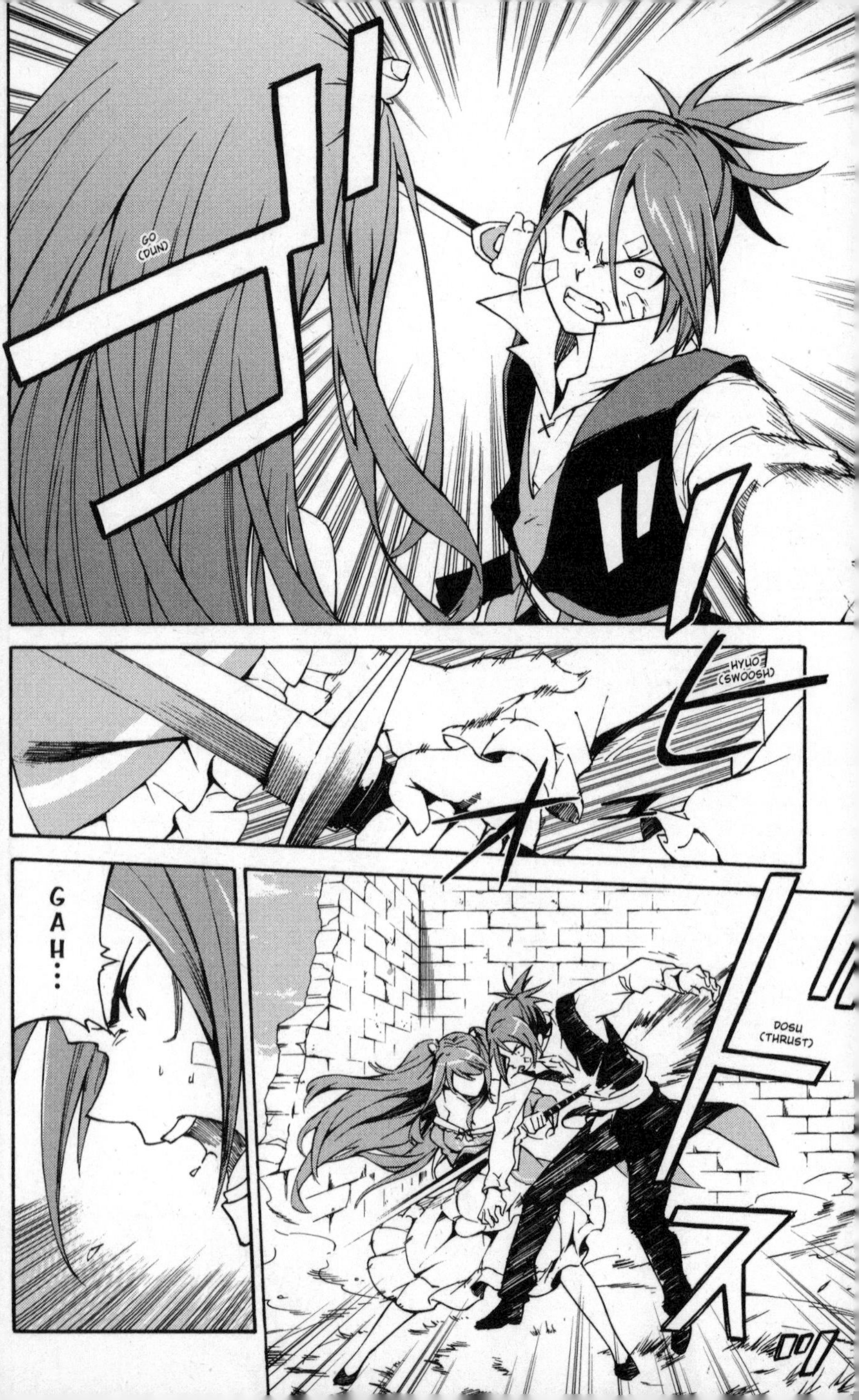
GO (DUN)
HYUO (SWOOSH)
DOSU (THRUST)
GAH...

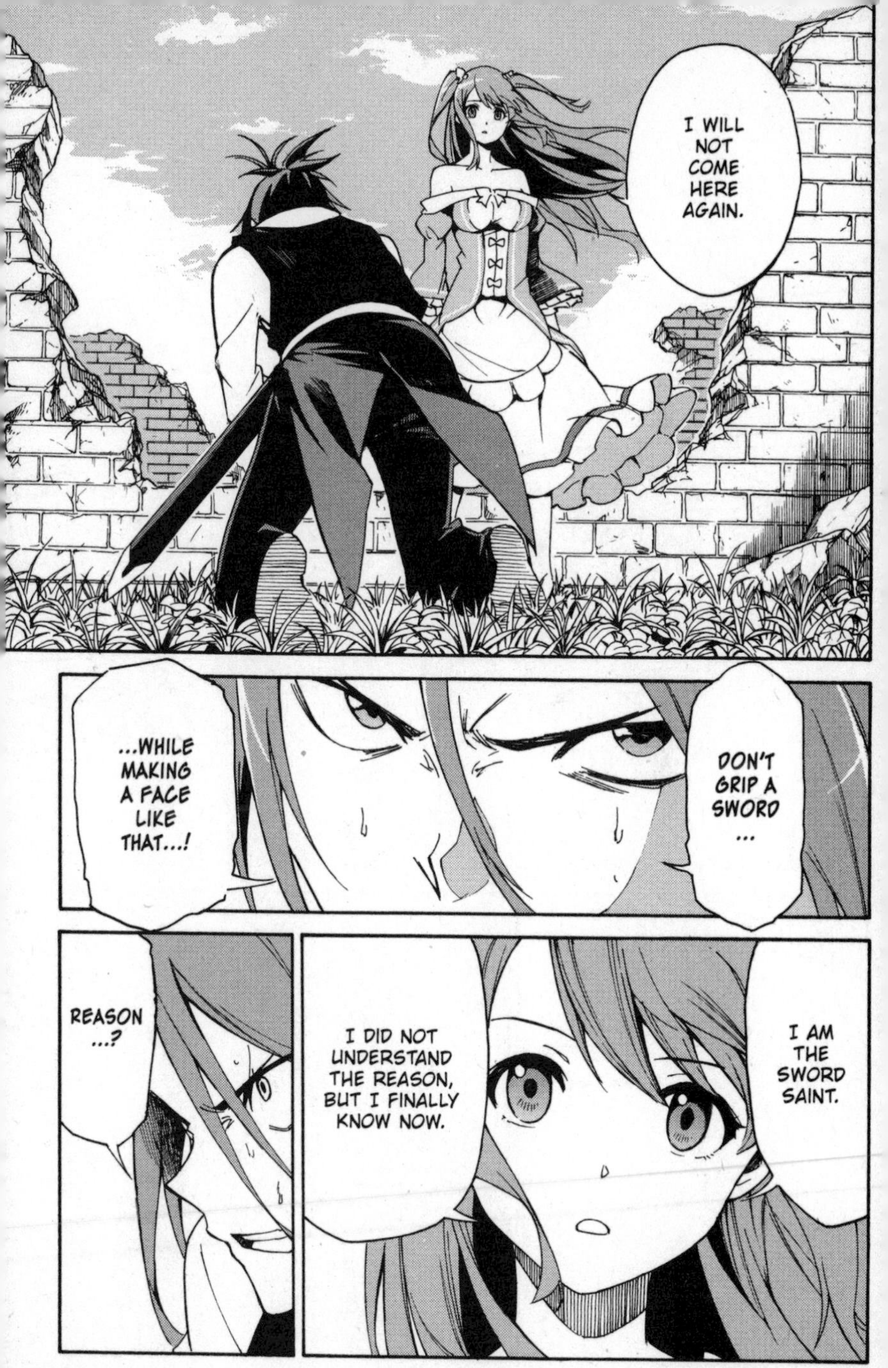
I WILL NOT COME HERE AGAIN.
DON'T GRIP A SWORD ...
...WHILE MAKING A FACE LIKE THAT...!
I AM THE SWORD SAINT.
I DID NOT UNDERSTAND THE REASON, BUT I FINALLY KNOW NOW.
REASON ...?

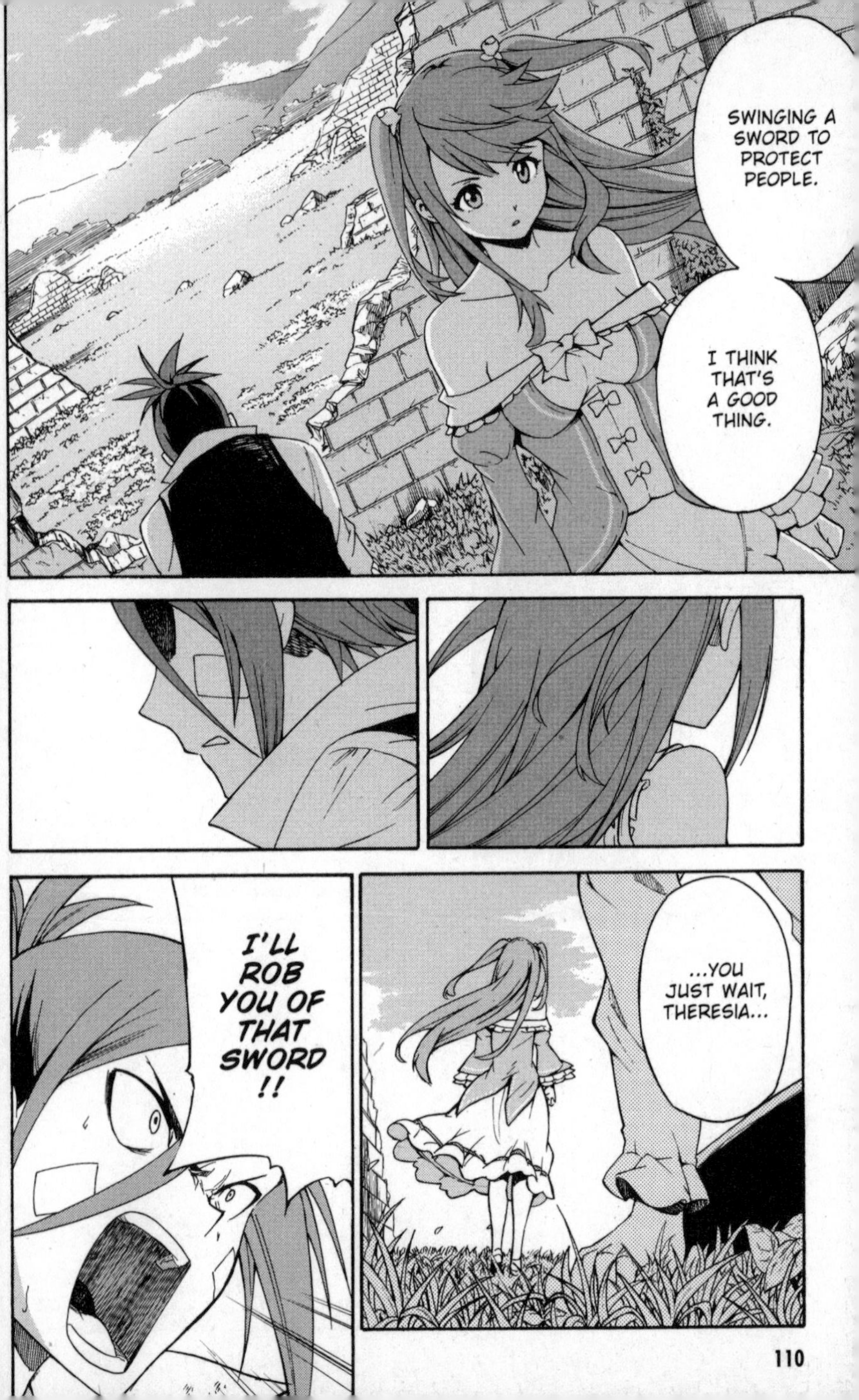
SWINGING A SWORD TO PROTECT PEOPLE.
I THINK THAT'S A GOOD THING.
...YOU JUST WAIT, THERESIA...
I'LL ROB YOU OF THAT SWORD !!

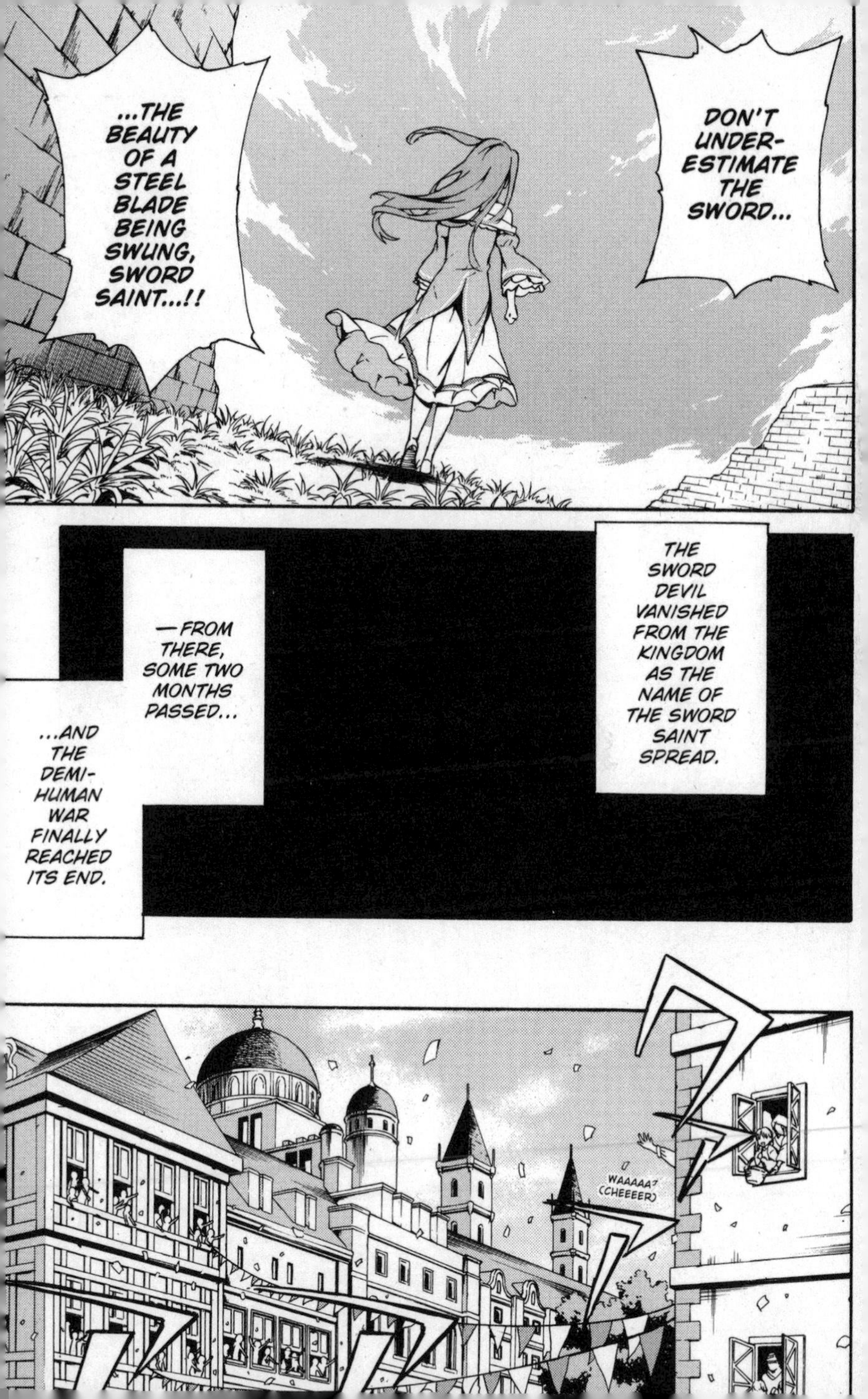
DON'T UNDER-ESTIMATE THE SWORD...
...THE BEAUTY OF A STEEL BLADE BEING SWUNG, SWORD SAINT...!!
THE SWORD DEVIL VANISHED FROM THE KINGDOM AS THE NAME OF THE SWORD SAINT SPREAD.
—FROM THERE, SOME TWO MONTHS PASSED...
...AND THE DEMI-HUMAN WAR FINALLY REACHED ITS END.
WAAAAA (CHEEEER)

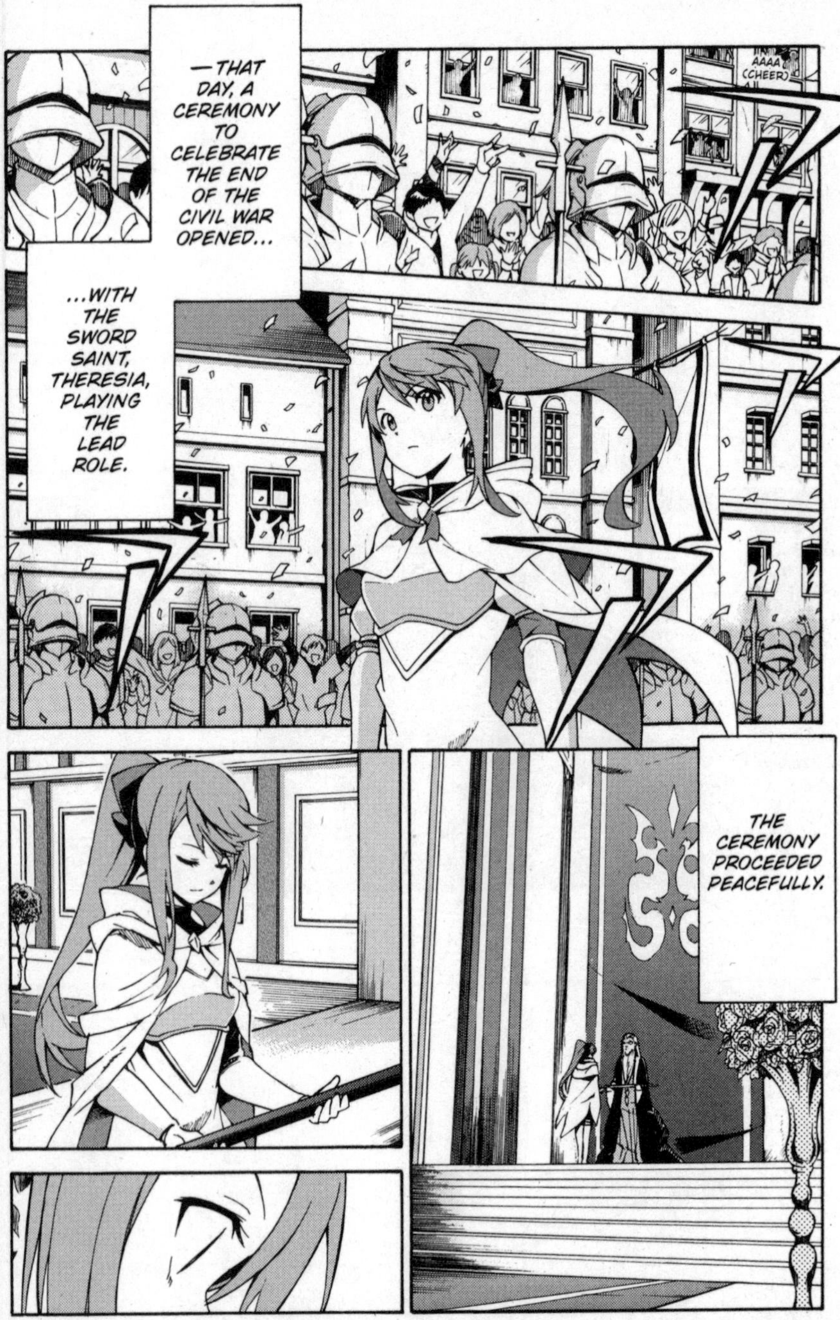

—THAT DAY, A CEREMONY TO CELEBRATE THE END OF THE CIVIL WAR OPENED...
AAAA (CHEER)
...WITH THE SWORD SAINT, THERESIA, PLAYING THE LEAD ROLE.
THE CEREMONY PROCEEDED PEACEFULLY.

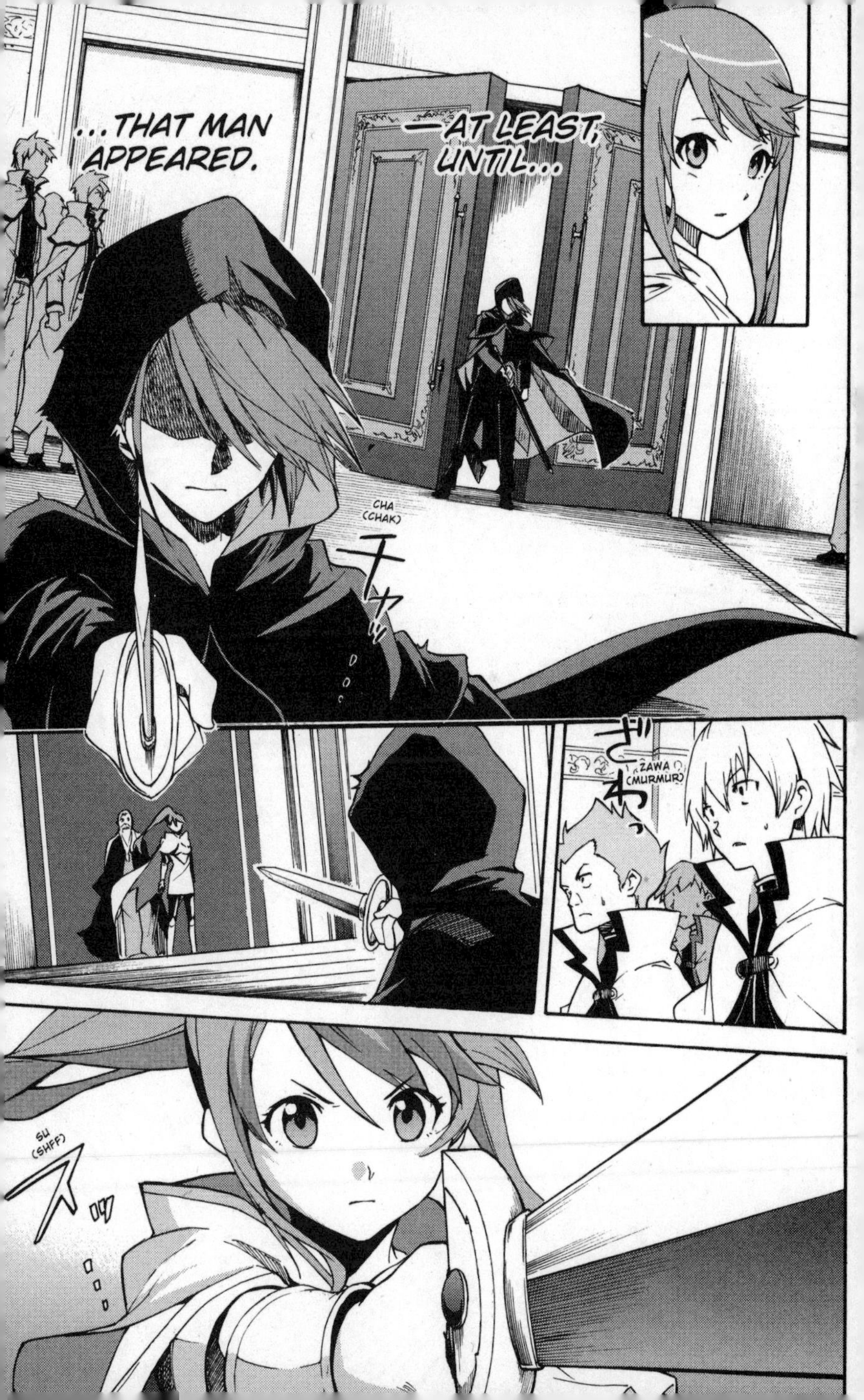
—AT LEAST, UNTIL...
...THAT MAN APPEARED.
CHA (CHAK)
ZAWA (MURMUR)
SU (SHFF)

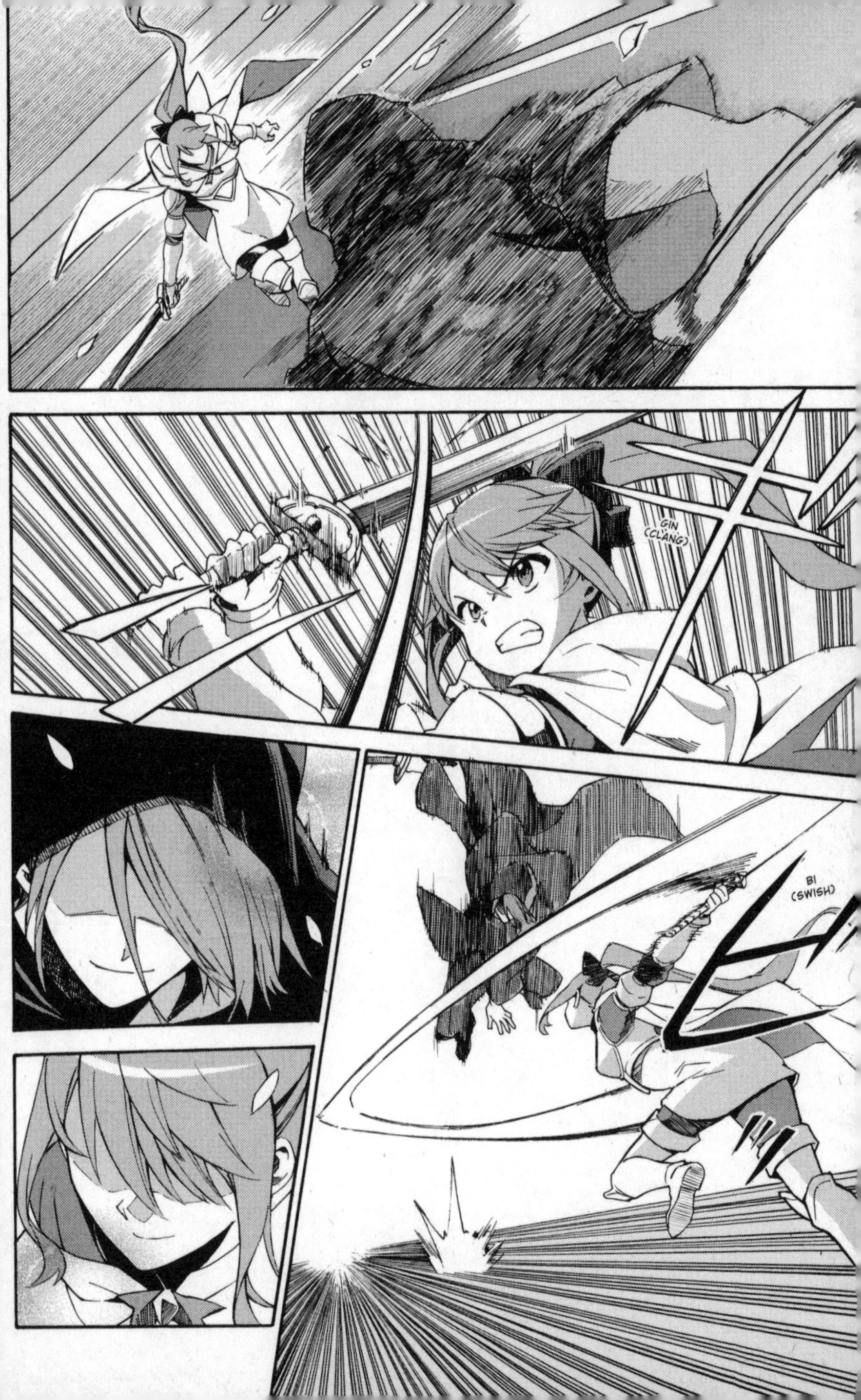
GIN
(CLANG)
BI
(SWISH)

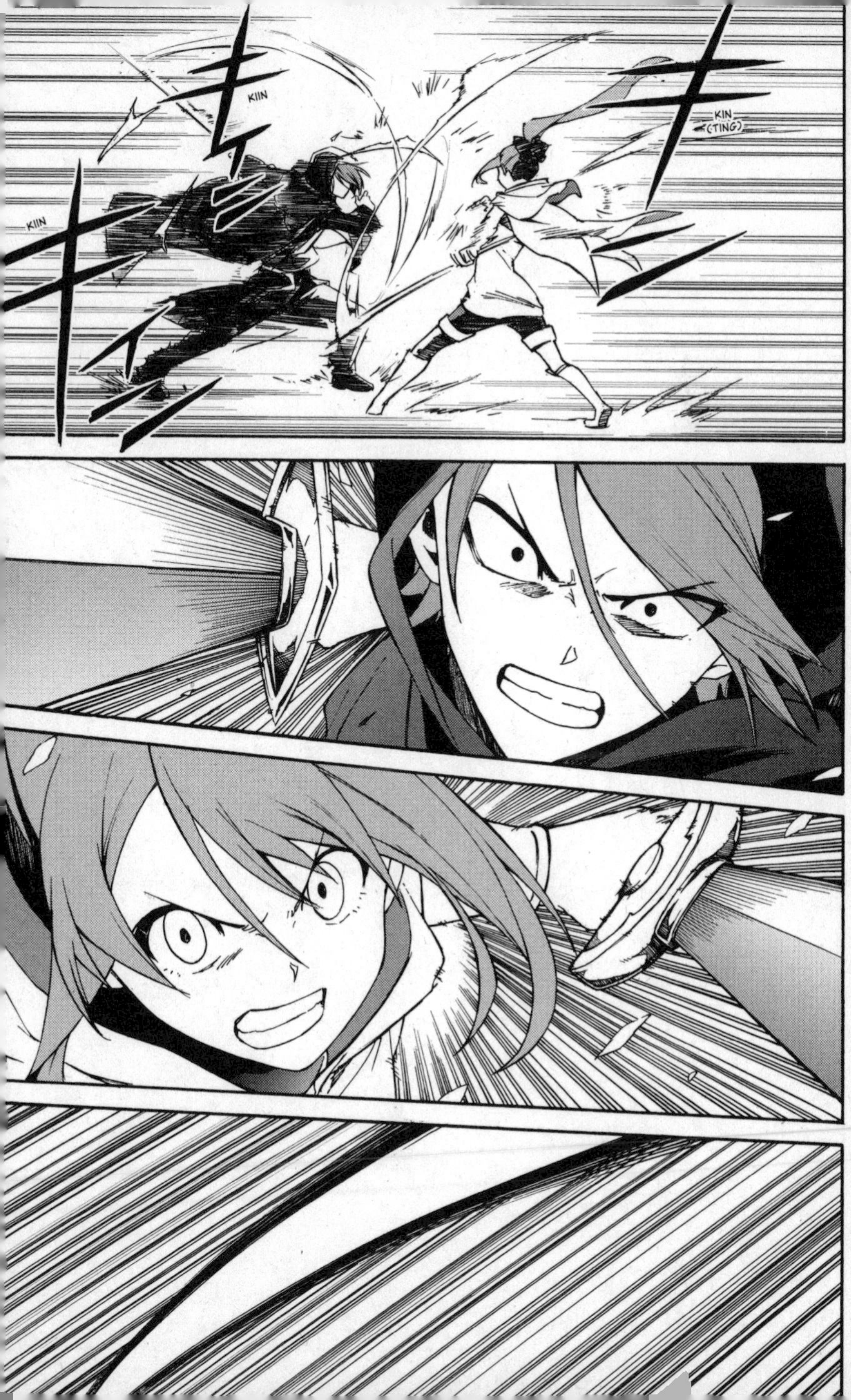
KIN
(TING)
KIIN
KIIN

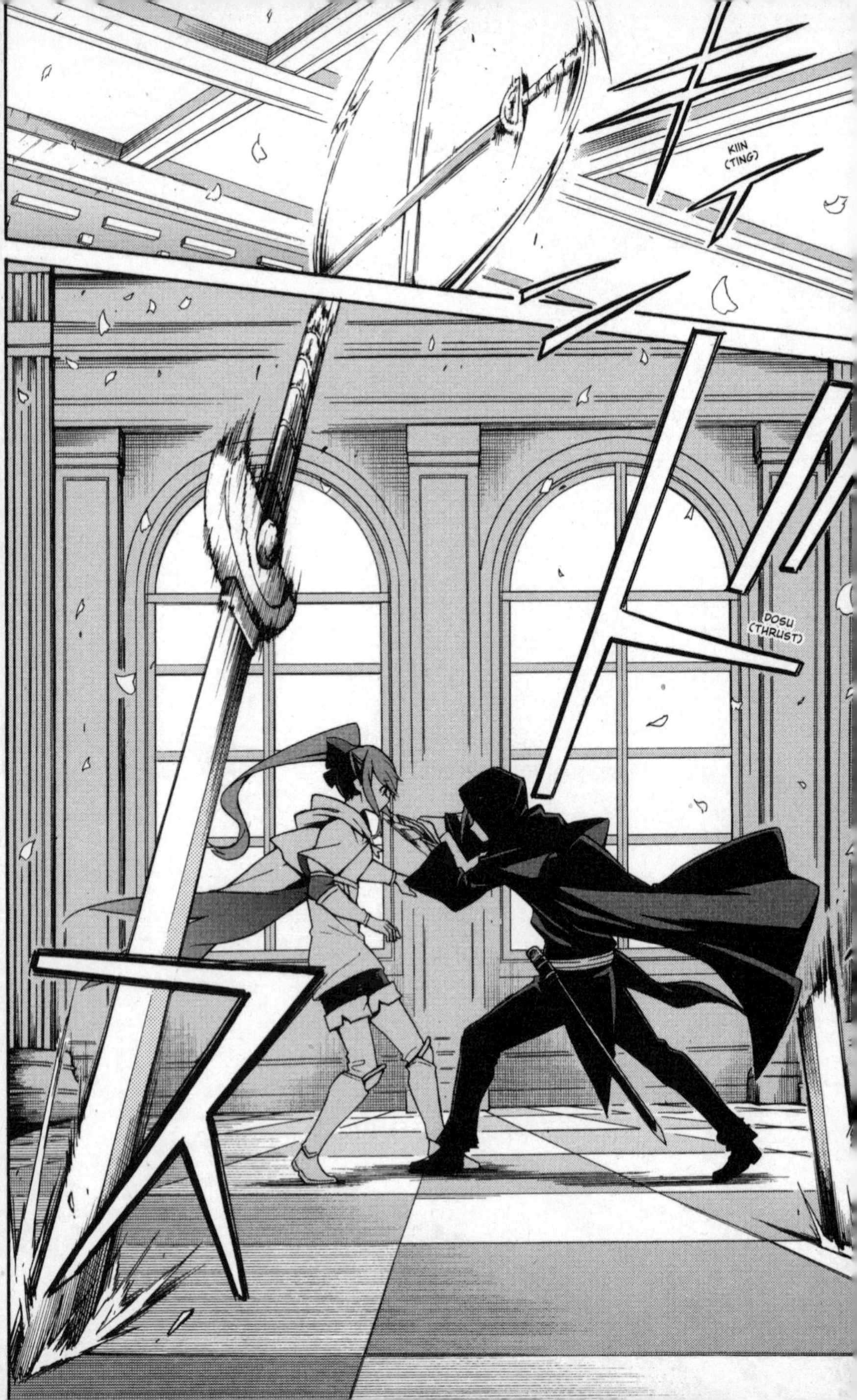
KIIN
(TING)
DOSU
(THRUST)

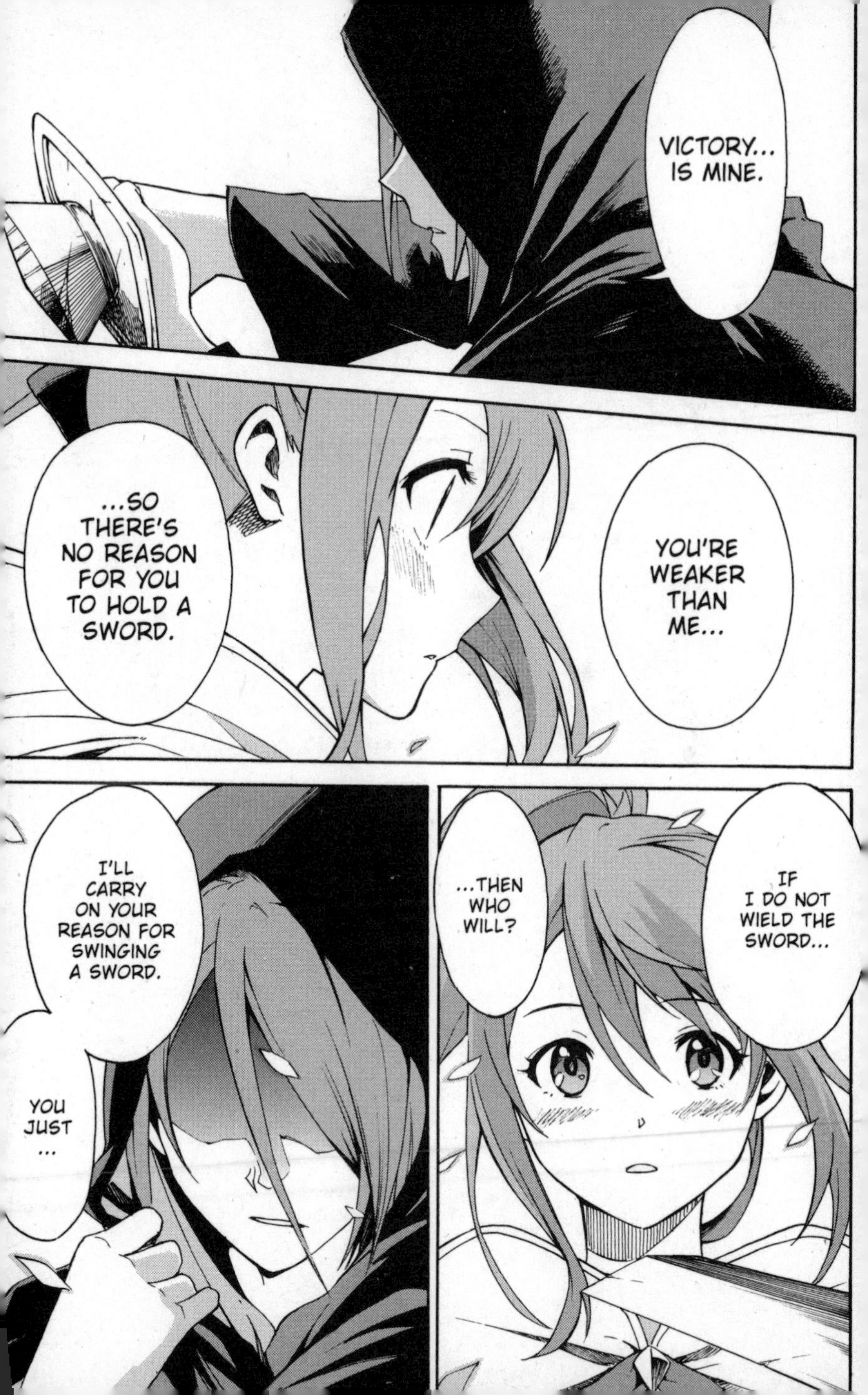
VICTORY... IS MINE.
YOU'RE WEAKER THAN ME...
...SO THERE'S NO REASON FOR YOU TO HOLD A SWORD.
IF I DO NOT WIELD THE SWORD...
...THEN WHO WILL?
I'LL CARRY ON YOUR REASON FOR SWINGING A SWORD.
YOU JUST ...

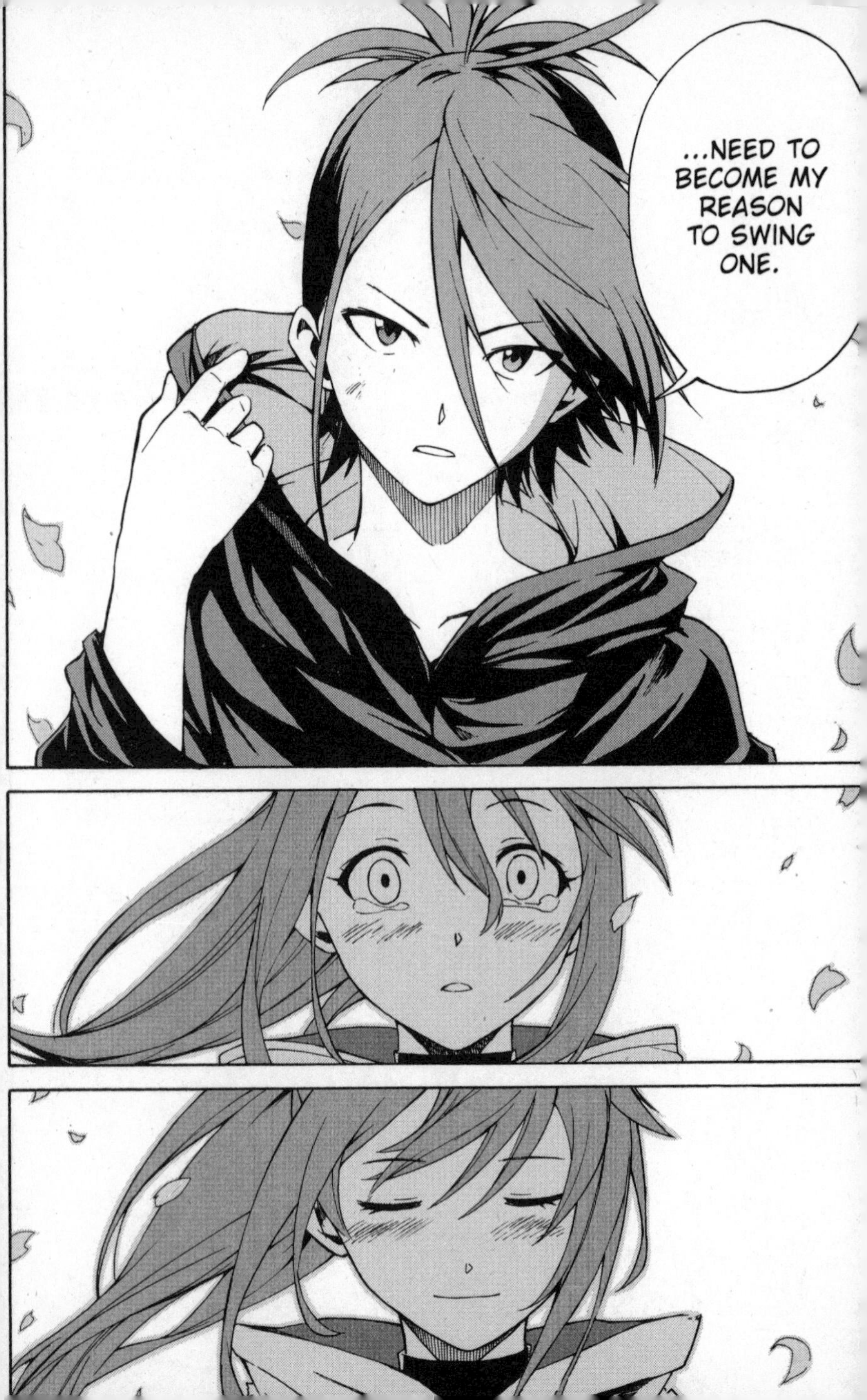
...NEED TO BECOME MY REASON TO SWING ONE.

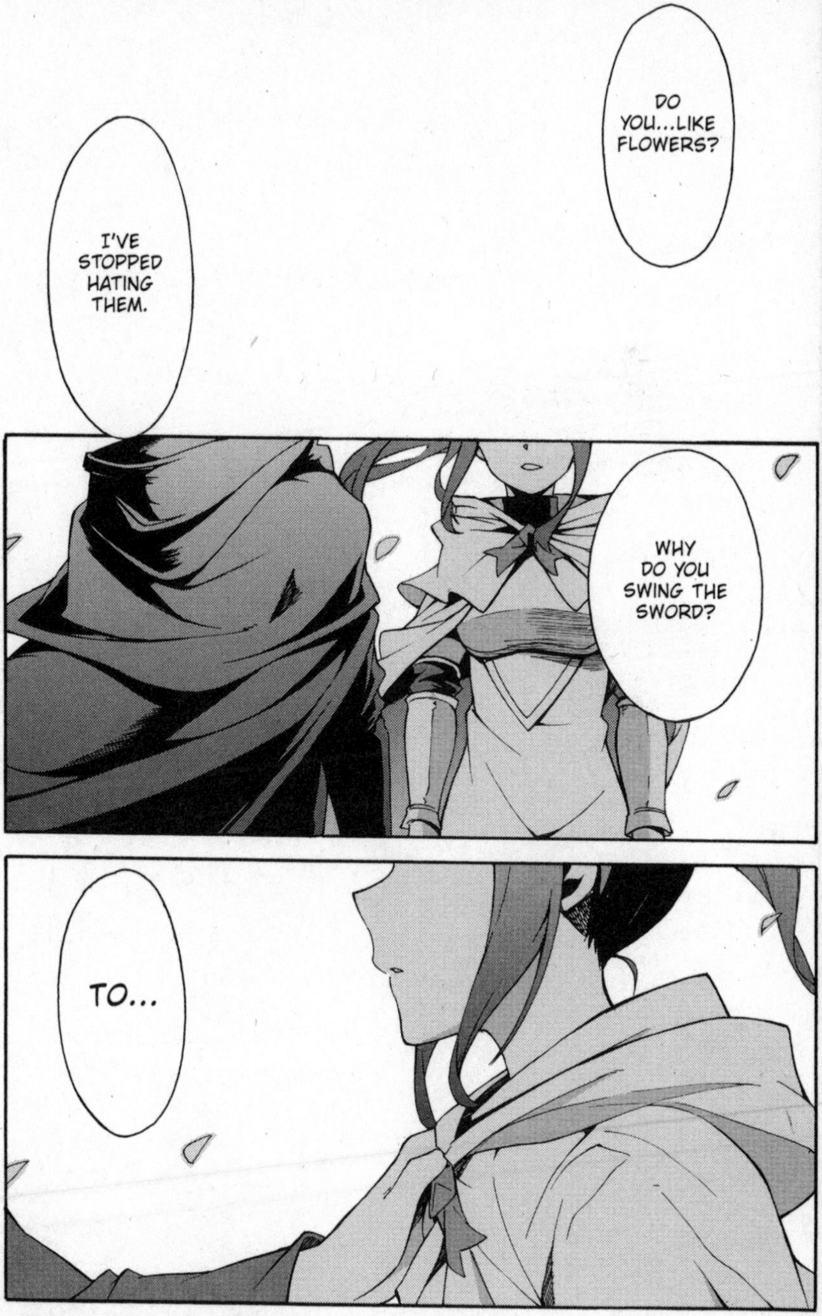
DO YOU...LIKE FLOWERS?
I'VE STOPPED HATING THEM.
WHY DO YOU SWING THE SWORD?
TO...

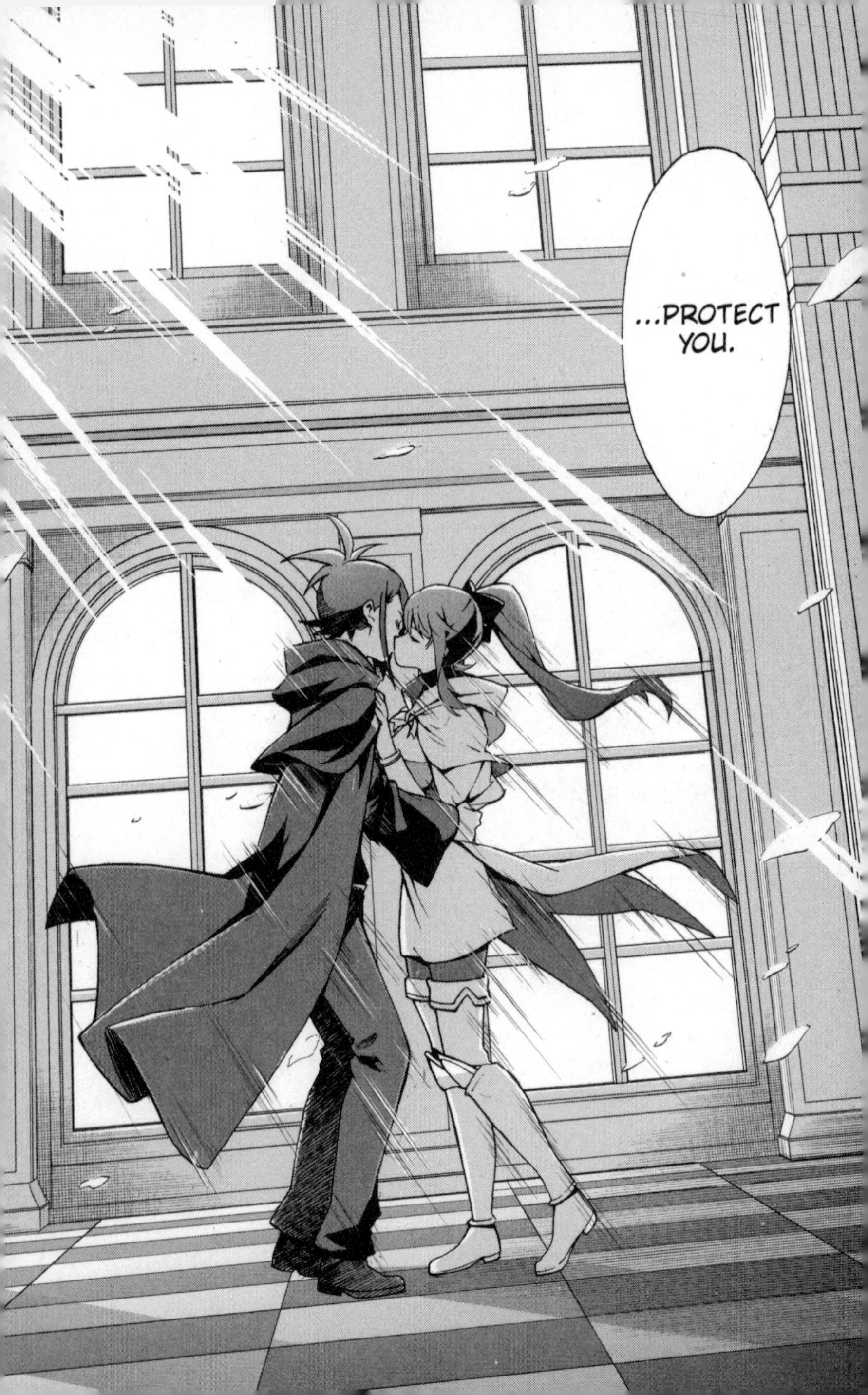
...PROTECT YOU.

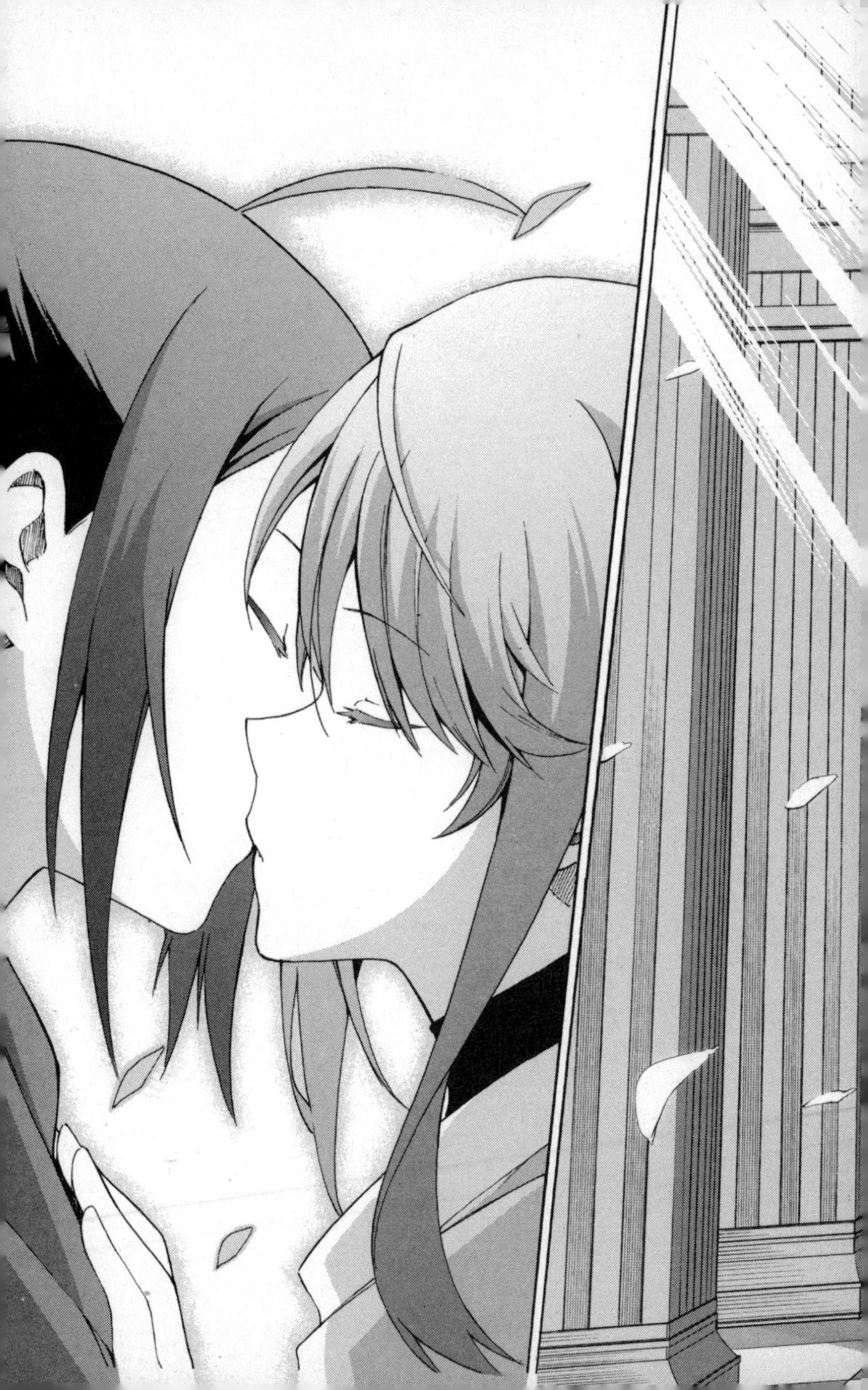

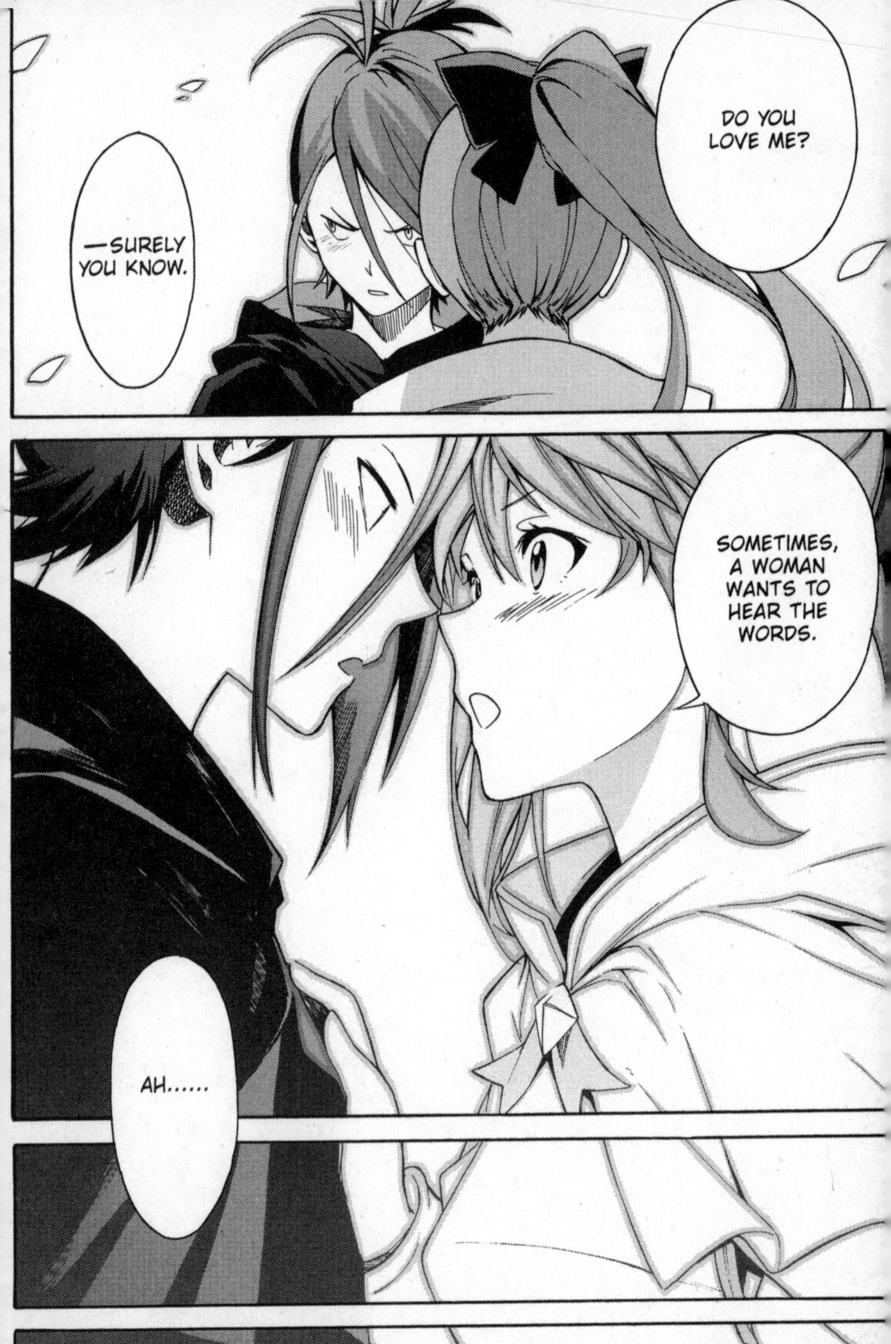
DO YOU LOVE ME?
—SURELY YOU KNOW.
SOMETIMES, A WOMAN WANTS TO HEAR THE WORDS.
AH......

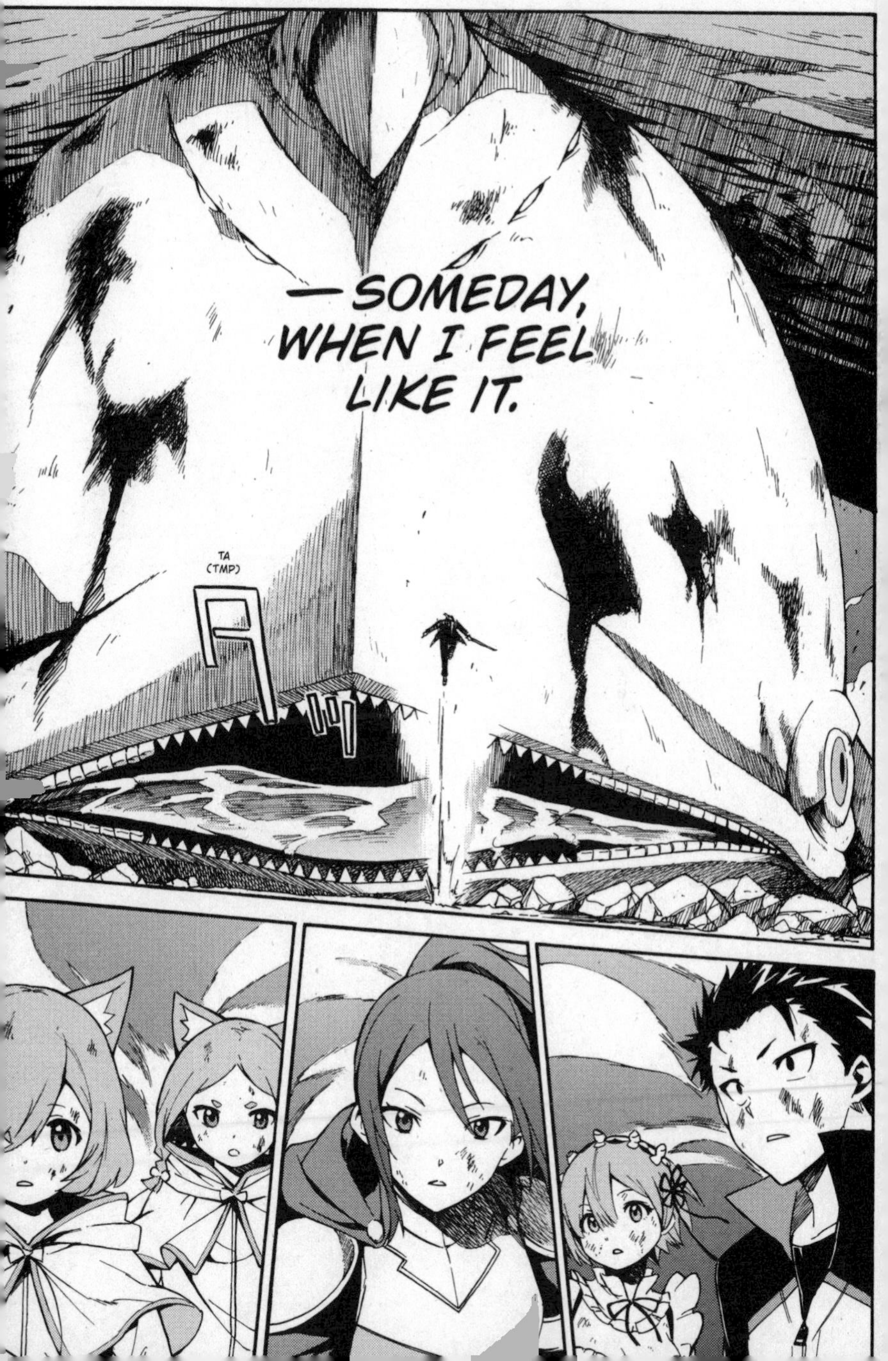
—SOMEDAY, WHEN I FEEL LIKE IT.
TA (TMP)

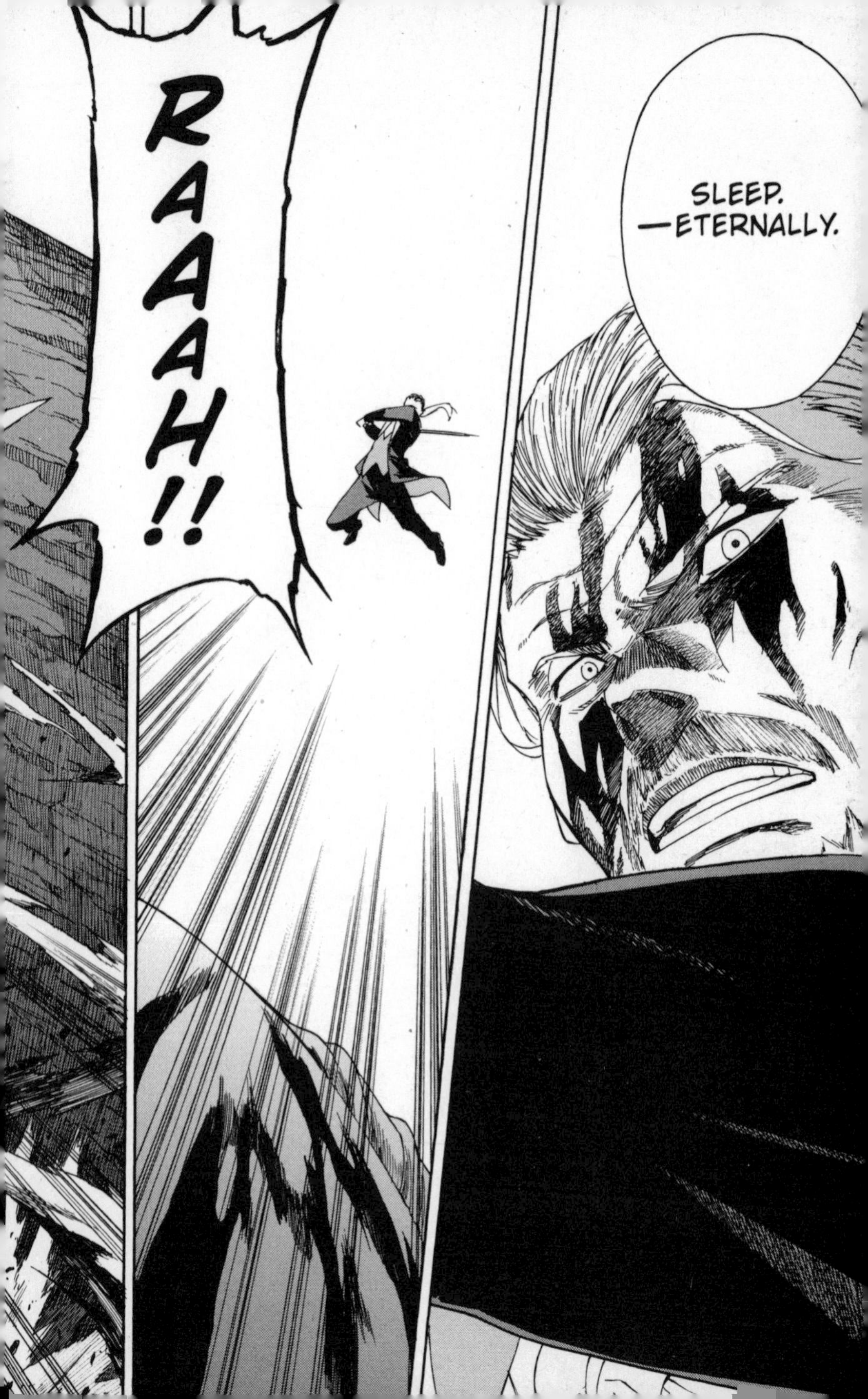
SLEEP.
—ETERNALLY.
RAAAAH!!

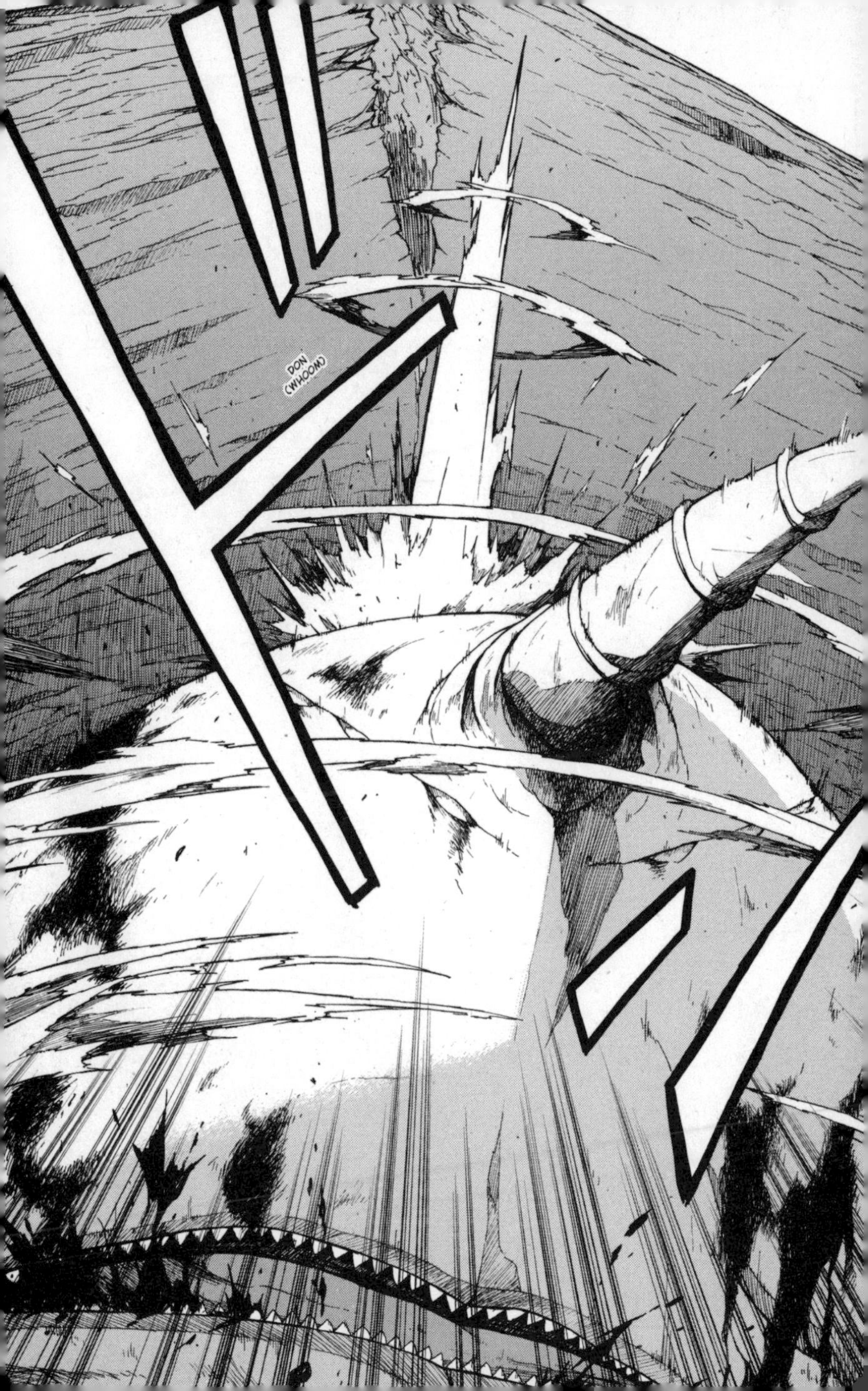
DON
(WHOOM)

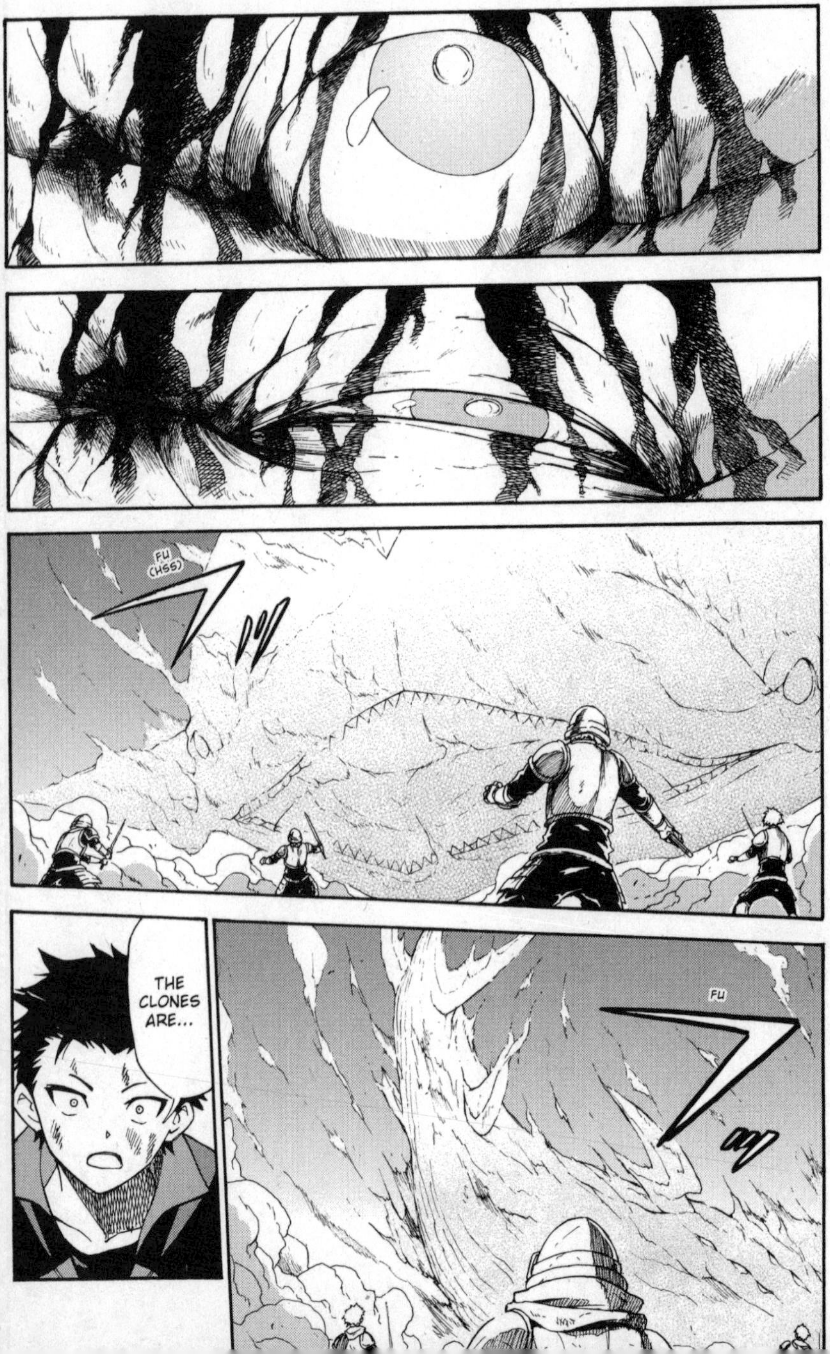
FU (HSS)
THE CLONES ARE...
FU

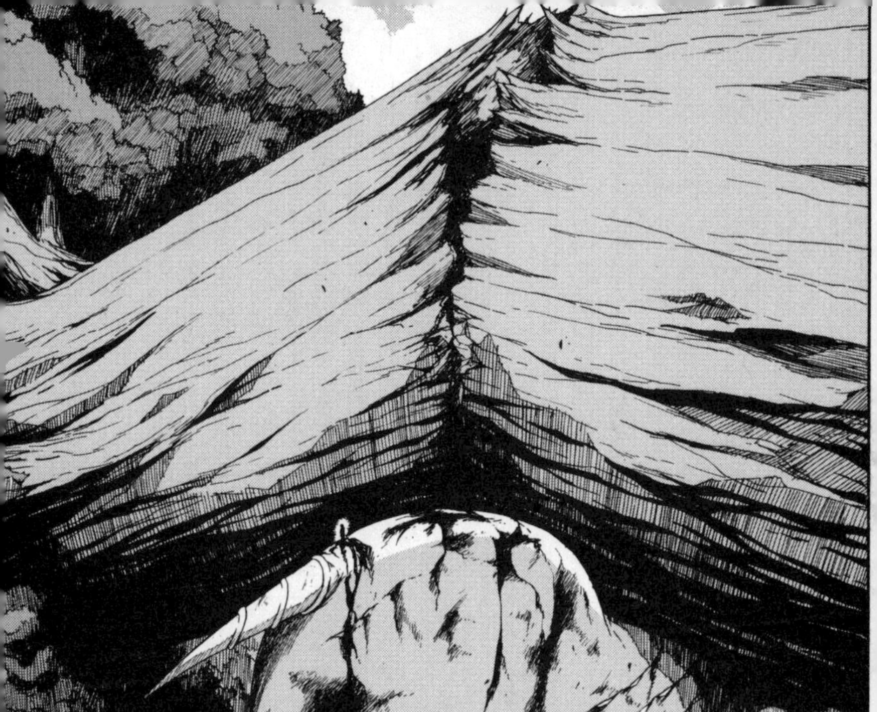
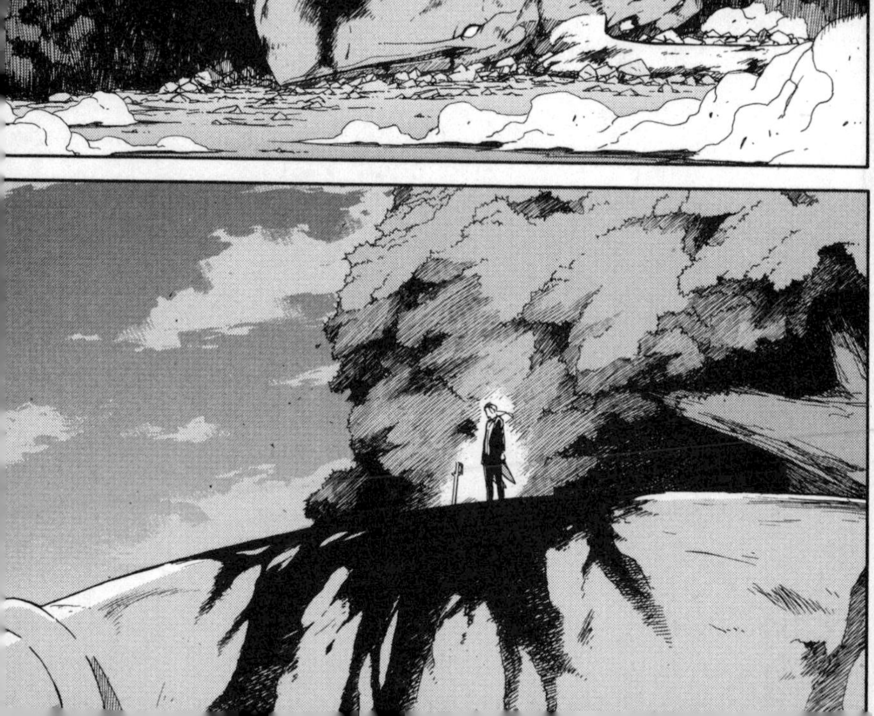

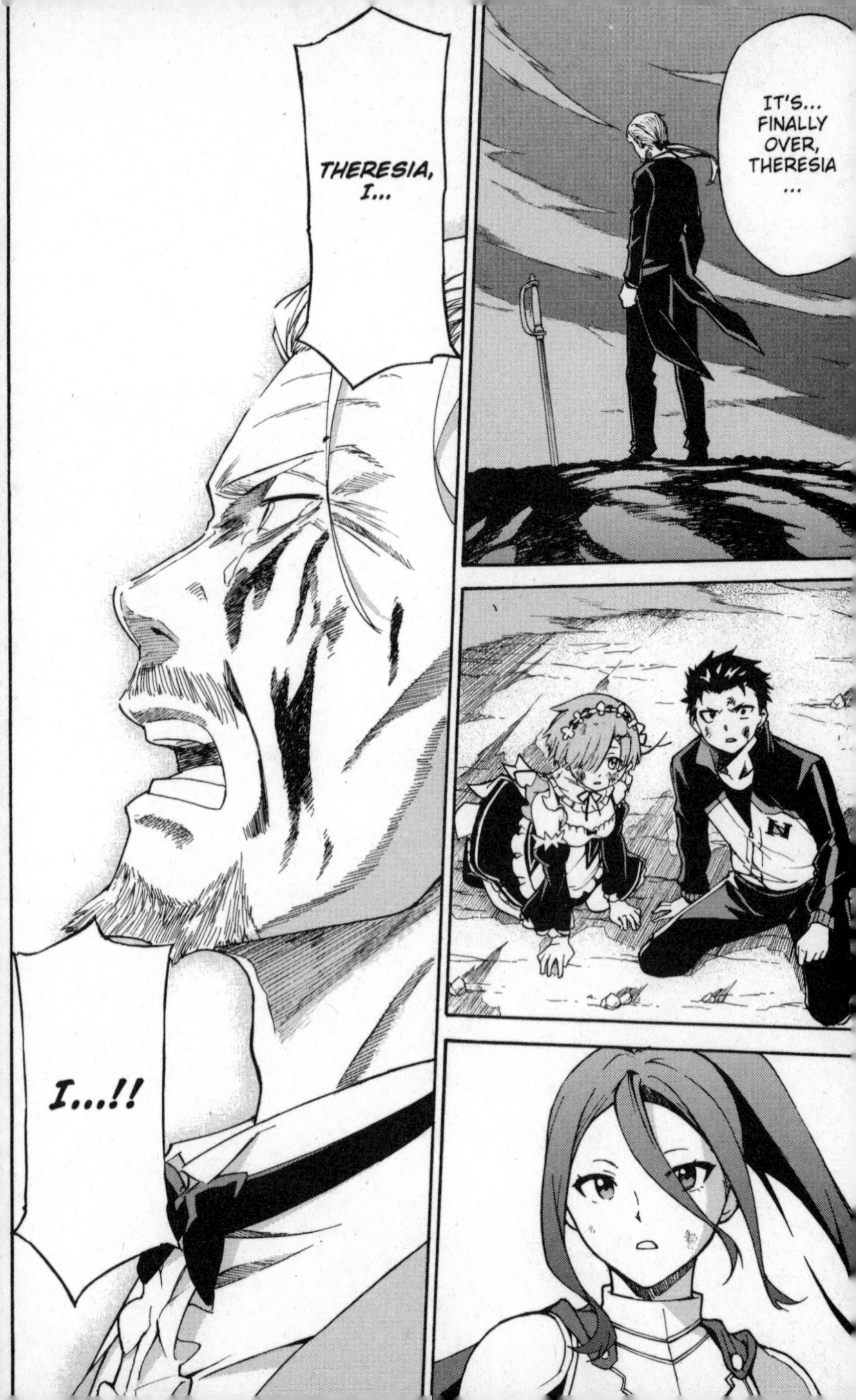
IT'S... FINALLY OVER, THERESIA...
THERESIA, I...
I...!!

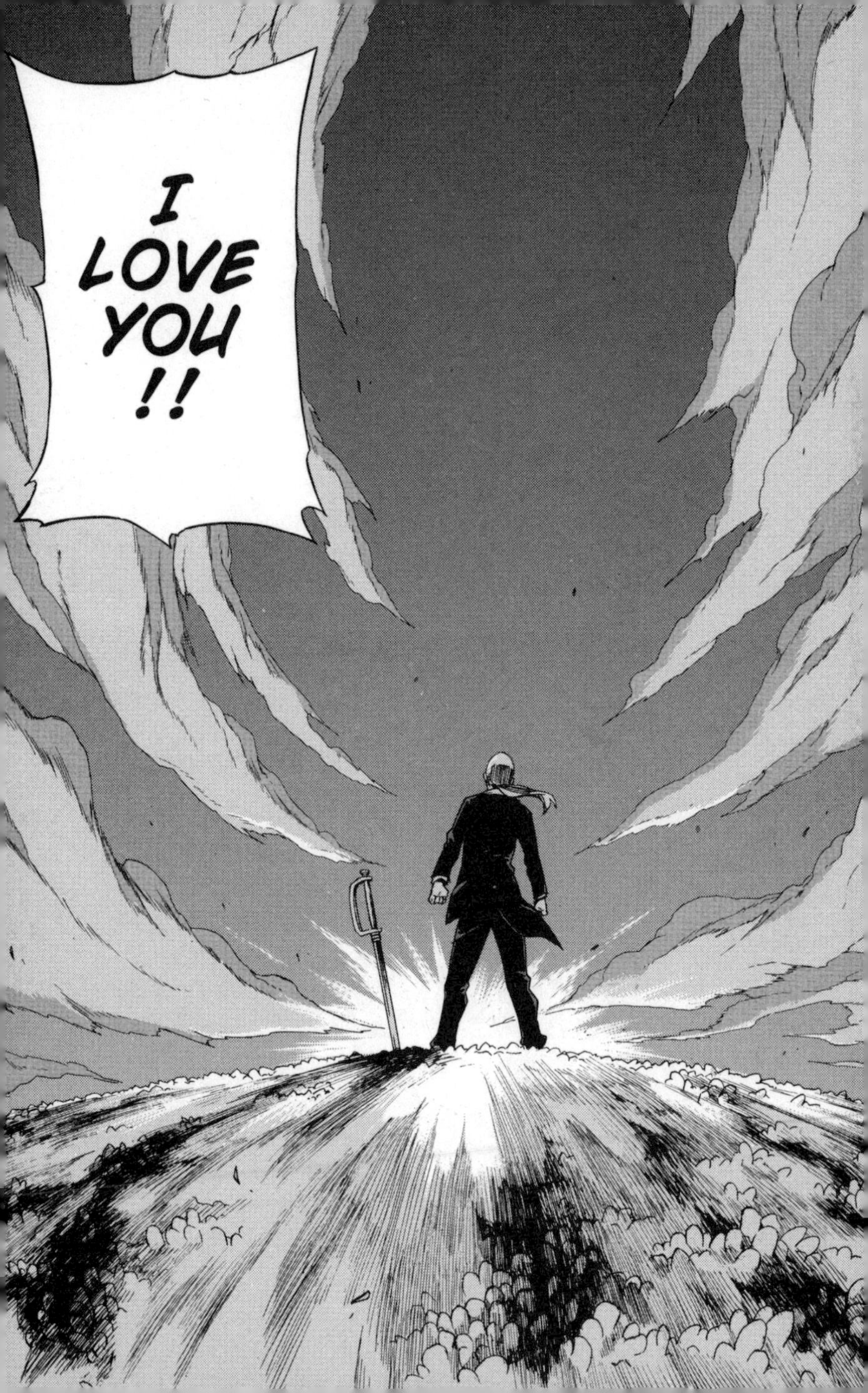
I LOVE YOU!!

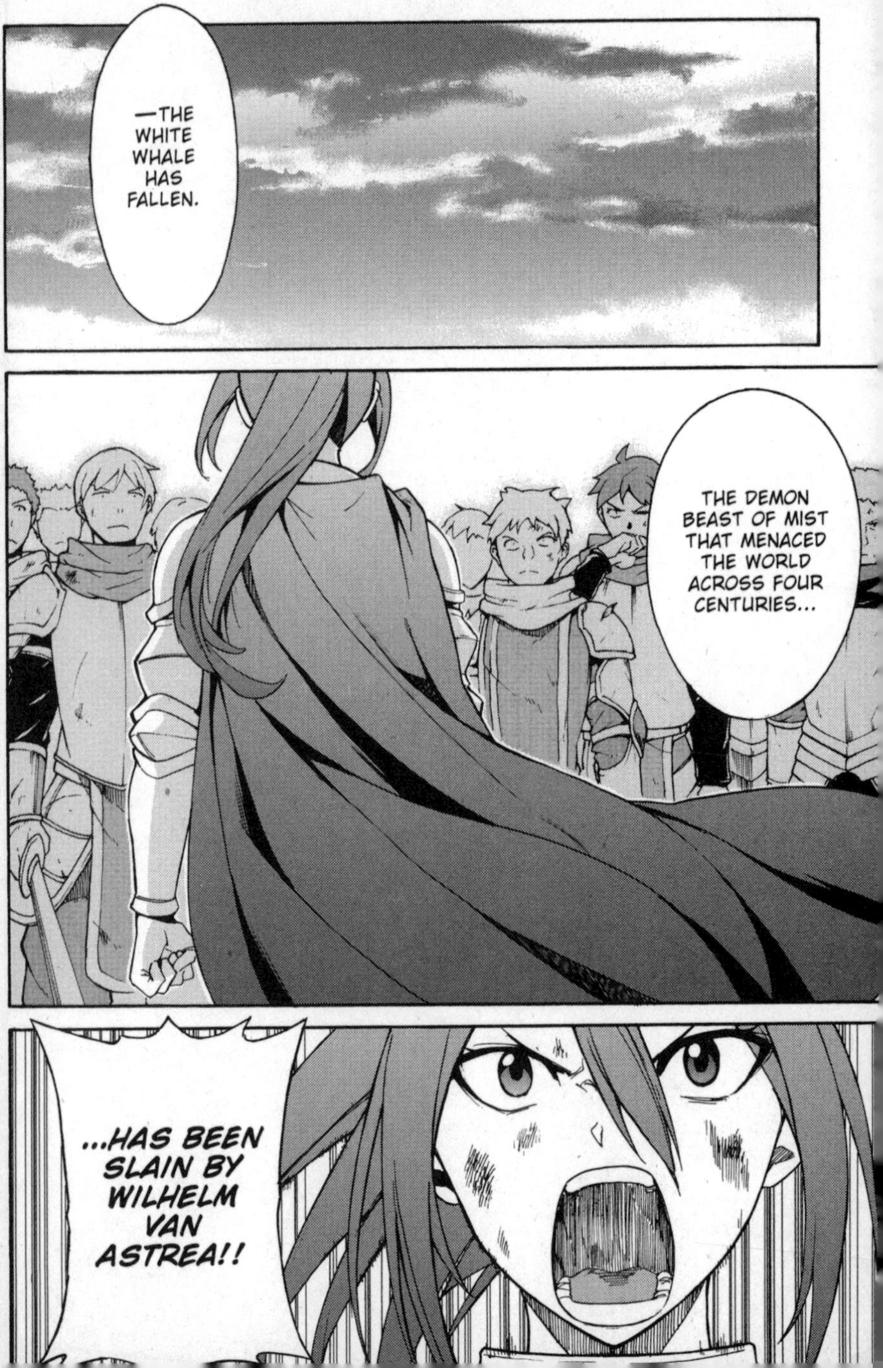
—THE WHITE WHALE HAS FALLEN.
THE DEMON BEAST OF MIST THAT MENACED THE WORLD ACROSS FOUR CENTURIES...
...HAS BEEN SLAIN BY WILHELM VAN ASTREA!!

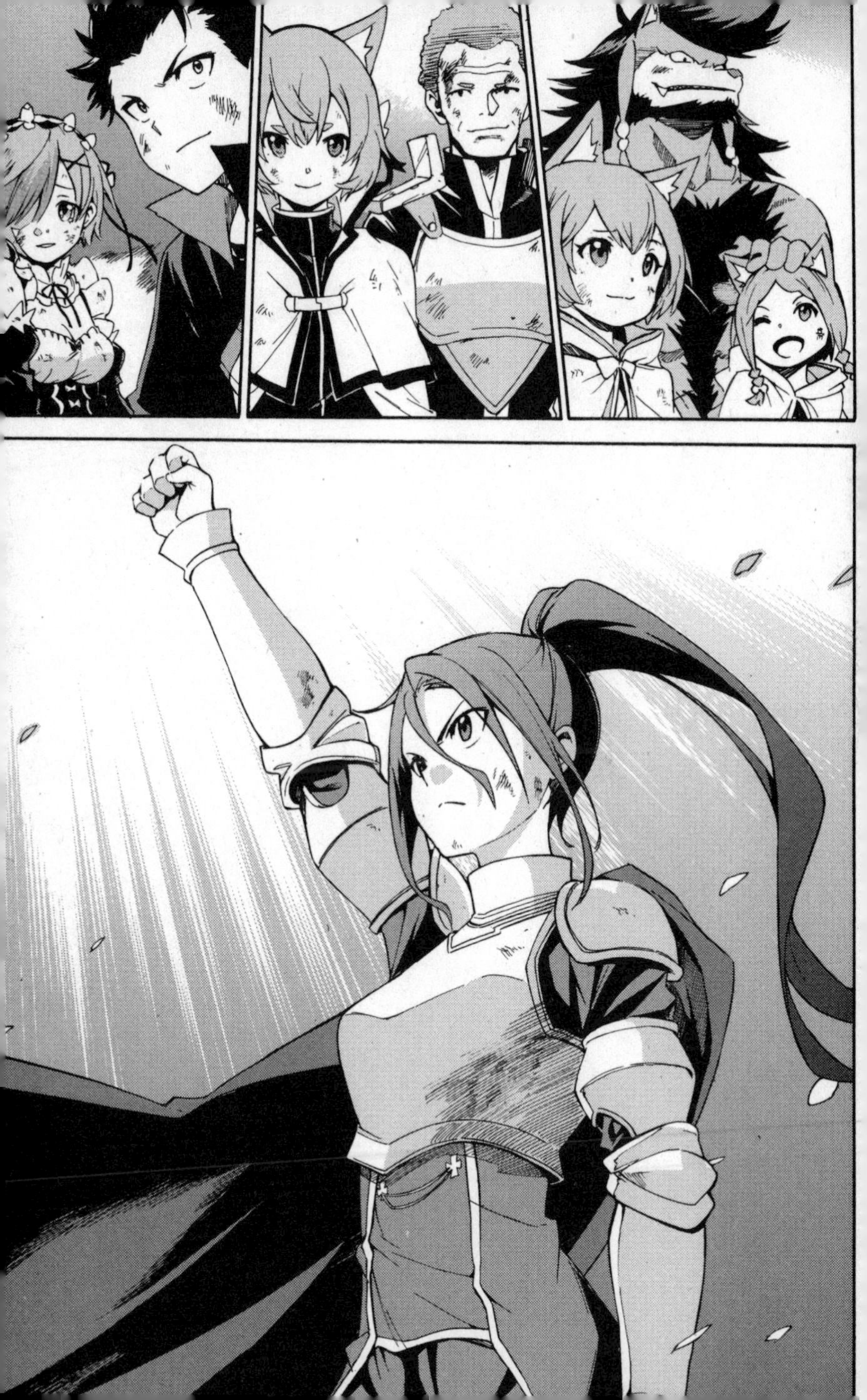

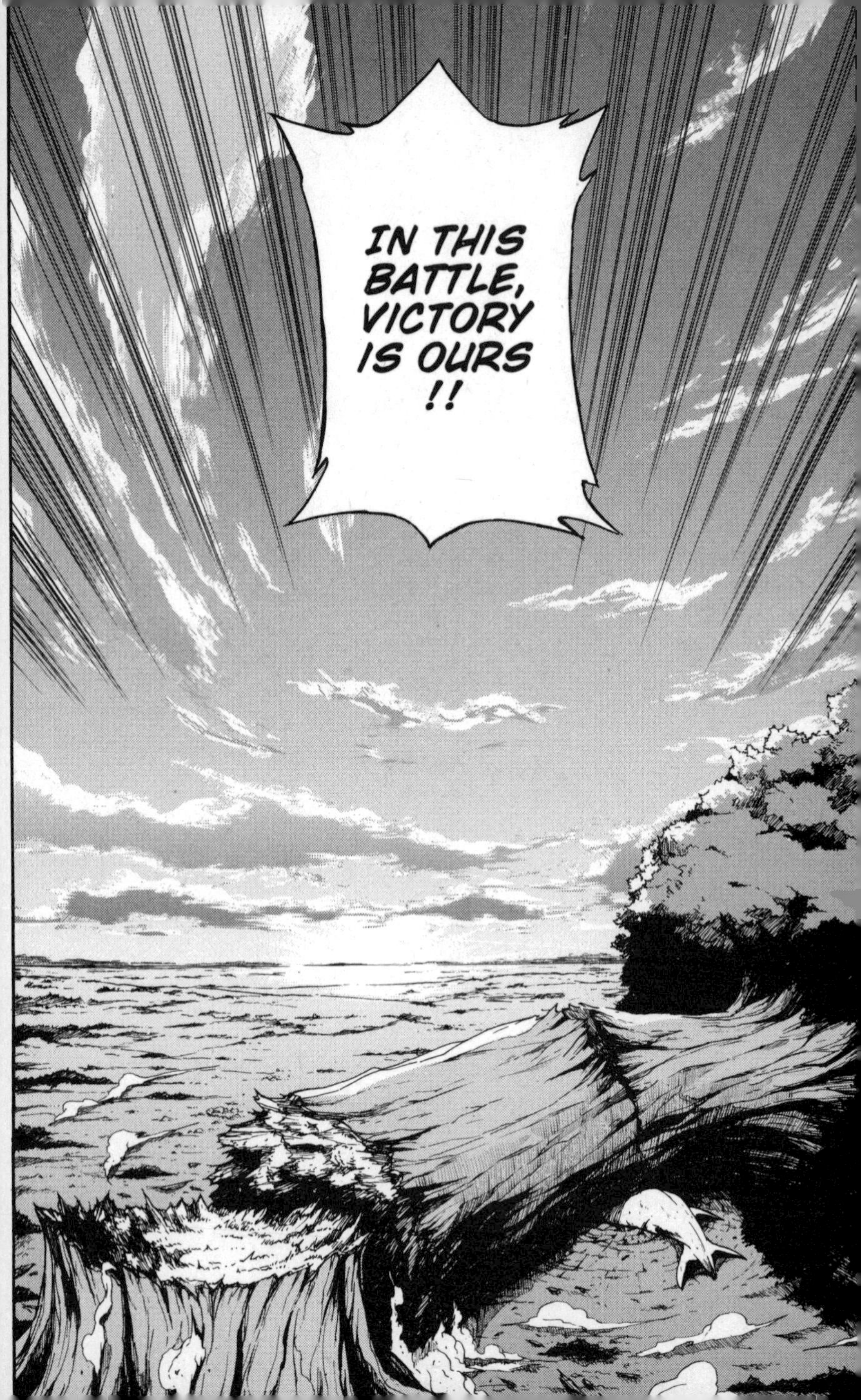
IN THIS BATTLE, VICTORY IS OURS !!

Truth of Zero

The only ability Subaru Natsuki gets when he's
summoned to another world is time travel via his own
death. But to save her, he'll die as many times as it takes.

Re:ZERO -Starting
Life in Another World-

Re:ZERO
-Starting Life in Another World-

Truth of Zero

The only ability Subaru Natsuki gets when he's summoned to another world is time
travel via his own death. But to save her, he'll die as many times as it takes.

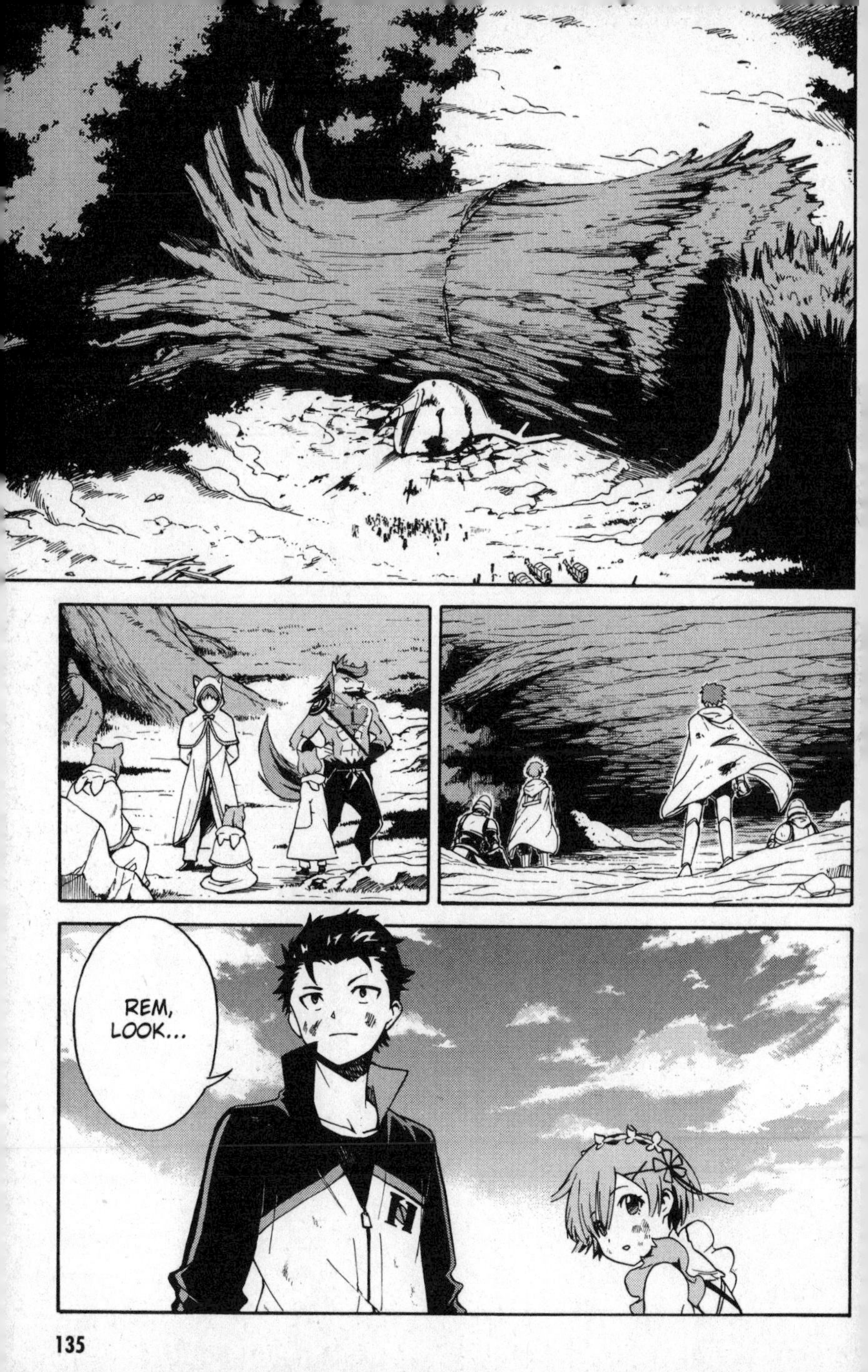
REM,
LOOK...

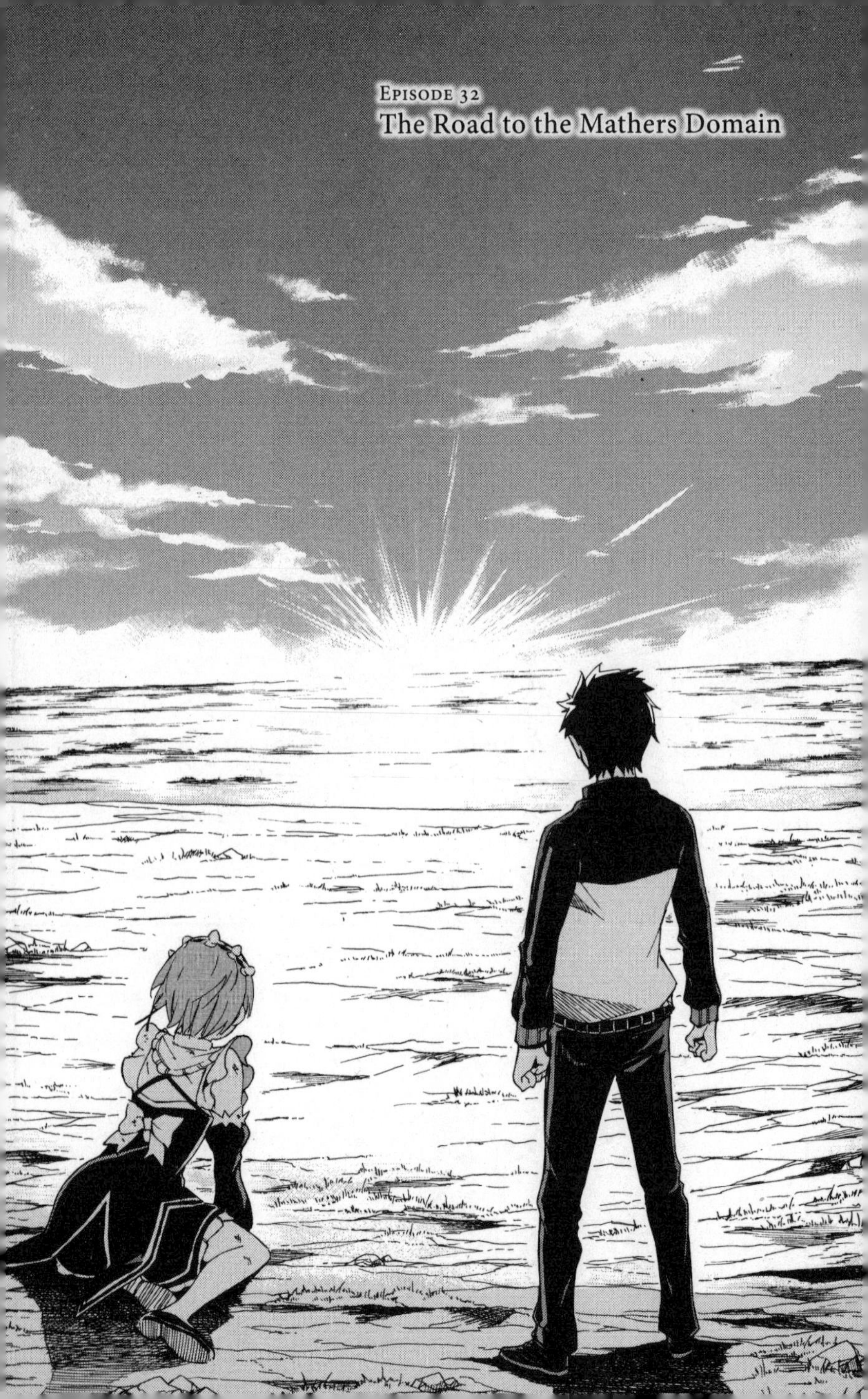
Episode 32
The Road to the Mathers Domain

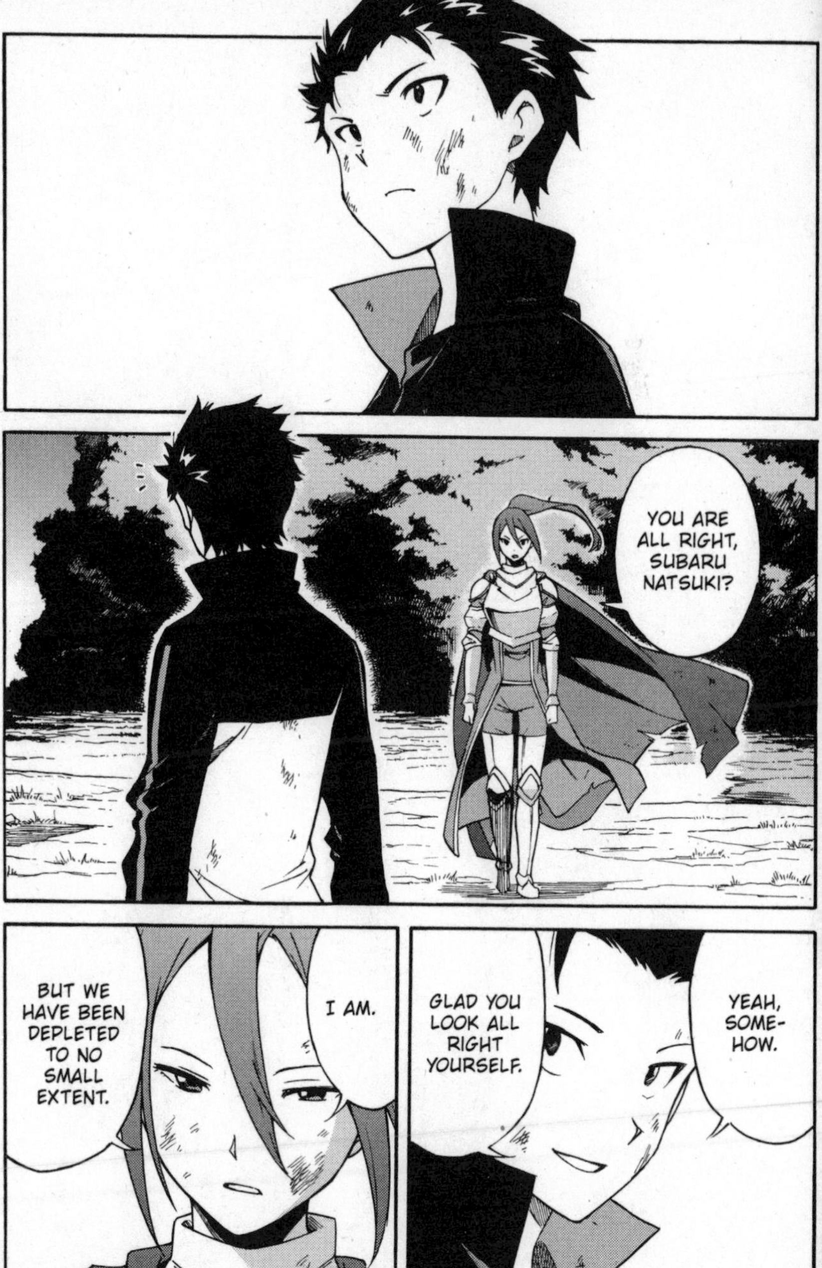
YOU ARE ALL RIGHT, SUBARU NATSUKI?
YEAH, SOME-HOW.
GLAD YOU LOOK ALL RIGHT YOURSELF.
I AM.
BUT WE HAVE BEEN DEPLETED TO NO SMALL EXTENT.

NOR WILL THOSE SLAIN OR ERASED BY THE WHITE WHALE RETURN.
I THINK YOU DID PRETTY WELL, CRUSCH.
YOUR POPU-LARITY SHOULD SHOOT EVEN HI—
HUH!? DOES THIS MEAN ...
...I MADE THE ROYAL SELECTION WORSE FOR US!?
YOUR FACE HAS BECOME RATHER DARK.

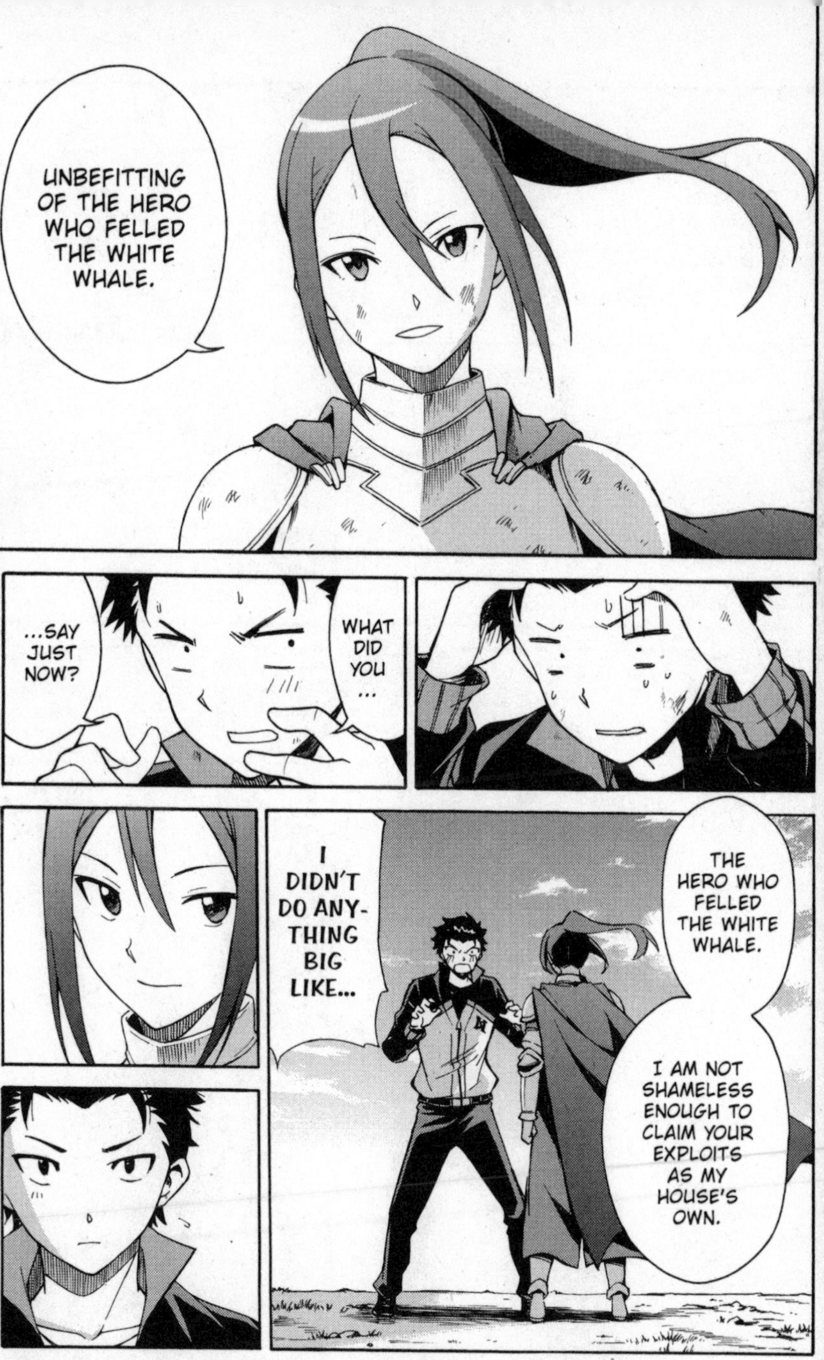
UNBEFITTING OF THE HERO WHO FELLED THE WHITE WHALE.
WHAT DID YOU ...
...SAY JUST NOW?
THE HERO WHO FELLED THE WHITE WHALE.
I DIDN'T DO ANY-THING BIG LIKE...
I AM NOT SHAMELESS ENOUGH TO CLAIM YOUR EXPLOITS AS MY HOUSE'S OWN.

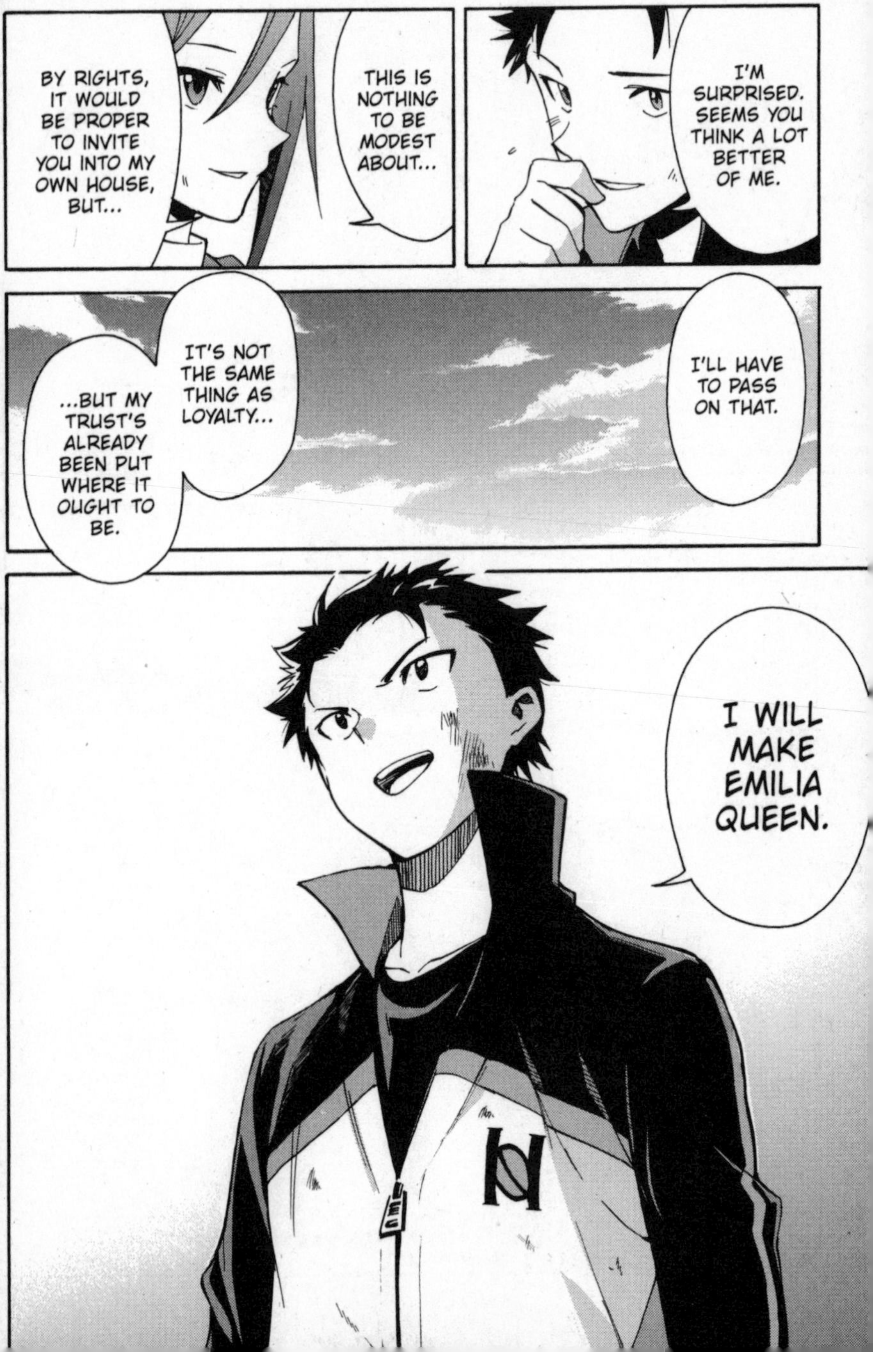
I'M SURPRISED. SEEMS YOU THINK A LOT BETTER OF ME.
THIS IS NOTHING TO BE MODEST ABOUT...
BY RIGHTS, IT WOULD BE PROPER TO INVITE YOU INTO MY OWN HOUSE, BUT...
I'LL HAVE TO PASS ON THAT.
IT'S NOT THE SAME THING AS LOYALTY...
...BUT MY TRUST'S ALREADY BEEN PUT WHERE IT OUGHT TO BE.
I WILL MAKE EMILIA QUEEN.

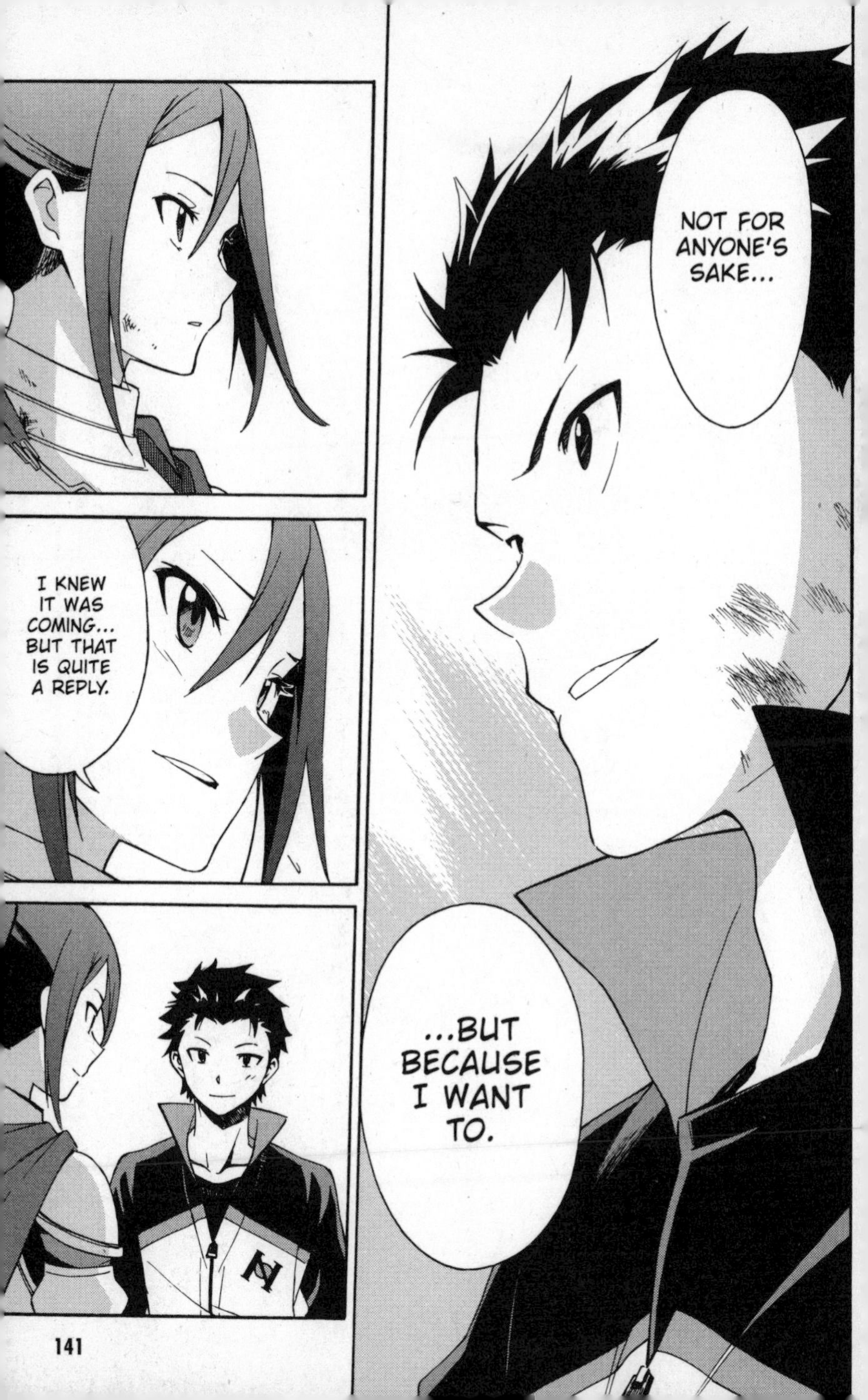
NOT FOR ANYONE'S SAKE...
...BUT BECAUSE I WANT TO.
I KNEW IT WAS COMING... BUT THAT IS QUITE A REPLY.

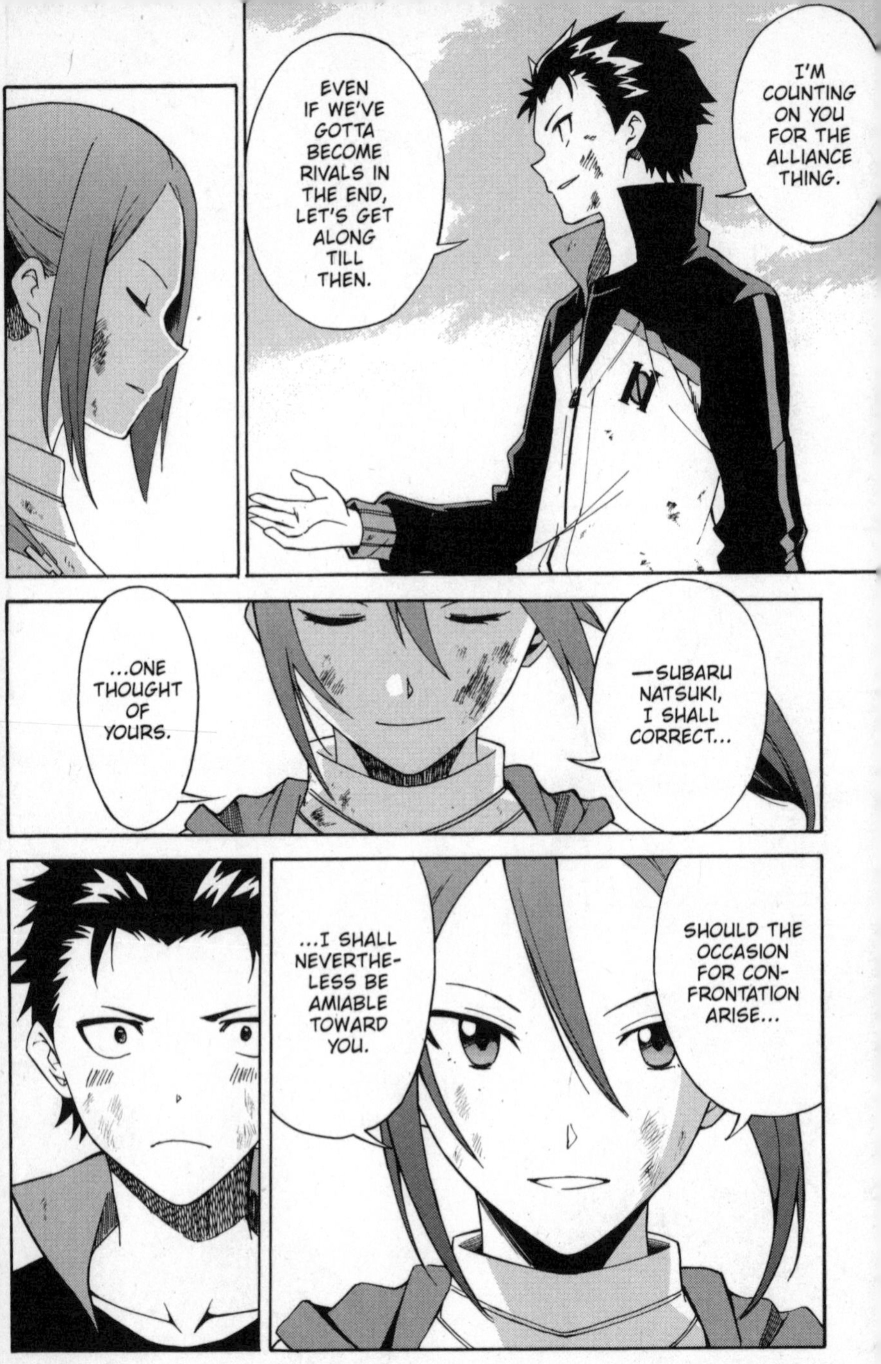
I'M COUNTING ON YOU FOR THE ALLIANCE THING.
EVEN IF WE'VE GOTTA BECOME RIVALS IN THE END, LET'S GET ALONG TILL THEN.
—SUBARU NATSUKI, I SHALL CORRECT...
...ONE THOUGHT OF YOURS.
SHOULD THE OCCASION FOR CON-FRONTATION ARISE...
...I SHALL NEVERTHE-LESS BE AMIABLE TOWARD YOU.

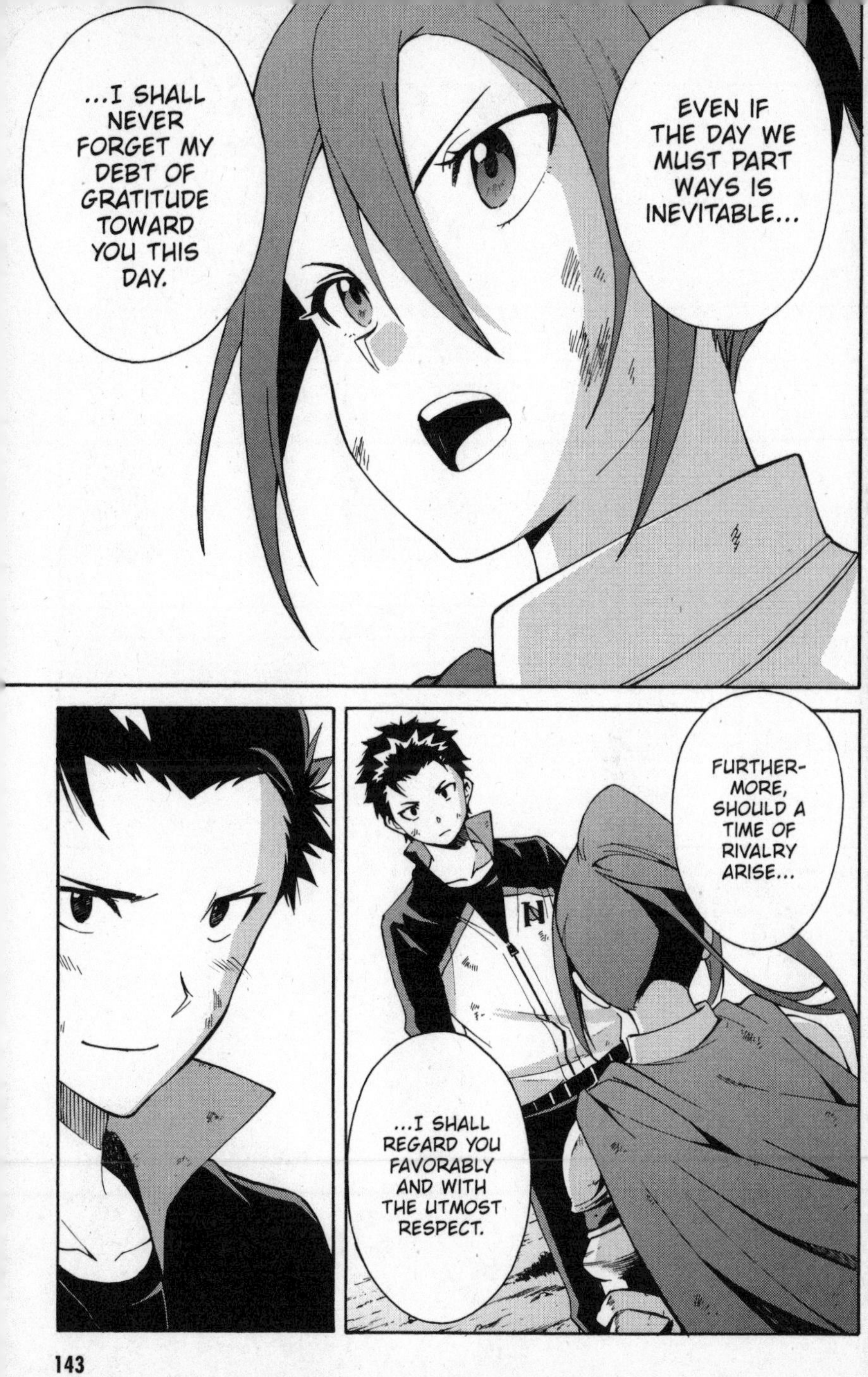
EVEN IF THE DAY WE MUST PART WAYS IS INEVITABLE...
...I SHALL NEVER FORGET MY DEBT OF GRATITUDE TOWARD YOU THIS DAY.
FURTHER-MORE, SHOULD A TIME OF RIVALRY ARISE...
...I SHALL REGARD YOU FAVORABLY AND WITH THE UTMOST RESPECT.

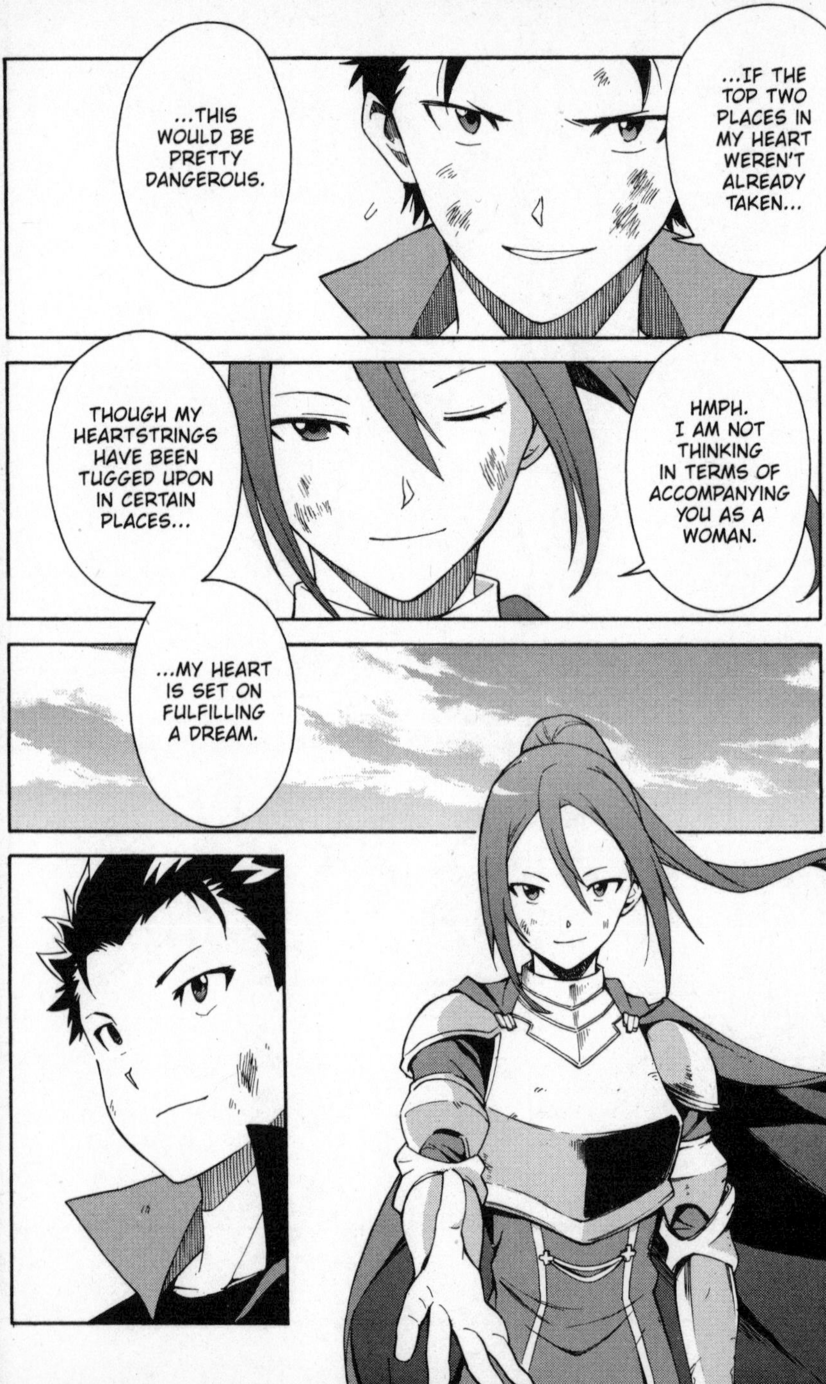
...IF THE TOP TWO PLACES IN MY HEART WEREN'T ALREADY TAKEN...
...THIS WOULD BE PRETTY DANGEROUS.
HMPH. I AM NOT THINKING IN TERMS OF ACCOMPANYING YOU AS A WOMAN.
THOUGH MY HEARTSTRINGS HAVE BEEN TUGGED UPON IN CERTAIN PLACES...
...MY HEART IS SET ON FULFILLING A DREAM.

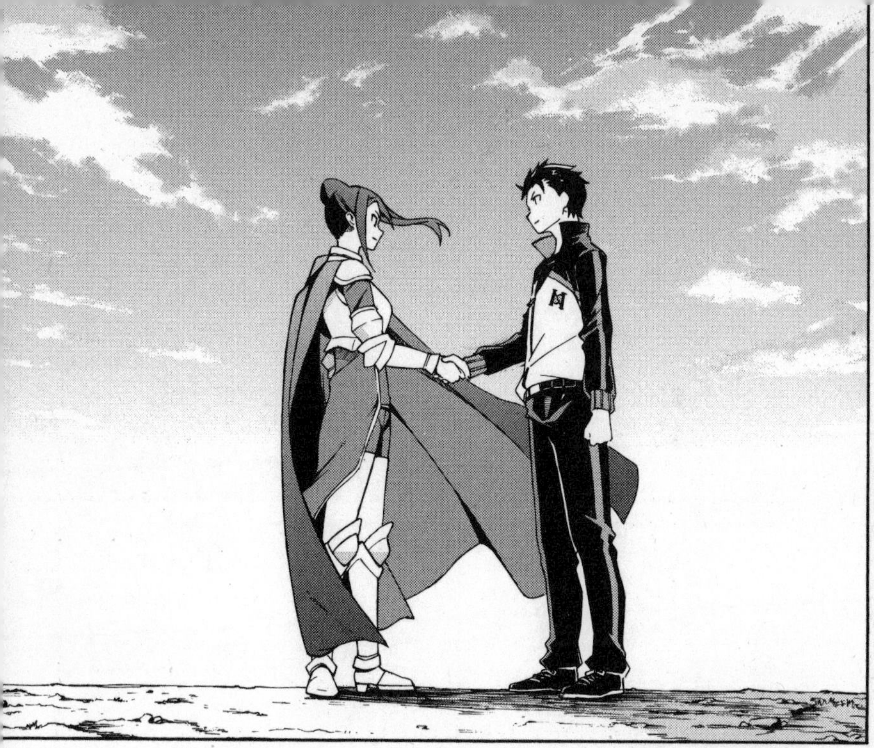
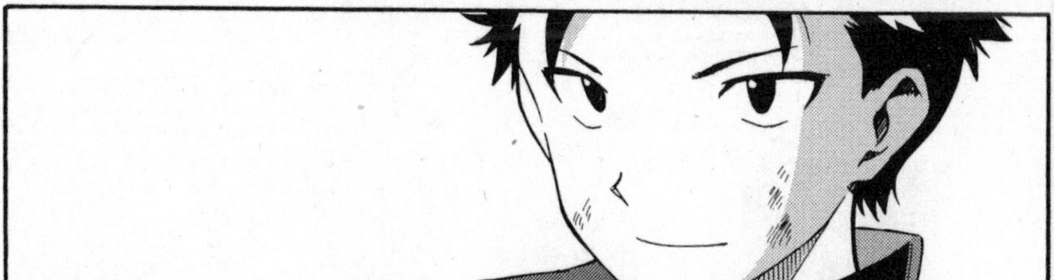
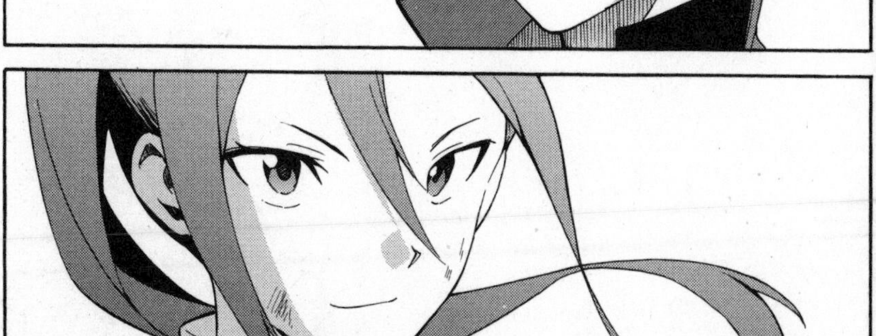

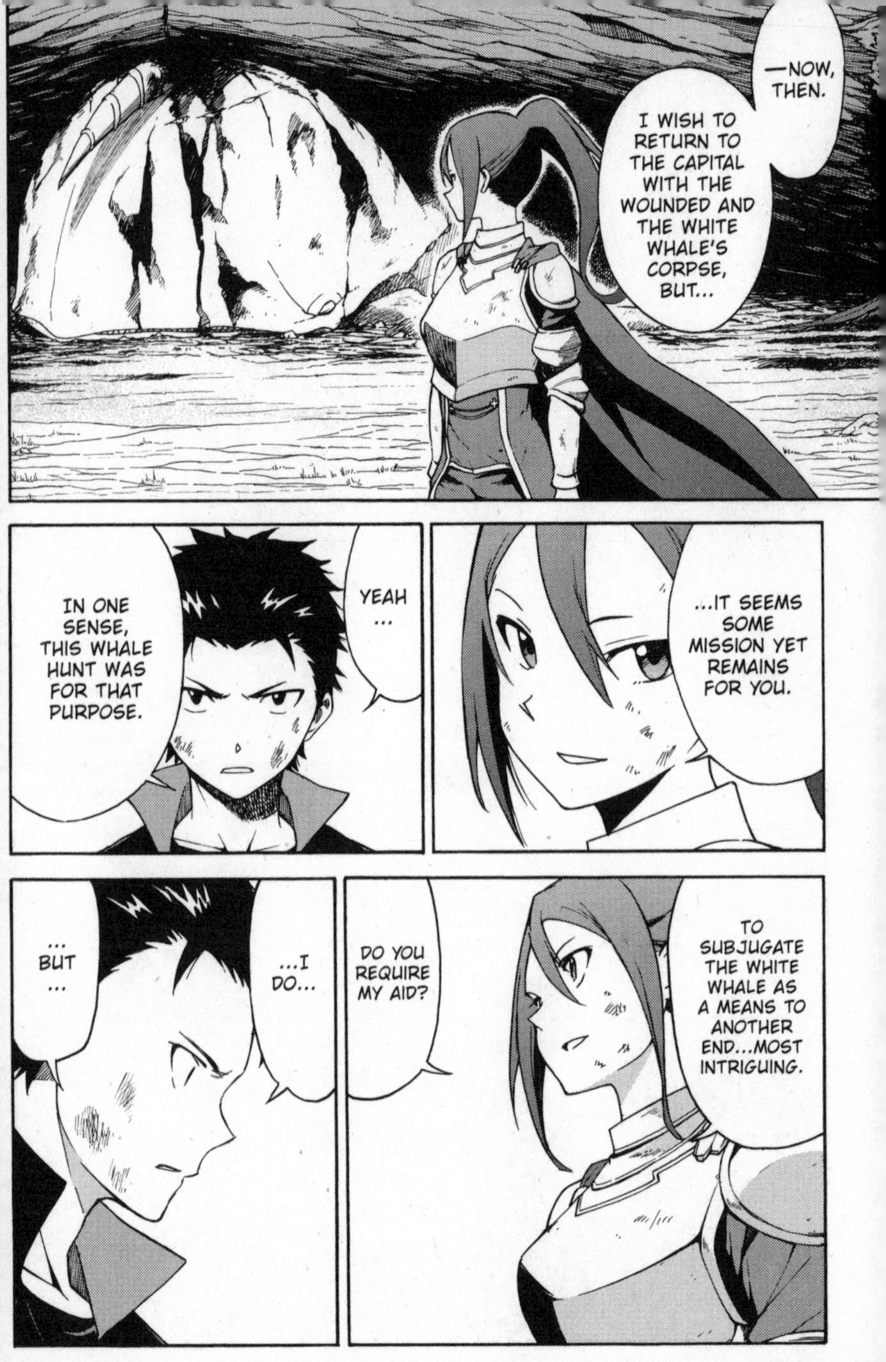
—NOW, THEN.
I WISH TO RETURN TO THE CAPITAL WITH THE WOUNDED AND THE WHITE WHALE'S CORPSE, BUT...
...IT SEEMS SOME MISSION YET REMAINS FOR YOU.
YEAH ...
IN ONE SENSE, THIS WHALE HUNT WAS FOR THAT PURPOSE.
TO SUBJUGATE THE WHITE WHALE AS A MEANS TO ANOTHER END...MOST INTRIGUING.
DO YOU REQUIRE MY AID?
...I DO...
... BUT ...

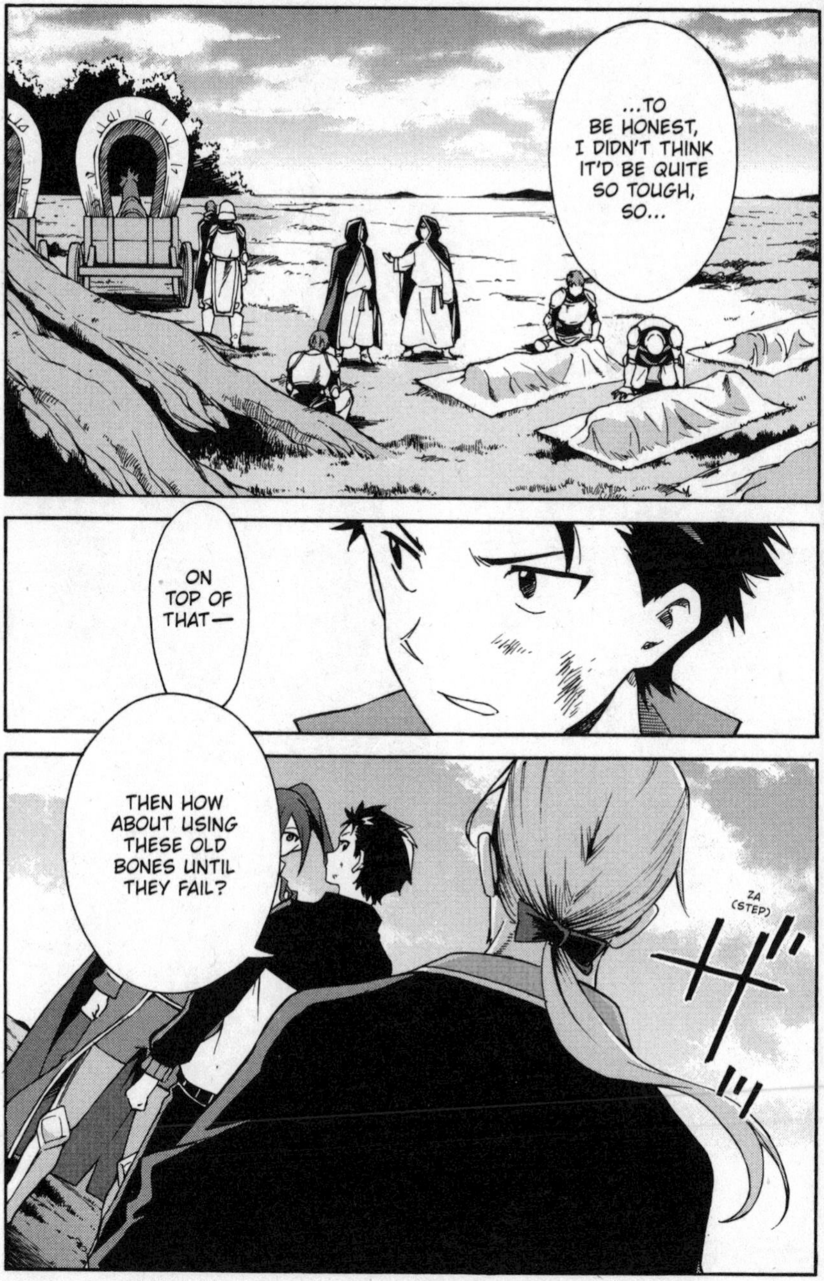
...TO BE HONEST, I DIDN'T THINK IT'D BE QUITE SO TOUGH, SO...
ON TOP OF THAT—
ZA (STEP)
THEN HOW ABOUT USING THESE OLD BONES UNTIL THEY FAIL?

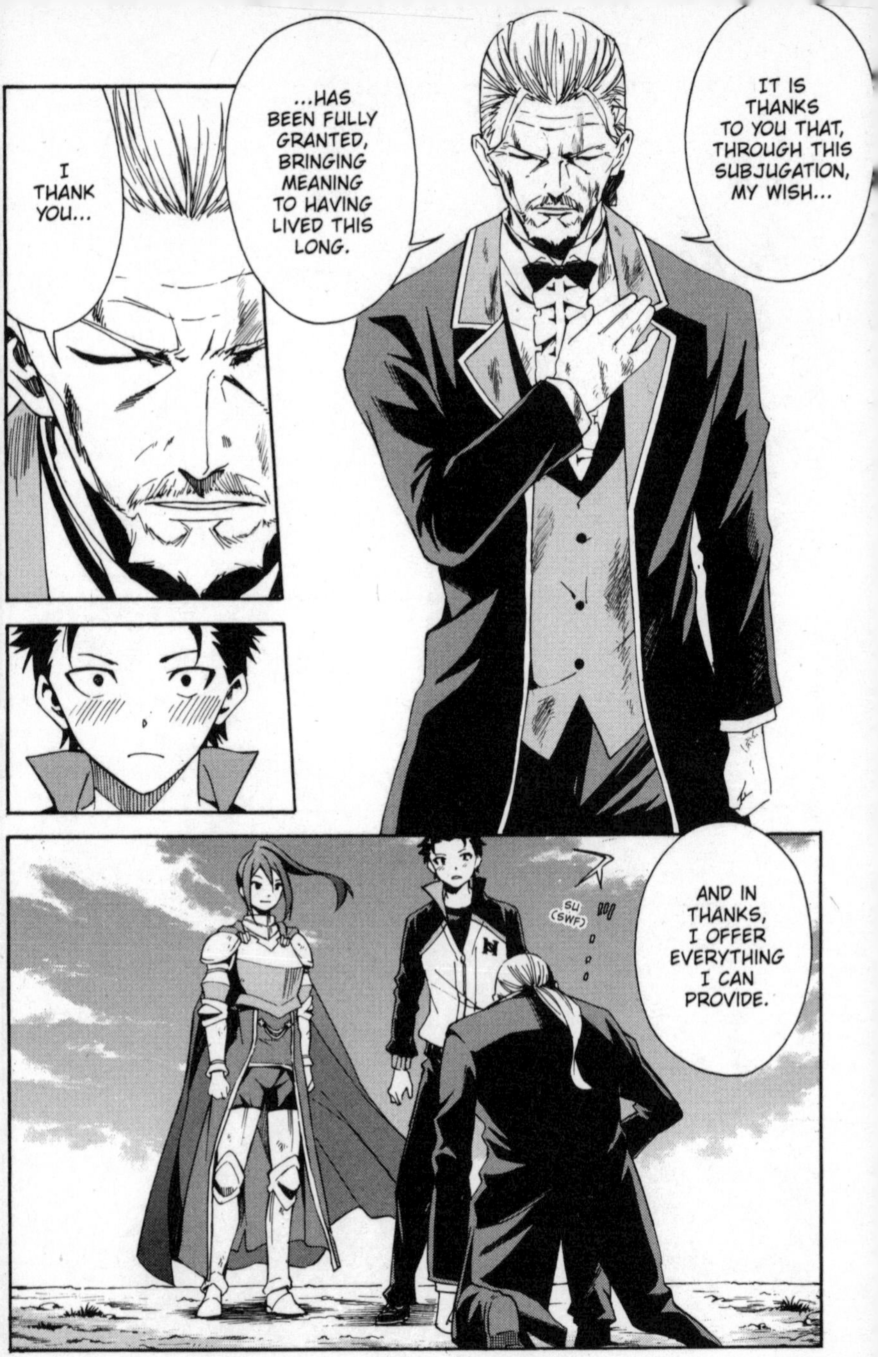
IT IS THANKS TO YOU THAT, THROUGH THIS SUBJUGATION, MY WISH...
...HAS BEEN FULLY GRANTED, BRINGING MEANING TO HAVING LIVED THIS LONG.
I THANK YOU...
AND IN THANKS, I OFFER EVERYTHING I CAN PROVIDE.
SU (SWF)

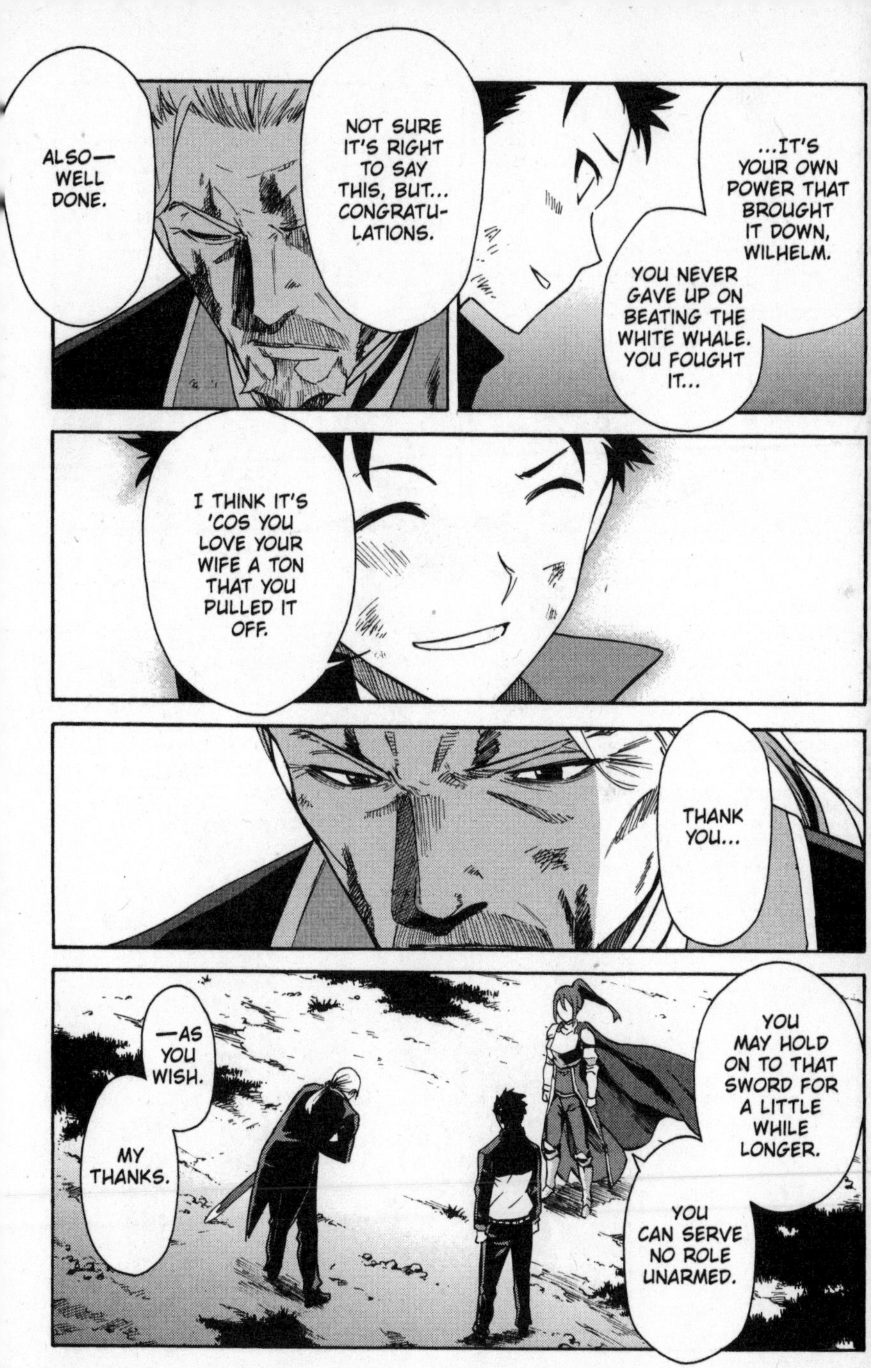
...IT'S YOUR OWN POWER THAT BROUGHT IT DOWN, WILHELM.
YOU NEVER GAVE UP ON BEATING THE WHITE WHALE. YOU FOUGHT IT...
NOT SURE IT'S RIGHT TO SAY THIS, BUT... CONGRATULATIONS.
ALSO— WELL DONE.
I THINK IT'S 'COS YOU LOVE YOUR WIFE A TON THAT YOU PULLED IT OFF.
THANK YOU...
YOU MAY HOLD ON TO THAT SWORD FOR A LITTLE WHILE LONGER.
YOU CAN SERVE NO ROLE UNARMED.
—AS YOU WISH.
MY THANKS.

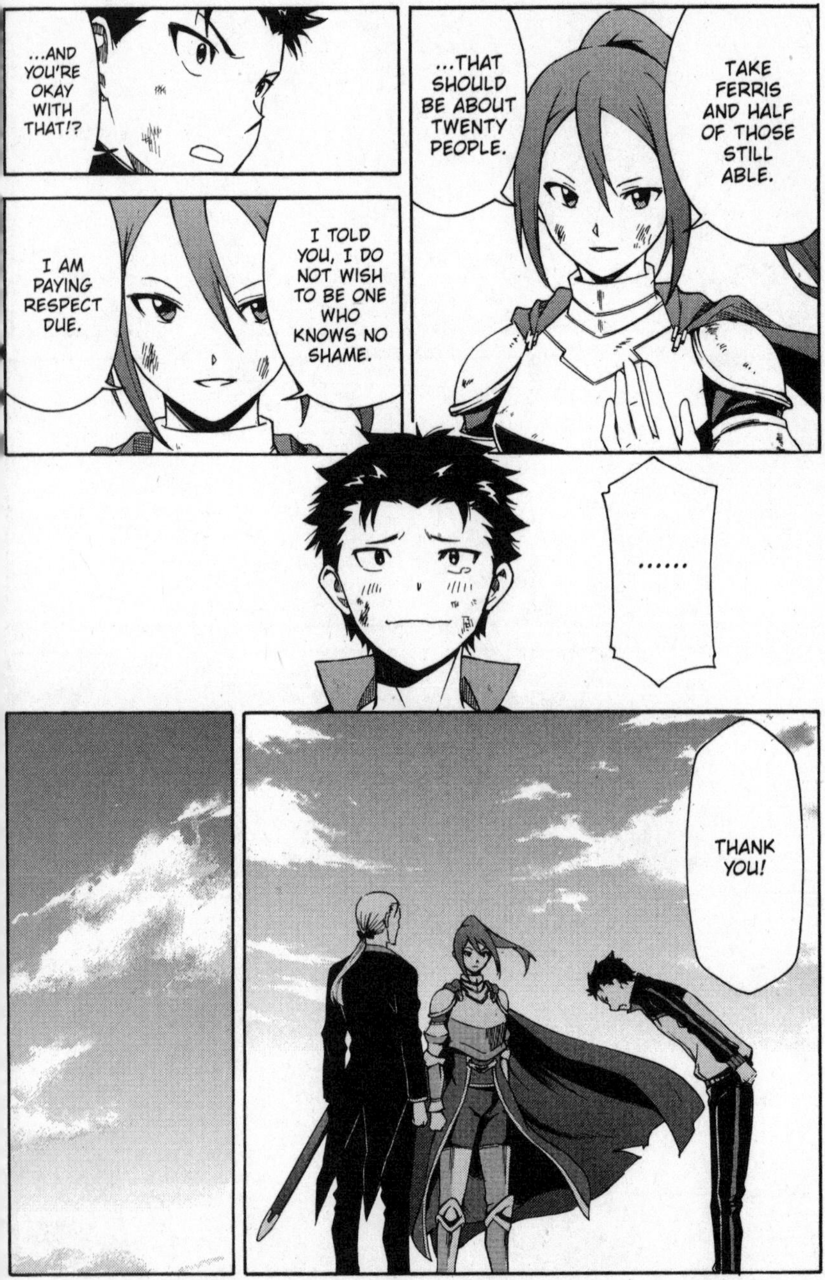
TAKE FERRIS AND HALF OF THOSE STILL ABLE.
...THAT SHOULD BE ABOUT TWENTY PEOPLE.
...AND YOU'RE OKAY WITH THAT!?
I TOLD YOU, I DO NOT WISH TO BE ONE WHO KNOWS NO SHAME.
I AM PAYING RESPECT DUE.
......
THANK YOU!

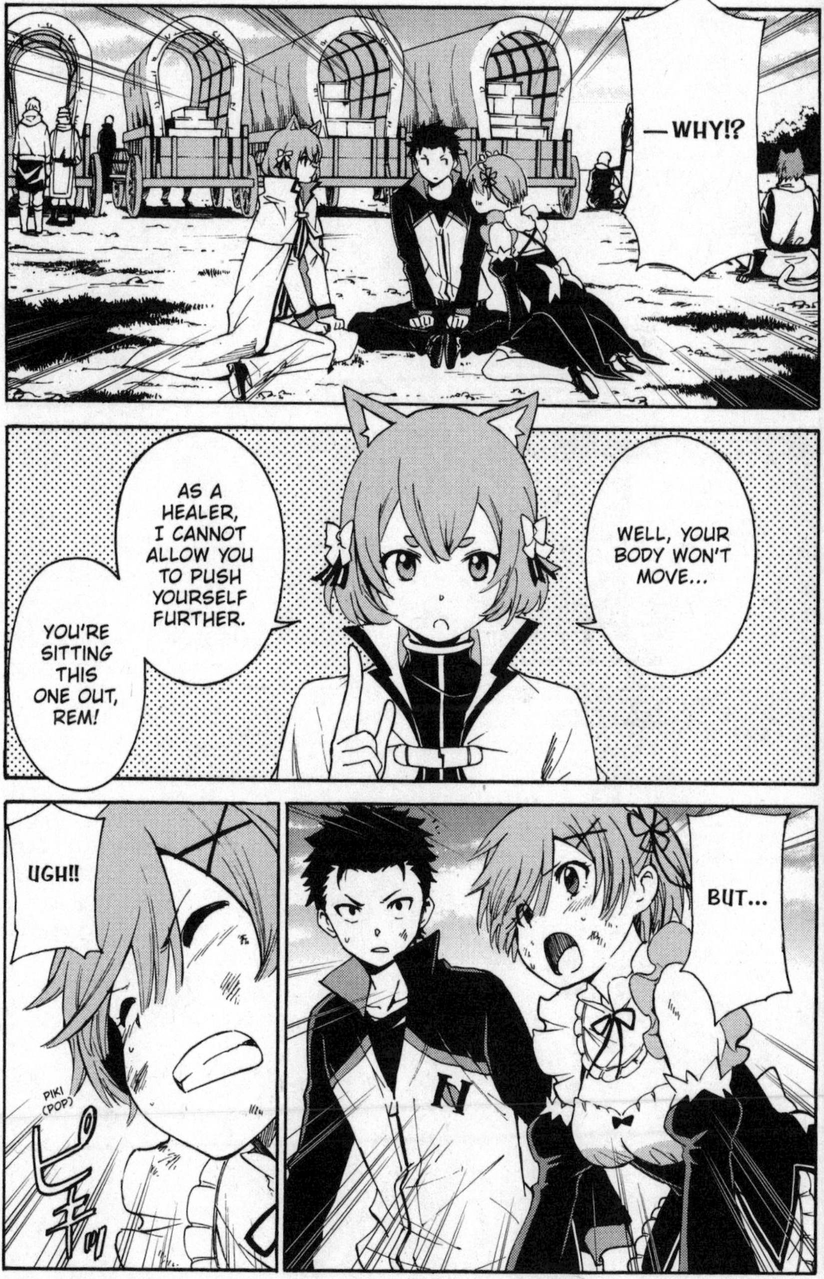
—WHY!?
WELL, YOUR BODY WON'T MOVE...
AS A HEALER, I CANNOT ALLOW YOU TO PUSH YOURSELF FURTHER.
YOU'RE SITTING THIS ONE OUT, REM!
BUT...
UGH!!
PIKI (POP)

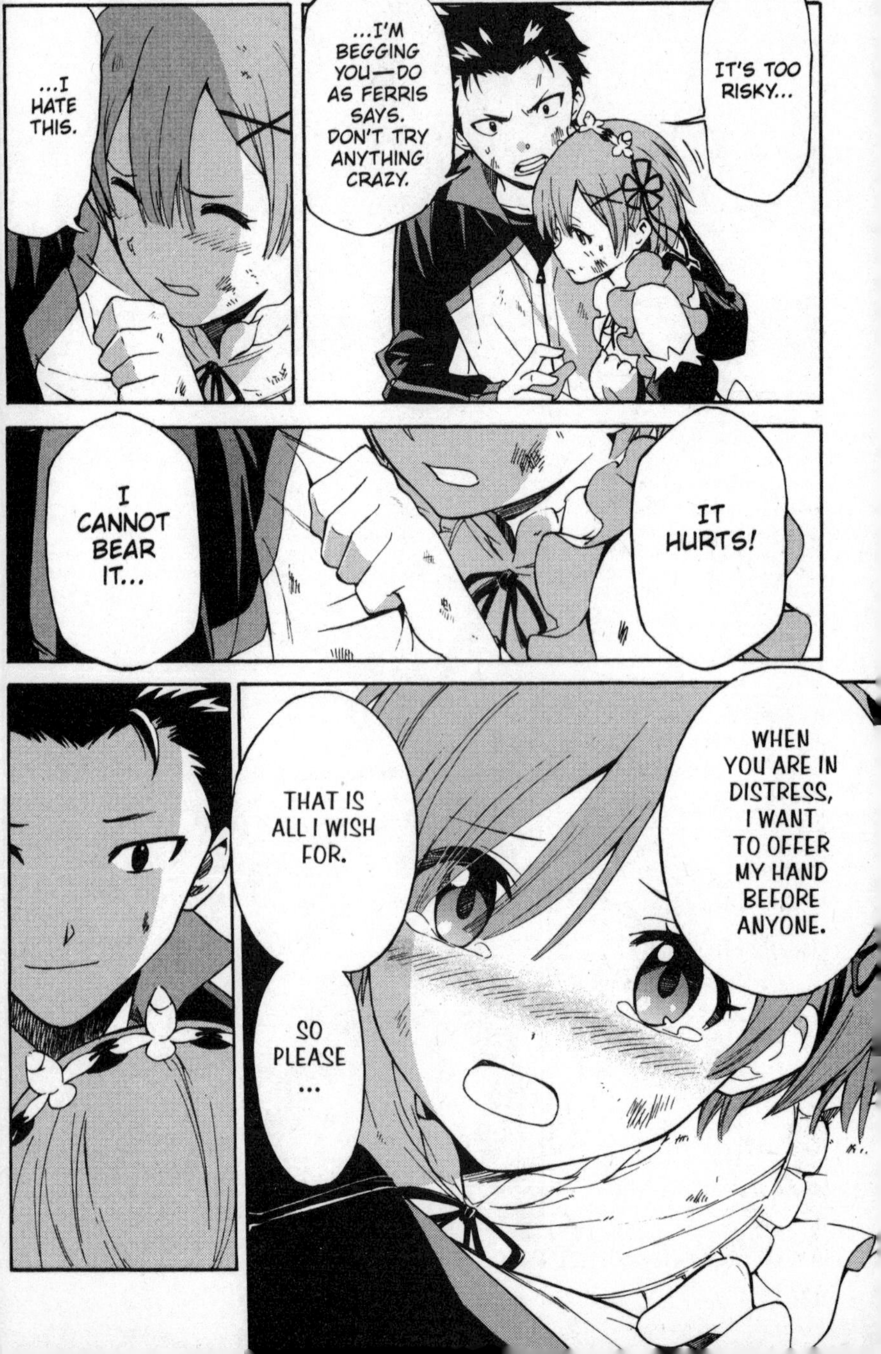
IT'S TOO RISKY...
...I'M BEGGING YOU—DO AS FERRIS SAYS. DON'T TRY ANYTHING CRAZY.
...I HATE THIS.
IT HURTS!
I CANNOT BEAR IT...
WHEN YOU ARE IN DISTRESS, I WANT TO OFFER MY HAND BEFORE ANYONE.
THAT IS ALL I WISH FOR.
SO PLEASE...

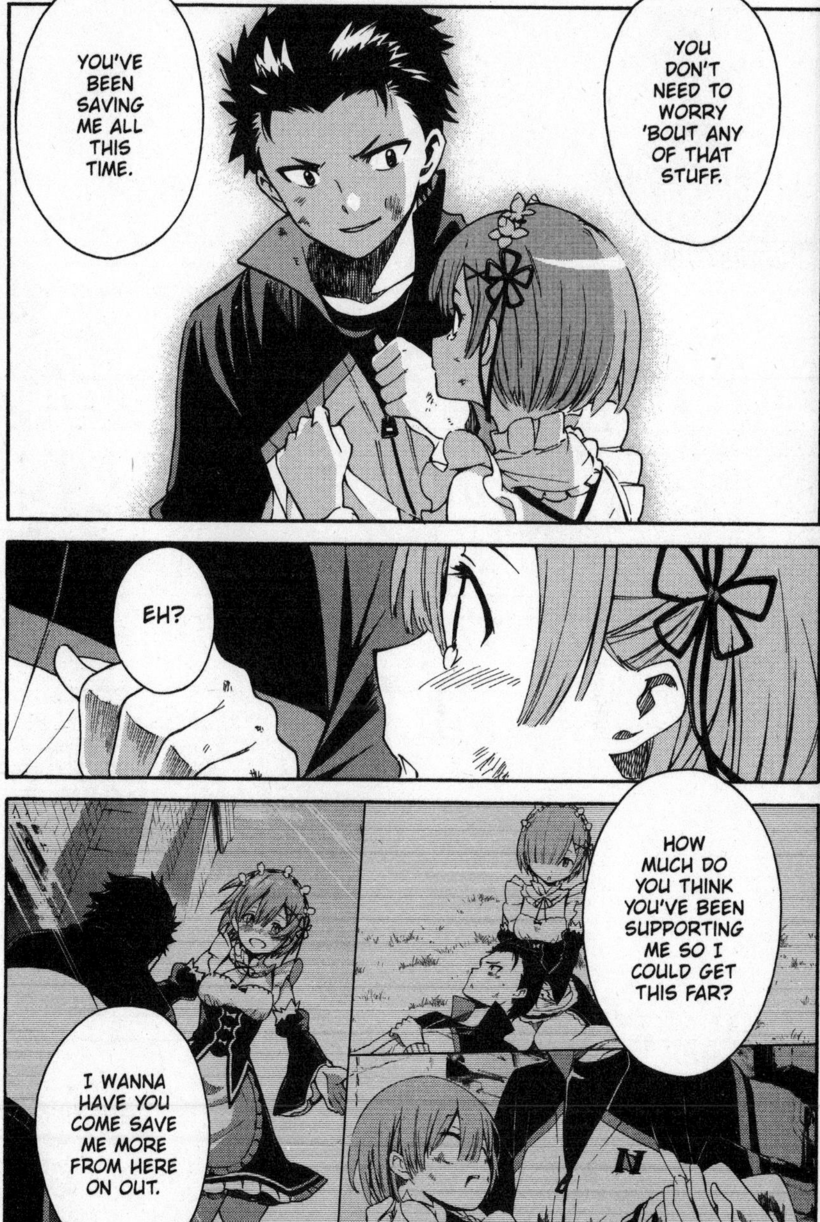
YOU DON'T NEED TO WORRY 'BOUT ANY OF THAT STUFF.
YOU'VE BEEN SAVING ME ALL THIS TIME.
EH?
HOW MUCH DO YOU THINK YOU'VE BEEN SUPPORTING ME SO I COULD GET THIS FAR?
I WANNA HAVE YOU COME SAVE ME MORE FROM HERE ON OUT.

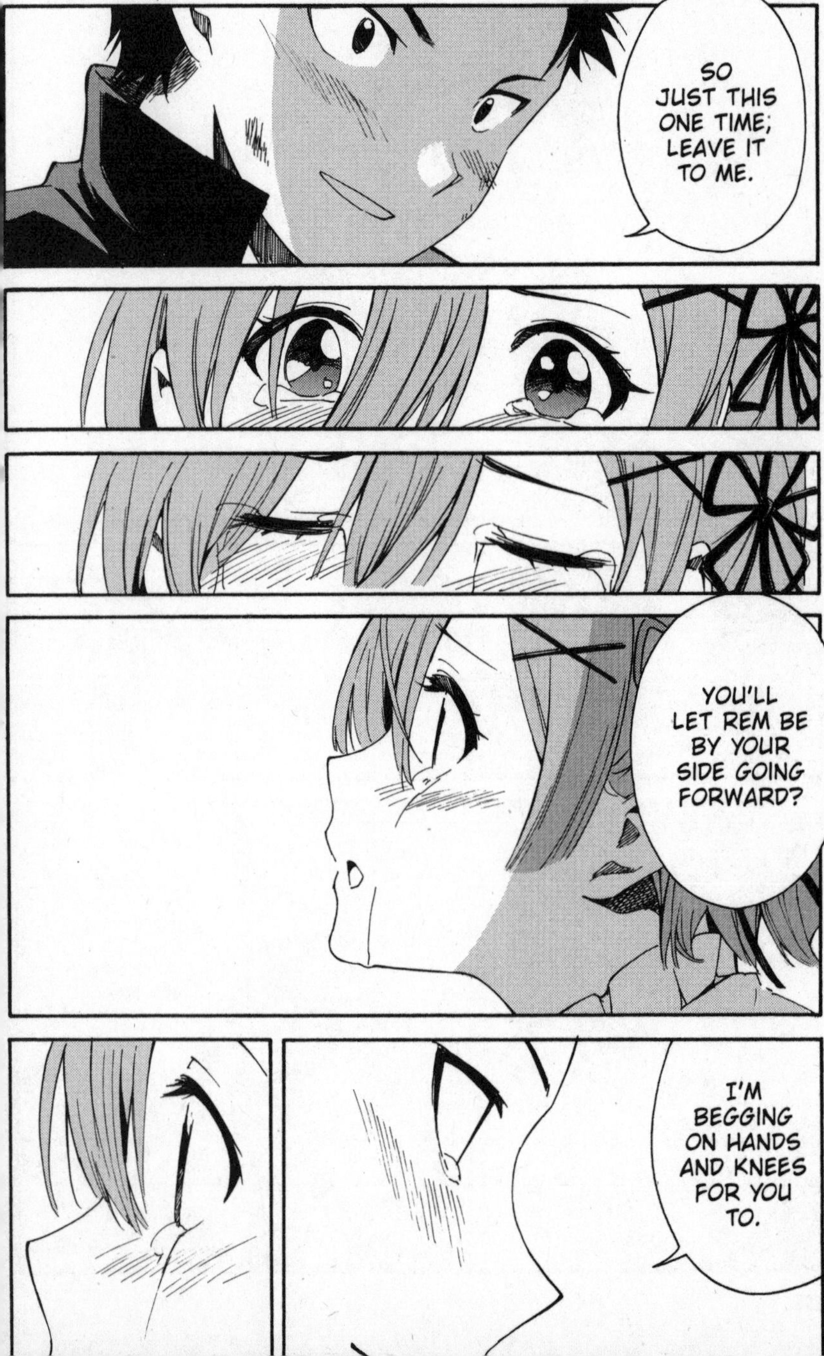
SO JUST THIS ONE TIME; LEAVE IT TO ME.
YOU'LL LET REM BE BY YOUR SIDE GOING FORWARD?
I'M BEGGING ON HANDS AND KNEES FOR YOU TO.

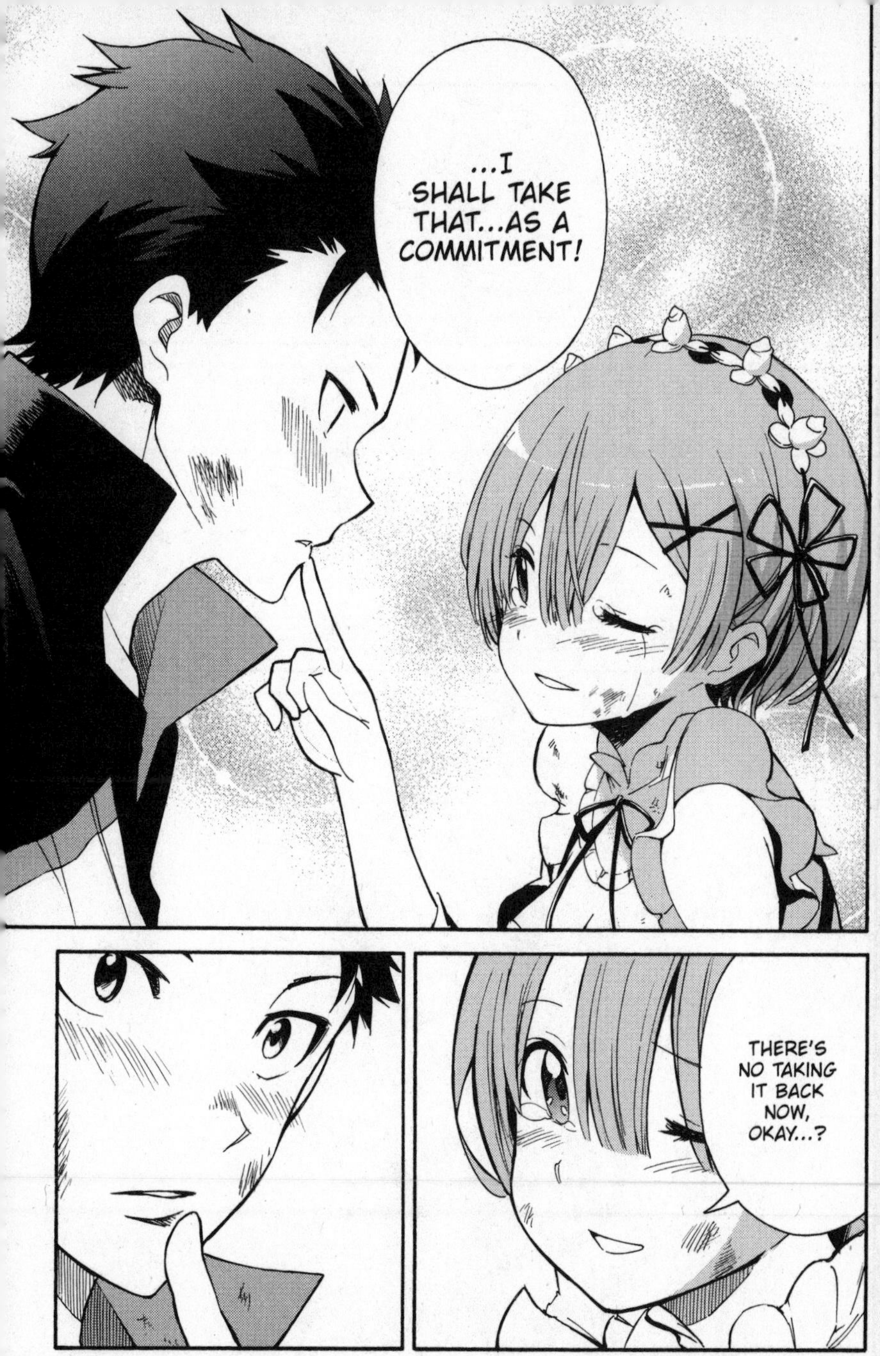
...I SHALL TAKE THAT...AS A COMMITMENT!
THERE'S NO TAKING IT BACK NOW, OKAY...?

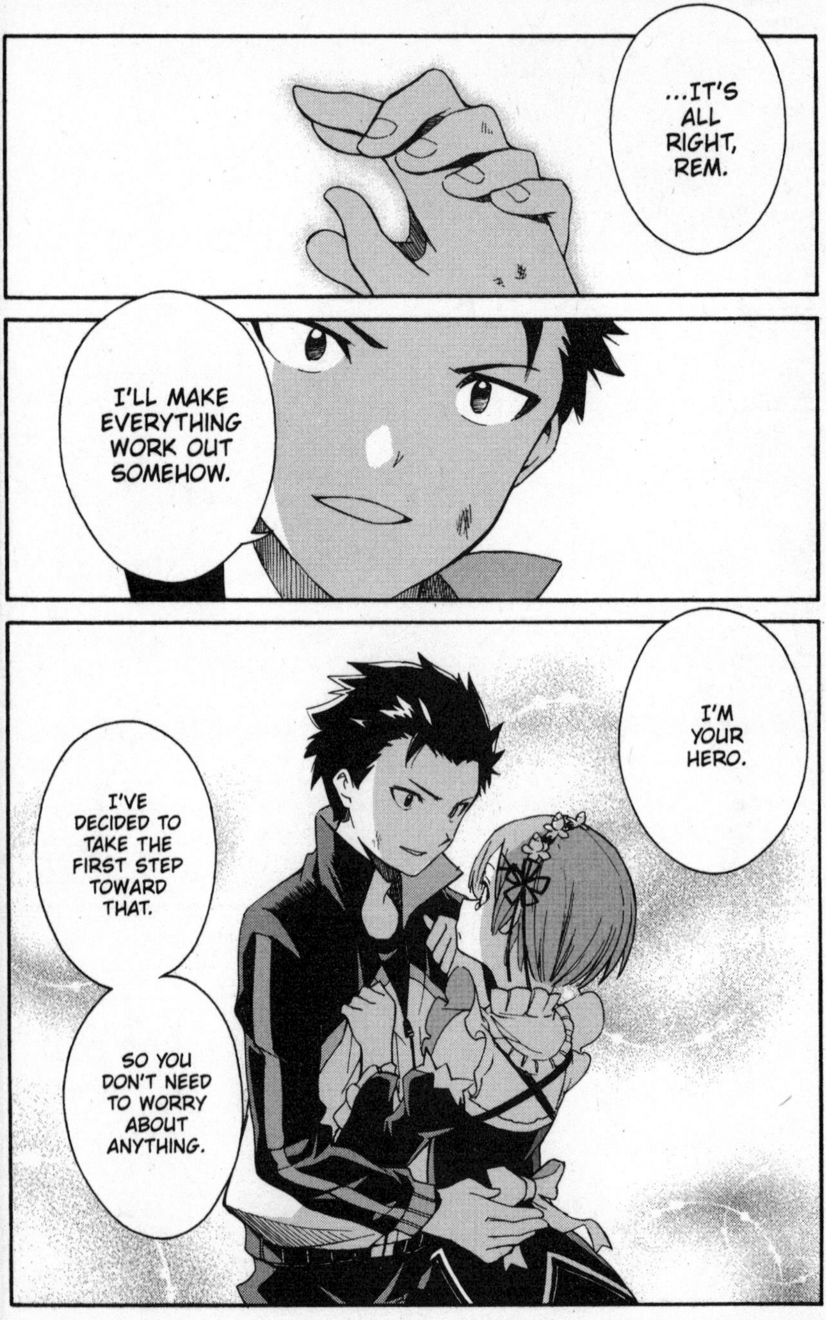
...IT'S ALL RIGHT, REM.
I'LL MAKE EVERYTHING WORK OUT SOMEHOW.
I'M YOUR HERO.
I'VE DECIDED TO TAKE THE FIRST STEP TOWARD THAT.
SO YOU DON'T NEED TO WORRY ABOUT ANYTHING.

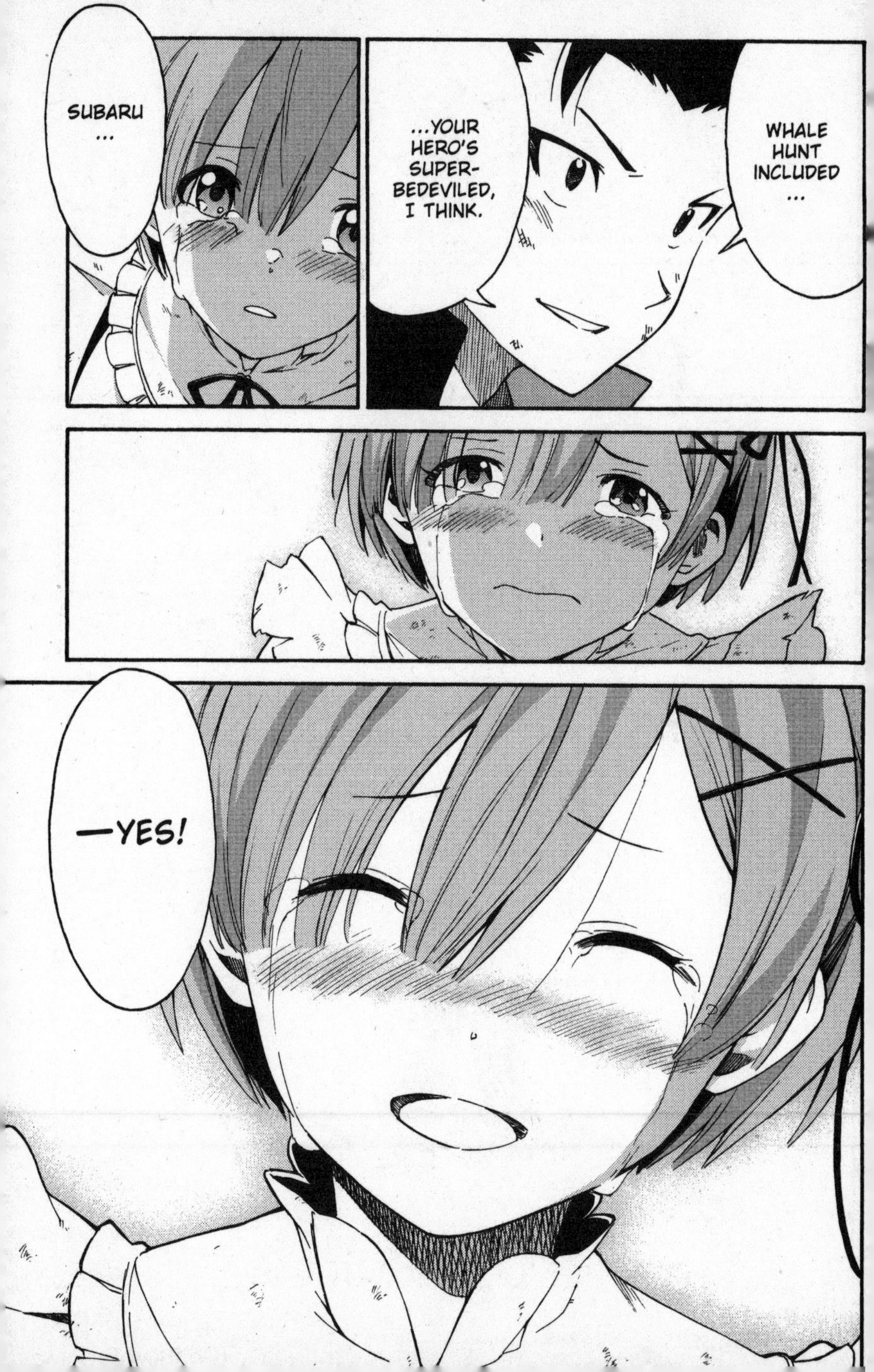
WHALE HUNT INCLUDED ...
...YOUR HERO'S SUPER-BEDEVILED, I THINK.
SUBARU ...
—YES!

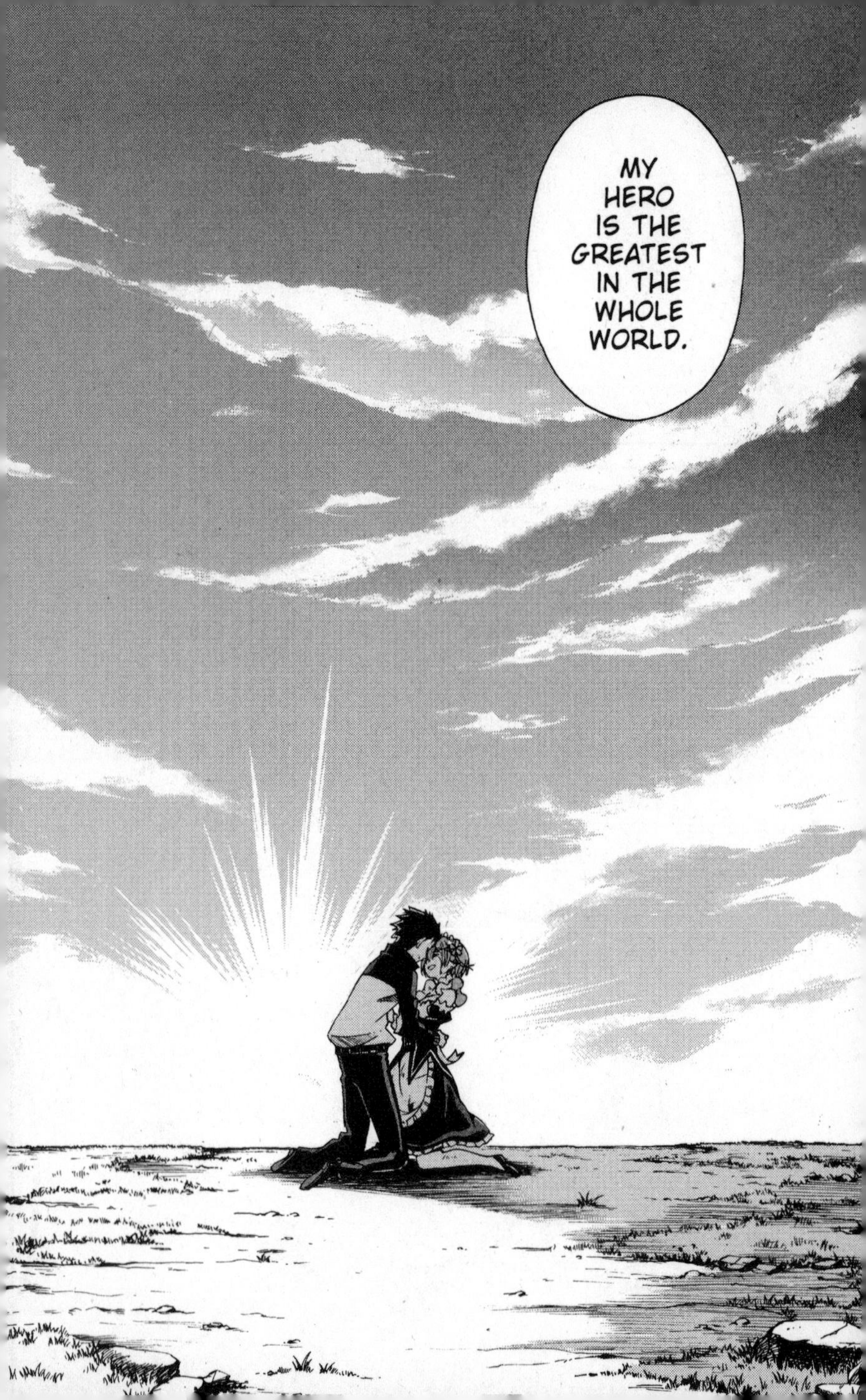
MY HERO IS THE GREATEST IN THE WHOLE WORLD.

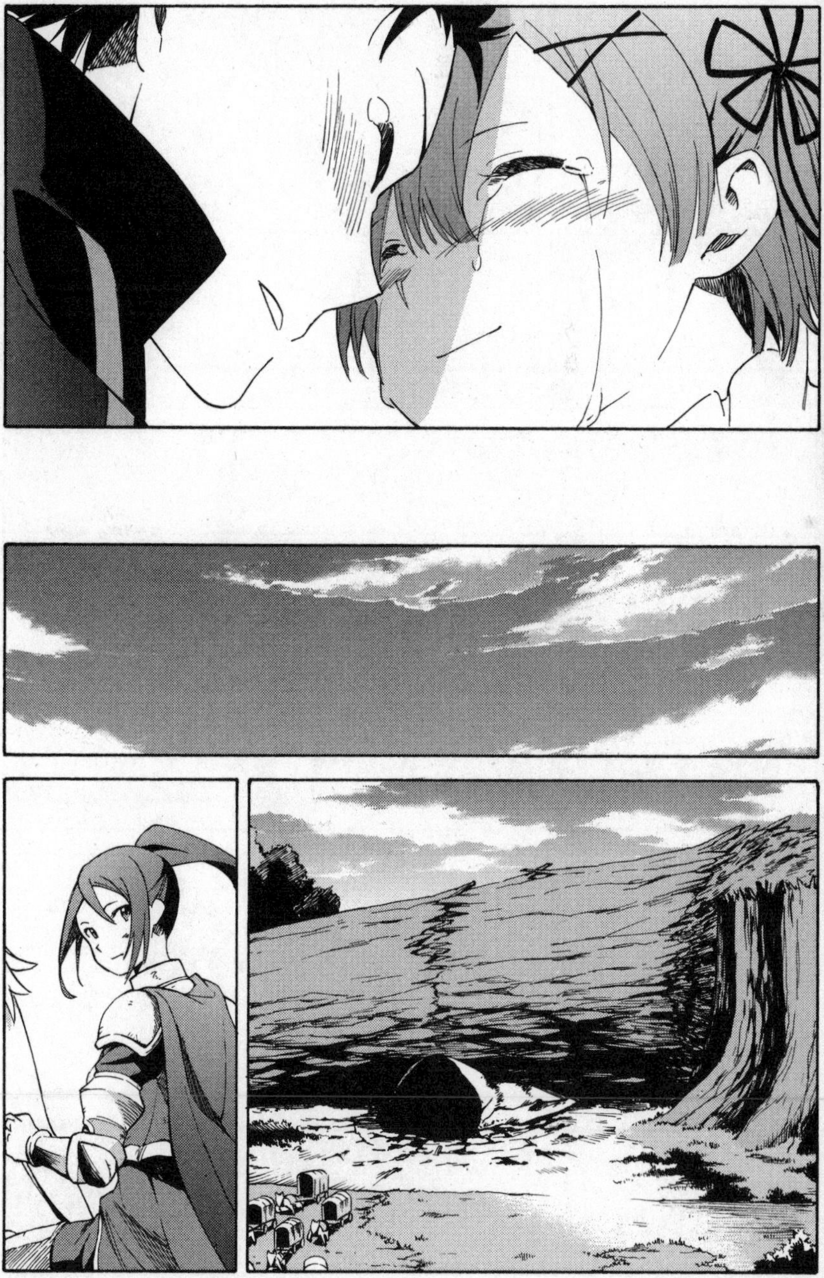

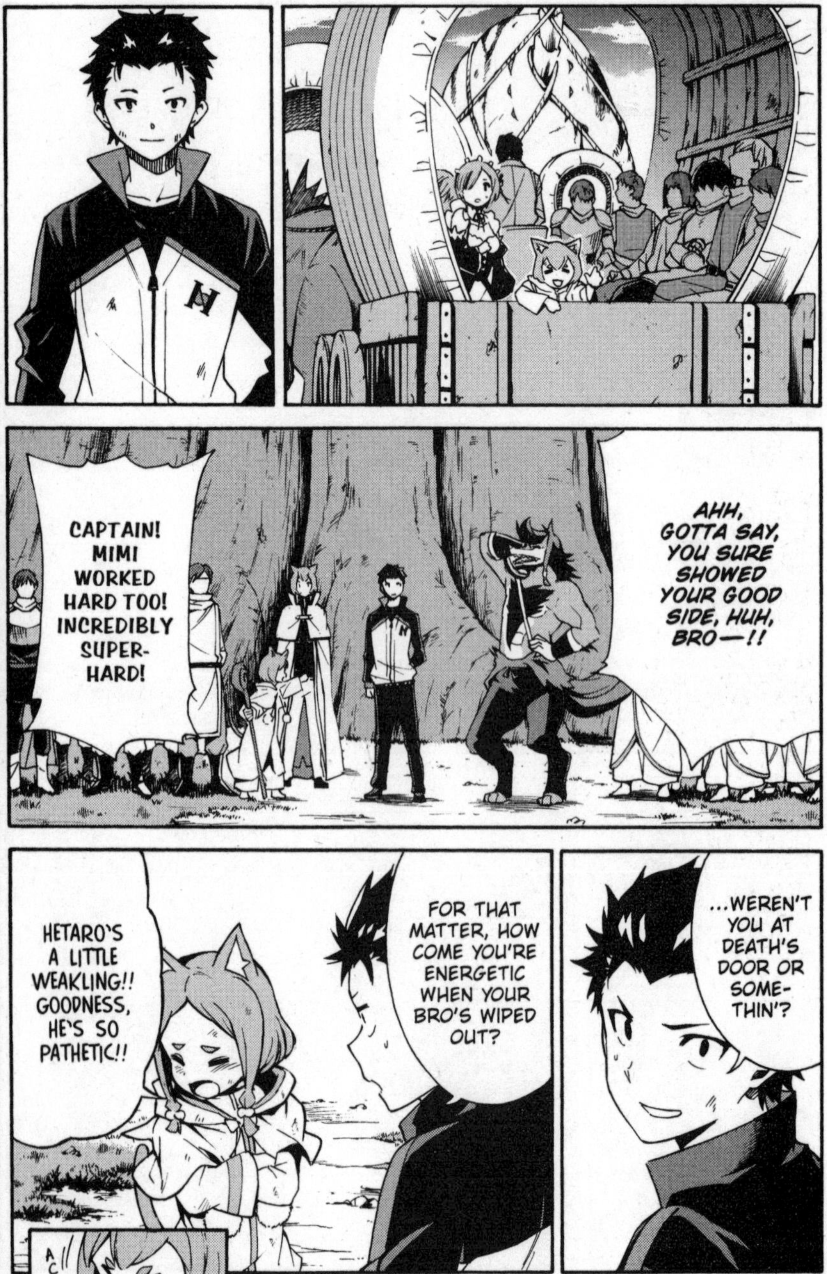
AHH, GOTTA SAY, YOU SURE SHOWED YOUR GOOD SIDE, HUH, BRO—!!
CAPTAIN! MIMI WORKED HARD TOO! INCREDIBLY SUPER-HARD!
...WEREN'T YOU AT DEATH'S DOOR OR SOME-THIN'?
FOR THAT MATTER, HOW COME YOU'RE ENERGETIC WHEN YOUR BRO'S WIPED OUT?
HETARO'S A LITTLE WEAKLING!! GOODNESS, HE'S SO PATHETIC!!
ACHOO!

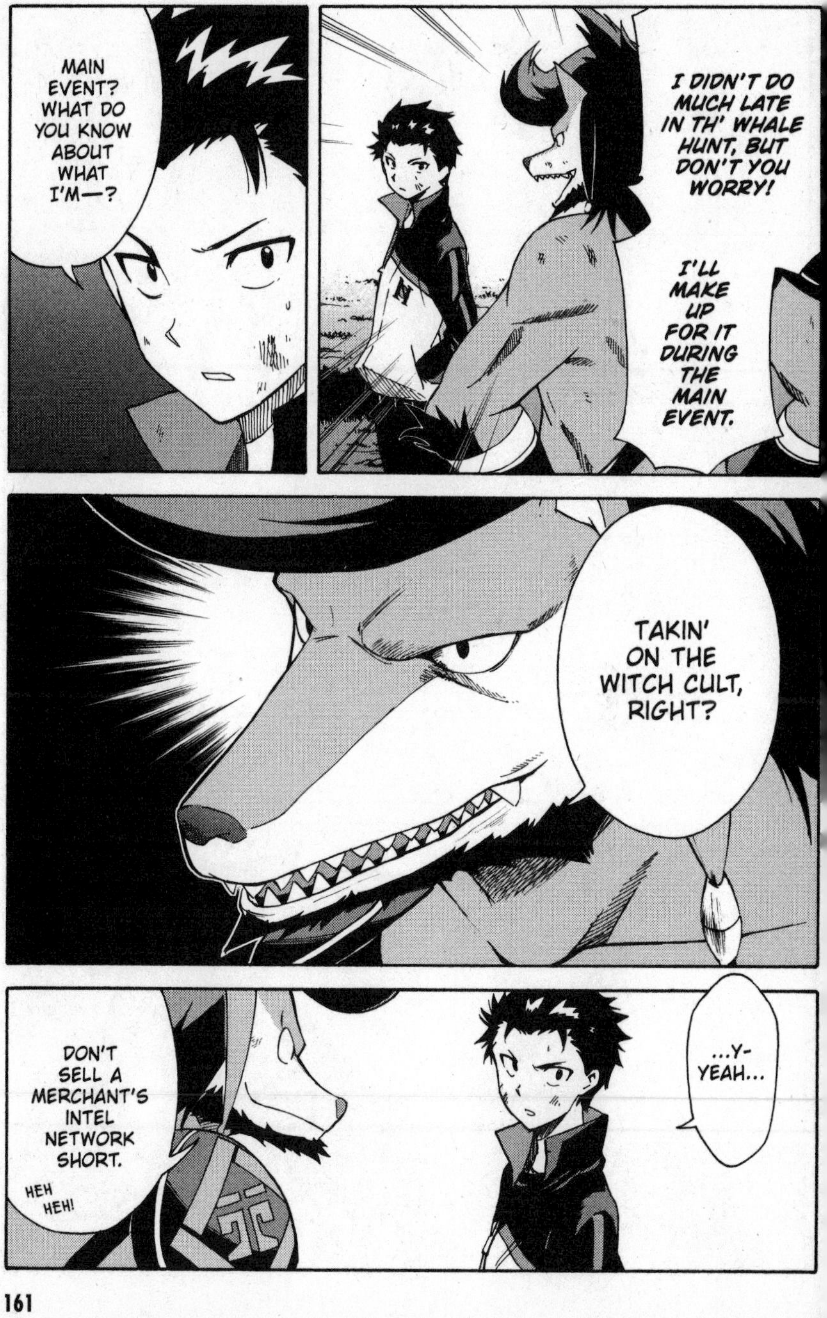
I DIDN'T DO MUCH LATE IN TH' WHALE HUNT, BUT DON'T YOU WORRY!
I'LL MAKE UP FOR IT DURING THE MAIN EVENT.
MAIN EVENT? WHAT DO YOU KNOW ABOUT WHAT I'M—?
TAKIN' ON THE WITCH CULT, RIGHT?
...Y-YEAH...
DON'T SELL A MERCHANT'S INTEL NETWORK SHORT.
HEH HEH!

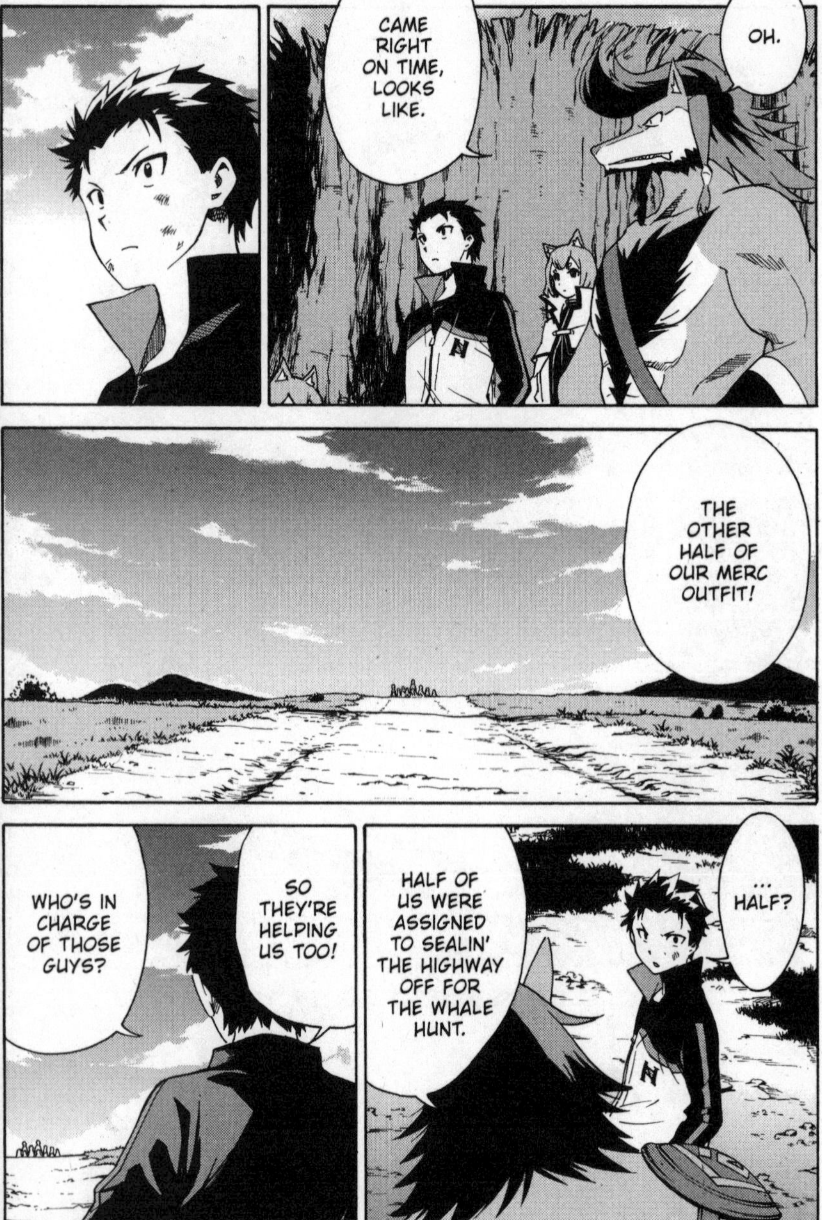
OH.
CAME RIGHT ON TIME, LOOKS LIKE.
THE OTHER HALF OF OUR MERC OUTFIT!
...HALF?
HALF OF US WERE ASSIGNED TO SEALIN' THE HIGHWAY OFF FOR THE WHALE HUNT.
SO THEY'RE HELPING US TOO!
WHO'S IN CHARGE OF THOSE GUYS?

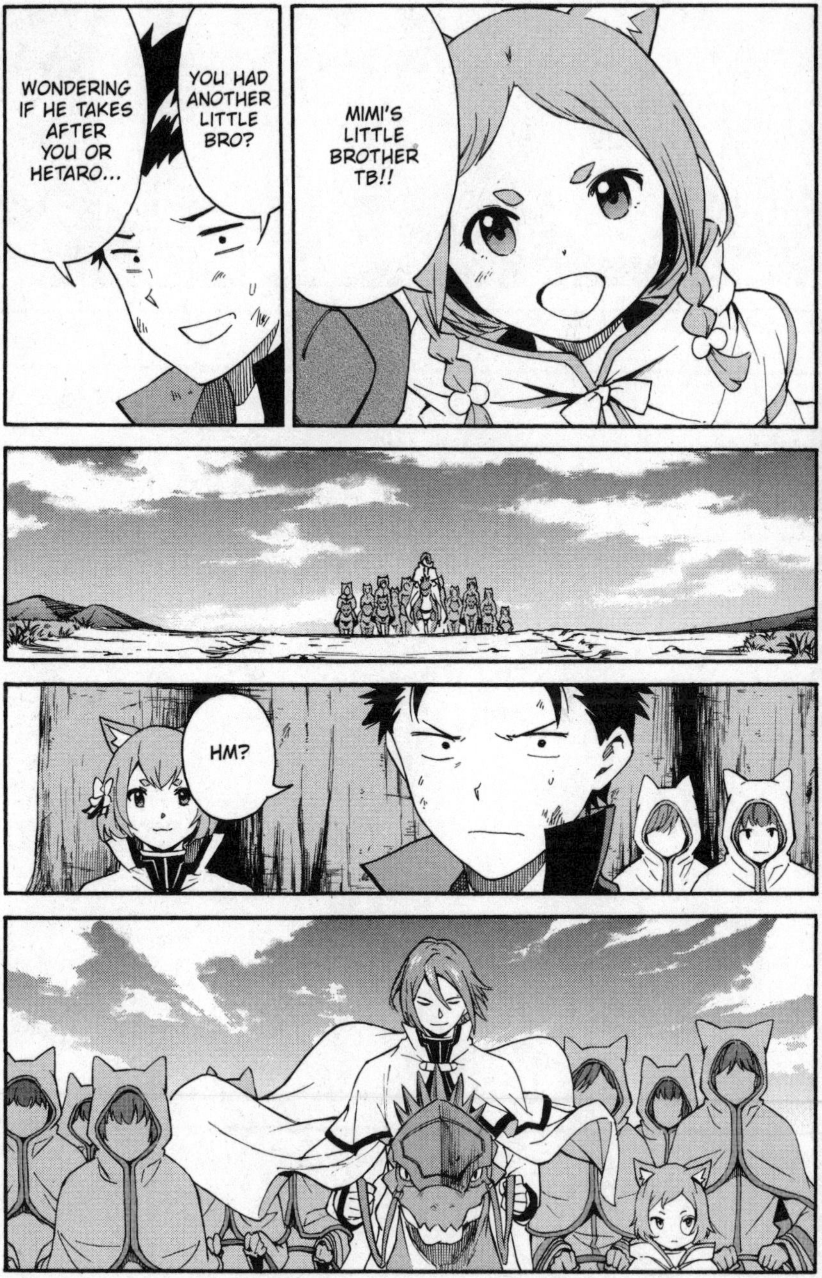
MIMI'S LITTLE BROTHER TB!!
YOU HAD ANOTHER LITTLE BRO?
WONDERING IF HE TAKES AFTER YOU OR HETARO...
HM?

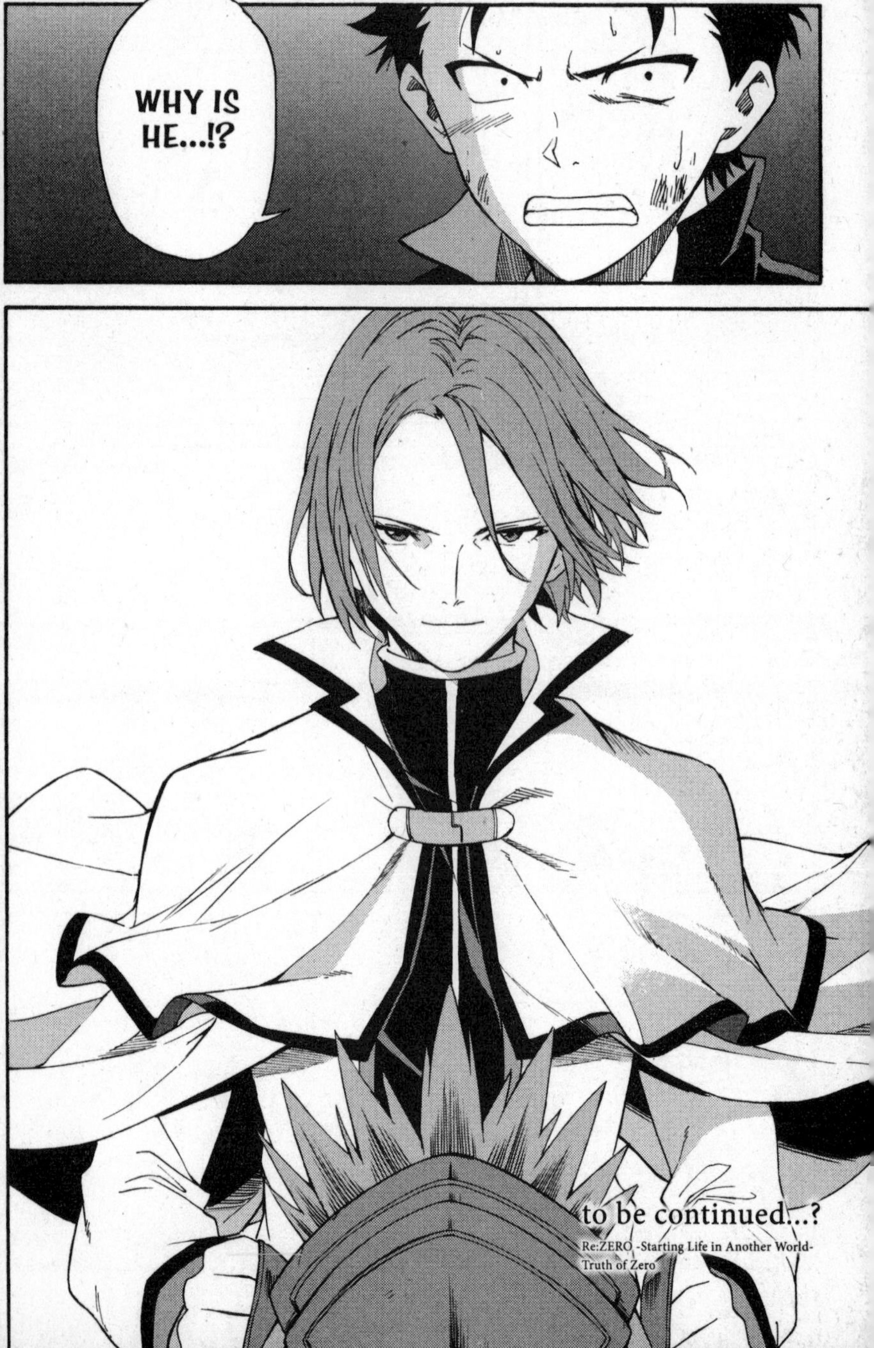
WHY IS HE...!?
to be continued...?
Re:ZERO -Starting Life in Another World-
Truth of Zero

Re:ZERO -Starting Life in Another World-

Truth of Zero
The only ability Subaru Natsuki gets when he's summoned to another world is
time travel via his own death. But to save her, he'll die as many times as it takes.

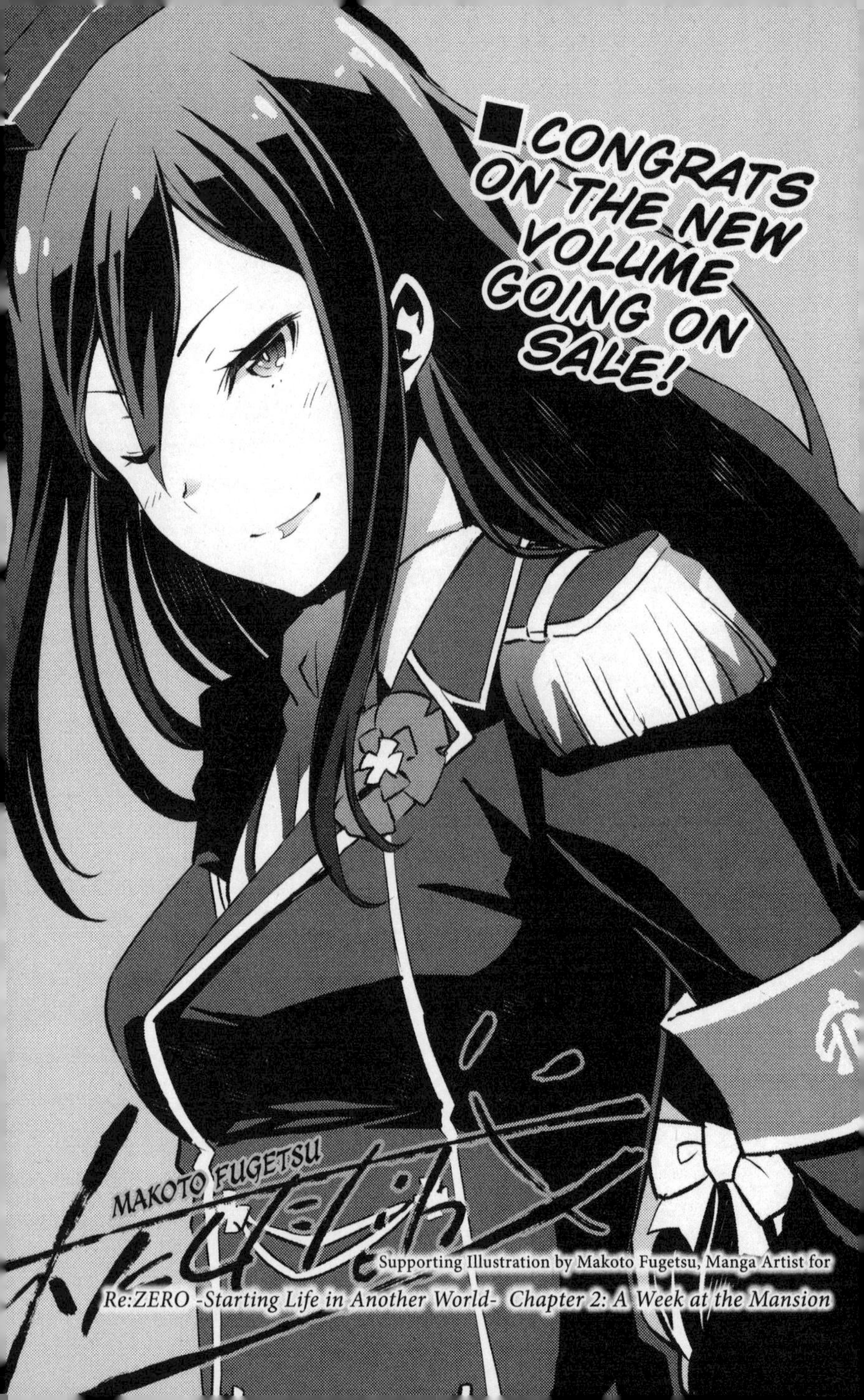
CONGRATS ON THE NEW VOLUME GOING ON SALE!
MAKOTO FUGETSU
Supporting Illustration by Makoto Fugetsu, Manga Artist for
Re:ZERO -Starting Life in Another World- Chapter 2: A Week at the Mansion

Illustration by Shinichirou Otsuka (Character Designer)

Re:ZERO -Starting Life in Another World-

Supporting Comments from the Author of the Original Work, Tappei Nagatsuki

Daichi Matsuse-sensei! Congratulations on Volume 7 of this *Re:ZERO* comic going on sale!

Thank you very much for using nearly an entire second volume to draw the conclusion to the "Battle of the White Whale"! From the beginning, I thought the vigor of your *Re:ZERO* drawing skills held no half measures, but as you continued to capture the full course of the battle, I felt you raised its intensity to the very utmost!

You've done such a wonderful job drawing the contents of Subaru Natsuki's restart "From Zero", Wilhelm's showdown with his mortal foe, and numerous other highlights.

However, just like in the story, it's out of the frying pan and into the fire for you, Matsuse-sensei (LOL).

With the real fight with the Witch Cult's Bishop of the Deadly Sins and other developments still to come, *Re:ZERO* Chapter 3 is finally approaching its grand finale, so best regards from here on out!

I will enjoy watching henceforth how Subaru Natsuki will confront the greatest travails of his life in another world!

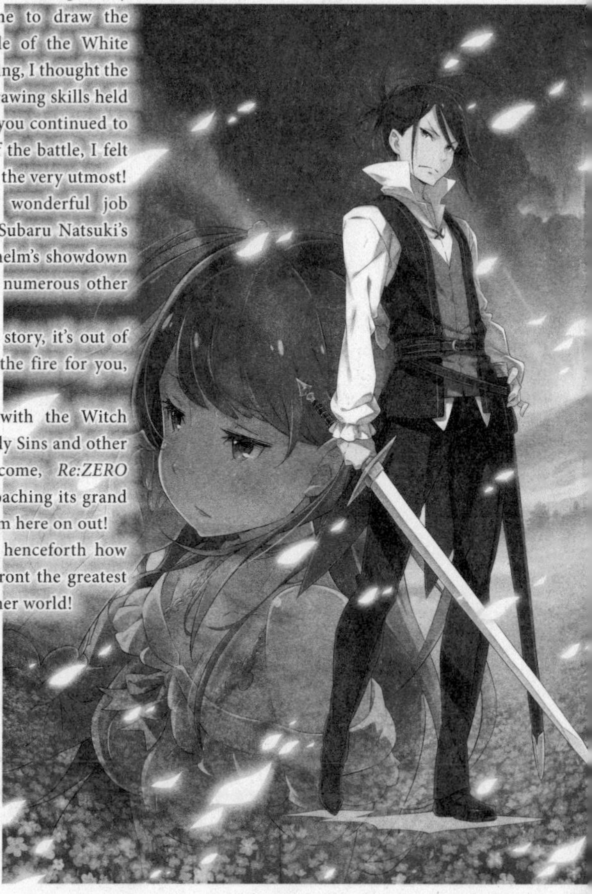

Re:ZERO -Starting Life in Another World- Chapter 3: Truth of Zero

ARTIST COMMENTS

Thank you very much for picking up Chapter 3,
Volume 7 of the comic version of *Re:ZERO*.
In this volume, they were finally able to subdue the White Whale.
As I drew the subjugation of the White Whale,
I think I myself grew along with Subaru and company.

Among the characters who appear during the Battle of the White Whale,
I have come to like Crusch more and more.
Personally, I really liked the part with Subaru passing by Crusch
in the final scene where the Great Flugel Tree fell.

Next volume, the battle against Petelgeuse begins.
I will strive to make things even more thrilling than to date,
so please continue buying!

Daichi Matsuse

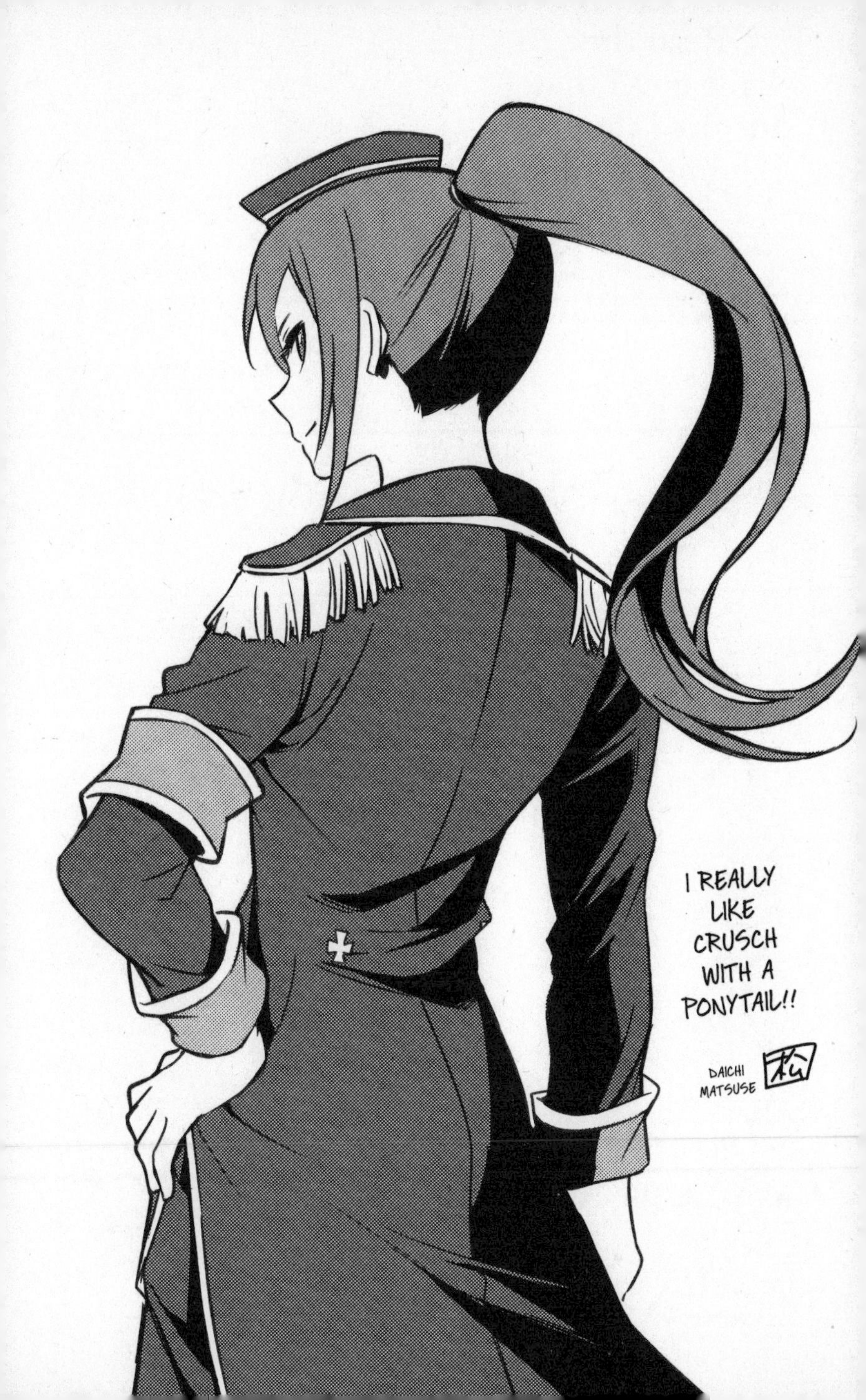
I REALLY LIKE CRUSCH WITH A PONYTAIL!!
DAICHI MATSUSE

Read the light novel that inspired the hit anime series!

Also be sure to check out the manga series!

AVAILABLE NOW!

www.YenPress.com

Re:Zero Kara Hajimeru Isekai Seikatsu
© Tappei Nagatsuki, Daichi Matsuse / KADOKAWA CORPORATION
© Tappei Nagatsuki Illustration: Shinichirou Otsuka/ KADOKAWA CORPORATION

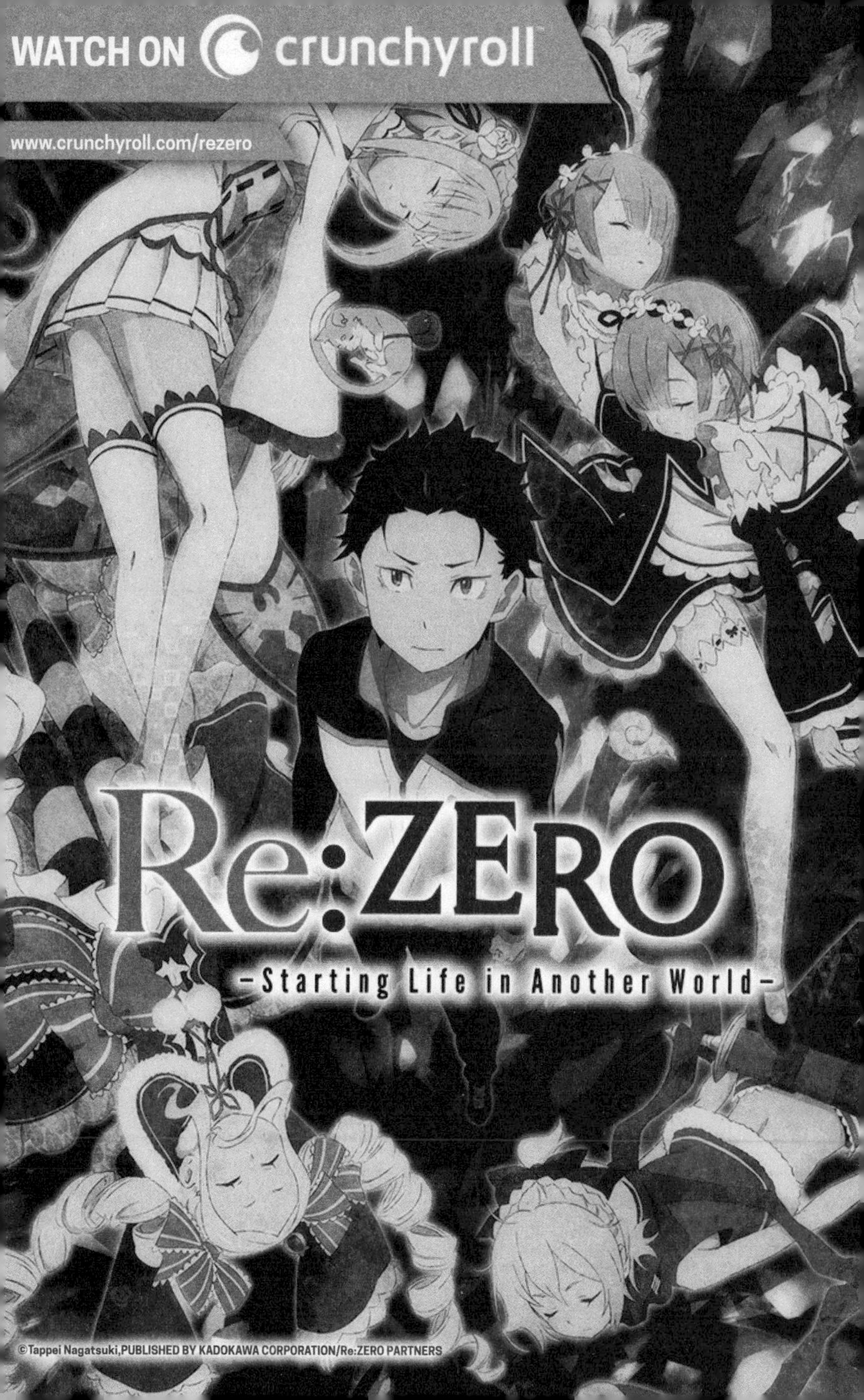
WATCH ON crunchyroll
www.crunchyroll.com/rezero
Re:ZERO
-Starting Life in Another World-
©Tappei Nagatsuki,PUBLISHED BY KADOKAWA CORPORATION/Re:ZERO PARTNERS

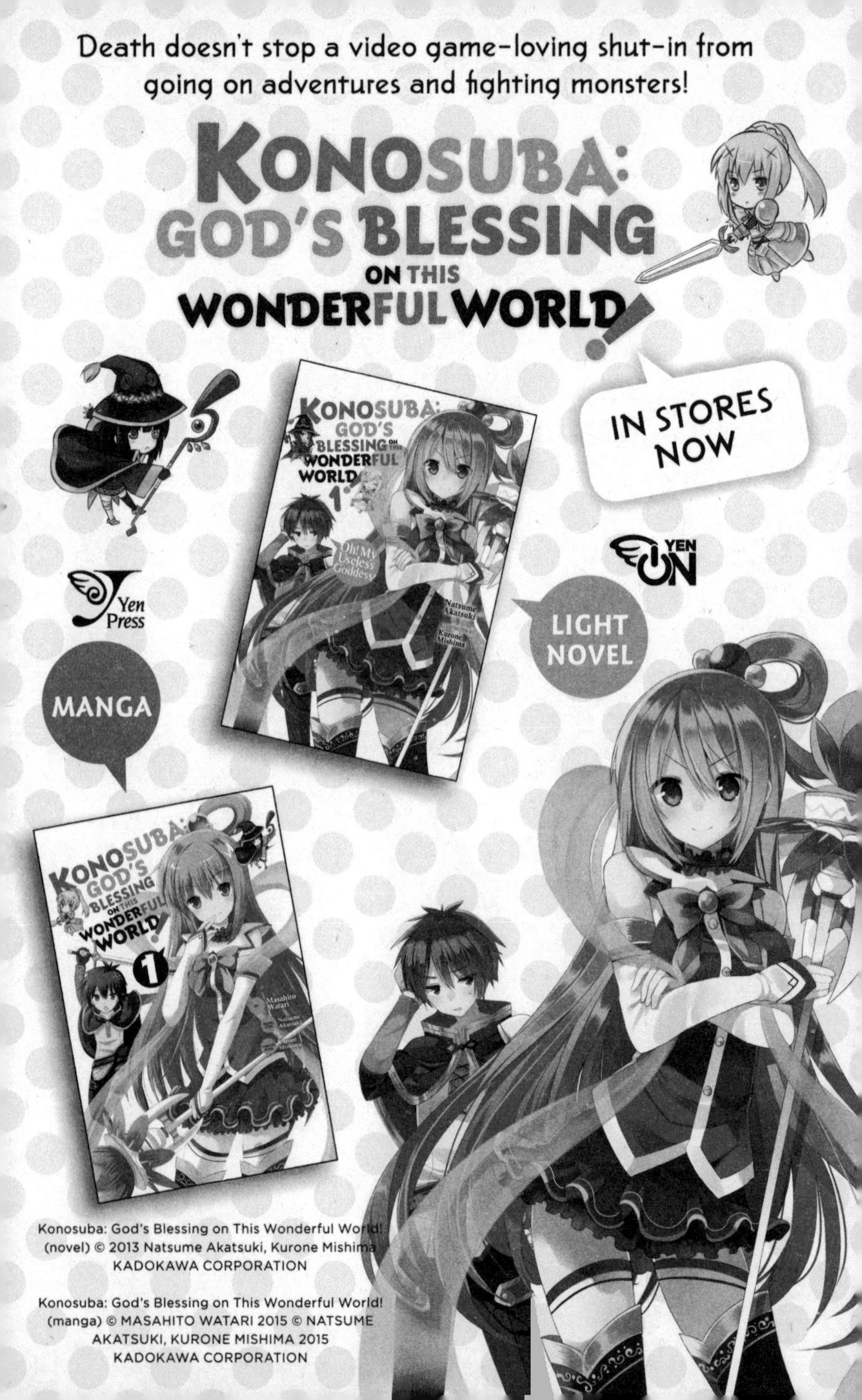
Death doesn't stop a video game–loving shut-in from going on adventures and fighting monsters!
KONOSUBA: GOD'S BLESSING ON THIS WONDERFUL WORLD!
IN STORES NOW
YEN ON
LIGHT NOVEL
Yen Press
MANGA
Konosuba: God's Blessing on This Wonderful World! (novel) © 2013 Natsume Akatsuki, Kurone Mishima KADOKAWA CORPORATION
Konosuba: God's Blessing on This Wonderful World! (manga) © MASAHITO WATARI 2015 © NATSUME AKATSUKI, KURONE MISHIMA 2015 KADOKAWA CORPORATION

IN THIS FANTASY WORLD, EVERYTHING'S A GAME—AND THESE SIBLINGS PLAY TO WIN!

A genius but socially inept brother and sister duo is offered the chance to compete in a fantasy world where games decide everything. Sora and Shiro will take on the world and, while they're at it, create a harem of nonhuman companions!

No Game No Life ©Yuu Kamiya 2012 Illustration: Yuu Kamiya
KADOKAWA CORPORATION

No Game No Life, Please! © Kazuya Yuizaki 2016 © Yuu Kamiya 2016
KADOKAWA CORPORATION

LIGHT NOVELS 1–6 AVAILABLE NOW

LIKE THE NOVELS?

Check out the spin-off manga for even more out-of-control adventures with the Werebeast girl, Izuna!

Follow us on

f 𝕏 t 🐦 📷   www.yenpress.com

The ISOLATOR ▼ Manga

©REKI KAWAHARA/
NAOKI KOSHIMIZU

The ISOLATOR ▼ Light Novels

©REKI KAWAHARA
ILLUSTRATION: SHIMEJI

THE ISOLATOR

▶▶▶ ACCEL WORLD Manga

©REKI KAWAHARA/HIROYUKI AIGAMO

Art: Hiroyuki Aigamo
Original Story: Reki Kawahara
Character Design: HIMA

▼ ACCEL WORLD Light Novels

©REKI KAWAHARA ILLUSTRATION: HIMA

©KEIICHI SIGSAWA
©REKI KAWAHARA
©TADADI TAMORI

©REKI KAWAHARA ILLUSTRATION: KOUHAKU KUROBOSHI

◀ Kawahara's newest series:

SWORD ART ONLINE ALTERNATIVE GUN GALE ONLINE
MANGA AND LIGHT NOVELS

Dive into the latest light novels from *New York Times* bestselling author REKI KAWAHARA, creator of the fan favorite *SWORD ART ONLINE* and *ACCEL WORLD* series!

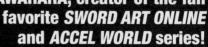

SWORD ART ONLINE Light Novels ▼

©REKI KAWAHARA   ILLUSTRATION: abec

©REKI KAWAHARA   ILLUSTRATION: abec

SWORD ART ONLINE Manga ▼

©REKI KAWAHARA/
TAMAKO NAKAMURA

©REKI KAWAHARA/TSUBASA HADUKI

©REKI KAWAHARA/NEKO NEKOBYOU

©REKI KAWAHARA/KISEKI HIMURA

©REKI KAWAHARA/CSY

©REKI KAWAHARA/TSUBASA HADUKI

©REKI KAWAHARA/KOUTAROU YAMADA

abec Artworks ▶

Featuring original, full color artwork from multiple
Sword Art Online manga and light novels.
A must for any *Sword Art Online* fan!

©abec ©REKI KAWAHARA

www.YenPress.com

PRESS "SNOOZE" TO BEGIN.

DEATH MARCH
TO THE
PARALLEL WORLD RHAPSODY

MANGA

LIGHT NOVEL

After a long night, programmer Suzuki nods off and finds himself having a surprisingly vivid dream about the RPG he's working on...only thing is, he can't seem to wake up.

YEN
ON

www.yenpress.com

Death March to the Parallel World Rhapsody (novel) © Hiro Ainana, shri 2014 / KADOKAWA CORPORATION
Death March to the Parallel World Rhapsody (manga) © AYAMEGUMU 2015 © HIRO AINANA, shri 2015/KADOKAWA CORPORATION

BUNGO
STRAY DOGS

Volumes 1-10
available now

BUNGO
STRAY DOGS 01
Story by KAFKA ASAGIRI   Art by SANGO HARUKAWA

If you've already seen the anime, it's time to read the manga!

Having been kicked out of the orphanage, Atsushi Nakajima rescues a strange man from a suicide attempt—Osamu Dazai. Turns out that Dazai is part of a detective agency staffed by individuals whose supernatural powers take on a literary bent!

BUNGO STRAY DOGS © Kafka ASAGIRI 2013
© Sango HARUKAWA 2013
KADOKAWA CORPORATION

www.yenpress.com

Yen Press

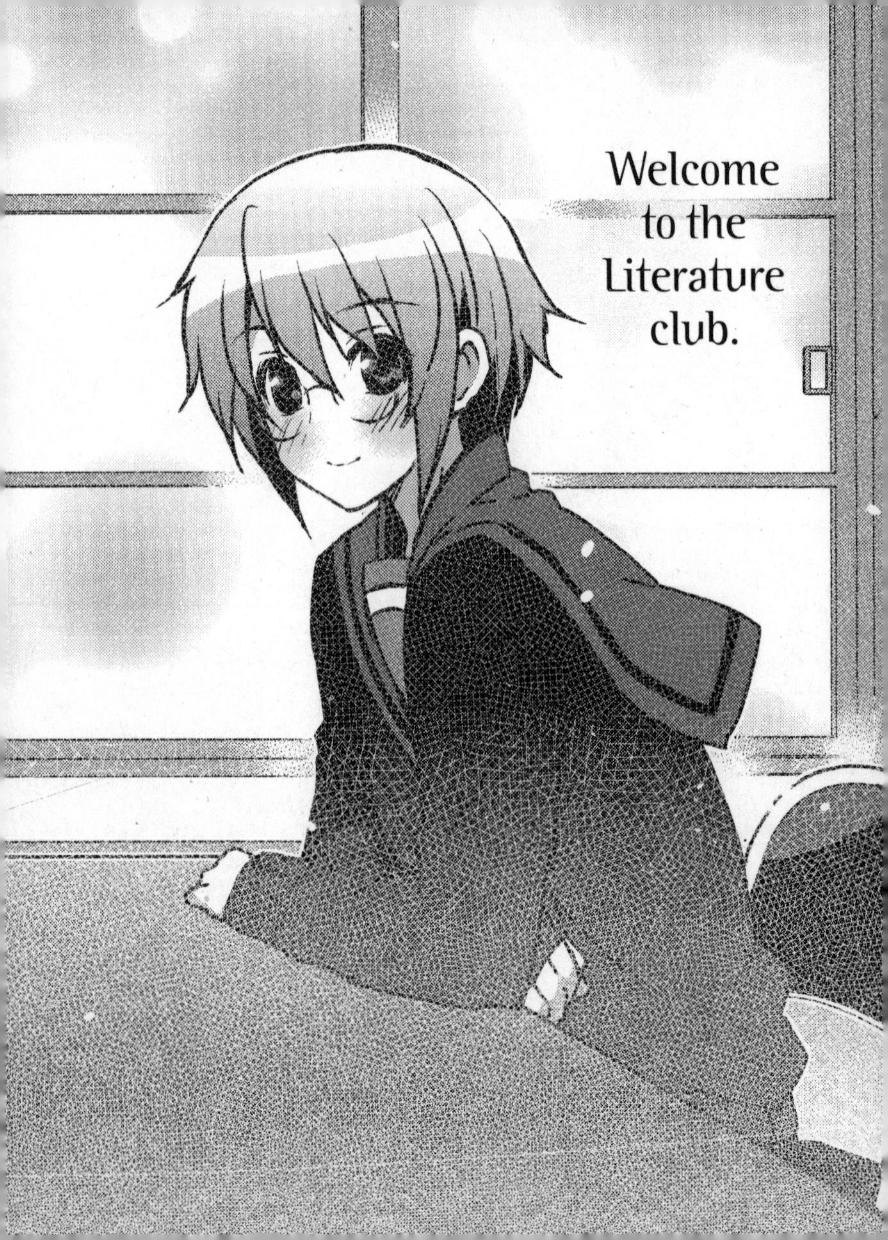
Welcome to the Literature club.

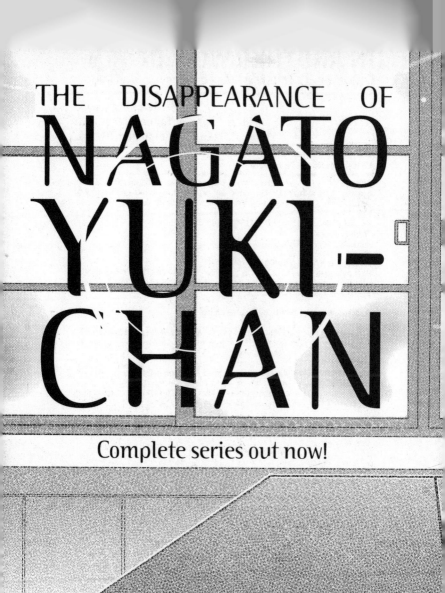

THE DISAPPEARANCE OF
NAGATO YUKI-CHAN

Complete series out now!

STORY: **NAGARU TANIGAWA** ART: **PUYO** CHARACTERS: NOIZI ITO

RE:ZERO -STARTING LIFE IN ANOTHER WORLD- ⑦
Chapter 3: Truth of Zero

Art: **Daichi Matsuse**
Original Story: **Tappei Nagatsuki**
Character Design: **Shinichirou Otsuka**

Translation: Jeremiah Bourque
Lettering: Rochelle Gancio

This book is a work of fiction. Names, characters, places, and incidents are the product of the author's imagination or are used fictitiously. Any resemblance to actual events, locales, or persons, living or dead, is coincidental.

RE:ZERO KARA HAJIMERU ISEKAI SEIKATSU DAISANSHO
Truth of Zero Vol. 7
© Daichi Matsuse 2018
© Tappei Nagatsuki 2018
Licensed by KADOKAWA CORPORATION
First published in Japan in 2018 by KADOKAWA CORPORATION, Tokyo. English translation rights arranged with KADOKAWA CORPORATION, Tokyo through TUTTLE-MORI AGENCY, Inc.

English translation © 2019 by Yen Press, LLC

Yen Press, LLC supports the right to free expression and the value of copyright. The purpose of copyright is to encourage writers and artists to produce the creative works that enrich our culture.

The scanning, uploading, and distribution of this book without permission is a theft of the author's intellectual property. If you would like permission to use material from the book (other than for review purposes), please contact the publisher. Thank you for your support of the author's rights.

Yen Press
1290 Avenue of the Americas
New York, NY 10104

Visit us at yenpress.com
facebook.com/yenpress
twitter.com/yenpress
yenpress.tumblr.com
instagram.com/yenpress

First Yen Press Edition: May 2019

Yen Press is an imprint of Yen Press, LLC.
The Yen Press name and logo are trademarks of Yen Press, LLC.

The publisher is not responsible for websites (or their content) that are not owned by the publisher.

Library of Congress Control Number: 2016936537

ISBNs: 978-1-9753-0401-0 (paperback)
       978-1-9753-0402-7 (ebook)

10 9 8 7 6 5 4 3 2 1

WOR

Printed in the United States of America